SPECIAL MESSAGE TO READERS

This book is published under the auspices of

THE ULVERSCROFT FOUNDATION

(registered charity No. 264873 UK)

Established in 1972 to provide funds for research, diagnosis and treatment of eye diseases. Examples of contributions made are: —

A new Children's Assessment Unit at Moorfield's Hospital, London.

•

Twin operating theatres at the Western Ophthalmic Hospital, London.

•

A Chair of Ophthalmology at the University of Leicester.

•

The establishment of a Royal Australian College of Ophthalmologists "Fellowship".

You can help further the work of the Foundation by making a donation or leaving a legacy. Every contribution, no matter how small, is received with gratitude. Please write for details to:

THE ULVERSCROFT FOUNDATION,
The Green, Bradgate Road, Anstey,
Leicester LE7 7FU, England.
Telephone: (0116) 236 4325

In Australia write to:
THE ULVERSCROFT FOUNDATION,
c/o The Royal Australian College of
Ophthalmologists,
27, Commonwealth Street, Sydney,
N.S.W. 2010.

I've travelled the world twice over,
Met the famous: saints and sinners,
Poets and artists, kings and queens,
Old stars and hopeful beginners,
I've been where no-one's been before,
Learned secrets from writers and cooks
All with one library ticket
To the wonderful world of books.

© JANICE JAMES.

WHERE OLD BONES LIE

What do you do when you think your ex-lover has murdered his wife? That's the question archaeologist Ursula Gretton puts to Meredith Mitchell in the hope that Meredith's friendship with Chief Inspector Alan Markby might cast some light on her dilemma. Markby is dismissive of Ursula's suspicions concerning the disappearance of Dan Woollard's wife — until a woman's body is found near the site Woollard and Ursula have been excavating. Markby is faced with a tangle of conflicting clues — and when a second body is found, it is clear the web is growing ever more complex.

ANN GRANGER

WHERE OLD BONES LIE

Complete and Unabridged

ULVERSCROFT
Leicester

First published in Great Britain in 1993 by
Headline Book Publishing Plc
London

First Large Print Edition
published October 1995
by arrangement with
Headline Book Publishing Limited
London

British Library CIP Data

Granger, Ann
    Where old bones lie.—Large print ed.—
Ulverscroft large print series: mystery
I. Title
823.914 [F]

ISBN 0–7089–3391–2

Published by
F. A. Thorpe (Publishing) Ltd.
Anstey, Leicestershire

Set by Words & Graphics Ltd.
Anstey, Leicestershire
Printed and bound in Great Britain by
T. J. Press (Padstow) Ltd., Padstow, Cornwall

This book is printed on acid-free paper

' ... history ... the register of the crimes, follies and misfortunes of mankind.'

Edward Gibbon

Prologue

FOR some time after she left, he waited for a letter, watching out for the post van from the top of the old rampart. He took special care to sit there on Tuesday mornings because he had a theory that she'd write at the weekend and post it Sunday evening or early Monday. She must know he'd be worrying that she was all right and had somewhere to live and money, so he was confident the letter would come.

Sitting up there early in the day on the damp grass, all the colours of the surrounding countryside seemed newly washed. Because the wind blew chill across the earthwork, he wore the last pullover she'd knitted for him, tracing the cable pattern with his fingers and remembering how she'd sat by the window in the good light to knit it.

He knew that at fourteen years old he wasn't a child and ought to be able to manage without her, just as she'd said.

But he still felt a strange pain inside him when he thought about her.

He saw the little red box-like van most mornings, rattling along the road down there, past the quarry. Sometimes there were letters for the farm. The van turned up the hill and, his heart pounding, he'd race to intercept it. But the driver would only shake his head, smiling, and speed on. There was no letter for him. The awful emptiness returned as, trousers creased and damp from dew, he made his way down to the road to await the school bus.

On the evenings of such days he'd surreptitiously riffle among the opened mail jammed behind the mantelpiece clock to see if she'd written to his father. But if letter there had been, his father had hidden it away, perhaps because it was precious to him, too. He longed to ask. He'd have liked to know if his father shared his pain. But since on both accounts he'd most likely have got short shrift, he kept his questions and his feelings to himself.

One Tuesday when he awoke he knew in his heart that his letter would never come. He wondered if it was his fault and he'd done something to upset her. He didn't go out early to wait on the rampart that day, or any day ever again. He got on with the business of growing up. But he never forgot her and he hoped that, wherever she was now, she was happy there and perhaps, just occasionally, she thought about him.

1

THE travellers rattled along the main road in a small convoy of vans, trailers and converted buses. Some vehicles were little more than metal hulks, more rust than paint, held together by hope and defiance, others were gaudily decorated with brightly coloured flowers. In all of them, aged engines coughed throatily as they coped with the incline. Clouds of black exhaust fumes stained the clear late summer air and filled it with a pervasive stench of oil.

Suddenly a raucous blast on the horn of the purple bus leading the file signalled that a sought-for landmark had been sighted, and the vehicles behind responded in a joyous cacophony.

Here the road crossed the lower slope of Bamford Hill. To the right the ground fell away, to the left it rose steeply to open pasture, patched with fields of rippling wheat. With a predatory roar the purple bus quitted the road to turn left up a rough track signposted 'Motts Farm'. The others followed with squeals of tortured metal.

Their leader veered left again off the first track, thrusting through a gap in the bordering hawthorn hedges. Triumphant, he lurched at the head of his tribe across dry grassland towards a curious turfed rampart which crossed the hillside horizontally half way up.

They were not the first arrivals. A band of archaeologists had already established themselves here and had excavated a warren of trenches. They had been toiling assiduously beneath the sun but now leapt up, open-mouthed, to watch aghast as the invaders surged past them up the hill to the rampart, blaring horns and belching fumes. Below the grassy mound the wild assortment of vehicles drew up in two parallel lines like so many siege machines and finally halted.

Out swarmed the bushy-bearded men and long-skirted women, the youth of both sexes in tattered jeans, the children of all ages, the dogs excited and barking. Even a goat was decanted from its own wheeled pen. With the ramshackle efficiency of all nomads some began to dismantle the tangled hedgerow for firewood; others, armed with buckets, climbed a far fence to draw water brought down to a cattle trough by rickety pipe and tap arrangement, sending surprised cows cantering away in all directions.

Finally a large, black labrador-cross trotted downhill to the archaeological dig, plumped himself down, scratched vigorously and, with pink tongue lolling, surveyed the appalled workers in a neighbourly manner.

But already opposition was on its way. A battered Land-Rover was bumping down the hillside from where chimney tops poking above the rise marked Motts Farm. It disappeared behind the rampart and then abruptly reappeared on top of the ancient earthwork.

Two men jumped out, a curiously contrasted pair. The appearance of the elder, tall, spindly yet sinewy, his nose high-bridged, his grey locks whipped into a tangled halo by the stiff breeze, suggested an Old Testament prophet. The shotgun in the crook of his arm served only to bring the image up to date.

The younger was squat and stocky in build, wearing strong brown corduroys and a baggy grey-green pullover which made it seem as if the component parts of him had been scooped up from the surrounding landscape. He now stepped forward, cupped his hands to his mouth and yelled: "You — are — trespassing!"

"Stop breaking down that hedge or I'll blow your bloody heads off! Get off our land, off our land!" the grey-haired man bellowed. His voice rose to a scream as he took the shotgun from under his arm and grasped it ready for use in both hands.

"Hold on, Uncle Lionel!" the other said curtly. "Let me handle this!"

Some authority in the younger man's voice temporarily prevailed over his companion. The wood gatherers had left their task to join the other travellers and form a silent, motley crowd. Across the invisible line between the opponents stepped a bearded spokesman.

"We're only taking out dead wood. We're not breaking it down."

"I can see with my own eyes what you're doing!" Lionel Felston shouted, and the shotgun barrel jerked dangerously.

His nephew Brian again put out his hand to forestall his enraged uncle. "You're trespassing! I'm asking you to leave our land. I'm asking you politely for the one and only time. Now get your women and kids together and get out!"

Another traveller, shaven-headed and wiry in torn jeans and with three gold earrings all in one earlobe, pointed down the hill to the archaeological site.

"What about them, then? Aren't they trespassing, as you call it?"

The bearded traveller's voice had been educated but his was imbued with a nasal urban whine.

"No! They're excavating the site with our permission. You don't have our permission and you're sure as hell not going to get it! You can just clear off!" Brian snarled at him.

"You going to make us?" asked the wiry one, grinning evilly.

"You're darned right I am!" Lionel Felston raised his gun.

"You only have the right to use

9

reasonable force," the bearded man said calmly. "Threatening us with a shotgun isn't reasonable. If you blast off with that, you're in trouble."

"Don't you quote the law at me!" Lionel snapped. "This is private land! Our land! I've seen what you people can do in other places and you're not going to do it here! Leaving filth, destroying crops, injuring beasts — "

The shaven-headed traveller sniggered, gaining himself a swift reproving glance from his better-spoken companion.

"We'll dig proper latrine pits and clear up after us. We'll take our rubbish away. You're not using this piece of land. We aren't in anyone's way. Why don't you just let us stay here a few days in peace? We've got our families, our children with us. We need somewhere to stay for a few lousy days, that's all!"

"Few days!" Lionel's lean features contorted. "I'll blast you all to kingdom come first!"

A sudden extra-strong gust of wind caught the words and sent them swirling away high into the sky where gulls flown inland to forage swooped and dived on wide white wings, uttering their strange screams. It was almost as if the souls of all those who had fought and died on the rampart cried encouragement to the latest adversaries to face one another on this ancient place of blood.

2

AT risk to life and limb.

Ursula Gretton wished that confidence-sapping phrase had not forced itself into her mind. She'd been riding her bike about Oxford for years, although it had become more and more of a self-inflicted obstacle course as the traffic grew ever denser, drivers less tolerant and the exhaust fumes more noisome. A car cut in front of her and Ursula wobbled. A double-decker bus behind her tooted. The woman on the pavement alongside her, encumbered with shopping and pushchair, glared. Ursula gritted her teeth and cursed Dan. He'd better have a good reason for getting her out here!

She cursed her ancient, rickety bike too, but palaeontologists seldom had much spare cash. Not unless they were working on a particularly prestigious site, preferably funded by some generous corporate body, and intended writing a definitive book on the subject. Not just working for the Ellsworth Trust, a small independent educational trust with particular interest in Dark Age archaeology and admittedly limited financial resources.

The last was particularly significant because the Trust was funding the Bamford Hill dig. All the other trusts approached had been unable to help. The Ellsworth, by reason of its charter, had been willing, but its resources were stretched and calls on them various. Of course, if Ian . . .

Dan said, perhaps this time with reason, that Ian Jackson was on to something and could well be right about there being a more important burial than any yet discovered. Dan had been largely responsible for chivvying the Trust into supporting the dig thus far.

Dan said. As if she'd not had enough trouble already from listening to what Dan Woollard said.

More fool me! thought Ursula, sticking out her left arm. And not just for riding a bike along this road on a Saturday. More fool me for getting into this mess!

She turned into the side road with a sense of relief. To be honest, the heavy traffic scared her. She slowed, seeking the house and spotting it, took her feet from the pedals and coasted to a stop. Putting down one foot and holding the bicycle upright beneath her, she eyed the frontage dubiously. Whatever it was, surely he could have explained on the phone?

Ursula dismounted, manoeuvred the bicycle between parked cars, pushed it across the cracked pavement, through the space where a gate ought to be and propped it up in the tiled forecourt against the bay window. Then she carefully threaded the safety chain through the front wheel and locked it, although who in his right mind would want to pinch this old heap of scrap she couldn't imagine.

These houses had once been modest residences built for late Victorian trades-people and office workers. Now they had a sort of cachet and the 'chattering classes', as some dubbed them, had moved in. As an address the street was 'all right', and the prices here had risen out of all reasonable proportion to the type of property. Most houses had been carefully renovated by the new owners. This one hadn't. Its paintwork peeled. Its net curtaining had a grey tinge. Natalie wasn't a housewife by inclination or talent and Dan never noticed that sort of thing.

Ursula pushed at the bell and sighed.

She heard his footsteps echoing along the hall towards her, conjuring up a picture in her mind of the unfurnished, uncarpeted passageway. Why they had to live like this, goodness only knew. Natalie must surely make good money from those steamy novels. Perhaps the state of the house simply reflected that of their marriage.

The door opened and he exclaimed, "Sula!" his broad face lighting up with pleasure.

"Hullo," she mumbled.

"I — I'm glad you came, after all." He gave her a truly pathetic look that only succeeded in making her cringe.

"This had better be a real emergency, Dan. I told you, I wanted this weekend to write up my notes."

"It is!" He sounded grim. Perhaps it was, after all.

Ursula put one foot over the threshold and then paused. "Is Natalie home?"

"No, gone to Bamford to see her mother."

"Oh." Fatally she hesitated.

"Well, don't turn and run!" he said angrily, "I'm not going to attack you! Anyway, Ian's on his way over." He glanced at his watch. "He'll be here in about ten, fifteen minutes. I'll stick the kettle on."

Humiliated by the transparency of her doubts, she followed him down the hallway to the sitting room at the back of the house. The sun fell on this side in the mornings and still shone brightly through the window into what had been turned by the Woollards into an all-purpose study. On one side stood Natalie's desk, strewn with pages of print. On the other was Dan's. The suggestion was of a couple working in harmony. As with so many other things about Dan and Natalie, it was false. But the room had a comfortable disorder and nice old horsehair-stuffed chairs. Ursula

16

sank down in one of them, putting her shoulder-bag down on the floor by the side of it. Dan could be heard rattling cups in that kitchen of theirs which looked as if it belonged in a church hall. Suddenly nervous, she got up and began to wander round the room. She crossed to Natalie's desk and peered down at the stack of printed sheets.

"Are these the proofs of Natalie's new book?"

He shouted "Yes!" and then swore, probably burning himself on the handle of the kettle.

There was a note lying on top of the stack of proofs. It was from Natalie's editor and read 'Sorry these are late. Would appreciate having them back by the 12 August. Thanks'.

It was the eighth of the month already. If Natalie was going to get these proofs back on time she'd have to get a move on. Hardly a good moment to scoot off and visit her mother unless she'd been called away urgently. Ursula called out, "Is Natalie's mother ill again?"

"What?"

Dan's voice sounded near at hand and

Ursula realised she needn't have shouted. "Natalie's ma!" she repeated more clearly but in a lower voice.

"Oh, Amy. I don't know. She rings up and Natalie drops everything and rushes off to Bamford. I don't know. Don't care frankly."

"She's getting on, I suppose, over seventy?"

"There's nothing wrong with her, if that's what you're thinking, but she likes Natalie dancing attendance. I used to — we used to argue about it. Now Natalie does what she wants — in that as in everything else." He handed her a mug.

"Thanks." Ursula retired with the coffee to her chair. "What's all this about?"

"Ian will explain. We've got an emergency on our hands." He grimaced. "It takes that nowadays, doesn't it? To persuade you to meet me anywhere but at the dig? Working, that's the only time I see you. It could all change, you know. I could — make things different."

"If there's an emergency, just stick to telling me about it!" she said curtly.

"There's no point in me going through it and Ian going over it again and he's got more up to date information than I have. Briefly, we've got visitors."

Ursula groaned. Any excavation was liable to be hindered by this kind of outside interference, sometimes well-intentioned, mere curiosity, sometimes not. "Treasure-seekers? Idiots with metal detectors?"

They were the worst. If they found anything, they made off with it and valuable clues to the date and nature of the site were lost.

"No, New Age travellers. Lorries and dogs and kids, the lot. Thirty or more people in all at a conservative estimate, tramping all over the place. Lighting fires. Kids chasing each other. Dogs digging holes."

She stared at him in horror. "On the site?"

"Slap bang above us on the hillside — between us and the rampart. Ian will tell you the rest."

She was frowning. "But what about the Felstons? Can't they make them leave? Surely the Felstons don't want hippies

19

camped on their land?"

"Of course they don't, and we had a very hairy confrontation, I can tell you, with old Lionel Felston brandishing a shotgun and Brian reading the riot act. It didn't do any good. Apparently they have to get an injunction."

The doorbell rang again. "Ian!" Dan said starting towards the door.

Ursula began, "Are Karen and Renee on their own at the site — ?"

But Dan had disappeared into the hall and could be heard letting Ian Jackson into the house. Within moments the curator of Bamford Museum, short, red-faced and sandy-haired, erupted into the room.

"Sula? Dan's told you, I suppose? What, Dan? Oh, tea, coffee, anything." Jackson flung himself into a chair, his tan tweed jacket hitching itself up behind his ears. "I'm sorry I'm late but I made a detour via Bamford first. I called by the police station and had a chat with the senior man there. He's a chief inspector called Markby."

Ursula started, opened her mouth and then closed it again.

20

"I stressed the urgency and how important the dig is to the museum and asked him to send a few of his blokes along to get these New Age people to move on. It seemed simple enough to me. But he was no help at all! Just said he'd look into it, but it depended on the circumstances and sometimes confrontations didn't help, could turn violent and we wouldn't want a punch-up right by the site, would we?"

Jackson grabbed the mug Dan handed him. "I rather lost my rag. I told him, 'I paid my Poll Tax and when I ask for help from my local cop shop I expect some action!' He said he sympathised. I told him he could keep his sympathy and did he realise that the museum was a cultural oasis in that benighted town of his?"

He fell momentarily silent again. Dan had perched himself in ungainly fashion on the edge of Natalie's desk during the tirade. Ursula's eye wandered back to the stack of uncorrected proofs.

She asked quickly, "What about the Felstons?"

"They say they can't afford an injunction. But we can't rely on rapid police action! Old Lionel's liable to blow someone's head off! It couldn't be worse and someone has to do something!"

He leaned forward, slopping his tea. "I don't want to be unfair. The spokesman for the convoy, Pete, is a reasonable sort of bod. But I really don't think we can rely on all the others. There's a peculiar character who keeps wanting to see the skeleton, lurks round trying to lift the corner of the tarpaulin while we're not looking. I tell you, Sula, we'll all need eyes in the back of our heads while they are there and we'll get no work done! We'll spend all our time on look-out while the Felstons and the travellers play King of the Castle. No way can we leave the site unguarded until they're gone and that's flat! And I mean, at night as well."

Silence fell. Ursula broke it tentatively. "What about the works trailer?"

"I've thought of that. We could fix up a couple of beds in it, no problem. I think if they knew there were a couple of us staying on the site all night it would do the trick. They're not dangerous, if you see what I mean. It's just that they might meddle or go walking over the dig. It's keeping a physical presence. I thought you and I could sleep there tonight, Dan. But tomorrow I can't because the baby's teething and I don't like to leave Becky all on her own."

"I can sleep there tomorrow night as well," Woollard said.

The other two looked at him questioningly and he reddened.

Ursula asked bluntly, "What about Natalie?"

"I told you, she's in Bamford with her mother."

"I'll take a turn," Ursula said, "Monday night, Tuesday too if you like. Perhaps Karen would stay over with me then."

Jackson had been fiddling awkwardly with his mug. "Look, I've got a favour to ask of you two. I mean, you're directly connected with the Trust. I'd rather we kept this all under our hats for a bit. There's no point in worrying the Trust with it. If the Ellsworth find out a hippy convoy is living there, they might think things were going on that shouldn't be."

He flushed. "I mean, drugs and so on. They do have drugs, don't they? Those sort of people? Or the Trust might think we couldn't work properly in those circumstances."

"We can't," said Dan briefly.

"Besides which," Jackson's voice rose, "I've only just asked them for an extension. We're at such a tricky stage. You both know I believe we can find Wulfric's burial. A Saxon chieftain with all his apparel! Think what it would mean to Bamford Museum!"

Jackson's face alternately glowed with enthusiasm and grew wistful with longing. "I thought I had the Trust convinced. They were pleased when we found one complete skeleton but when it wasn't Wulfric's they started to get sceptical we'd ever find his burial pit. I know you've both been backing me up and I'm grateful. But I'm painfully aware we haven't found anything I can show the Ellsworth to support my theory. I must have more time and nothing must happen to shake the Trust's confidence any further."

He set down his mug. "Well, I'll get

back to Bamford and see what I can organise for tonight. Then we'll get a roster going until the convoy has moved on." Jackson was making his way out of the door as he spoke. Dan accompanied him and their voices drifted in from the hall, discussing the need for sleeping bags and methylated spirit stoves.

Ursula sighed. It was all very well offering, but she really didn't fancy sleeping out on the hillside, cheek by jowl with an encampment of unknown hippies with the aim of keeping them at bay. Nor would Karen's company be an unmixed blessing.

She put her hand down by the side of the chair and felt for her shoulder-bag. Her fingers touched unzipped leather and she rummaged for her handkerchief. It was a moment before she realised something wasn't right and looking over the edge of the chair realised that she had her hand not in her own bag, but in someone else's. Unwittingly she had placed her shoulder-bag down on the floor by another. Curious, she picked the other one up. It was open so it wasn't really prying just to peep inside.

A leather wallet containing credit cards, a lipstick, a notebook, biro, a purse, two supermarket receipts, car keys . . .

Dan was coming back, having seen Ian out. Ursula dropped the bag and grabbed her own as he came in.

"I'd better be going now." She stood up.

"You don't have to dash off, you know, Sula."

"I told you, my notes — "

"You can take five minutes to talk!" He almost shouted the words and they echoed in the room.

"What about?" Ursula asked quietly.

He hunched his shoulders and said sullenly, "Us."

"There isn't any 'us'. I told you, it's over. It was nice while it lasted, but it was a mistake."

Obstinacy set his battered features into uncompromising lines. "I told you, Natalie and I are through! It's just that she won't admit it. But she will agree to a divorce if you and I just face it out."

"I don't want you to get divorced on my account. I wouldn't marry you if you did. For God's sake, Dan! We

26

went through all this nearly a month ago! I thought you'd begun to accept that we're absolutely through, finished!" She knew she sounded exasperated but it was like talking to a brick wall. "But no! You and Natalie, you really are two of a kind! Neither of you listens to a word anyone else says!"

"I love you!" he yelled at her, his face scarlet. He took a step forward, his hands held out and then seemed to recollect himself and halted, his arms falling back by his sides.

"You don't! You just think you do! If you'd just think about it objectively, you'd realise you haven't been in love with me for ages!"

"That's rubbish!" he retaliated. "What's more, I won't believe you no longer love me! If only Natalie weren't here — "

"Well, she isn't here!" Ursula snapped. "And I'm going as well."

"I won't let you go," he said fiercely. "Not walk out on me, not after everything!"

She had reached the door but turned at the suppressed fury in his voice and looked back at him. He stood in the middle of the floor glowering and with such real rage in his eyes that for a moment she felt quite afraid of him. From here she could glimpse the handbag poking out from behind the chair. It had to be Natalie's, didn't it?

"How long has Natalie been at her mother's?" she asked, wishing she'd taken the elementary precaution of finding out where Natalie was before coming here today.

"I — three days now." He turned his head aside.

"When's she coming back?"

"I don't know and I don't care! It would suit me if she never comes back! You don't know what living with her is like! And since I've met you, Sula, it's been agony, knowing that — "

Ursula interrupted him. "Dan, nothing's happened, has it?"

"Other than I fell in love with you, what should happen?"

"For the last time, stop talking like that! You sound like one of Natalie's books!" That was unkind and she didn't want to hurt him. She wanted his honesty — if he had any. "I meant, has anything, anything other than usual, happened between you and Natalie?"

"For God's sake, stop harping on about Natalie!" His face had reddened and his bushy beard seemed to bristle. The undusted recesses of the hall echoed to his voice. "What are you trying to do to me? I love you and you said you loved me! We're here alone and Natalie's gone!"

"Gone where, Dan?" Despite her care the words leapt out as an accusing snap.

"I told you, to her mother's! Maybe she won't come back! If she didn't — "

"How do you mean, didn't?" Suspicion crackled in her voice.

"I mean, if she didn't, we could be together like this always! Things can change, just as I said. I can make them change. Think about it, Sula." His voice sank and he took a step forward.

Automatically she recoiled as he whispered, "I'd do anything if it would mean you and I could be together, anything, I swear!"

"Stop it!" She turned and fled, hurrying down the hall, her fingers fumbling at the latch of the front door. "I didn't want to work on this dig when I heard you were involved because I knew you'd just keep on and on about us!"

Her fingernail broke on the stubborn latch. What was the matter with the thing, was it stuck?

"It was only because Ian couldn't get anyone else and the Trust asked me — "

Thank God, the door came open at last! She almost fell over the step and out into the forecourt.

"Wait, Sula!" he called.

But she'd already unchained her bicycle and was pushing it out into the road. She heard him still calling her name as she cycled away, her head spinning and a new and terrifying suspicion growing slowly in her brain.

"Stupid, stupid!" she muttered aloud as she pedalled along, head down. A car driver pounded his horn and shouted, unheeded by her. "Stupid, stupid! Red light!" She saw it just in time. Waiting for the traffic light to change to green, she repeated, "Stupid!" aloud one last time.

But it wasn't the last time she'd think

about it, that horrible, unspeakable, unbelievable but not impossible notion which had lodged itself so disagreeably in her head. Crazy as it surely must — must! — be, it wouldn't go away.

3

MEREDITH MITCHELL stretched out to wiggle her feet against the duvet, luxuriating unashamedly in Saturday morning idleness. Today, for once, she needn't dash out to fight her way from Islington to Whitehall on the tube, there to sweat frustratingly over a Foreign Office desk. Today she could just lie here, the clock radio muttering faintly by her ear, and contemplate the pleasant prospect that not only was there no office today: there was no office for the next whole week.

The short leave ahead wasn't a void. She'd planned several small but important visits. To the hairdresser for a really decent cut. To the dentist for an overdue routine check. More interestingly, she meant to shop at leisure for new clothes, taking her time, lunching out. It was all going to be —

Rattle, scrape, click.

Meredith sat up with a start and an

unpleasant pounding in her heart. The duvet promptly slithered to the floor and exposed her bare limbs to a cool draught. She swung her feet over the side and let them dangle as she strained her ears. There must be some innocent explanation. A bird had perhaps come down the chimney. It had happened before.

But the noise came from the other side of the bedroom door, out in the narrow hall. It was a small flat and it didn't belong to her, it was owned by an FO colleague at present away in South America. Cramped and unlovely the flat might be, but it was handy and she had the good fortune to live in it alone.

But not alone at this moment. Someone was at the front door and had just managed to get it open and was entering the flat.

There was a thump as some heavy object landed on the floor and a muttering of a male voice. It was eight forty-five on a Saturday morning. Did the burglar think the flat empty?

Meredith stood up cautiously, toes feeling for slippers as she pulled on a dressing gown. The telephone was in the hall. It was unlikely that she would be given sufficient time to use it, even if she reached it. The most practical action would be to get out of the flat altogether and in the safety of the outside world, raise help.

A silence on the other side of the door indicated that the intruder had moved into a different area of the flat and it was only a matter of moments before he tried the bedroom. Meredith pulled open the door. Yes, the hall was empty, although a large canvas grip lay on the floor. It looked already crammed full which was odd. The living room door was ajar and someone could be heard moving in there and more muttering. Her heart pounding, she skirted the grip and stretched out her hand to the main door catch. As she did the living room door swung fully open and a dark figure filled the aperture. She found herself confronting a stained, sweaty young man wearing a leather jacket, jeans, trainers and forty-eight hours' growth of beard.

Meredith gave a shrill squeak. Then, her hand dropped to her side, her heart dropped back from her throat to its normal position and, her voice rising to an outraged howl, she demanded: "What on earth are you doing here? You're supposed to be in South America!"

"It's my flat!" said Toby simply. He hoisted the canvas grip and slung it into the living room ahead of him. "I got sent home, *persona non grata*."

"You would be!" she said resignedly.

She followed him into the living room. He'd shed his jacket and was stepping out of his trainers. He threw himself on the sofa, propping a pair of grubby socks on the arm, and announced, "I'm whacked. I had to come via Paris, the only flight I could get. They were on strike." He closed his eyes. "It's not my fault. It was one of those diplomatic squabbles. The UK sent home one of theirs so they slung out one of us and my name came out of the hat." He opened his eyes. "Any coffee going?"

"No! I was in bed! You scared the living daylights out of me! You could have at least rung the bell!"

"Whaffor? Had my own key. I really could use a cup of coffee."

Meredith resisted the impulse to retort that as he was so anxious to point out it was his flat, he could make his own. He was probably genuinely shattered by his journey. She made her way resentfully to the kitchen. As the coffee began to bubble into its glass jug and fill the air with its aroma, an unwelcome thought struck her. "You don't think you're going to stay here, do you? You leased me this flat!"

"I didn't know I was going to need it myself then, did I?" He'd managed to drag himself from the sofa to the kitchen table and sat there hopefully.

Meredith simmered as Toby munched his way happily through a huge bowl of cornflakes. "Toby, you can't stay here. I've got next week off, I was planning so much . . . "

"I've got to, where else can I go? I've got to report at the FO on Monday morning. You go ahead. I won't be in the way," he went on in his optimistic way. "You can carry on using the bed and I'll have the Put-U-Up in the living room. I'm still famished. Any chance of a boiled egg?"

"Boil it yourself!" There were limits.

In the bathroom, a pile of crumpled socks and Y-fronts festered quietly under the dripping cold tap. Meredith went back to the kitchen. "It won't work, Toby. You're untidy and messy! You've put dirty washing in the tub and I was going to take a bath. The flat's too small for us both."

"We'll manage. I'll take the wash to the launderette some time."

Later, as she was getting dressed, a blast of rock music assaulted her ears. The phone rang and she heard him pick it up.

"What? Who?" he yelled above the racket before bawling, "It's for you!"

Meredith stalked out and grabbed it from him. "Hullo?"

"What on earth is going on there?" Alan Markby's voice burst into her ear. "Who was that?"

"Oh, Alan, hang on! Toby! Turn that music down, I can't hear a word!" But Toby had shut himself in the bathroom and she had to see to it herself. A blessed calm fell. She went back to the phone and explained briefly the nature of the problem.

"You're not telling me he's going to live there?"

"He's been thrown out of his posting and he's back in London for the foreseeable future and didn't have time to make arrangements." Cupping her hand over the receiver, she hissed, "It's a nuisance but it is his flat and he's moved himself in! I can't throw him out, so what else can I do?"

"Tell him to go and find a B and B, that's what! And while you're about it, get his key off him. He signed a lease agreement! You're paying him a generous rent and the tenancy most definitely doesn't involve sharing with him! Hold him to it! It's not your fault he got booted out."

"But I can't make him go if he won't. I mean, he isn't to blame."

"Meredith!" said Markby's voice belligerently. "Don't think I'm jealous or suspicious or anything like that. But he's taking advantage of your good nature. If you let him stay there, you'll regret it!"

Toby threw open the bathroom door and, to the accompaniment of running water, appeared, a towel draped round his midriff. "D'you mind if I use your soap? I was thinking, now I'm back we could ring round a few friends and throw a bit of a party tonight!"

Meredith's hand tightened round the receiver. "I don't need anyone to tell me what I already know!" she said grimly into the phone.

★ ★ ★

The following Sunday afternoon Ursula sat in Oxford in the little back bedroom which had been converted to her personal study. She was meant to be typing up her notes on the skeleton at the dig, but she sat at her desk before the window and stared unseeingly out into the garden.

She had been quite unable to quash that frightening notion which had leapt into her mind the day before. Surely it was just too horrible? How was it she could even think such a thing possible of Dan? Because, she told herself, behind her suspicion lay a gnawing personal guilt which invited inevitable disaster.

She had put herself squarely in the wrong, painted herself into a corner with

39

no way out. Ursula jammed a fresh sheet into the platen. At moments like these she panicked, trapped, remorseful, hating herself, hating Dan, longing to be free. Most of all hating the inaction, wanting to do something about it all. But what?

At the time it had seemed so different and she had had no doubts at all about the rightness of her actions. Dan and Natalie were known to have a rocky, tempestuous marriage, a puzzle to outsiders. Like the half-furnished state of their home, their marriage appeared incomplete and neglected. Yet both could be meticulous, Natalie in her books and Dan in his work. Ursula hadn't been surprised that Dan was unhappy and, on reflection, was perhaps flattered that he'd chosen her to confide in. She could see now a kind of vanity in her attitude. Natalie had failed Dan: but she, Ursula, would heal the wound.

She'd discovered her error fairly soon. Dan's constant whingeing, as it soon began to appear, revealed itself as a practised form of emotional blackmail honed to perfection in his dealings with his wife and now turned on Ursula. He wanted all her time and attention, was both jealous and possessive and, she suspected, not always quite truthful. Or rather he had the capacity to see things in such a way that he always appeared in the best light. A quarrel was never Dan's fault, always the other person's. A delay was always because Dan had been held up by others. A mix-up over labelling was because the light was poor in the works trailer and Ursula's handwriting illegible. So it went on.

Doubtless Natalie practised the same sort of emotional pressure on Dan and the two of them existed in a mutually tormenting relationship. Too late Ursula had discovered that no matter what outward appearances might suggest, no one knows the truth about a marriage except for the two people locked in it.

At that point Ursula had decided that she wanted no part of any of it. Getting away from Dan, however, especially as they were working together, was another matter.

Ursula doodled on her notepad. Natalie. Was Dan telling the truth? Or was she being fed yet another version of events as filtered through Dan's mechanism for adjusting reality to suit himself? Even now, she tried to play fair and give him the benefit of the doubt. Natalie's mother did live in Bamford. Ursula had seen the house. Amy Salter was sometimes ill and had been known to phone her daughter urgently to come and help out. It made sense.

But not the unfinished proofs. Not the wallet of credit cards and not the car keys.

And what had he meant? He could make things change? Was that just Dan talking or had he already done something, did he know something had altered?

Let's face it, she couldn't even pretend she was working. She tidied her papers away and went downstairs to put her head round the door of her father's study. "Dad?"

"What's that, darling?" her father muttered, busy at his own work.

"I need to go out for a couple of hours. Is it all right if I take the car? You won't need it, will you, this evening?"

"Car?" He raised his head, turned and stared at his daughter vaguely. "Oh, yes, car . . . by all means take it."

"I won't be late home."

He was already lost in his books again. They were an academic family and had been a large and happy one. But Ursula's mother had died; her sisters had married. Somehow she'd just carried on, living at home where it was so comfortable and convenient, cheaper too, existing in an easy-going relationship with her father and perhaps, for all her twenty-nine years and formidable qualifications, never really growing up.

So Ursula told herself as she backed the car out and set off to drive to Bamford. She was a cautious motorist and it took her an hour, even on the motorway for most of the trip. Bamford was a place of Sunday evening quiet. A bell summoned worshippers to Evensong and people hurried in ones and twos towards church or chapel. The pubs were still closed.

Ursula parked in the empty back street several yards down from Amy Salter's house and sat watching the place, uncertain what to do next. These were terraced cottages with frontages right

43

on the pavement marked by well-scoured stone door steps. They were all tidily kept with freshly painted doors and gleaming polished brasswork. They had net curtains. They had bowls of fruit or flowers positioned dead centre in the middle of the front ground floor windows between net and glass. They were the epitome of respectability of an old-fashioned kind. She could hardly go and rap on the door and inquire after Natalie's whereabouts outright, perhaps causing needless alarm and leaving herself open to accusations of malicious rumour-mongering. And what if Natalie were there? Even opened the door? What could she say? How could she meet her eye?

She tapped nervously on the rim of the steering wheel. Then, without warning, the door of the Salter house opened. Amy Salter, neatly dressed and obviously in blooming good health appeared, fidgeted with her handbag and then closed the door behind her. She set off briskly down the street. She had not, Ursula noted, called out to anyone within the house before leaving.

When Amy had turned the corner

out of sight, Ursula jumped out of the car and walked determinedly towards the green-painted door and rapped the fox's head brass knocker. The sound echoed within in the way it only does when a house is empty. Nevertheless she tried again and even lifted the letterbox, stooped and shouted "Natalie?" through it. Nothing. Ursula moved to the front window, flattening her nose against the pane, but the net blind obscured the room behind.

Suddenly the first-floor sash window of the next door house flew up and a woman's head appeared. "Was you wanting Mrs Salter, dear?"

"Er, yes . . . " Ursula looked up, shielding her eyes.

"She'll have gone to evening service, All Saints church. Always does, regular as clockwork, 'cepting when she's not well."

"Oh, I see. Er — Mrs Woollard, that's Mrs Salter's daughter, she isn't staying here, I suppose? I really wanted her."

"Natalie you mean? Oh no, dear. I'm sure she's not. I can't rightly remember when I last saw her."

45

"Right. Thanks."

The window slammed down. Ursula beat a retreat to the car. If you wanted to get up to any skulduggery, it wasn't wise to do so in a street like this where neighbours seemed to know your every move.

But was this skulduggery? And if so, what should she do about it?

And then, out of the blue as she drove home, she thought, 'Meredith! Of course'!

★ ★ ★

Meredith, late that Sunday evening, was tidying the flat. Toby had just gone out, and while he'd been there she could only observe the mounting chaos all around. Now, muttering furiously to herself, she beat cushions, collected up sheets of newspaper scattered on the carpet, washed cups, cleaned the bath and raced the elderly inefficient vacuum cleaner around.

Eventually she flung herself on the sofa and announced aloud, "I am NOT going to put up with this!"

46

At least she'd talked him out of the party on the Saturday night but the idea had only been postponed. His friends, he had pointed out, would expect it. Clearly word of his return had spread throughout the metropolis and the phone had been ringing for him all today.

Even as she thought about this, it rang again. It was impossible to ignore its shrill insistent cry. Meredith snatched it up and snarled, "He isn't here! He's gone down to the pub."

"Meredith? Is that Meredith Mitchell? I hope I didn't get you out of bed. It's Ursula Gretton."

Meredith snapped alert. "Oh sorry, Sula. Are you in London? I thought you'd planned to go on some sort of dig this month."

"I did, I have — I'm phoning from home. The dig's got problems and so have I. Meredith, are you still friendly with that chief inspector at Bamford? I know he's still there."

"Alan Markby, yes. Only friends!" Meredith paused, remembering the final sharp exchange over the phone on Saturday morning. "At least, I think

47

he's still talking to me!"

"Is he easy to talk to? Does he listen or does he jump in and start asking endless questions?"

"What's wrong?" Meredith asked crisply.

But she'd put Ursula on the defensive. "Nothing! Well, yes, perhaps something. I'm not sure. I'd like advice and I thought about your friend at Bamford. Ian's already been in touch with him about the trouble at the dig and I thought perhaps I could make an informal approach. I just want, well, reassurance, I guess."

"Who's Ian? What trouble?"

"Ian Jackson, curator of Bamford Museum and leader of the dig. We've worked so hard there this summer and now it's all under threat." Meredith heard Ursula heave a sigh. "I've promised to sleep out there tomorrow night in the works trailer. We're taking it in turns for as long as it's necessary. Goodness knows how long that will be! On top of everything else, having to spend my nights in that caravan is the last thing I need. I'm going to ask someone to share the duty with me, but no one is really keen."

"Hold on!" An idea leapt into Meredith's brain. "Caravan? You're sleeping in a caravan and you want someone to keep you company? I'm on!"

"Oh no!" Ursula sounded distressed. "I didn't mean to suggest that! You've got your own work and problems."

"I'm off work for a week but I do have problems, believe me! The idea of leaving them behind for a few days is wonderful!"

"It wouldn't be wonderful here. The circumstances are fairly unpleasant and it's not a proper holiday caravan. It's a grubby old trailer full of our work stuff."

"At the moment," said Meredith grimly, "I'd contemplate sleeping on a park bench!"

4

"MORE coffee?" suggested Ursula. "A liqueur or a drop of brandy?"

"Thanks but no. I'll fall asleep."

Meredith's fear that she was going to doze off was well-founded. Toby had returned at midnight and played his rock music till one. She had risen early to drive down here. Roast lamb with mint sauce and summer pudding with cream had finished her off. Now she and Ursula sat in the family's pleasant garden and the warm sun was having the effect of a drug. She made a renewed effort to attend to the problem under discussion.

"I could tell you a thing or two about uninvited guests!" she muttered.

"Not like our New Age lot! They're very hard to shift. The law is so tricky. They're in possession, that's the problem. Of course it is trespass, but that's a civil matter and the police aren't keen to be too heavy-handed. There are small children in that convoy and it could turn violent. But having them so close to the dig could be a disaster."

"I do sympathise, believe me!" Meredith had a mental picture of Toby sprawled asleep on the Put-U-Up, the empty beercans in the waste bin. She told Ursula about Toby. "Although it's not quite the same. But he's there and he obviously means to stay there."

"I bet your policeman doesn't like that!"

"I don't like it! Incidentally, Alan isn't 'my' policeman! And I do quite like Toby. He's just incredibly messy and noisy."

"Then we've both got problems." Ursula paused and fiddled with a spoon. "I shouldn't have bothered you with mine, bringing you all the way here from London. I've told everyone I'm writing up my notes at home today. I couldn't face the others, especially Dan."

"That's what friends are for." Meredith eyed her. "I was desperate to get out of the flat so this visit is a lifeline! But if you've changed your mind about telling me about the other thing . . . because there is something, isn't there? And it matters more than the other?"

"Yes," Ursula said almost inaudibly. "I haven't changed my mind. I must talk to someone, if only to you." She shook her head miserably. "I've been such a fool."

"That's been said a few times! If it's a tale of the heart, give it time. It's the only cure."

"It's not like that. Time could be important."

Meredith listened as her friend told her tale.

"You could be getting into a stew over nothing, Sula," she said when Ursula had stumbled awkwardly to the end of her story. "Married couples do quarrel and one or the other can walk out either temporarily or for good. It's embarrassing and people ask questions so the other one makes an excuse. Dan said his wife had gone to her mother at Bamford. The fact that you've established she didn't, doesn't necessarily mean anything sinister."

"I know! But she's been gone several days now and if that was her handbag I saw she hasn't credit cards or car keys.

And don't forget the proofs! However rickety the marriage, Dan and Natalie are both of them dedicated to their respective professions. Natalie wouldn't let her publisher down." She paused. "You couldn't just have a word with your policeman about it?"

"It isn't his patch. He's miles away at Bamford. It's not his business."

"He might suggest something!"

"He's not an agony aunt!" said Meredith exasperated at the thought of Alan's reaction. "I think you should first try talking to Dan again. Tell him you're worried. The worst he can do is laugh."

"He wouldn't laugh. He'd lose his temper. He hates me to mention Natalie. And he's not the sort of person you can talk to. He tells lies!" Ursula concluded bleakly.

Meredith reflected wryly that she'd made too many mistakes of that sort herself to wonder how an intelligent woman like Ursula could fall for a man who, by her own account, was so obviously flawed. There was something fatally attractive in a rotten character and the world was full of women who could testify to that.

"The thing I had with Dan," Ursula was saying, "while it lasted, it was . . . how can I explain it?"

"A real fireworks show," supplied Meredith. "Lots of passionate clinches and floating about on Cloud Nine in between. You don't have to explain it, Ursula. We've all been there. The trouble with floating on the clouds is that they're so damn high up. When you fall off it hurts."

Ursula leaned forward. "But Dan's still on his cloud, if you see what I mean! He's adamant he still loves me and no matter what I say to him, he persists in believing I really love him and that it's only because of Natalie that I want out. It's frightening. He's so intense. And it makes me feel so bad about accusing him — "

As she broke off, Meredith asked gently, "Accusing him of what?"

She saw her friend's face turn a ghastly grey-white and felt cruel. But if Alan was to be asked about this, he had to be told just what Ursula thought had happened.

If it meant forcing Ursula to confess to a suspicion she hardly dare to think, so be it.

Ursula had put up both hands to push back her hair in a nervous gesture. "I don't know! But I think I know when he's telling lies, and he's lying now! Talking to him is useless! I'm nearly driven out of my mind by it! Of course, I don't mean he deliberately harmed Natalie! I was thinking more of a quarrel, an unfortunate accident. Perhaps I'm making even more of a fool of myself than I already have." She jumped up and began to gather up the coffee cups.

"Well, that's one possibility certainly," Meredith said calmly. "But this is still what you want me to tell Alan Markby? That Dan may have harmed his wife?"

"Yes! No! Meredith, I don't know what to do. I thought if I asked you to speak to Markby it would be informal, not actually saying something has happened, only that perhaps!"

"Sula!" Meredith said sharply. Her friend froze with the tray in her hands. "If I speak to Alan about this, it's telling the police. Because that's what Alan is, a policeman. He never forgets it and he wouldn't forget it this time. Vague accusations would be wasting his time. He'll insist on something specific. And if you make a specific charge, it's on the record, one way or the other! So before I speak to him, are you sure in your own mind that you want me to do it?"

Ursula's chin wobbled but she said firmly, "Yes."

"Even though we may be talking about murder? Because if the worst came to the worst, that's what we would be talking about and to pretend otherwise is to hide from reality!"

Almost inaudibly, Ursula mouthed, "I know."

There was a silence. "All right, then," Meredith said. "I'll talk to him."

Ursula began to move away with the tray. She looked back with a sad smile. "I do know that if Dan even suspected I'd been talking to you like this, he'd never ever forgive me."

★ ★ ★

56

Alan Markby wove his way carefully between the early evening press of bodies in the lounge bar of The Bunch of Grapes, a brimming glass in either hand.

"Right!" he said, reaching his destination safely and depositing the glasses on the ring-stained table. "One draught cider. So, what's brought on this sudden interest in archaeology, or is it Ursula drumming up volunteers?"

Meredith picked up the cider with thanks and began her carefully prepared explanation of Ursula's dilemma. She'd had time to work out what to say during the long drive to Bamford in the late afternoon and it had sounded sensible enough then. Now she wasn't so sure and Alan was looking unconvinced, frowning beneath the fair hair which flopped over his forehead, his lean angular figure hunched on his chair in an attitude of scepticism that was achingly familiar.

She felt that twinge in the chest and wobbling in the stomach that is half pleasure and half pain which, she knew, wouldn't be cured by a dyspepsia pill. She wondered for the umpteenth time if she was being wise. Not just in taking up

Ursula's cause, but in coming here and seeing Alan again. It was all too easy to let oneself be swept away by good old human urges. But once you'd got the sex out of your system, what then? That was the problem.

Perhaps it was a good thing she could talk to someone else. Besides, she was pretty sure he was going to raise the little matter of Toby in the flat and if she could head him off with Ursula's troubles, so much the better.

"Ursula's situation is a little more complicated than that," she said.

He had his nose in a beer glass so he couldn't make any comment which was probably just as well. But his eyebrows wiggled alarmingly and he shot her a very sharp look over the rim. Meredith plunged into her tale before he could get his breath.

"And that's about it," she said when she'd explained about the missing Natalie Woollard. "She thinks he's telling lies and she's worried."

He had listened in silence. Now he uncoiled from his hunched posture, squared his shoulders and asked, "You want my professional advice? Don't get mixed up in it!" He saw protest well up in her face and held up a soothing hand. "It seems clear to me that the Woollards have had an almighty quarrel, probably about his involvement with Ursula. The wife, who sounds a flamboyant character, has flung out of the door and decided to bring her husband to heel by going incommunicado. The situation isn't so unusual as you and Ursula seem to think. I've known a number of such cases where the wife has stomped off, yes, even without her handbag. He now feels embarrassed and guilty and is covering up by telling people his wife has gone to see her elderly mother in Bamford. Mrs Woollard will come home when she's good and ready. Or she'll sue for divorce from a distance and her husband will hear from her lawyers."

"I still think it's odd!" Meredith persisted. "All right, I've said something similar to Ursula already. But wherever Natalie is, she's without personal belongings and left urgent work unfinished on her desk."

"What's urgent? Your work or your

marriage? In normal circumstances she wouldn't leave her work, but circumstances aren't normal, are they? She wasn't reasoning when she went. She went in a red haze of fury and burning for revenge, you bet! Tell me when Ursula finds signs the floorboards have been taken up or Woollard starts repainting the place in the middle of the night!"

"Alan!" Meredith warned. "Are you taking this seriously?"

A passer-by bumped into Markby's back and apologised. The chief inspector hitched his chair nearer the table.

"See here," he went on, a touch of irritation entering his voice, "I've been through all this myself! Not, I hasten to say, that I was playing around like Woollard! But Rachel was forever storming out and then storming back in again a few days later. She used to go and stay with girlfriends. Women's version of the old school tie. The first few times I wasted effort ringing round and they'd coo, 'Rachel? Oh no, I haven't seen her!' Then I twigged that they lied through their teeth and Rachel was sitting on the sofa behind them knocking back their gin

and mouthing, 'Don't tell him I'm here!'
So I wised up and sat tight when she
did a runner. She always came back."
He finished his narrative on a slightly
gloomy note.

"Bet she didn't leave her credit cards
behind!"

"How do you know Natalie hasn't got
at least one with her, or a cheque-
book? How do you know she isn't
with friends? You don't and neither
does Ursula. Of course her absence is
causing problems. But it's not a crime to
be inconsiderate or to decide you don't
want to be found. And it's not difficult
to disappear if you really want to. We
live in a free society, you know. If we
were in a country of identity papers,
residence permits, policemen on every
corner, it would be different, but not
here, believe me! You can go anywhere,
give any name and provided you don't
commit a crime thereby, there's nothing
to stop you. And people do it. They
walk out of their houses and their lives
without warning. They say they're going
to buy a pint of milk and are never seen
again. A few of these are suicides. Very

few are murders. Mostly they're people who have been under intolerable pressure for years. One day they just flip. They leave spouses, children, parents, jobs and income, obligations and memories. Especially the last. To start again with a clean slate and to do it without having to explain first to your associates and dependents, it's tempting! That's why they don't take anything! No documents of any nature to tie them to the past and give a lie to the new identity. Nothing which makes them feel obligated to the life and the people they've left behind! Nothing to remind them and give them doubts."

"And you think Natalie Woollard's done this?" Meredith asked, impressed despite herself. "Had a sort of brainstorm and resolved on a clean break even if it is traumatic?"

Markby took a deep swig of his pint. "Not a complete break. More a symbolic gesture to warn her husband. As for Ursula's fears, your friend, if you ask me, is suffering from a combination of conscience and a fertile imagination. She thinks this row is all about her. She's afraid of getting the blame. After all, she was playing with fire, wasn't she?"

"No! She thought she was in love with Dan and she believed him when he said his marriage was as good as over!"

"And now she's not in love with him, doesn't believe a word he says and is anxious to see his marriage survive! So she's changed her mind, Meredith! She wants out! Only he's still keen and he isn't letting go so easily. Ursula's in a spot. Of course she wants his wife to turn up and reclaim the erring husband. Woollard frightened into good behaviour. End of affair, all neat and tidy. Ursula free."

"You don't sound very sympathetic towards Ursula!" Meredith said reproachfully.

"I don't have to be!"

She leaned forward, causing the table to rock, and Markby hastily rescued his pint. "You wouldn't by any chance be suggesting that Ursula's trying to get some sort of petty revenge on Dan or just using this to get rid of him when he's being persistent? Because I can tell you here and now she wouldn't do that! She knows she's making a serious accusation and she doesn't do it lightly!"

"And I can tell you that whenever the police appeal to the public for help in identifying a criminal, the phone lines are jammed with calls from women who think the guilty man may be their husband or boyfriend! They often have the flimsiest reason for saying so and not the slightest scruple in naming the poor bloke! They're only too keen to think the worst! But before you pour cider all over me, I'm not saying your friend is either vindictive or neurotic! I'm saying she just doesn't understand how odd human behaviour can be!"

Meredith drummed her fingertips on the tabletop in an expression of impatience. "No use asking you to set an inquiry in motion, then?"

"I can't! You should know better than to ask. It isn't my patch anyway."

"Natalie's mother lives in Bamford, a Mrs Salter. I've got her address. You could go and ask her — "

"No! There's no evidence of a crime! Just another 'domestic'. Colourful but commonplace and slightly tawdry. Please leave it alone."

"I can't. I'm spending a week in a trailer with Ursula on Bamford Hill and it's bound to be discussed." Meredith sighed. "I wish the wretched woman would come home!"

"You see? You really don't think there's any foul play! In your heart of hearts, you think Natalie is just playing silly-buggers."

"Well," Meredith confessed unhappily, "when I listen to you, yes. But Ursula isn't feather-brained, Alan. She's very intelligent."

"Intelligence never had anything to do with commonsense. And if you want further evidence of that, whose crack-brained idea is it that you two should sleep in a trailer on Bamford Hill alongside a camp of hippies? Ursula's! Ursula should stick to old bones!"

"All right, then! Can we talk about the hippies? Why don't you move them on, so we don't have to sleep out there? Ursula and the others are very worried."

He scowled. "I know. Jackson is pestering the life out of me! So are the Felstons. An awkward pair, those two. Trespass is a complicated business. As I understand it, the Felstons normally keep the track to the hillside blocked to prevent access by cars, but they removed the barrier to let the archaeological team on. They also gave permission for the team to set up a trailer and a temporary residence. They even had water taken downhill from the farm by pipe. I've told them to cut that off."

"They have, and it's a nuisance for Ursula and the others, too. They used it to wash bits of pot and themselves! It's a mucky job."

He hissed in exasperation and scratched at his fair hair. "The most desirable thing is to persuade the hippies to leave of their own volition, but we all know they won't. So what am I supposed to do? Go up there with a bunch of coppers and throw them off by force? They're not averse to a punch-up, your peace-loving New Age friends! Next thing is the press are taking pictures and it even gets on local TV! No, let the Felstons' solicitor get them an injunction, or hope the hippies agree to move on. They know the drill.

They'll hang on till the last moment and then up and away. They're past masters at brinkmanship. It'll all sort itself out. Keep everything cool. Believe me, I've handled these situations before. Patience pays off."

"And in the meantime they damage the dig!"

"Have they done so yet?"

"Well, no, I don't think — "

"There you are then! Your pal Ursula exaggerating again!"

"You've got something against Ursula!" Meredith said angrily. She leaned forward, hazel eyes flashing.

"No, I haven't, but I'm a busy man and I can do without people raising false alarms! Missing wives! Vulnerable ancient sites! D'you think we've nothing else to do over at Bamford police station?"

"Have you any idea how pompous you sound sometimes? I don't know why I bother to ask you for any help!" Meredith declared, spilling cider in her agitation.

"I do! You let other people unload their problems on to your shoulders! It's a legacy of your days as a consul! You think you've got to help all these people.

You don't! And what's more, you soon find you can't help, so you zoom over here and try and unload it all on to me! And while we're on the subject of consular connections, is that fellow still at the flat?"

"Toby? Yes. It's his flat."

"It's leased to you, sole occupation. Turf him out!"

"Oh yes? You can't throw off the hippies because of legal technicalities and you don't want to be bothered! And I'm supposed to throw out Toby, who's a colleague and an old friend!"

"What sort of friend?" he demanded suspiciously.

"Well, we've worked together, very closely at times. He used to be my vice."

"There was a time I'd have said I knew what you meant by that. Now I'm not so sure!"

"Oh for goodness sake! You're not going to be jealous!" She got to her feet, scooping up her shoulder-bag. "I haven't got time to sit here squabbling! I've got to get out to Bamford Hill. I've told Ursula I'll meet her at the site."

68

"I strongly advise you in my official capacity not to spend the night out there!" Markby said stiffly.

Frustrated in her endeavours and sensing a nagging suspicion he might just be right, the various disquieting emotions combined to trigger Meredith's temper. "And I strongly advise you to mind your own business! I asked for your help and you refused it. So now I'll do things my way!"

"When did you ever not!"

They glared at one another.

"Have you got a proper sleeping bag?" Markby asked more calmly.

"Yes, thanks. And Ursula's got a camping stove out there so we can make hot drinks."

"Make sure it's on a stable, level surface. I've known those trailers go up in flames like tinderboxes."

"We're not a couple of dimwits! I got all my girlguide badges in my day and went to camp, thank you very much. We know what we're doing!"

"Be prepared!" said Markby unkindly.

5

MEREDITH calmed down as she drove out of town towards Bamford Hill. She had forgotten how lovely this countryside could be. Now, on an August summer evening, golden and mild as the sun sank slowly, colouring the horizon rose, she felt a timeless peace sweep over her. Red sky at night, shepherd's delight! she heard a voice from her childhood whisper in memory.

The new-found serenity allowed her to review the day's events with detachment. Alan was probably right about Natalie Woollard and it was foolish to have squabbled over something which was such an everyday occurrence. A domestic. She pulled a wry face. At least she'd kept her promise to Ursula.

She could now see the outline of the hill a little way off, veiled in a mauve haze. Soon she discovered that the road ran across the base of it so that to her right the terrain rose steeply and to her left it dropped away. She slowed, looking for the right-hand turning which Ursula had described. It should be marked, indicating Motts Farm, and Ursula had explained that after taking it, she must then turn left off it on to the track up the hill to the site.

"Follow the ruts left by all those hippy vans!" she had said grimly.

Ursula was going to be disappointed when she learned of Markby's negative reaction to her story. Disappointed but probably not surprised.

Meredith's progress had dwindled to a crawl, and now she drew in to the side of the road, and stopped to take a quick look at the sketch Ursula had given her. She peered through the windscreen. Yes, there was a turning on the right and an illegible wooden sign. But there was also a turning here on the left, just by her stopping place. A large board was nailed up and read:

QUARRY. CAUTION. DOMESTIC TIPPING ONLY.

Trees obscured the quarry edge. Between them she could see lengths of barbed-wire fencing. The drop was dangerously close to the road. Curious, she got out of her car, slamming the door, and walked a few steps down the dirt track between the trees to investigate.

The thin fringe of trees ended and with startling suddenness an old quarry was revealed at her feet. It had gouged a great wound in the landscape. But kindly vegetation had veiled its scarred flanks now that stone was no longer being extracted. A wide gravelled track in good repair led down to the bottom where the tip itself sprawled untidily across the broad flat floor.

Huge metal rubbish skips were piled high. In addition, either because the skips were full or because they couldn't be bothered to use them, visitors had left their junk in piles about the quarry floor, everything from garden clippings to old furniture. There was even a three-piece suite down there, set up incongruously in a circle as if in a drawing room.

For Meredith it held out the lure of a bazaar offering strange, eclectic bargains. She longed to climb down and view closer but hadn't the time. Turning her head she saw among the trees at the top beside the road, overlooking the track down to the quarry floor, a tumble-down cottage. Its thatched roof was rotted and eaten away by mice. Its walls were repaired with sheets of corrugated iron, its windows dusty, its surrounding fence collapsed about an overgrown garden. She supposed it disused, but she supposed wrongly.

Suddenly its peeling door flew open and an elderly man appeared. Seeing her, he let out a squawk and began to hobble rapidly towards her with the aid of a stick. He seemed nimble enough for all his lameness, his stout girth and age which could have been anything from sixty plus. He wore a plush waistcoat over a dirty collarless shirt, corduroy trousers, stout boots and to finish the ensemble, a trilby hat.

"Hang on!" he was croaking. "I'm coming!"

Oh, dear! thought Meredith, taken aback. Does he think I've come to visit him?

He had reached her and leaned on his stick gasping, his cheeks purple and his eyes bulging. "I heard the car!" he managed eventually. "I heard you a-slamming the door. What you got, then?"

Meredith blinked. "Got?" she asked cautiously.

He screwed up his red-rimmed little eyes and drew in his mouth making a sucking noise.

"Justa minute!" he muttered. "I'll put me teeth in."

He fumbled in his pocket in the plush waistcoat and produced a set of antique porcelain dentures which he first spat on, then rubbed the saliva across with his thumb, and finally inserted in his mouth.

"Thash better!" he said indistinctly. "Allus better with me choppers in!" He snapped his mouth shut. The teeth clicked together and then opened up. "I'm called Finny. What you got?" White porcelain jiggled up and down in his mouth as he spoke.

"Mr Finny!" said Meredith impulsively. "Have you thought of asking your dentist to adjust those teeth? I'm sure they could be made more comfortable."

"Never got 'em from no dentist!" he said, looking shocked. "I got 'em from down there, where I gets everything else!" He pointed with his stick towards the quarry floor. "These are good 'uns! Don't know why anyone would throw 'em away!" The teeth were rattling like castanets now. "People!" said Finny with disgust. "They throw away things like you wouldn't credit! Good stuff, beautiful! I furnished my cottage from what I got down there."

Meredith glanced dubiously at the dilapidated hovel he called home. It was probably worse inside than out and she hoped she never had to cross its dingy threshold.

"There's a beautiful sofa and chairs down there now," said Finny wistfully, leaning on his stick and gazing down at the three-piece suite below them. "Uncut moquette upholstery, wooden frames, metal castors. I just ain't got the room for it. Crying shame. When the rain comes that'll be ruined. You don't want a three-piece suite, do you? Lovely condition. I'll let you have it for a fiver."

Meredith did not point out that it wasn't his to sell. "I'm afraid not," she said, "and I haven't come to throw anything away."

"Not got anything?" Finny spluttered. "What are you doing here, then? Oy! You're not from the council? Not come about me cottage?"

"No," she assured him.

He looked only partly convinced. "They wants to pull it down, and me to go into one of them flats in Bamford!"

"It would be more convenient, Mr Finny." More hygienic, too. She'd spotted a sentry-box-like edifice among the garden weeds which was undoubtedly a wooden seat and bucket privy.

"I ain't going!" said Finny sulkily. "I got a lovely home of me own, full of beautiful things. I does very well by meself here. Anyway, I keeps an eye on the tip for them. They oughta be grateful to me, they did!"

He stamped his stick on the ground. "What you come poking about round here for if you've got no rubbish? You sure you're not the council?"

76

"I'm sure. I only stopped to look."

"You ain't a new district nurse? No — " He edged closer and inspected her. "You ain't a nurse. They got uniforms. Mine comes out once a month and cuts me toenails and trims me corns. I got bad feet . . . Well, I can't stand gossiping!" Finny concluded. "Not if you ain't got no junk. Can't understand it. Everyone's something to throw away."

"As soon as I have, I'll bring it here," she promised.

He brightened. "Ah, give me a shout before you take it down there. Then if it's summat good we'll unload it here and I haven't got to go dragging it up here again. And mind, if you knows of anyone what wants a nice three-piece suite, I got one down there, only wants the castors oiling. A tenner."

He hobbled back to his cottage, turned in the doorway to shout, "Uncut moquette!" before saluting her with his stick and slamming the door.

Meredith beat a hasty retreat to her car and drove off, turning up the track on the other side of the main road leading to the hillside.

"Hippies on one side, Finny on the other. Ursula and I in a trailer in between!" she said aloud. "A desirable residence and pleasant neighbours!"

★ ★ ★

As she approached the dig Meredith saw a reception committee lined up, four people and a black labrador-cross dog. The setting sun elongated their shadows so that the five dark strips on the turf resembled the spread fingers of a giant hand reaching out towards her.

The three women and one man were standing together before a ramshackle trailer, as if they'd been engaged in some discussion which they'd broken off at her approach. The limitations of the trailer as bed and breakfast accommodation were all too obvious from this first sight of it.

Meredith could not but be aware too of the New Age camp. It was further up the hillside just beneath the swell of a sizeable rounded turfed bank running for some distance in either direction. Lines of washing fluttered between the decrepit collection of vehicles, lending an incongruous domesticity to the scene.

Her former equanimity deserted her before this whiff of reality and it was with some apprehension that she switched off the engine. Ursula was running towards her, her long dark hair flying. She'd changed her clothes since Meredith had parted from her after lunch and now wore stained jeans and a tartan shirt beneath a sleeveless wool waistcoat unbuttoned and flapping as she ran.

Meredith wound down the window as Ursula stooped panting to gasp, "Glad you found us all right!"

"No problem. Except for meeting a funny old man down there on the other side of the road. He thought I was looking for a refuse tip."

Ursula swept back a curtain of dark hair with a dusty hand, leaving a smear of dirt on her forehead. "That's Finny. Mad as a hatter but harmless!"

As Meredith got out of the car, Ursula whispered, "What did Markby say about — about that?" She jerked her head towards the hippy encampment.

Meredith could both smell and hear it now. The breeze blowing down from the rampart towards them brought on it the chatter of voices, bark of a dog, thin wail of a baby and the odour of woodsmoke and dirty engine parts.

"Not much joy, I'm afraid. Nor about the other matter," she added cryptically.

"Okay, we'll discuss it later."

They exchanged glances. Looking towards the trailer, Meredith murmured, "Is that Dan?"

But the sandy-haired stocky man she indicated was already striding purposefully forward, cutting off Ursula's reply and supplying his own answer.

"Hullo!" He thrust out a stubby hand. "I'm Ian Jackson, curator of Bamford Museum! You're Meredith Mitchell. Welcome to our scene of operations. Only nothing's happening at the moment owing to that lot having parked themselves up there and Chief Inspector Markby sitting on his backside in Bamford station doing nothing about it! Ursula says you're connected somehow with Markby, right?"

His eyes bored into hers and he didn't wait for an answer. "If you are, I'd be grateful if you'd twist his arm and get

80

him to do something! He seems more worried about their welfare than ours!"

Ursula drew a deep breath and said resolutely, "Give her a chance, Ian! You know Markby has his own way of handling the situation and Meredith can't help that!"

"I only mean — "

"He only means," interrupted a small dark girl with a puckish face, "that he'd like to see the cavalry arriving over the hill there to send our hippies flying in full retreat!"

"Oh, very funny!" said Jackson sourly.

The dark girl's American accent was clear to Meredith's ear and Ursula hastened to perform introductions. "This is Renee Colmar, an American colleague. And this is Karen Henson who's also helping out!"

Jackson gave a strangled snort. Renee threw him a look of ill-concealed irritation but produced a bright smile for Meredith. "Hi! Welcome to our happy little family, Meredith. Come to put your head on the block?"

"Cut it out, Renee!" said Ursula briskly but without rancour.

The other girl, Karen, moved forward awkwardly. An old-fashioned raffia garden hat, its wide brim decorated with faded flowers, had done little to prevent a sandstorm of freckles across her homely face and a suggested appearance of a freshly boiled lobster. Meredith sympathised, guessing how this beefy and rather unattractive young woman must suffer from exposure to the summer sun.

As if to underline the fact, Karen extended a hand at the end of an arm blotched with more patches of sunburn and dried scabs of pink calomel lotion. "Hullo," she muttered and looked down at the ground as if aware of her wretched appearance.

The dog added to his own greeting, pushing his nose into Meredith's hand. She patted his head. "Whose is he?" she asked Karen.

"None of us really," Karen said shyly. "He belongs up there, at the camp. But he's sort of joined us. He's very good!" she added defensively with a defiant look at Jackson. The dog flopped down by her feet and looked up at her, tongue lolling. Clearly he had appointed himself her devoted companion and relied on this new mistress to argue the case for his inclusion in affairs.

"I have to confess," Meredith told Jackson, "that I've never visited Bamford Museum even though I've been in Bamford often."

He looked rueful. "You and the world at large! We're not exactly packed out with visitors! The biggest crowd is when one of the local schools brings a party of children along as part of some project or other! I can't blame the general public. Flints and broken pots aren't of much interest to the layman. What we need desperately, of course, is something really dramatic!" He cast a wistful glance around the warren of open trenches and stripped earth. "That's why I'm here. This is, well, my great hope!"

Her first impression of him had been of an abrasive young man dominated by an *idée fixe*, but suddenly she found herself liking him.

"You spoke as if you expected to find something important."

"This whole undertaking is Ian's

brainchild!" said Ursula. "He talked the Trust into financing it. Tell her, Ian."

Jackson flushed, partly embarrassed and partly pleased by the recognition.

"If we don't come up with something spectacular soon, the Trust mightn't finance it much longer. And yet I know it's there — " He broke off and hunched his shoulders. "Maybe I didn't give you the best welcome just now, Meredith. But it's because I'm so damn frustrated with all this! Sorry if I sounded a grouch."

"I'd say you had good reason!" she told him, indicating the glorious chaos of the New Age travellers' encampment. It was certainly near enough to cause alarm and Jackson's concern was understandable. Since her arrival someone had attempted to start a fire with wood which was obviously still green, and smoke rose into the evening air between the trailers and heaps of rubbish in a series of dark grey belches. The distinctive pungent sulphurous odour wafted towards their group and she sniffed. It made her nostrils itch. Meredith felt a desire to sneeze come over her. She pulled out a handkerchief and rubbed at her nose.

"It'll get worse!" said Renee, observing her. "Believe me, we've been nearly smoked out! Well, better get on with it! Talk with you later, Meredith!"

She grinned, hunched her shoulders resignedly and turned away to recommence her interrupted work a few yards off. The soft persistent scrape of her trowel on gritty soil formed a descant to their further conversation. Karen made no move to join her, only shuffled awkwardly on the spot and reached out a hand to touch the dog's head as if to reassure either him or herself. Meredith wasn't sure which.

But they were all of them intruders on this landscape. Meredith tried to imagine the hillside without any of them cluttering it up. Quiet, with an air of melancholy. But not at peace. There was a restlessness about this primitive place. Here the wind would never be still. And who knew whether those who had lived in the shadow of the great mound or died on its slopes did not still wander here in spirit? Could one ever be sure that a sound was only the rustle of the wind in the longer grass? But although it was lonely, there was a habitation just over the horizon. She could see its chimneys. And further along, dominating the scene, was a strange stump of a building with battlements. Yet it did not look convincingly mediaeval and was more likely the brainchild of some eccentric Victorian, a folly pure and simple. Meredith, who had a weakness for such places, resolved to climb up there and examine it if she got a chance.

Jackson had seen how her gaze studied the horizon and he pointed at the long grassy mound overhanging the New Age camp. "That rampart's called Motts Castle. The name indicates a Norman motte and bailey but it's much, much older than that, an Iron Age earthwork."

"Ursula said something about Saxon remains."

He nodded. "After the Roman legions withdrew from Britain, raiders weren't slow to cross the sea and plunder the country. It was easy pickings and eventually they stayed and settled. They first appeared in this area in the late fifth century as pure marauders — " Perhaps unconsciously, Jackson glanced up the hill towards the ramshackle camp. " — and they were led by a Saxon chieftain called Wulfric."

"The local Britons put up an unexpectedly stiff resistance, making a stand here behind the old fortification. But Wulfric and his men overran the place and massacred the lot. However the Britons had the last laugh because Wulfric himself was mortally wounded by a poisoned spear. By 'poisoned' the chronicler probably refers to gangrene. In ancient times and right through the Middle Ages there's a lot of reference to poisoned arrows and so on, because it was the only way they could explain why some wounds putrefied and others didn't."

The speaker was now well away, his face glowing with enthusiasm. "Picture it! There'd been a battle, dead bodies all over the place including Saxon casualties. Wulfric's warriors were pagan and they set to work to bury their dead according to their particular tradition. They buried them here where they fell, because they were themselves going to move on once they'd finished and held a suitable wake!

"Some Saxon tribes cremated the fallen, others buried them with their weapons. Wulfric's lot were inclined to the latter. In the meantime poor old Wulfric's wound was turning green. They probably carried him to the nearest shelter. Certainly he'd have been weak and they wouldn't have moved him very far. There, in some requisitioned Romano-British farmhouse Wulfric lay watching his flesh rot, all alone because the stench of it kept others away. In the distance he could hear his men digging graves for their comrades, pretty sure they were digging one for him too. Although perhaps he was delirious."

Jackson shook his head and pointed at the hillside. His voice tense with excitement he went on, "Wulfric died we don't know where. But here, this is where they buried the poor blighter, I'm sure of it! Because this was the scene of his last victorious battle! He was their chief and they sent him off to the next world with all honours! Dressed in his best clothes and laid in the grave with his shield, his helmet and any other armour, his sword, his drinking cups and personal jewellery. If they'd had a successful expedition until then, they would have added his share of any loot collected elsewhere: coins, jewellery, gold or silver plate. Any and everything which belonged to him went into the grave with him and it's here!" Jackson's voice had slowly risen to fever pitch. "It's here, dammit!" He swept his arm over the surrounding landscape. "Wulfric the Saxon is lying here in all his burial splendour and I'm going to find him!"

Silence fell. At last Meredith ventured tentatively, "Ursula said you'd found a skeleton already."

"What?" Jackson turned and blinked at her. "Oh yes, we did but it's not Wulfric. It's probably one of his men. It's over here. Come and have a look before the light gets too bad."

He set off. Meredith and Ursula followed him, Karen and the dog bringing up the rear. Karen had been listening as Jackson spoke, nodding occasionally in agreement but keeping what appeared to be her usual silence. Lack of confidence, decided Meredith, picking her way along a wooden gangplank. A pity, but difficult to remedy.

"Here we are!" said Jackson in a brisk practical tone. He had stopped by a rectangle of tarpaulin pegged out on the ground. "Take that end, Karen!"

So he does know she's with us! thought Meredith.

Karen had scurried forward and stooped to release the nearer peg. Between them she and Jackson rolled back the cover. With that action a thousand or more years rolled back and a Saxon warrior again faced the light and air.

It was an extraordinary and, Meredith had to admit, a downright spooky experience. First the bones of the feet came into view, dry, dull and discoloured, frail. Then the shin bones, next the thigh bones slightly at an angle as if he'd been buried with his knees bent to one side. Perhaps they hadn't dug the grave long enough and couldn't fit him in straight. The pelvis next and then the crushed ribs and some scattered bones presumably of the left arm. The right arm bones were tangled in the ribs. Finally, lying where dark shadow crossed the corner of the grave ditch, his skull, gleaming in the gloom and surprisingly well preserved. There was an almost full set of yellow teeth although the jawbone had fallen off and lay to one side. The empty eye sockets gazed up at them in a manner which seemed to Meredith hostile, as if this fighting man of old still had the power to leap up and give them a nasty moment or two for daring to disturb his rest.

In fact so real was he now that she felt that if she looked up she'd see his silhouette standing on the earthen wall above them, watching.

Ursula spoke, perhaps sensing what was in her mind.

"He was tall, wasn't he? A six-footer. The bones of the left upper arm are back at the lab for tests. But this is a fighting man all right and judging by the state of his teeth he was in his prime, in his twenties. He was buried under his shield according to Saxon practice."

Meredith shivered. "Where's the shield?" she asked, staring down at the ancient bones.

"Gone away for X-ray treatment and

preservation. What's left of it, that is. Really only the metal central boss and some metal studs from the rim. It would have been made of wood and rotted. His spear was probably beside him but that's gone, rusted."

"It's spellbinding . . . " Meredith said quietly.

"Then imagine what Wulfric's grave must be like!" Jackson burst out. "A princeling's burial chamber which no one's ever found! If they had, there'd be some record of it. You don't dig up a treasure and no one knows!"

"Gives you the creeps, dunnit?" said a strange voice suddenly from above, and gave a hoarse, malicious chuckle.

They all jumped and looked up, startled. Uphill from them, several yards away and looking down on the skeleton, stood an unsavoury youth in torn denims with shaven head and ears festooned with gold rings. From the camp! thought Meredith in relief, stilling the unwarranted lurch of her heart and the shiver of superstitious awe.

"It's not to be disturbed!" Jackson shouted at him, colouring in anger.

The youth grinned evilly. "I ain't disturbed it. I like looking at it. It's int'resting!"

"Well, yes," Ursula broke in as peacemaker. "But really only interesting to people like me who mess about with old bones. It's Joe, isn't it?" she added.

"'S'right." Joe sat down on the turf cross-legged like some sort of imp. "This other bloke, then . . . You reckon they buried him here too wiv gold and that?"

So he's been up there listening for some time and we didn't realise it, Meredith thought, frowning. It was an uneasy realisation.

"It's only a theory!" Jackson howled, his face taut with emotion. "For God's sake, don't go digging around!"

"Free country, innit?"

"Look here, you could ruin — "

Ursula hastened to break in again. "Pete said the travellers wouldn't interfere with our work! It's highly unlikely we'll find anything you'd call valuable and if we did it wouldn't be immediately recognisable. It would have been buried over a thousand years. It wouldn't be any use to you."

The imp unfolded his spindly limbs and got to his feet. "Don't worry, I don't give a shit about old coins and that. Them bones, they're what interest me, see? Same as they interest you, love, all right?"

"Yes, all right," said Ursula, laughing despite Jackson's glare.

"Cheers, then!" Joe waved a hand in salute and ambled away towards the encampment.

"Miserable little ghoul!" snarled Jackson. "Why don't the Felstons get their solicitor on to it and get the blighters thrown off the hill? I can't understand what prevents them!"

Ursula hunched her shoulders. "You know the Felstons. They're a canny pair; they'd hate the idea of anyone knowing anything about their business. They say they can't afford the solicitor's fees. Personally I suspect they can, but they don't want to pay if the police will do it for free."

"If the police oblige!" Jackson exploded. "Markby told me that in his opinion the travellers 'will probably move on in a few days'. A few days! Does he realise what that necrophiliac of a spotty kid could do in that time? If he starts digging on his own account — "

There was a murmur of engine noise and the grinding of gears. A horn tooted. They turned and saw a dusty van lurching down the track towards the site.

Ursula touched Meredith's arm. "Now you can meet — "

But before she finished, Karen burst out loudly, "It's Dan!"

6

EVERYTHING Ursula had told her made Meredith very curious to see Dan Woollard but she tried not to show her eagerness. As it was, even knowing nothing about him, he would have made a striking impression.

A burly bear of a man, he wore a plaid shirt, denims and high laced combat boots. She thought he looked more like a lumberjack than an archaeologist. He came towards them, bushy eyebrows raised questioningly, and she heard Ursula beside her making the introductions. Meredith put out her hand.

His massive paw closed on it. "Nice to meet you!" he said. "Sula told us you'd be coming down to keep her company out here. You'll be okay in the trailer but I'm still against the two of you staying here. That lot — " He jerked his head towards the travellers' camp. "They're unpredictable. For all we know they've got drugs up there. They could get as high as kites and come waltzing down here in the middle of the night. If you think anything like that is happening, then you and Sula get the hell out of it as fast as you can! Don't stay to argue."

"Stop making such a fuss, Dan!" Ursula said sharply. "You stayed here last night and nothing happened to you."

"I'm not saying it will happen, only that it could!" He glared at her. "And I'm a bloke and pretty solidly built as well. You two, it's different."

"We're perfectly capable!" Ursula told him.

Now that she'd had a moment to observe him closely Meredith was already revising her first impression of him. At first sight one thought of strength. There was certainly physical strength. But the mouth framed by the beard was surprisingly weak, and she wondered if he was aware of it and the facial hair had been grown to disguise an unsatisfactory feature. There was also something petulant in his manner, something she couldn't quite identify for the moment.

But he seemed affable enough and now he turned to her. "I see you've been taking a look at our body in the grave!"

Jackson, who had been showing signs of unease in the background, burst out, "We'd better get it covered over before it gets too dark to see what we're doing! That little yob Joe was here again! He pokes and pries, snoops about. Now he thinks there's a treasure to be found! It gets worse and worse!"

Dan hunched his shoulders. "Ease up, Ian. The little squirt won't come around if someone's here. At least," he glanced at the two women again, "I hope not!"

He began helping Jackson to replace the tarpaulin over the skeleton and Ursula and Meredith made their way back to the trailer. Karen, who had been hovering and listening with her eyes fixed on Woollard, followed them.

Renee was already there, packing her things together for the day.

"Well, rather you two than me!" she said cheerfully. "I think the guys should do it."

"Don't you start!" said Ursula. "Dan seems to think they're all going to rush down here in the middle of the night after supper of magic mushroom stew and overturn the trailer."

"They might!" Renee was not one of nature's comforters.

Karen murmured in her self-effacing way, "I'll get my, stuff out of the trailer. You won't want it in there with you."

She climbed the step and disappeared inside. Curious to see the place where she was to spend the night, Meredith followed her. Ursula remained outside talking to Renee.

Inside the caravan was a mess but an organised mess. There was a temporary long trestle table set up in the centre taking up most of the room and laid out along it in neat piles pieces of bone and pot. There was also a chipped enamel washing-up bowl full of muddy water and a sponge. Karen was moving a stack of labels and clearing pens and sticky tape out of the way.

"I've been cleaning and labelling up," she said apologetically.

"Tricky job."

"Not as tricky as being outside in the trenches. I've got two left feet." She hunched her shoulders in dejection.

"I stepped on something again this afternoon and Ian bawled me out. He's put me on indefinite duty in here where he reckons I'll do less harm."

"I expect he'll relent. He's obviously very worried about the site now the hippies are camped here, and he's probably lost his temper unintentionally."

"No." She turned clasping a sheaf of papers to her smock. "He doesn't want me on the dig. If he wasn't short of people he wouldn't have me."

Embarrassed and not knowing how to reply, Meredith mumbled indistinctly.

"Everyone knows. You'll see it too if you stay. I don't mean to damage anything! I do try to be careful! Everyone gets angry, except Dan, that is! He's always nice to me." There was a wistful note in her voice.

Hmn, thought Meredith. Aloud she said, "I dare say we'll be quite comfortable in here tonight."

It was an optimistic statement. The set-up was Spartan. There were two bunks with sleeping bags, a calor gas picnic stove, a small tin kettle and an assortment of mugs.

"Renee says the site's haunted." Karen flushed at seeing Meredith's surprised expression. "Sorry, that was tactless! I don't suppose it is. It doesn't do for archaeologists to believe in ghosts, does it? Disturbing the dead all the time as we do! I must go now."

Alone Meredith squeezed her way down the caravan between trestle table and bunk examining the assorted finds of the dig. But one piece of pot looked very much like another to her. One or two were patterned in herringbone design. One, a little larger and set to one side, showed part of a primitive figure scratched in the clay before firing. It looked and probably was rather rude.

The sound of a step and a rocking of the trailer made her turn her head. The American girl, Renee, materialised, arms akimbo in the doorway.

"I came for Karen's bag! She forgot it. She'd forget her head if it wasn't fixed to her neck!"

Meredith looked round and picked up a well-used canvas rucksack. "This one?"

"Yes, thanks." Renee moved forward

101

to take it but then stood with it gripped tightly in both fists, eyeing Meredith speculatively. "Karen's been talking to you about Jackson?" It wasn't a question but a statement. "It isn't her fault, you know, the things which happen when she's around. It's his. He makes her nervous. He doesn't make me nervous because I'm a whole lot tougher than she is. She can't look out for herself. So I do it for her. She's a good kid."

Meredith said firmly, "Yes, I'm sure she is."

Renee hunched her shoulders. "Jackson's half way to plain nuts, in my opinion! Not that anyone ever asks me what I think!"

"Karen said," Meredith picked up her last sentence, "that you think the site's haunted!"

Renee gave a little snort. "It's weird, let's put it that way. The whole hill is a strange place. You feel as though you're being watched. It's difficult to explain."

"Why do you and Karen stay if the situation isn't pleasant?"

"We joined the dig for the practical experience. These kinds of excavations aren't a dime a dozen, you know! We were really pleased, both of us, to get the chance. But we didn't join to get bawled out every five minutes. Wulfric, Wulfric! That's all we get from Ian. You'll see!"

She vanished abruptly and her place was taken almost immediately by Ursula, looking equally flushed and annoyed.

"Dan's being stupid. What can happen to us?"

"Nothing, I hope!" said Meredith, wondering if the atmosphere around here was always so fraught and if so, how they ever managed to get any work done.

"Absolutely! Nothing happened to him last night! They're all leaving now."

The sound of car engines confirmed her statement. Meredith went to the door and put her head out. Karen and Renee had already left and Jackson was just driving away. Dan was getting into his van. He paused, seeing a figure in the trailer doorway. But when he recognised Meredith he merely raised his hand in salute and got into his van. She waved but she knew she wasn't the one he'd hoped to see. She watched him drive off.

7

IN the trailer Ursula had lit an oil lamp to dispel the growing gloom. Now she was unpacking a cardboard box and putting tins of soup and beans on the table.

"It's all a bit primitive but we'll have some supper! I've got bread rolls and some cheese and ham."

"Soup and a bread roll will do me fine. That was an enormous lunch you cooked today at your home!"

"Still, we have to spend the evening somehow, so we might as well eat." Ursula was fiddling with the calor gas stove.

"What can I do?"

"Nothing really. There's a little radio somewhere but reception isn't good out here. You did manage to have a word with your police boyfriend, you said."

"I really wish you wouldn't call him a boyfriend. He is a friend but he isn't a boy. I don't even see him that often!"

Meredith was sorry to snap, but it was a constant problem that people misunderstood her relationship with Alan. Possibly this was because neither Alan nor Meredith herself had yet succeeded in quite sorting out what that was or where it was going: if indeed it was going anywhere.

She climbed up on one of the bunks and clasped her knees with her arms. "Alan wasn't very charitable, I'm afraid. He thinks Natalie will turn up of her own accord — when she's good and ready. It isn't his area anyway. He reckons it's just a domestic squabble. No one has officially reported her missing. Mrs Salter, if she had any doubts about her daughter's whereabouts, would probably have gone to him as Bamford is her local station, but she hasn't. Dan doesn't look worried to me. I know you're concerned, Ursula, but well, after talking to Alan — "

"You think I'm imagining it? I don't blame you. Tomato all right?" Ursula held up a tin. "I keep telling myself I'm imagining it. But the atmosphere's getting very tense. Everyone's wondering. Perhaps you didn't notice tonight, but you will tomorrow. No one asks Dan about Natalie any more. No one wants to bring up the subject."

"Tell me about Karen."

Can-opener in hand, Ursula looked up in surprise. "Why Karen?"

"She seems shy. She said she'd been taken off the dig and put in here out of harm's way, labelling and washing pots. She seems rather keen on Dan."

"Pah!" said Ursula crossly. "She's smitten. I feel sorry for her. She's very bright in other respects. She has a brilliant degree and has been working for her master's at an American university. She met Renee there and they decided to try to get summer practical work in England. The Ellsworth was pleased to take them on. But Karen seems to have five thumbs on each hand. Ian's got a bit fed up with it."

"But he seems to think she'll be all right in here!" Meredith gestured expressively at the trestle table laden with potsherds.

"Unless she knocks the whole lot over, which is quite possible, yes. Oh, curse this can-opener! What's the matter with the thing?" She redoubled her efforts and panted, "I think Ian makes it worse. He watches poor Karen like a hawk, waiting for her to do something wrong and when inevitably she does, he pounces and tells her off in front of everyone. I've told him he shouldn't do it. But Ian's completely wrapped up in this dig. He's got Wulfric on the brain. I think that if he'd relax, if we'd all show a bit more confidence in Karen, and if the general atmosphere around here weren't so tense, what with hippies and this business of Natalie, Karen wouldn't be so clumsy. She's very sensitive."

"And worried about Dan?"

"Probably." Ursula frowned. "I hope she doesn't get mixed up with him. I mean, if he goes off me and looks for another shoulder to cry on. She couldn't cope. Dan isn't easy and Karen hasn't got, you know, any notion about men. I doubt she's ever had a boyfriend." Ursula gave a snort. "Look who's talking, you might say! Much I turned out to know about it. What do you think of Dan?"

"I've hardly had time to judge. A good-looking man. Pleasant manner. I can understand — " She broke off awkwardly.

"My falling for him? Yes, so can I — sometimes. He can be very pleasant if he's in the mood. He's also got a lousy temper when he isn't, and a conviction the world's against him. Lord knows why. The Ellsworth, the Trust which employs us both, thinks very highly of Dan. I get the feeling that when the present Director retires, they'll hand Dan the administration of the Trust."

"So, I suppose he ought to be treading carefully, as far as his private life's concerned. These registered bodies are generally sensitive about their reputations."

Ursula leaned forward, her eyes burning with eagerness. "Exactly! You see, Meredith, there isn't proof I can show your Mr Markby, but the situation is set up for something like this! Suppose Natalie found out about me and was set to make a great fuss? She could do it. Suppose Dan in a temper picked up a paperweight or something and just lashed out at her with it, or pushed her and she fell and hit her head? He'd panic. He'd try and hide the body. He'd pretend nothing had happened. He'd say Natalie was away on a visit. Of course he wouldn't get his story perfect because he isn't an habitual criminal! But he does have this way of adjusting the truth . . . "

"So where is it, the body?" Meredith objected. "Any signs of digging in the back garden?"

"All paved over. Just a yard with a few tubs of dead-looking shrubs. Neither Dan nor Natalie is a gardener. Anyway, even if there were any earth out there, he wouldn't go digging in it. It would be immediately obvious and a neighbour might see. Those are terraced houses, all the back yards overlook one another."

"Saw the body up? Take it out a bit at a time in plastic bags?" Meredith pulled a face. "Sorry to be gruesome, but it just isn't easy to dispose of a body in the middle of town. Out in the country, well, perhaps. If I do have a theory, just an idea, about this, it's that — just possibly — some accident has happened to Natalie since she stormed out and has prevented her return. I do think the time's come for either you or Jackson to insist that Dan report his wife missing."

"Alive or dead," Ursula said fretfully, "she ought to have turned up by now if her disappearance was genuine. I just have this gut feeling, and a bloody awful feeling it is, that she's dead and Dan — "

"Oh hell!" This last cry was accompanied by a yelp as Ursula leapt back and the tomato soup can shot across the table, fell on its side and began to ooze a steady red stream on to the trailer floor.

Meredith rescued the can as Ursula seized a rag and began feverishly to mop up. But the scarlet stain seemed imbued with a life of its own, creeping across every surface and leaping magically over gaps so that the merest touch resulted in a rash of crimson fingerprints appearing in fresh places all over the caravan. The sweet smell of canned tomato filled the air. At that moment there was a sudden sharp knock at the trailer door.

They stopped work to stare at one another startled. Meredith knelt on the bunk and peered out of the dusty little window. Outside in the twilight two dark shapes stood still and silent. One was tall and shaggy. The other seemed to be clad in fluttering draperies. Behind them a network of trenches ran in a darker pattern against the grey ground. The grave with the skeleton could not longer be made out. Meredith swallowed and tried to dismiss superstitious fears.

"Visitors!" she said, she hoped normally. "I'll let 'em in."

"We're from the camp! On behalf of all of us!" said a voice in the gloom as she opened the door. The shapes outside became reassuring flesh and blood but the announcement was a little ominous.

The trailer rocked and bounced beneath the added weight as they clambered up the steps. The man came first, dressed in an old Aran sweater, and corduroys. The woman wore a long skirt, grimy at the hem, and, Meredith was amused to note, men's sturdy work boots. Both had shoulder-length loose flowing hair, the man's confined under a greenish hat. He sported a straggly beard. They edged carefully round a gory footprint on the trailer floor but neither queried it.

They did look taken aback as Ursula advanced to greet them holding out scarlet smeared hands, clots of nameless horror slithering over her wrists and up her forearms. "It's Pete and Anna! Do sit down. Sorry about the mess!"

Now the girl asked crisply, "Have you cut yourself? We've got a first-aid box in our bus."

Ursula explained and the visitors sat down side by side, turning a critical stare on Meredith. There was a distinct odour of woodsmoke clinging to their clothes and it began to permeate the air of the caravan and displace that of spilled soup. The girl looked ultra self-assured and slightly aggressive. The man was more diffident.

"Nice to meet you," said Meredith not quite knowing what was expected.

The girl replied in her surprisingly loud, clearly articulated voice. "We came to see if you were okay. Also the travellers have talked it over and want to make something clear."

They exchanged glances and the man, Pete, took up the conversation. "We appreciate your work and we wouldn't interfere or do any damage. We know Joe was here earlier but he doesn't mean any harm. He wouldn't touch anything. He understands."

"Does he?" Ursula asked sceptically.

"We don't interfere with anyone else's lifestyle!" Anna snapped in her county voice. "We just ask that no one interferes in ours! Joe knows the rules. But we want you to understand that."

Meredith asked, "Has he been travelling with your convoy long?"

They exchanged glances again. "Not long," Pete said.

"Where does he come from?"

But she had asked too many questions. She saw their faces freeze.

"We don't ask people that," Anna said shortly.

"It doesn't matter where they come from," Pete added. "Or where they're going. That's not the purpose of life. We're in communion with Mother Earth. We allow her to regulate our lives with her seasons."

Meredith felt it wouldn't be helpful to become embroiled in a discussion about the specific nature of life's purpose or what part Mother Earth played in it. She looked at Ursula for help.

Ursula broke the awkward silence by asking, "Would you like to stay for supper? I've got other tins of soup and I won't chuck the next lot round the place. You'd be very welcome."

Perhaps they took this as a hint to leave or perhaps they just didn't want to stay. Possibly they'd lost confidence in Ursula's culinary skills. They both stood up and spoke in unison. "No thanks. We must get back."

At the door Pete turned to repeat, "You needn't worry about Joe."

"Don't fall in the trench," warned Ursula. "Break an ankle or anything."

They only chimed, "Good night!" and then they were gone.

"Well!" said Meredith. "That was a very civilised social call."

Ursula bit her lip. "Do you suppose they could hear anything through the door?"

"If they did, I think they'd keep it to themselves. They don't bother with life outside the convoy, just as they said."

"Dan would say," Ursula muttered, "that it was a recce. They came to see just who was staying here overnight."

"Then they know," Meredith answered. "We are."

★ ★ ★

Brian Felston stood in the doorway to the kitchen at Motts Farm and watched his uncle. The farmhouse wasn't that old, 1920s-built and of uninteresting design. Nothing the two men had done to the interior had made it any more attractive or inviting. It was a bachelors' home for two working men. The only pictures on the walls were one of *Ruth and Naomi* in faded sepia tint and another of Winston Churchill, cut from a magazine and framed by Lionel long ago in patriotic spirit. There were no cushions or crocheted mats or vases of flowers. There were a few ornaments, dusty and cracked, which had been put there by Brian's mother when she and his father had lived here. Anything even slightly decorative had belonged to her.

Brian couldn't remember her very well. She'd left when he was fourteen. Just put on her hat and coat one day and walked out. He didn't blame her for that even though he'd missed her. She'd had a dog's life. He understood and had even felt guilty about it. If he had been older he could have helped her, perhaps, protected her. But he'd only been a child and forced to stand idly by until she'd upped and helped herself. She'd done right.

Brian, surveying his uncle, thought how Lionel, in the dreary ordinariness of the kitchen, looked out of place by about a hundred years. He sat at the deal table reading by the light of an art deco lamp (that had been Brian's mother's!). It had only a low-wattage bulb and there was no other light on in the room. Outside it had grown dark and dark within too, thrown like a cloak around the old man who sat in a pool of mottled orange, green and purplish blue thrown by the coloured glass lampshade. He looked quite isolated in time, space and attitude.

The old chap wasn't reading his Bible tonight but a stout volume of Victorian sermons. There was nothing wrong with his eyesight. Even in this poor light he needed no spectacles but he followed the lines with his forefinger and his lips moved soundlessly forming the words. This didn't signify poor reading skill but was, Brian knew, because his uncle liked the sense of weight and authority the solemn, high-flown language conveyed. He revelled in its archaic turn of phrase and colourful imagery.

They had a television in the house but the old man never watched it, convinced it showed nothing but half-naked cavorting women. Even attempts to get him to watch the weather forecast failed because Lionel had once seen a woman presenting that. Anyway, he knew what the weather was going to be by looking up at the sky.

Plenty of people would have thought the old man eccentric but Brian didn't consider him that. He knew he was a first-class farmer and it was only in this one respect that he was out on a limb, unlike others. And Brian was used to that, having lived his entire life to a background of Lionel's denunciation of human fleshly pleasures. All the same it made life difficult, especially just at the moment. If the old man even suspected . . .

Brian felt the sweat break out on his brow. He also experienced a pang of resentment. Hadn't he the right to live his life as he wanted? Had any chance of happiness always to be spoiled by the fire and brimstone notions festering in the old man's brain?

He moved quietly across the kitchen, passing behind his uncle's chair. The old man didn't look up. Brian went into the outer closed porch where they kept coats and footwear and stooped to lace up the strong boots he wore round the farm. He pulled on a thick jacket and reached for the flashlight kept on a hook.

As his fingers touched it his uncle's voice came harshly from the kitchen and Brian froze.

"Where're you going off to, then, this time of night? Stock's all settled. I checked it."

"I'm just going along the ridge, Uncle Lionel. See what those hippies are up to."

A gusty sigh came from Lionel but his voice croaked loudly like a raven's. "Fornication, that's what it is!"

"What?" Brian heard his own voice

yelp. He edged towards the outer door and grasped the handle in his sweating palm.

"Fornicating they are! Carrying on like beasts, only beasts does it by way of nature and aren't to be blamed!"

Imprudently Brian muttered, "People do it by way of nature too!"

The old man's hearing was as keen as his eyesight. "You cleanse your mind of them thoughts, Brian!" His fist crashed on the table and the lamp rocked. "Don't you be corrupted and led into temptation! Them as go astray fall into the pit, the pit of everlasting fire!"

Brian jerked open the back door and the fresh night air struck his face with a welcome, liberating blast. He felt it cool the sweat on his forehead.

"You going as far as the old folly?" called his uncle.

Now what had made the old chap ask that? wondered Brian uneasily. Lionel never went near the folly himself. Surely . . .

As casually as he could he shouted back, "I might. If they're still stirring down at the camp I might sit up there for a bit and keep watch."

"Stay away from that camp! It's a nest of evil!"

"All right, Uncle Lionel, take it easy!" Brian spoke the words automatically and in relief. He pulled the door closed.

The moon spread her silver light and he didn't need any help to see his way. Hands in pockets, Brian strode sturdily across the yard, calling a word of reassurance to the chained dog, and set off up the track which led to the ridge. He was a man with a task but there was a spring in his step which suggested he was looking forward to it.

★ ★ ★

Despite everything, a certain spirit of adventure had entered Meredith's heart. Besides, the bunk wasn't nearly so hard as it looked and the sleeping bag snug. It had been a long and confused day and exertion and fresh air combined like a knockout draught. She fell asleep immediately although she had thought she wouldn't.

But it was not a peaceful sleep. Her

brain churned. For some reason she dreamed about Finny and his teeth. In the dream he'd lost them and she was helping him look for them. Then she saw something gleaming on the ground and, thinking she'd found the elusive dentures, stooped to pick them up. But it was the broken jaw bone from the skeleton that she found herself holding and with a gasp of horror, she hurled it from her in her dream and awoke.

It was very quiet and very dark. Earlier, before she'd gone to sleep, there had been a certain amount of noise from the camp, babies crying and music. Someone up there played a fiddle and the scraped tunes had drifted towards them on the night air, together with the crackle and spit of a wood fire blazing up and turning the night sky rosy pink. In a curious way, it had been rather romantic, conjuring up a picture of colourful gypsies and throbbing violins, not upperclass girls slumming it in hobnailed boots, with shaven-headed dropouts about whom no one knew anything.

Now, lying in the darkness filled with the unease from her dream which wouldn't leave her, Meredith found herself straining her ears for any sound. On the other side of the trailer regular breathing told her that Ursula slept. She peered at the illuminated dial of her wristwatch and saw that it was just before three in the morning. Perhaps before long it would begin to be light. She would be glad to see the dawn and hear the first twitter of birdsong.

It was cold now in the trailer and the sleeping bag couldn't disguise it. Meredith put out a hand and touched the trailer's metal wall. It was filmed with condensation. Trying not to make a noise and disturb Ursula, she knelt on the bunk with the sleeping bag pulled round her and tried to see out, rubbing more condensation from the little window.

Silvery moonlight bathed the scene outside. The trench pattern was etched jet black like a gigantic puzzle-maze which ought to have some meaning, long-lost like that of carvings on a jungle temple. The distant hedgerow and trees were silhouetted against the inky sky like a cut-out paper frieze. She unlatched the window, pushing it open and pressing her face to the gap to get a breath of air and a better view.

Up at the camp among the vans and trailers the remains of the fire still flickered erratically, shooting up stabs of yellow and sending pale smoke curling into the night sky. Her eye rose above the camp, above the dark mound of Motts Castle, to the skyline and the black stump of Motts Folly.

And then she saw it, quite distinctly, a flash of light up there at the folly. Meredith blinked and waited. A moment or two later she saw it again. Someone was awake and a-prowl, up there on the skyline. Who was it? And at this time of night? She waited quite five or six minutes but didn't see the light again. Perhaps after all it had only been an escaping spark from the dying fire and the poor visibility had made it look as if it came from the folly.

The wind was getting up. The silhouetted trees swayed and bowed like courtly dancers. There was a dull flap of cloth from out in the darkness on the site which made her jump and she realised that Dan and Ian had failed to secure the tarpaulin sufficiently. The wind had seized a loose edge and was shaking it mischievously. It flapped again, making a short angry snapping sound as if the warrior lying beneath had decided to get up from his grave-bed and walk around for a while, stretching his bony legs.

She shut the window, snuggled down into the sleeping bag again and tried to go back to sleep. The wind soughed around the caravan and rocked it gently. Every so often she thought she caught the sound of twigs cracking, movement outside. She could still smell the woodsmoke. Either it had drifted in through the opened window from the dying bonfire or Anna and Pete had left it behind them.

Eventually, wondering vaguely what Mother Earth thought about it all this digging up of her ancient secrets, she fell asleep.

8

ALAN MARKBY, walking briskly into town in search of lunch the following day, was attracted by the faint dirge-like scrape of a fiddle. The music, if that's what it was, did not sound as though it came from a radio perched on someone's shoulder or through the open window of a parked car. Curious, he followed the sound and found it originated from the recessed doorway of some shuttered shop premises.

There were two of them, a boy and a girl. It was difficult to say how old they were but certainly little more than twenty. The fiddleplayer was a scrawny youth in tattered jeans, in Markby's view distinctly undernourished. The girl could have been as scrawny as the youth but there was no way of telling. She was quite shapeless, a swaddled form wrapped about with enough petticoats and shawls to model as one of those wooden Russian dolls, strong boots at one end and a pink face tied round with a headscarf at the other. As he watched she opened her mouth and began to sing.

At least, no doubt that was the intention. Just as the purpose of the display was to beg for coins. Markby was not musical himself and, well aware of it, inclined to be tolerant of the tastes of others. But on this occasion he had to admit the sound produced was awful. The fiddler had a rudimentary knowledge of his instrument but apparently no ear. As for the singer, someone had evidently told her that folksongs were to be bellowed out in an unmelodious howl, scorning conventional musical presentation.

They were not, unsurprisingly, having much success. Pedestrians hastened by, looking appalled. No one threw any money into the upturned cap on the pavement. Markby wondered whether to act the heavy-handed guardian of the law and move them on. But they weren't obstructing the thoroughfare nor importuning the passers-by other than by an assault on the ear. Markby decided to leave them to it for the time being and walked on, glancing at his watch.

It had just turned twelve, but he was hungry. The Bunch of Grapes was only a few yards further down the road and did a very acceptable home-made soup and crusty bread. He wended his way there.

Established in a corner with his soup and his pint, his thoughts inevitably turned to Meredith with whom he had been in this very pub early the previous evening. He didn't see nearly as much of her as he'd liked to, especially since she'd taken on that flat in London. A flat now invaded by its male owner who threatened to take up residence. Markby grimaced at his beer. It was annoying that now she was in the area again for a week, she would be spending her time out at Bamford Hill. He wondered how she was getting on at the dig. He hoped she and the other one, Ursula, had had an undisturbed night out there.

In fact the presence of the travellers had been seen by him as an urgent matter since their arrival, despite the soothing noises he'd made to Ian Jackson. He wanted at all costs to avoid unpleasantness. There would certainly be young children in that convoy. Force was not the answer.

But Markby was well aware that if the convoy didn't move on soon, voluntarily, he was going to have to do something about it. It might be a good idea to drive out there this afternoon and have a word with their leaders. And at the same time, look in on Meredith.

Markby sipped at his beer. Thinking about all this and especially about Meredith, he recalled the story she'd told him about Dan Woollard and the missing wife. If indeed Natalie Woollard were a genuine missing person. It was quiet in the pub at the moment and Jenny behind the bar was idly wiping down the counter and obviously willing to chat. He got up to return his empty soup bowl and replenish his glass and leaned on the counter while she filled the latter.

"Have something yourself," he invited.

"Thanks!" She'd been in the business a long time. She never refused this kind of offer because it was money in the till, but she didn't confuse it with an opportunity to take alcohol. Bar staff need clear heads. She poured herself out a bitter lemon. "Cheers!" she said amiably.

"Do you ever get much chance to do any reading, Jenny?"

"I've got the *Sun* somewhere," she said vaguely. "If you want today's newspaper."

"No, I mean books. Do you ever read books? Don't suppose you get much time."

"Oh, I love a good book!" She rested her plump forearms on the bar. "I can't be bothered with television. Give me a really good paperback and I'm happy!"

"Ever read anything by a lady called Natalie Woollard?"

"Oh yes! I like her books! The last one, it was about this woman photographer for a top magazine who went out somewhere in some mountains to get some pictures and got captured by tribesmen and this tribal chief, he took one look at her and — "

"Yes, yes!" said Markby hurriedly, having got the message as to the sort of book Mrs Woollard wrote. "Good book, then?"

"Really smashing. She's a great writer. Mind you, she don't leave nothing to the imagination, if you know what I mean.

Tells you every blooming move and this chap in the mountains, he knew a few moves too, I can tell you! I read bits of it out to Len. He said he'd never heard of anyone doing some of them. He reckoned they were physically impossible and he didn't fancy trying in case he ricked something." She looked regretful.

"I see," said Markby. Two more customers came into the bar. "Well, I must get hold of a copy obviously."

"I'll lend you one of mine!" she offered, moving away to serve the newcomers. "I've got all her books."

"Thank you." He hoped she'd forget this kind offer.

Walking back to the station, however, he again reviewed what Meredith had told him. He felt he had been a little ungracious, dismissing Ursula's suspicions out of hand. Meredith had taken them seriously and at the very least he ought to have given equal consideration to her complaint. Pompous, she'd called him. Markby disliked that and thought it unfair. But he realised she had been disappointed in his response. He felt that he'd let her down somehow.

He put his hand in his pocket and his fingers touched a scrap of paper. Opening it out, he saw it was Natalie's mother's Bamford address, given him by Meredith. It gave a further nudge to his conscience. It might be worth just checking with Mrs Salter. If nothing else, he could tell Meredith, honestly, that he'd done something about it, and it might help restore him to her good books.

Accordingly, when he walked into his office he said to Sergeant Pearce, "Pop along to Old Mill Street if you've got time this afternoon. Go and see a lady called Mrs Salter." Briefly he explained. "Just find out when she last saw her daughter and don't alarm her. Make up some reason."

"My girlfriend reads those books," said Pearce unexpectedly.

"Then you've got a ready-made excuse for calling. Buy a copy out of petty cash and take it with you. Ask Mrs Salter if she'll get her daughter to sign it. Your girlfriend is Natalie's greatest fan and so on, and you want to surprise her with a signed copy for her birthday. I'm going out to Bamford Hill and have a word with those New Age travellers. Two of them are busking in town. We're going to have to move them on."

★ ★ ★

Many years in his profession had made Markby finely attuned to subtle nuances in his reception wherever he went. As he got out of his car at the site of the dig he reflected wryly that it was a long time since a group of people had met him with such a mixture of emotions clearly written on their faces as they gathered about him.

Meredith's face lit up. That was nice. The young woman by her, a surprisingly handsome young woman, looked surprised but also pleased. Was that Dr Gretton? Never having met her, he'd imagined the palaeontologist to be a dowdy female with spectacles. He'd been wrong.

There was another girl there, much more the type he'd imagined as an archaeologist, sturdy and awkward and wearing a mud-stained smock and a funny old garden hat. This girl was looking at him in a kind of dismay. And a dark girl with a snub nose who was staring at him as if he were something she'd just dug up and couldn't identify. Then there were the men. A couple of youngsters who clearly were just helpers showed hardly any interest at all. But the other two men presented a different kettle of fish. The tall bearded man was probably Woollard. This wasn't difficult to deduce because the chief inspector had met the other, Ian Jackson.

Jackson was hurrying towards him. "Chief Inspector! Thank goodness you're here! Are you going to do something at last?"

Markby overlooked the implied rebuke. "Good afternoon, Mr Jackson. I've come to take a look at the situation at first hand, as you see."

But as he spoke he was looking towards Woollard. It was always difficult to detect an expression through a beard but he could have sworn that Woollard had looked quite alarmed when Jackson hailed the visitor by his rank. Now Woollard had relaxed a little but still stood back, watching warily.

"How did you get on last night?" Markby asked Meredith.

"Fine. This is Ursula, Dr Gretton, who asked me down here."

Markby shook hands with the handsome girl. She had a firm grip and a level gaze which he found quite disconcerting. Her long dark hair was tied back with a ribbon, she wore no make-up and the tight jeans emphasised her slim hips and long legs.

She spoke. "We did have a social visit from a couple of the hippies. They came to see how we were."

"They were quite nice," said Meredith. "But a bit smelly. I don't mean body-smell, I mean woodsmoke. We couldn't get it out of the caravan after they'd left."

"But you weren't disturbed at all during the night?"

Ursula shook her head vigorously but he noticed slight hesitation on Meredith's part before she said, "No, it was very quiet."

"No damage has been done to your work, then?" Markby turned back to Jackson.

134

The curator said fretfully, "Everyone keeps saying that! But it's not the point. How can we work properly when we have to keep looking over our shoulders! Even that's a nuisance, that dog!"

He pointed to a black labrador-cross which was tied to a wooden stake by a length of rope.

The girl with the smock said quickly, "He's no trouble really, Ian!"

"He isn't ours, for pity's sake, he's theirs! But he seems to have tacked himself on to us! But my chief worry is the one called Joe. We can't keep him away from the skeleton."

"Oh yes, you told me about that. Colonel Harbin, the coroner, mentioned the skeleton to me at dinner the other night. He was quite tickled by it all. Said it was the first time he had to sit on a Saxon warrior." Markby smiled faintly. "I think that's now his stock dinner table joke."

Woollard spoke for the first time, "I'm glad the old boy thinks it funny!" he said loudly. "We don't. We're bloody fed up with the situation!"

"Dan . . . " the girl in the smock

said anxiously with an apologetic look at Markby.

"I expect you are. Mr Woollard, is it?"

He saw suspicion flash into the man's eyes. "Yes!" Woollard said defensively.

"You and Dr Gretton represent the Trust which is financing the work, I understand."

"That's right — and I'm going to have to tell them about this soon. I should have told them before."

"You mean they don't know about the travellers?"

Jackson said, "I asked Sula and Dan not to tell the Trust. I was afraid they'd pull the plug on us. Chief Inspector, there's so much at stake here! The future of Bamford Museum hangs on this! We've got real possibilities of finding something exciting here!"

"Then perhaps I'll just walk up there and have a word with your neighbours."

As he passed Meredith she murmured, "Thanks for coming. I felt I'd let Ursula down."

"I thought I'd let you down. Anyway I need to see the travellers for myself.

Meet you at the pub tonight about seven, okay?"

She nodded. So that was all right. He'd see Meredith tonight.

* * *

At first sight the camp appeared deserted. Markby stood at the edge of it and surveyed the scene. He wondered where they all were and felt a twinge of unease at their absence. A large round blackened area in the centre of the collection of ramshackle vehicles showed where a fire had burned the night before. Wisps of smoke still rose from the fragments of charred wood. Babies' nappies fluttered in the breeze. A pile of rubbish under a nearby hedge mouldered beneath a cloud of buzzing flies. From behind a hedge a distinctive odour rose announcing the presence of a communal latrine. He exclaimed in disgust, "Tsk!"

Then a voice behind him spoke. "Can we help you?"

He turned. Two young women of starkly contrasted types had materialised. One was a self-assured young person in a long skirt and heavy boots. The other was in jeans, with cropped hair and her bare arms covered in a profusion of tattoos.

"Chief Inspector Markby, Bamford police," he said firmly. "I'd like to have a word with whoever's in charge here."

"This is a collective!" said the girl with the long skirt.

"Then I'll talk to you, if I may."

They both stared at him. Then the girl said, "Go and find Pete, Lily. He ought to hear this."

Lily, the inappropriately named tattooed female, disappeared behind the trailers. Markby had come across so-called collectives before in multiple house-squats. In practice he had found that there was always some dominant personality in charge, whatever the theory of the thing. There were leaders and followers in life. The girl with the long skirt and aggressive stance was a giver of orders, born to it. Expensive private education produced that kind of confidence and authority, and the cut-glass accent. Lily of the tattoos, for all her apparent non-conformity, was a follower, probably of poor background and ill-educated, easily influenced.

"Could I know your name?" he asked.

"Anna Harbin," the girl said shortly. "Not, incidentally, that I have to tell you or that it's any business of yours."

"This camp is very much my business, Miss Harbin. You're not, by any chance, related to Colonel Harbin, the coroner?"

Her mouth twitched in exasperation. "He's my great-uncle."

"Does he know you're living like this?"

"Like this?" Her eyes mocked him briefly. "Oh yes, though he probably keeps quiet about it. Not the thing, you know. Awf'ly embarrassin'!" She was a good mimic and had old Harbin off to a T. Markby hid a smile.

"He doesn't actually know I'm here at this very spot and I'll thank you not to tell him! Does it make any difference? Uncle George being a coroner?"

A young lady with connections. She might scorn it but yes, whether she liked it or not, it did make a difference.

"Not to me," said Markby mildly (although that wasn't strictly true). "But ultimately to you, yes, I suppose it will."

Her eyes flashed. "How?"

"Because a young woman like you has somewhere to go when she eventually gets fed up with living like this." He indicated the surrounding squalor. "Family who will rally round. Your friend Lily probably doesn't."

He'd hit on a raw nerve. Plainly furious, she shouted, "I wouldn't go running home no matter what happened! This is my life. I don't want to go back. I never will! They wouldn't have me, anyway!"

He could have argued this out but he didn't want to, nor had he to, for Lily had returned with a bearded man in a green trilby hat and an old Aran sweater.

"I'm Pete Wardle," said the newcomer. "You're from the police, Lily says."

Markby introduced himself again. "You're going to have to move on, you know," he said.

"We're not doing any harm."

"That's debatable. The owners of the land say you're destroying hedges for firewood, your dogs are running loose amongst stock. I can see heaped rubbish which I suppose, when you move on, you intend leaving behind, to disfigure the landscape and constitute a hazard to livestock, walkers and picnickers. I can also see that you've destroyed a large area of grazing grass with your fire."

"That will grow over again once we've left!"

"With weeds, not grass. This morning," Markby went on before Pete could interrupt, "I observed two of your number begging in Bamford. Now I'm giving you fair warning. I won't allow it. I left them busking in the street today but when everyone gets back here tonight, tell them that if any of them are seen begging in the town after today, they'll be charged."

"What harm does it do?" Anna snapped.

"I'm only here to make clear the law's point of view and tell you what I intend, Miss Harbin."

"Stop bloody calling me that!"

He ignored her. "I want this entire convoy out of here inside twenty-four hours. Is that clear? Good morning!"

He left them glaring furiously after

him. If they do move on, he thought, it won't be for fear of the law. It'll be because young Anna there will be worrying I'll tell her family where she is! And what Anna Harbin wants, I fancy the others will do!

Now that he was out here, he might as well make a clean sweep of it and call on the Felstons. The farm was less than a mile away just over the rise and walking across the fields was pleasant in the sunshine. He climbed a stile and set off for the distant roofs.

★ ★ ★

He wasn't the only visitor that day to Motts Farm. There was a car parked in the yard and voices came from a barn. Within a beast lowed sadly as if in discomfort.

Markby put his head round the door and found both Felstons and the local vet standing ankle deep in soiled straw around an unhappy black and white cow.

"Wondered when one of you police fellows would dare show your face up here!" Lionel Felston greeted him sourly.

"See this?" Brian Felston dispensed with any greeting and pointed at the cow. "She's eaten some filth or other those New Age blighters chucked out and it's damn near poisoned her!"

"She'll be all right," said the vet. He was washing his hands in a bucket of water. He stood up, dried them and began to pull on his jacket. "But keep her in here and if she seems no better by tomorrow, give me a call. Hullo, Markby!"

They all moved out into the sunshine. "You're sure about the cause of the animal's illness?" Markby asked the vet.

"As sure as I can be. I've been down to the field where the cattle are grazing and there's a fair bit of rubbish been chucked over the fence from the camp."

"I've just been to the convoy," Markby said. "And told them to move on."

"If they don't get off my land soon, I'll go down there and move them off with a blast or two from a shotgun!" Lionel growled.

"I wouldn't advise that, Mr Felston!" Markby said sharply.

Lionel lunged forward and shook a

balled fist under his nose. "Then you stir yourself and do something! I pay my taxes! Gets nothing for it! I know where my money goes, it goes into social security what that lot live off! And I'm supposed to do nothing while they poison my beasts and break down my fences? Just sit here while down there they're fornicating and carrying on with no shame! Them layabouts of fellows and trollops of girls! Some of 'em educated enough to know better! It's a scandal! It's a downright affront to decent, God-fearing, hard-working folk!"

"All right, Uncle Lionel!" Brian pulled his uncle away. "We'll let the police handle it." He patted the older man's shoulder.

Lionel spat to one side and made off stiffly across the yard.

Brian turned to Markby, his face lined with worry. He didn't look as if he'd had much sleep lately. "Look, Mr Markby," the farmer said. "He's serious. And I'm serious, too. The animal is okay but we could just as easily have lost the beast if what she'd eaten had been more dangerous. If more of them had eaten it, we could have had half the herd down! I don't have to tell you what that would have meant in loss of milk production and vet's fees!"

"I do understand," Markby said. "Your uncle is obviously very upset. I hope you can persuade him that taking matters into his own hands really wouldn't be a good idea."

Brian looked even more harassed. "You've seen for yourself how the old man is and heard him! I can't keep him on a tight leash much longer. We're working men and to get an injunction costs money! If your lot doesn't move them on soon, I can't answer for the result! Just you mind that, Markby! There'll be bloodshed!"

He turned and strode away in the wake of his uncle. Markby stood thoughtfully in the yard looking after him until Brian disappeared.

"Not got your car, Chief Inspector?"

Markby turned, startled. He'd forgotten the vet.

"Yes, but it's right down at the bottom of the hill. I left it at the archaeological site."

"Then I'll give you a lift down the track and drop you off there."

"Thanks." As the vet's car lurched down the uneven track, Markby asked, "You must know the Felstons quite well. You're their regular vet, I suppose?"

"Yes to the last question and no to the first. I don't think anyone knows the Felstons well. I've known them quite a long time but that's not the same thing at all!" the vet said frankly.

"True. But would you say that old Lionel was likely to go down to the camp and blast a shotgun off at anyone?"

"Bah!" The vet was negotiating a pothole and it was not clear whether it was that or the question which elicited an exclamation of irritation. "If you're asking my opinion, I think Lionel's a damned old fool! Cracked, to put it bluntly. Reads his Bible a lot. Not that it's a bad habit, don't get me wrong! But he interprets scripture strictly according to his own understanding of it and his understanding isn't very great. Very apt to sound off about Sodom and Gomorrah is Lionel. Any shrink would probably tell you that an obsession with brimstone

146

religion of that sort is nearly always an obsession with sin. For 'sin' read 'sex'. Sexual misbehaviour is the main object of Lionel's rambling. There's very little charity in his religion but plenty of being cast into outer darkness. Generally speaking, I think Brian has him under control. I wouldn't worry unduly if I were you. Don't know about at full moon!" The vet chuckled. "Wouldn't surprise me a bit if old Lionel didn't go dancing around naked then!"

"Lionel never married?" Markby asked curiously.

"No, never that I know of. Makes it worse, of course. His brother, who started up the farm with him, married. That was Brian's mother. There was some story there, something happened, a scandal of some sort. I don't know the details. Years ago, before my time. One or two of the old people on farms around here remember it and drop a hint from time to time. Brian's mother walked out, I believe, and left the two men and the young boy, as he was at the time, to get on with it by themselves."

"What about Brian? Does he work for

his uncle or is it a straight partnership?"

"Partnership. They own the land together because when Brian's father died, Brian inherited his share. I feel a bit sorry for Brian who's a nice chap but very shy. I think — " The vet broke off and glanced sideways at his passenger. "I won't gossip."

"I wish you would. How I deal with the hippies may depend very much on how the Felstons will react to what I do."

"What I was going to say wouldn't affect that. I was only going to remark it's a pity Brian never married. Probably just too shy to go chasing after girls. Living with Lionel must have put a dampener on Brian's love life."

"But you'd say Brian was a level-headed type of person?"

"Reasonably. Although anyone living under the same roof as Lionel must be sorely strained at times. I'm surprised Brian is as sane as he is!"

They had reached the bottom of the track. "Well, here we are!" the vet said, stopping the car.

Markby got out. "Thank you."

The vet leaned across to call through the window. "Just get those raggle-taggle nomads off the land and you won't have to worry about either Lionel or Brian!"

Markby lifted a hand in acknowledgement and farewell. But privately he was worried. Everything the vet had said indicated that either of the Felstons might prove unpredictable. Old rancour, pent-up frustrations, distorted thinking . . . it made a nasty and potentially dangerous brew.

9

"I'LL be happy to ask my daughter
to sign your book, sergeant!" said
Mrs Salter. "More tea?"

Pearce declined the tea. He'd already
drunk three cups. "Does Mrs Woollard
come back to Bamford often?" he asked.
"I dare say she's busy, what with the
writing and so on."

"Natalie's a very good daughter!" said
his hostess firmly. A slight frown marred
her forehead. "A little forgetful at times.
I mean, she does forget to phone or write
from time to time. I have to ring up and
remind her. Of course, that husband of
hers . . . " Amy Salter fell silent and
settled the tea-cosy over the pot. Abruptly
she went on, "He's not a local man. I
wish Natalie had married a local man.
She would have come home more often.
But there, I suppose the young men in
Bamford weren't what she wanted."

"See her recently?" asked Pearce. "Very
nice cake, this."

150

"Thank you. I'll wrap a piece up for you to take with you. No, I haven't seen Natalie lately. But that's because she's in London."

"Oh, is she?" asked Pearce startled.

"Yes, it's publicity, you know." Mrs Salter spoke the word self-consciously. "They have to do it. She's visiting bookshops and some other things and staying in London for a week or two."

"She's phoned you from there, I expect," probed the devious Pearce.

Again that faint frown wrinkled Amy Salter's brow. "No, she must have forgotten again. They keep her so busy. I did ring Dan, my son-in-law, and he told me Natalie's in London. I do wish Natalie wouldn't go away. My health isn't good. I do like to think she's near at hand so that I can pick up the phone and give her a call, you understand."

Pearce thought he did understand. He glanced at the clock ticking softly on the mantelpiece between a pair of Staffordshire china dogs.

"Must be off. Sorry to have taken up so much of your time."

"Not at all, sergeant. I'll just wrap up that piece of cake."

* * *

Later that evening this information was relayed by Markby to Meredith in the lounge bar of The Bunch of Grapes.

"It's fishy!" said Meredith firmly. "I told you Ursula wasn't imagining it. He's told two quite different stories. He told her his wife was in Bamford with her mother. The mother says he told her Natalie's in London. One of those stories has to be a lie and I bet both are!"

Markby looked unhappy. "There still could be a quite straightforward explanation."

"What?" she demanded in exasperation.

He was spared having to reply. A hand came over his shoulder and put a luridly jacketed paperback book on the table in front of him.

"There you are, Mr Markby!" said a cheerful voice. "There's the book you wanted. I said I'd lend it you!"

"Oh, thanks, Jenny!" he said weakly.

152

"Hope you enjoy it!" She bounced off back to the bar.

Markby reached for the book but was too slow. Meredith had tweaked it away in triumph.

"What's this you're reading? I didn't know you were a secret fan of bodice-rippers!"

"I'm not! Give it here, for crying out loud!"

But she had spotted the author's name. She looked up, merriment fading in her face and that direct look which he rather dreaded entering her eyes. "This is one of Natalie's! You did take what I said seriously!"

"No, I just was, well, curious. I got chatting to Jenny at the bar and she seemed to think I wanted to borrow the wretched thing! I mean, it's hardly in my line!"

"Don't know. Might be a good yarn at that." Meredith was riffling through the packed pages. She returned to the title page and gave a frown. "This publishing house, Toby's got something to do with that. I mean, not Toby himself. An uncle or godfather or something. He told me so once."

"Toby?" Markby asked suspiciously. "Do you mean that character who's in the flat?"

"Yes, have you got a couple of tenpence pieces? I'll give him a call on that phone over there. He might not have gone out for the evening yet."

"What on earth for?"

"Because," said Meredith patiently, "Toby can check for us whether Natalie is really doing the publicity rounds in London. Her publisher would know. I'll get Toby to sound out his uncle and to phone you directly with the answer."

"Just be careful what you say to your friend Toby. I don't want the publisher to think there's a major problem with one of his best-selling authors! Just remember this'll probably prove a mare's nest."

"Toby will think of something!" said Meredith cheerfully. "He's very enterprising!"

"Then get him to enterprise himself into finding somewhere else to live!" Markby said crossly.

★ ★ ★

She was lucky enough to catch Toby just before he set off on his evening's social whirl.

"When are you coming back?" he asked.

"Not before next week at the earliest! Have you found somewhere else to live?"

"Of course I haven't. This is London! I'm not going to live in some one-room slum when I've got a perfectly good place of my own! Anyway, I'm nicely settled in now."

Meredith dismissed an image of the general state of the flat and concentrated on matters in hand. "Listen, Toby, I want you to do something for me, if you would." She explained about Natalie Woollard.

"I'm lunching with my uncle tomorrow as it happens," Toby said. "I'll sound him out. I'll tell him you're a fan of this lady. No problem."

"It's all organised!" said Meredith when she returned to Markby. "Leave it to Toby!"

He grunted and sipped his beer.

* * *

155

Driving back to the site that night, Meredith found herself wishing that she and Ursula hadn't volunteered to spend a second night out on the hillside. They'd been comfortable enough the night before and had no trouble. But it was an eerie spot and the proximity of the travellers unsettling.

She slowed down seeking the unlit turning in the twilight. It was as well that she did for, without any warning, the twin beams of headlights blazed through the gloom and a vehicle roared out of the narrow exit and on to the main road. It made a sweeping turn and rocketed away into the night in the direction of Bamford.

It was impossible to be sure in the darkness but it had looked like Dan Woollard's van.

With a feeling of unease Meredith drove up to the site and with more haste than normal parked her car and got out. Light shone from within the works trailer and Ursula's car was parked alongside. Meredith paused to glance up the hill towards the camp nestled under the lee of the rampart.

The travellers had built up their fire again. She could hear it crackling and smell the smoke. Its rosy glow hung over the scene and the trailers and lorries were black cut-out shapes against it. It was a primitive scene. All nomad camps must look like that. The Saxon warrior in the grave, had he been able to look up there at this moment, wouldn't have found the scene strange. An encampment of adventurers, something as old as time. The fiddler was playing again, a lament or what sounded like one. On the night air it was immeasurably doleful. Meredith hurried for the light and warmth of the site trailer.

She pulled open the door and called anxiously, "Ursula?"

Ursula's head appeared above the table on which the potsherds lay, startling Meredith considerably. Her face was flushed and her long dark hair hung untidily around it.

"Oh, it's you!" she exclaimed. "I thought it might be — Dan was here!" She hesitated and added starkly, "We quarrelled."

"I thought it was his van which passed me." Meredith climbed into the trailer and saw for the first time that the floor was littered with sheets of paper, and Ursula's reason for being on her knees was to collect them up again.

"Bad luck," said Meredith, stooping to help.

Ursula peered under the table at her, a sheaf of papers clutched to her chest. "Bad luck, nothing! Dan's bad temper! He chucked my notes all over the place. They're all muddled up. Thank God I numbered the sheets!"

"Did he hit you?" Meredith demanded.

"No. I thought he was going to. He came at me and I picked up that marker peg over there. I don't know what I was going to do with it. It's got a pointed end so Dan must have thought he was going to get a nasty jab and he backed off, swept all my papers on to the floor and then rushed out."

"He did lie to you about his wife visiting her mother. Mrs Salter hasn't seen her. She, Natalie's mother, seems to think her daughter's in London. I've got someone checking it out."

Ursula sat on the bunk with her hands full of creased sheets of notes and looked miserable. "Dan swears everything is all right. He makes me angry but he also makes me feel, well, guilty. As if I'm being unjust. He's so damn good at that, making you feel you're being unfair to him. I don't know what to think." She paused, and borne on the night air came the distant screech and wail of the fiddle.

"If he'd just stop playing that damn thing!" Ursula clapped her hands to her ears. "It's like a funeral dirge!"

★ ★ ★

Not surprisingly Meredith didn't sleep well. She dozed fitfully and at one point awoke completely, hearing the noise of a car engine. Fearing that Dan Woollard had decided to come back, she knelt on the bunk and peered out of the trailer window. But she was too late. There was the faintest flicker of headlights through the undergrowth on the far side of the site, bordering the track then the silent blackness of night. Perhaps one of the hippy vehicles.

Across the trailer Ursula, also awakened,

159

whispered, "What is it?"

"Nothing, just those travellers driving about at night for some reason or other."

She heard Ursula sigh in the darkness. "I'm being punished, aren't I? For playing around with a married man. Poor Natalie, I wish I knew where she was. If I did know, I think I'd go and apologise. Life with Dan can't have been easy all these years and the last thing she needed was me making it worse!"

Meredith dozed fitfully for the rest of the night, a prey to bizarre nightmares. In one she imagined herself roused by a bright light and a distant roar. The camp's bonfire raged out of control engulfing them all in its flames. As she struggled desperately to beat them out, she saw with horror that her arms streamed with blood. She rubbed at it and it turned out to be only tomato soup. Meredith awoke with dry mouth and throbbing head.

★ ★ ★

The following day saw the beginning of a promised heatwave. At breakfast time

160

it was already hot and sticky. By mid-morning the archaeologists were toiling in irritable silence, Ursula and Dan at opposite ends of the site, ignoring one another. Meredith, scraping carefully with her trowel in her allotted ditch, wiped the sweat from her brow and wondered if the past really was worth all this effort.

In Bamford, Alan Markby sat at his desk and worried about the plants in his greenhouse. He'd opened a ventilation pane and covered the roof area with green cloth but he was sure when he got home he'd find they'd all collapsed with heatstroke. So concerned was he, that he rushed home at lunchtime to check and, sure enough, they all drooped miserably. He opened another ventilation pane, fussed around them like a nanny round a brood of ailing charges and got back to the office late.

He'd just sat down at his desk again when the phone rang.

"A Mr Smythe is calling from London, sir. He wants to speak to you on a private matter. Shall I put him through?"

"Smythe?" snapped Markby. "I don't

161

know any — Hang on! Yes, I do. Put him on!"

Shortly after that, a voice said suspiciously, "Is that Chief Inspector Markby? This is Toby Smythe."

"This is Markby! Is this about Natalie Woollard?"

"That woman novelist Meredith asked me to check on. I had lunch with my uncle. He's her publisher. I spun some tale about Meredith being a fan. I didn't think he'd swallow my being a fan! She, the Woollard female, doesn't appear to be in London just at the moment. Or if she is, my uncle doesn't know of it, so she can't be doing publicity signings or anything."

"Thanks," said Markby, wondering if he really wanted to know this. It wasn't his business, after all, much as Meredith seemed determined to make it so. "I don't suppose it matters but I'm obliged to you, anyway."

"No sweat," said Toby's voice laconically.

"How's the flat hunting?" Markby asked.

"What flat hunting? I've got a flat. I'm staying there with Meredith!"

162

"Like hell you are! She leased it from you, sole occupancy."

"Listen, Markby!" Toby's voice grew anxious. "I don't want you to get the wrong idea about me and Meredith. We're just friends."

"Friends in a very small flat! Find yourself another place, Smythe!" He slammed down the phone.

* * *

Finny's teeth lurked in a tumbler of water on the draining board by his kitchen sink where they looked like a weird specimen in an eighteenth-century collector's cabinet of curiosities. Their owner always gave them a rinse after eating.

Finny himself was washing up, something which didn't take him long. During the Second World War the government had impressed on beleaguered Britons the importance of growing and eating their own vegetables. Young Finny had taken this advice to heart.

He had lived for years on carrots, onions, turnips, cabbage and potatoes grown in his garden. As age rendered digging and hoeing more arduous, he had gradually abandoned cultivation of all of these except potatoes on which Finny now lived almost exclusively. It made cooking simple and cut down on the shopping.

"Potaters fer me breakfast, potaters fer me dinner and potaters fer me tea!" he had proudly informed the district nurse.

She had protested that this diet ought to be augmented in some way. Recalling her words now as he rinsed his saucepan, Finny muttered, "Vittymin pills! I don't need no vittymin pills! Stands ter reason, what good could those diddy little tablets be to anyone? Potaters, that's what does you good!"

On this triumphant note he upended the saucepan on the draining board alongside the tumbler, wiped his hands on a grimy scrap of towel and fished the teeth from their watery retreat. He thrust them into his mouth, took a few practice snaps in the air to make sure the dentures were secure, put on his hat and made for his front door. He was ready for an afternoon's work, even though it was going to be very hot down there on the quarry floor this afternoon.

Rolling slightly from side to side in his uneven gait, he made his way down the gravel track into the cauldron of trapped heat which was the quarry. The rocky sides sent out waves of it and the air was scarcely breathable. Everything shimmered in a haze which made judging distances and objects a matter of guesswork.

Finny's intention was to spend the afternoon in one of the dumped armchairs, set up in the shadow thrown by a metal skip. There he'd waylay intending tippers. Otherwise, as he knew well, they'd go tipping the stuff any old where. But as he reached the bottom of the track, he saw to his anger and dismay, that others had got there before him. They'd descended unheard as he ate and, what was worse, they were unashamedly clambering over the rubbish and sorting through it.

Finny, squinting through the heat haze, saw four of them, and a more rum-looking bunch he couldn't have imagined. And taking liberties with his tip! He broke into a lumbering run.

"Oy! What d'you think you're doing? You jest get off there!"

The four stopped removing boxes from the top of the pile and turned to face him. One, whom Finny had assumed from the cropped hair and tattoos to be a boy, was revealed to be a girl when she spoke.

"Mind your own business, grandad!"

"Don't you give me no lip, you saucy little, baggage!" howled Finny. "This is my business. This is my tip!"

"No, it isn't," said the girl. "It's the council's!"

Finny wasn't having that. "See that cottage up there? That's mine! I've lived there forty year. I were quarryman here when stone was still dug and ended foreman. Now I mind the quarry like I always done! This is my job!"

"Take no notice of him, Lily," said another girl, wearing a long, cotton skirt. "He's batty."

"You listen to me!" yelled the furious Finny. "Yes, you there, the one what speaks posh and got her petticoats trailing

166

in the dirt! Who are you calling batty? That's not allowed! It's against the law!"

"It's all right, grandad!" said a scrawny youth with earrings. "We're just looking to see if there's anythin' useful for us, see?"

"I do see!" bellowed Finny. "Thieving, that's what you're doing! That's all new stuff tipped there. I ain't had time to go through that myself!" His tirade came to a choking stop as the teeth slipped and had to be readjusted.

"There's a roll of carpet hidden under all this stuff, Pete!" said the girl in the long skirt. "It's tied together but it looks quite good, I can't see any holes. It would make a tent cover. Pass me over the penknife and I'll cut the string round it so we can open it out. Come on, Joe and Lily! Give me a hand to drag it free!"

"You leave that alone!" Finny scrambled over the accumulated debris and stood guard over the carpet, his face purple and his fists clenched.

"Look," reasoned the man called Pete. "It's no use to you but it might be some use to us. Why don't you just let us unroll it to see if it's got holes in it? If it has, we don't want it."

"You can't have it, anyway!" muttered Finny. "'Tisn't yours."

"It'll rot, lying here. We could make use of it."

Finny eyed him. "All right, you can unroll it careful and look at it. But I'm not saying you can take it, mind! I'm not saying I'll give me permission!" He stooped and peered at the carpet. "Bit o' Wilton, that. Nice quality."

"It's donkey's years old!" said the girl in the long skirt, exasperated. "You can see it's all faded and worn."

"And the old bloke's donkey's years old as well!" quipped the earringed one.

"Yes, I am!" growled Finny. "And when I was a lad, your age, no self-respecting young feller wore jewellery like a bit of a girl!"

"Take no notice of him!" ordered the long-skirted girl. "You take that end, Pete."

She reached down and grabbed the end of the roll. The next second she

168

gave a piercing shriek and leapt back. A long, sleek, slightly hump-backed shape dashed from the interior of the rolled carpet and whisked away amongst the rubbish with a clattering of claws. It dislodged an empty paint tin in its flight which clattered away.

Finny gave a high-pitched cackle of glee. "Ah, that made you jump, didn't it, Miss Plum-in-her-mouth! Old rat, that was. I seen 'em here as big as cats. You wouldn't want one of they running up them long skirts of yours, I bet!"

"Hang on!" said Pete. "I'll just give it a kick to flush out any others!" He struck the roll with his boot whilst his friends stood nervously clear.

"You cut that out!" shouted Finny. "You're damaging it!"

"Shut up!" snapped the girl. "Okay Pete. Lily and I'll hold this end and you and Joe roll it over."

Pete was still probing the middle of the carpet roll with his boot. "It feels as if there's something in the middle, something solid."

"Oh, come on!" she ordered impatiently. The two girls grasped the edge of the carpet and heaved while the two men pushed at the roll to unravel it. It flopped over once awkwardly. The move put it at the top of a slope. Suddenly the carpet began to unroll under its own impetus, slapping over and over with increasing speed. With the last turn it lay spread out in the sunshine and the thing which had been hidden inside it was revealed. It slithered out and continued to travel on for some distance, bouncing over and over until it came to rest among the debris at the foot of the pile.

"Gawd . . . " whispered Finny.

"It's — it's a body!" Pete's voice was hoarse and disbelieving.

"It's a mannequin!" argued the girl but sounded uncertain.

They edged forward in a huddled group. It was indeed a woman's body. She lay with her sightless eyes looking up at the pitiless sun which beat on the quarry. She was clothed but her legs were bare and her feet shoeless. Feet and calves were marked with red scratches and teethmarks.

The tattooed girl screamed once and then pressed her hands over her mouth.

Joe croaked, "Let's get out of here!" and turned to run.

But the long-skirted girl seemed suddenly galvanised into action. "No, we've got to inform the police!"

"You stupid bitch!" Joe snarled. "I suppose you want us to tell your old uncle or whatever he is, so he can come out and hold a bleedin' inquest on it!"

"Yes, of course there will have to be an inquest!" she said vehemently.

"And us giving evidence, I s'pose?" He spat. "You can, if you like. But I'm not and neither is Lily. C'mon, Lil! And you two better get movin' too!" He jabbed a finger at the girl. "P'lice will be round here like flies and more than likely trying to make out we done her in!"

Pete, ashen-faced, grabbed the girl's arm. "Come on, Anna! Joe's right! We've got to alert the camp and get out of here!"

"We've got to report a body!" she insisted.

"Anna, d'you want your family to find us?"

She hesitated, then whirled and

advanced on Finny who stood motionless, staring at the corpse.

"Where's a telephone? Have you got one in your cottage?"

He stirred. "'Course I haven't got no telephone! Pub's got one, quarter of a mile down the road."

"Then you go there and tell the landlord to phone the police, do you understand?"

"Come on, Anna!" urged Pete. The others were already climbing the steep path to the top of the quarry.

She gathered up her long skirts and ran after them, shouting over her shoulder, "Fetch the police, you silly old man!"

Left alone, Finny blinked and automatically put up a hand to check his dentures. The gesture reassured him and he sidled forward to stoop over the body.

"You all right, missus? You ain't had a drop too much?"

No, she wasn't drunk, she was dead all right. Someone had dumped a dead body on his tip! Talk about taking diabolical liberties! Just come out here and chucked a body on his tip! Unthinkingly Finny stooped and grabbed the corpse by the shoulder.

In response and without warning, the corpse flung up a straight stiff arm and its outstretched fingers scraped across his face.

Finny squawked, leapt back, and then turned and hobbled at top speed out of the quarry to fetch help.

Behind him, all alone on the floor of the quarry, the corpse lay with arm raised and one hand pointing up at the sun. Now things were quiet again, the rat crept out of the rubbish and lifted his pointed snout to sniff the air, whiskers twitching.

10

BY the time Markby and Sergeant Pearce arrived at the quarry Finny was seated on a wooden kitchen chair at the gate of his cottage. Leaning on his stick, he was watching with a jaundiced eye as the police vehicles lurched past him down the track to the quarry floor. Markby stopped his car and got out.

"Mr Finny? You reported finding the body, is that right?"

Finny scowled. "More of 'em! How many more is there going to be? Messing around down there on my tip and very likely won't clear up after you, neither! You in charge?"

"The body!" Markby repeated loudly.

Finny bridled. "I reported it, ah. But I never found it, not strickly speakin'. Them tramps did that. They undone the carpet and out she rolled. I never touched that carpet, never had no chance! I told 'em to leave it be. They had no business

174

meddling with it. It's my tip! I sort all the stuff out careful. You tell your fellers that before they going chucking things all over the place! Bit of Wilton, that carpet was. And another thing, don't you going taking stuff away, not without letting me know!"

"When did the carpet appear on the tip?"

Finny raised his stick and jabbed at the air to accompany his calculations. "I never seen it yesterday so it weren't there. Early this morning a feller brought some stuff and I had to deal with him so I hadn't got round to checking the tip before them tramps got to it. When they dragged it out I saw straight off it was Wilton. I don't get so much Wilton. Gets a bit of Axminster and a lot of that nylon rubbish with the foam back. You can't beat Wilton."

"This man you mention, you're sure he didn't bring it?"

"Didn't you listen? I checked what he brought! I never saw that carpet come. Anyway, you don't want to ask me all this," Finny went on grumpily. "You go and ask them tramps."

"The New Age travellers? We can't just at the moment."

Finny narrowed his eyes. "Scarpered, have they? I heard a lot of traffic noise earlier up on the road."

"Yes, they've scarp — gone. We'll find them." Markby dragged the interview back to its subject. "I know this is distressing, Mr Finny." Not that the old blighter looked in the slightest bit distressed! "Did you get a look at the dead woman?"

"Ah, I did," said Finny. "Stiffening up, she were. Never seen her before, not as I recall."

"Did you move the body?"

"No! I give it a shake in case she weren't dead, just drunk."

"Rolled up in a carpet?"

"How do I know? Folks does all sorts of daft things when they're drunk. As soon as I touched her, on the shoulder here," he tapped his own shoulder, "up shot her arm and near hit me in the eye! Gave me a very nasty turn. I had to walk down the road to the pub and get the landlord to tellyphone you. My feet aren't made for much walking."

"I see." Markby eyed him thoughtfully. "We'll need all this in a written statement, Mr Finny. If I send a constable along now, we can get it all taken down while it's fresh in your mind."

"I don't forget things like a lot of old folk do!" Finny snapped.

"Still, no time like the present, eh? And I've got just the person for you to tell it to." Markby beckoned to a figure in the distance. "A very nice young lady called WPC Morgan."

"Oh?" said Finny brightening. "Best if she come on in the house with me, then. No point in sitting out here in the heat and dust!"

* * *

"I suspect we'll find she's been throttled," Dr Fuller said.

It was unbearably hot down in the quarry and the nature of the task made things worse. The body had been removed to the ambulance but rigor had now completed and the arm still stuck up in the air making it difficult to manoeuvre the corpse. In the ambulance it had been draped with a sheet but the raised arm pushed this up to a triangular tent shape.

"Are you sure?" Markby asked doubtfully, crouched with Fuller beside the bier. "Her face didn't look distorted."

"Of course I'm not sure!" said Fuller testily. "I haven't had a proper look at her yet. She wasn't strangled with a ligature which would have led to congested features. No, a manual, hands-on job and it wouldn't take much pressure. It can be very quick, just a matter of applying pressure in the right places. It's often accidental. I've always impressed on my children that they should never grab anyone round the neck in fun. Rigor is complete. Died late yesterday evening? I'll get a look at the stomach contents later. Find her shoes?"

"Not yet. I've got more officers coming and we can organize a search of this tip."

"Rather you than me!" Fuller said cheerfully.

Markby privately thought that unpleasant though the tip was, he'd still rather have that job than Fuller's.

"Before you take her away," he said. "There's someone I'd like to take a look and possibly identify her. It's just a hunch. I've sent Pearce up to the archaeological site to fetch the chap down here."

It was something more than a hunch. The pale dead face was eerily familiar. He'd last seen it, pert and smiling, on the back cover of a paperback novel. Arguing voices outside heralded Pearce and a loudly protesting Dan Woollard. Markby clambered out to meet them.

Woollard darted forward, looming over him, fists clenched. Pearce gripped his elbow expertly in response to the threat.

Woollard swore. "Tell your gorilla he needn't manhandle me! What am I, some sort of suspect? What's going on? Are you in charge? What d'you mean by dragging me down here? So you've found a woman's body! It's not my wife's! She isn't dead, she's — "

"We know she's missing," Markby interrupted. "And that she has been neither staying with her mother nor book-signing in London."

Woollard looked stunned. He growled,

179

"Who's been talking to you? Who, damn it? Listen, you'd better be careful — "

"And possibly, Mr Woollard, so should you! Now I realise this is distressing. But I'd be grateful if you would just take a quick look."

Woollard chewed furiously at his lower lip. "You're wrong, you know. And I'm going to take legal advice! I don't know who's been feeding you a bunch of lies — " He broke off and shook his shaggy head as if to clear it. "All right, where is it?"

The ambulance swayed and bounced beneath his weight as he climbed in. When Markby joined him there was very little room. Fuller withdrew to the far corner and waited impassively. He wasn't interested in who the woman had been, only in what had killed her.

Woollard stared at the steepled shape of the sheet. "What the hell — ?"

"Rigor!" said Fuller briefly.

Woollard swallowed and some of the aggression went out of him. "I just have to look at the face, right?"

"Right. Ready?" Fuller turned back the sheet.

This was always a bad moment for Markby when someone near to the deceased identified the body. It had to be done. But it must leave many people with an image which haunted them for the rest of their lives. Woollard's face looked stunned, grey, and he didn't need to ask the man. He knew.

Woollard said in a muffled voice, "Yes, that's Natalie." He paused and added pedantically, "That was Natalie, my wife." Almost with a kind of relief he added, "She's dead, then, after all!"

He had succeeded in shocking even unflappable Dr Fuller who drew the sheet back over the dead face with a quick, protective gesture.

"Okay," said Markby to him. "You can take it away now."

★ ★ ★

They watched the ambulance bump away across the quarry floor and climb the track to road level. Markby glanced round. Men were already combing the tip for evidence. The report of the body had come in shortly after his phone call from

181

Toby Smythe. The landlord of a nearby pub had called but explained that the information originated with the old man who lived above the quarry and that he was, in the words of the landlord, 'round the bend'. Nevertheless that nasty cold feeling had settled in Markby's stomach at the news and they had hurried out here at once.

The quarry seemed to Markby a curious, surreal sort of place in which anything might happen, and to expect a logical explanation would be vain. In the shade of a metal skip stood two abandoned armchairs, incongruously giving a genteel note to the scene. He glanced at Woollard who was wiping sweat from his face with a check handkerchief.

"It's hot, Mr Woollard, and you've had a shock. But perhaps we could just have a word?" He indicated the two armchairs. "Why don't we sit down over there?"

Woollard followed him wordlessly and slumped in a chair. Flies buzzed around them from the refuse in the skip above. Woollard gave the searching officers a listless look. "What are they looking for?"

"For clues or evidence. We'd like to find your wife's shoes. Do you happen to remember the kind she was wearing when you saw her last?"

"No. Probably sandals. She wore sandals all summer."

"Slip on or strap and buckle type? Heels or flat?"

"I don't know, I can't remember!" Woollard shouted. "Not straps, no. Slip on. I don't think she had any with buckles. I don't know about the heels."

"Thank you," Markby said. "That's very helpful."

Woollard clasped his huge hands loosely and stared down at the quarry floor. "We had a row. That wasn't unusual. We were always having rows. Ask anyone who knew us. She stormed out slamming the front door. I thought she'd come back in an hour or so and ring the bell. I knew she hadn't got her keys or any money. And she'd done it before. Generally she just walked round for a bit and when she calmed down, came home. When she didn't I assumed she'd gone to a neighbour. Then I thought she must have persuaded someone to drive her to

Bamford to her mother. Taken a taxi there maybe and got the fare off Amy." He looked up. "I did *not* kill her!"

"Didn't you phone her mother to check if your wife was there?"

"No!" Woollard's jaw set aggressively. "I thought why the hell should I? I thought she was trying to frighten me and get me running round in ever-decreasing circles! I was determined not to play her little game. I told you, she'd done it before and I was pretty sick of it! I don't expect you to understand!"

"I understand!" Markby said abruptly. He watched the men climbing over the tip for a moment. "When Dr Gretton asked where your wife was, you said she was with her mother."

"Yes, I didn't want Sula to think we'd quarrelled."

"Because the quarrel was about Dr Gretton?"

"Yes, if you must know!" Woollard gave a hiss of anger. "And at that time I still thought Natalie was probably at Bamford. But shortly after that Amy rang me and asked for her so obviously she wasn't. I had to put Amy off or she'd be ringing up every five minutes. Amy's like that. So I said Natalie was in London."

"But even after your wife had been missing for over forty-eight hours, you still didn't try to find her or report her missing? Didn't it seem odd to you that she hadn't communicated with her mother? The old lady might have been very worried."

Woollard gave an irritated hiss. "My mother-in-law likes — liked — to keep Natalie dancing attendance. She was for ever phoning and getting Natalie to dash over to Bamford on a wild-goose chase. It wasn't my family so not my business and it was up to Natalie to sort it out. Perhaps she thought she'd do that at the same time as frighten me. Give both Amy and me a scare and teach us a lesson, as she saw it!"

"You make your wife sound vindictive," Markby said mildly. "Was she?"

The man buried his face in his hands, something Markby always disliked and mistrusted a witness to do. It obscured the features, so often the image of the mind. "You don't — didn't know Natalie!"

Woollard's voice came muffled through

his fingers. Strong fingers and large powerful hands, thought Markby. As Fuller said, to throttle only needed pressure on the right places. It was often accidental. Had Woollard in a rage — ?

"Natalie was great at writing about emotional crises!" Woollard said suddenly. "In her books the hero and the girl would have a monumental quarrel and then, in the end, they always got back together again in a big reconciliation scene. She thought she could script our lives like that, hers and mine. She thought I was like a character in one of her books. She could move me around, make me speak the words she wanted to hear. She thought she could do as she pleased and I would always love her no matter what! You can have no idea how sick I got of that and how — how wearing it is. I was being worn down, destroyed."

"I've started reading one of your wife's books," Markby said.

"Have you? Then you'll understand how she thought. It's all there."

"I understand she left uncorrected proofs of her latest book behind when she walked out. Surely that's odd? Would she normally have done that?"

Woollard raised his head and met Markby's eye. "No. But this time I believe she really meant to scare me, and nothing else mattered. It wasn't normal, okay, but she wasn't normal at that moment. She was hysterical, shrieking, almost gibbering at me! I think she really wanted to make me suffer! She — she was vindictive, yes, you're right!"

"Because of your affair with Dr Gretton?"

Woollard's face reddened. "Keep Sula out of this!"

"Because of Dr Gretton?" Markby repeated remorselessly.

"Yes!" Woollard shouted, and Pearce, hovering discreetly in the background with a notebook, looked up.

"Sula's broken off our — our relationship," Woollard said unwillingly. "She doesn't mean it, I don't care what she says! I love her and she loves me! But she was worried about Natalie. She thought we'd hurt Natalie and, anyway, Natalie wouldn't divorce me, not without

187

raising a hell of a fuss and ruining Sula's reputation."

"And would your wife have done that?"

"Oh yes," said Woollard grimly. "She'd have done it." He suddenly realised the implication of his words and added fiercely, "But that doesn't mean I killed Natalie! You're trying to give me a motive!"

"Wouldn't you say you had one? Unless, of course, Dr Gretton really has ended this relationship of yours."

Woollard, realising the trap he was in, glowered. "I want my solicitor!"

"Fair enough. Sergeant Pearce will take you back to the station and we'll bring in your legal adviser."

He no longer wanted to talk to Woollard out here. It was hot and uncomfortable. The metal skip stank and radiated heat and the flies buzzed continuously. Besides, Woollard had now had time to pull himself together and take care that he didn't make unwary disclosures. Markby had to admit that the man had made a disagreeable impression on him. There was something distorted about his thinking, something self-pitying and obstinately self-justifying. Vain, too. He couldn't admit to himself that Ursula no longer loved him. Or did she? Markby would have to talk to her about that and insist on some straight answers.

Woollard had stood up and started to walk away with Pearce but suddenly he turned round and said,

"Sula does love me! Natalie said that she didn't. She said Sula had more sense than throw away everything she had for someone like me! Bitch!" The word exploded venomously from his lips.

Pearce met his chief's eye and Markby imperceptibly shook his head. There was no point in recording this last remark. Woollard had asked for his solicitor and, once he had done that, nothing he said before the lawyer arrived would be admissible as evidence. Pity, but there it was. If Woollard had said it five minutes ago, before asking for his solicitor . . . but he hadn't.

Woollard was talking again and Markby wondered if he knew that none of what he was saying could be used. "My wife was very talented. When she was in a good mood she was good company. I didn't love her, hadn't done so for some time, but I respected her as a writer. I didn't kill her."

Receiving no reply from the two police officers he stared out across the heaped refuse being carefully searched by intent figures.

"Rolled up in a carpet like — like Cleopatra! I ask you, it's grotesque! It's like — like something out of one of Natalie's books! It's as if she scripted the whole wretched thing herself!"

11

THERE was a police car parked at the dig and officers talking to a huddle of site workers. As Markby approached, Ian Jackson saw him and, breaking away from the group, ran to meet him.

The museum curator came to a halt, panting, his hair falling over his face. "What the devil's going on? Where's Dan?"

"Mr Woollard's gone to Bamford," Markby informed him. "There's been a death. No doubt the officers here have already told you."

"Yes, yes!" Jackson grew visibly more agitated. "Oh, for crying out loud! Haven't we had enough trouble? I thought when those travellers left everything was going to be all right! I thought we might get a bit of peace and quiet and be able to get on with our work! Then your people turned up. We're researchers into the past! What the devil can we tell you about this thing that's happened just now? We're not witnesses nor suspects! It didn't happen here! We don't know anything about it!"

"That's what we have to establish." Markby tried to be patient but clearly Jackson was not in a mood to listen to reason.

"Look here, Chief Inspector!" Jackson actually grabbed Markby's sleeve before thinking better of it and releasing it smartly. "You know what this dig means to me, to the museum! We've been held up in every conceivable way! Now we're to have coppers clumping all over the place in their size elevens! We can't help you people, can't you get that into your thick heads? And any scandal will finish us with the Ellsworth! They're already talking about cutting the funding — don't you lot realise you could ruin everything?"

"I don't think being abusive will help, Mr Jackson," Markby said firmly. "And if you let my men get on with the interviews, it will all be over and done the quicker and you can get back to work."

He left Jackson fretting and made his way to where Meredith stood waiting for him with a white-faced Ursula Gretton.

"You were both here last night, so I'll talk to you first," he said to Meredith. "And to you afterwards, if you don't mind, Dr Gretton. I'll use your works trailer if I may?"

"Feel free!" called Jackson sarcastically.

"He's upset, don't mind Ian!" Ursula said quickly. "Chief Inspector, who's dead? They said a body . . . " She bit her lip and fixed pleading eyes on him. "Is it . . . ?"

"We're not releasing the identity of the victim yet," he told her.

"But you know it? Oh God, it's Natalie!" She closed her eyes and swayed. Meredith grabbed her arm.

"I'm all right," Ursula mumbled. "It has to be Natalie, it is, isn't it?"

"Later, Dr Gretton, if you don't mind." Markby caught Meredith's eye and nodded imperceptibly at the trailer. Then he turned and beckoned to a woman constable who came across.

"Dr Gretton's unwell," he said. "Perhaps you could stay with her for a few minutes." He peered at the officer. "Morgan, isn't it?"

"Yes, sir."

"Did you manage to interview the old chap?"

"Yes, sir. More or less."

"Got it there?"

She handed him her notebook and he read briefly through Finny's account, then nodded and returned the book to Morgan. "Fair enough." He followed Meredith into the trailer.

"It is Natalie's body, isn't it?" she said immediately they were alone.

"Woollard's identified it." He sat down on one of the bunks and, after a moment's hesitation, Meredith sat down on the other and stared at him with hostile eyes.

"I told you Ursula wasn't making things up!"

"Let's leave Ursula out of this for a moment. I'll talk to her myself. We're not releasing the identity of the victim yet because someone will have to tell Mrs Salter. I'll do that. Woollard in his present frame of mind isn't the one to do it and I don't want the old lady hearing it from gossip first. So keep it to yourself. Now, you and Ursula were here overnight. Was there anything unusual? Did you hear any noise outside the trailer, traffic on the road at a late hour? Voices? Anything at all?"

"I was woken by a car, well, a vehicle of some kind, I don't know what. It was very late but I didn't check my watch so I don't know exactly what time. After midnight. Ask Ursula. She heard it too."

"She was here all night? I mean, you and she can vouch for one another?"

"Yes! You're not going to accuse either of us of murder?" Meredith's incredulity caused her hazel eyes to open wide in horror and her voice rose to fill the trailer.

"I've got to check all this kind of thing. Now, whereabouts was this car? Down on the road?"

She looked unhappy. "I think I saw its headlights over there." She pointed in the direction of the track. "I knelt on my bunk and looked out but I was too late. I thought at the time it must be one of the travellers' vehicles. They kept late hours up there at the camp."

"Think carefully. Where did it come from and where did it go?"

"It — it came down the hill from the direction of the camp. I didn't actually see it. I only saw headlights. At least, I saw a moving light through the hedge and heard engine noise. I put the two together and supposed the light to be headlamps. I could have been wrong."

"And how often did you hear it? Just the once. Did you see it going and coming back?"

"I only heard it once." She hesitated. "Honestly, Alan, I don't want to sound too certain. I only heard it once and maybe it was only the travellers. There was utter confusion up there at the camp after dark. A great fire sending up sparks and scraps of burning debris. Music. Kids yelling. I slept badly and dreamed, perhaps even dreamed the engine noise and headlights. The first night up here I woke up and thought I saw a light, but that was probably from the fire. So the engine noise last night, well I just can't swear that it was even real."

Markby asked grimly: "What time did they move out?"

"About an hour before the first police car arrived. It was very sudden. Ian was jumping about as pleased as punch because he thought his troubles were over! I thought they seemed in a heck of a hurry."

Markby snorted. "Has Woollard been here all day?"

"Dan? He came late, about eleven this morning but he's been here since. I mean, he was here until Sergeant Pearce came up a short while ago and fetched him. Have you arrested him?"

"No. He's just helping us. How was the atmosphere here? How did the others treat Woollard?"

"A bit warily. He's a funny sort of chap." Meredith frowned. "He's not the sort of person you'd go and chat to just to pass the time of day. No one spoke to him much unless it was about the work in hand, except for Karen. That's Karen Henson. She was talking to him, I think about that dog. The travellers have abandoned it, left it behind. I think Karen means to keep it and she

197

was telling Dan so. That's all."

"Is it?" he asked and waited.

"No, all right. When I came back from the pub last night Woollard passed me in his van. He'd been up here during the evening visiting Ursula. They quarrelled. When I got here she was picking papers off the floor. I gather he threw them there. For such a big chap he has a petty, spiteful sort of way with him."

Clearly Meredith didn't care for Woollard either. It was interesting, however, that her picture of him matched so well with Markby's impression.

He said, "Why don't you go and tell all this to detective constable Morgan? She'll write it down and you can sign it. Oh, and will you be going back to London now? I imagine the dig's suspended for the time being."

"I don't fancy going back while Toby's still at the flat. I'll take a room at The Crossed Keys and stay on for a bit. I'll phone the office and square it with them. It's a police inquiry, after all."

Meredith got up to leave but hesitated, looking down at him. She pushed back a hank of dark brown hair and asked defiantly, "Are you going to badger Ursula now?"

"I don't badger people!" he said a touch sharply.

"Don't you just! I'm not telling you your job, but this is a terrible shock to her." She saw his expression, and added, "All right, I'll shut up and ask her to come in!"

* * *

Ursula looked more composed when she entered the trailer. She took the seat vacated by Meredith and met his eyes evenly. Her own were cornflower blue, he noticed, and very striking. She was a remarkably attractive woman. She was looking a little puzzled and he realised he had been staring at her in open admiration.

Hastily Markby said, "I realise this is difficult for you, Dr Gretton."

"It's Natalie, then?"

He nodded. "But I must ask you not to tell your colleagues so yet. We want to inform Mrs Salter first."

"Poor old lady." Ursula paused. "And poor Dan."

He raised his eyebrows. "Poor Dan? You were suggesting to Meredith he might have done his wife some violence, weren't you?"

She nodded, her long dark hair falling round her face. "Yes, I know, but now — not like this! I mean, he didn't do this, kill her!"

"Forgive me, Dr Gretton," Markby said. "But you seem to have changed your tune!"

She leaned forward. "He wouldn't bring the body out here so near to the site! Right under our noses? Certainly he wouldn't leave it in that quarry! Put his wife's body on a rubbish tip? It's disgusting. Dan would have to be some kind of a monster!"

"The body," Markby said briskly, "was wrapped in an old carpet and not immediately visible."

She blinked. "A carpet?" There was a moment's silence whilst she considered this, frowning. Then she shook her head vigorously as if she'd convinced herself. "That proves it! Dan wouldn't have wrapped her body in a carpet! It's grotesque!"

"That's what he said," Markby observed. "That is actually the word he used."

She leaned back against the trailer wall and stared thoughtfully at him. "This is a stinker, isn't it?" she said suddenly.

"Yes. I suppose you could call murder that."

"Yes, I know. But this — I mean, I've put the finger on Dan, haven't I? I've been blathering to Meredith and she's been talking to you. God, what a fool I am!"

"I understand you have recently broken off your relationship with Mr Woollard."

"Yes, but — yes, I have."

"But he doesn't accept it, isn't that what you were going to say? I also understand he was here yesterday evening and there was a scene. He threw some papers on the floor."

"Meredith told you, I suppose. Yes, he did. It doesn't mean — oh God, I wish I never said anything! I haven't been thinking straight! It was different before this. I was just speculating and wondering. Now it's happened, I know

201

he couldn't have anything to do with it! Why didn't I keep my big mouth shut?" She clasped her arms across her body and rocked in misery.

Markby said gently, "Look, we're not here because of anything you said to Meredith, you know. We're here because a body was found in the quarry."

"You've taken Dan away!" she retorted accusingly.

"He's helping us."

"I know what that means!"

"With respect, no, you don't." He had succeeded in asserting his authority, and she was watching him with some caution, but also as someone prepared to acknowledge his definition of the situation. He felt oddly pleased about this and mentally ticked himself off. All right, she was a handsome girl. She was also one in a lot of trouble.

"Miss Mitchell says you were both awoken by the sound of a car during the night. Did you look out?"

"No. Meredith did. I don't think she saw much. I thought it was the hippies driving round. They kept late hours and made a fair bit of noise. Probably all smoking pot and dancing round the camp fire. There was a fiddler up there nearly drove me barmy scraping folk tunes half the night."

"I think I may have heard him in town," murmured Markby with some sympathy.

"I don't know that the car noise awoke me. I think I wasn't properly asleep. I was thinking about Dan. I don't know what time it was. Early hours. One o'clock? Something like that."

"Think carefully. Did you hear it once or twice?"

"Oh, only the once. I honestly wasn't paying that much attention. Too wrapped up in my own miserable little problems."

"Mr Woollard says his wife was vindictive by nature. Did you ever consider she might make your affair with her husband public?"

Ursula frowned. "Not for as long as she thought she could get Dan back. If she'd thought she couldn't get Dan back, she might have made a public fuss. But she could get Dan back, couldn't she? I mean, he and I were finished."

"The fact that you and he were

finished, as you put it, doesn't mean Mrs Woollard's husband was automatically going to return his affections to her!" Markby pointed out. "Woollard appears to think that the fact he was married influenced your decision to break off the liaison. Now that he's free, Dr Gretton, does it alter your feelings towards him?"

"No!" She jumped up, hair flying and fists clenched. "Finished means finished! What's the matter with you all? I can't seem to get it through to anyone! What do I have to do? Take out an advertisement in the local press? Just write it down in your notebook or whatever you do, can't you? And when you've done that, I'll answer any other question you want. But I won't answer any more about my relationship with Dan! I consider I've answered you fully already and any more prying on your part is just plain prurience!"

Markby said nothing at all to this and after a moment she heaved a deep sigh and threw herself down on the seat again. "I'm sorry. You're doing your job. I'm not making it any easier. But I'm not finding it easy. I'm pretty near cracking up. I wasn't just throwing a tantrum nor am I trying to hide anything. I know, however painful and embarrassing it is to me, every sordid detail of my affair with Dan is going to be made public now."

"Not necessarily," said Markby mildly. "Not if it isn't relevant to inquiries. We always have to sift through a whole lot of information and discard ninety per cent of it. We're like doctors and priests in the confessional. Nothing surprises us and there's little we haven't heard before."

"Now you really make me feel small!" She pulled a wry grin. "Okay. Let me make what you'd call a statement with regard to my feelings for Dan Woollard. I don't believe he killed his wife! I know I once thought he might have harmed her. But now I'm sure he didn't! It doesn't affect the ending of our affair which is still over! I don't love him any more! I can't help it if that makes me sound heartless or shallow. People fall out of love, don't they?"

"Yes," Markby admitted. "They most certainly do."

12

MEREDITH had given her statement to WPC Morgan, envying that competent young woman her professional detachment. Dismissed, she wandered away and stood with her hands in her jeans pockets, surveying the scene around her.

Jackson was over by the grave with the skeleton, together with two police officers. The tarpaulin had been partly turned back and the two uniformed men were staring down bemusedly at the bony occupant.

"The bloody coroner was informed!" Jackson howled, waving his arms. Your chief inspector knows all about it! No!" One of the officers had stooped to peer closer. "Don't touch it! It is a thousand years old, for God's sake!"

The young officer started back as if bitten, and his colleague asked with a wondering look at the surrounding excavations, "How many of these things

206

have you got buried round here, sir?"

Renee and the two young men who helped were sitting on the grass and whispering together. Karen Henson sat alone, but for her canine companion. She had put her arm round the dog's neck. Tears were trickling down her homely features and her nose was peeling in the sunshine. The raffia sunhat lay on the grass.

Meredith went across and stooped over her. "Cheer up!" she said awkwardly.

"They've taken Dan away!"

The dog gave a little whine at the wretchedness in his friend's voice and snuffled at her ear, venturing a little comforting lick with his pink tongue.

"Well it's — it's just routine. They're talking to all of us."

Karen didn't look convinced. She picked up her hat from the turf beside her.

Meredith, seeking to distract her, observed, "That's a lovely old hat. It must date from the Thirties. Where did you find it?"

Karen glanced at it. "In an attic. I like it because it's old." Her finger smoothed a raffia flower. "I like fashions of that time. They were romantic, all those slinky evening gowns and clinging skirts. No good to me because I haven't got the figure. They needed to be very slender and willowy. I suppose there were girls like me then, great lumpy things who couldn't wear decent clothes."

"Hey!" Meredith reproved her. "Don't talk about yourself that way! I'm five-ten but I don't go moaning about being tall. I look for the clothes which I hope suit me. Why shouldn't you look fine?"

The girl beside her cast her a surprisingly worldly look. It was one of suffering experience. "Because I wouldn't know how to wear the clothes if I had them! I look a mess in everything." She turned the brim of the hat in her hands. "That's why I like old things. They don't judge, do you know what I mean? It's as if they've seen everything and know everything and they're kind. There is a kindness in things, you know. That quarry down there — " She raised a calomel-daubed hand and pointed. "I've always thought that was a wonderful place full of rubbish, which isn't rubbish to people like us. In years to come, people will excavate that quarry one day to find out how we lived in our time."

"You'd get on well with Finny," said Meredith. "He thinks it's all valuable."

"I have talked to the old man. He's funny and nice." Her face clouded. "But I'll never think about it in the same way, not now this has happened."

Clearly inconsolable, Karen crammed on her hat and clambered to her feet. "No, stay!" she ordered the dog as he made to follow.

The labrador yelped his protest and whined as he watched his friend trudge across the turf. Meredith scratched his head.

"We can't help her, I'm afraid, old boy! Come on!"

The dog hesitated but then trotted after her as she walked away from the busy scene. She wished she hadn't elected to get mixed up in all this. It was a sordid business, after all. Murder always was. As was any crime, come to that, including those which were not actually on the statute books: the moral misdemeanours, the petty betrayals and vicious little acts of revenge.

She found that her feet had taken her off the site and through the gap in the hedge and that she was walking along the track up the hill. To her left now lay rutted earth, flattened and scorched grass and patches of oil, marking the abandoned travellers' camp. The rapidity with which it had been dismantled still left her bemused.

"Something's up!" Renee had called out. They had looked up from their toil in the trenches and seen a flurry of activity up here under the rampart. Almost at once the lorries and trailers, the converted buses and the old vans had started to leave, coughing and roaring their way down the track to the main road. As abruptly as they'd come, the travellers had left.

"Thank God!" Ian Jackson had exclaimed. "Let's hope that's the last we see of them!"

But even then Meredith had felt a twinge of misgiving. Why now? Why so sudden? Somehow when, later, she'd seen and heard the approach of the police cars, she hadn't been surprised. Although she, like the others, had first thought the police had come to move the travellers on, and the convoy had got wind of it and decamped first. But the police vehicles had stopped by the quarry entrance and from that moment on it was clear the troubles of the site weren't over. They were just about to increase.

Rubbish of all kinds had been left on the hillside by the fleeing travellers, truly an appalling mess. The large blackened area of destroyed turf which marked the fire was still smouldering, wisps of smoke rising from a few charred embers. A baby buggy, minus a wheel, lay upturned nearby. Cans, bottles, plastic bags and sacks, paper, food scraps, human refuse. The stench, already bad, would grow much worse within hours. The bluebottles had gathered above it in swarms and crawled across it, a legion of glistening insect scavengers.

The dog had begun to forage among the debris and calling him away, Meredith walked quickly on. At the summit a cool breeze brought a welcome fresh tang to the air. The path split here. The left-hand fork, the better maintained and wider, followed the line of the ridge and must end up eventually at Motts Farm. The right-hand spur soon dwindled to little more than a footpath and must lead to the folly. Meredith took it.

It was very quiet. Below she could see a whole hive of activity. The archaeological site, the main road with police vehicles clustered together and the chimneys of Finny's cottage sticking up through the trees. No wonder those who had first built a fort here had chosen this place. It commanded the approach on all sides.

Her footsteps fell almost silently on the track, half overgrown with short coarse grass. On either side a few bramble bushes stretched out prickly tentacles to snag the ankles of unwary walkers. A clump of nettles swayed to brush her arm with green jagged leaves sprinkled with stinging hairs. A butterfly fluttered past her nose. Then a shadow was cast long on the ground and, looking up, she saw the folly before her.

Meredith's first feeling was one akin

to disappointment. From below it had looked imposing, a great piece of mediaeval pageantry, a theatrical backdrop to stirring tales. That was no doubt how its creator had intended it should look. But close at hand it was just a solid piece of Victorian brickwork, rather unoriginal in inspiration, the more obvious sort of castle keep as appeared in hundreds of children's story books.

There should be a flaxen-haired princess leaning out of one of its arched windows about to let down her braids to act as a ladder for her lover and rescuer. But this Rapunzel's windows were glazed, hardly commonplace in mediaeval fastnesses and even here appearing a needless refinement.

The heavy oaken door had an iron latch. Meredith pushed it down, not expecting it to give. But to her surprise it opened beneath her hand and the door swung noiselessly inward. After a moment's hesitation, she entered.

The surprise of the folly lay inside, not outside its brick walls.

Quite simply, it wasn't just an empty shell, but furnished and habitable in a basic way. Its small square ground-floor room had a bare paved floor of pale York flagstone. There were a table and two chairs, an old-fashioned primus stove and a simple wooden cupboard. A venerable Victorian chaise-longue's carved scrolls still showed faint signs of once-splendid gilding. A sleeping bag had been thrown over it.

Meredith took a step inside and her foot kicked against some pebbles and sent them skidding across the floor. There were several small stones scattered around as if they'd been tossed in through the open door, and scrape marks on the paved floor where the dust had been disturbed. She gazed round her with increasing wonder. The glazing at the windows was now explained. Someone lived here or at least occasionally slept here.

A primitive wooden stair at the side of the room led up through a hole in the ceiling to a room above as she discovered on climbing it. But this upper chamber was empty and its dust undisturbed. From here more stairs led up again, probably out on to the parapet, but she didn't bother with them. They looked unsafe.

Returning to the ground floor, Meredith opened the cupboard door. It held a half-empty packet of cornflakes and a bag of sugar together with assorted oddments of crockery. She closed it thoughtfully and as she did, her eye caught a hint of colour. Fine scraps of some material had been swept or blown by the breeze from the open folly door half under the raised base of the cupboard. She crouched and fished out some ends of faded pink and blue straw.

The dog gave a low growl of warning. At the same moment there was a movement behind her. A voice demanded, "Who're you, then? And just what do you think you're doing here, miss?"

Meredith's fingers closed on the straw slivers and she whirled round guiltily.

A man stood in the open door. With the sun behind him he appeared as a solid black silhouette, stockily built and of middle height but featureless.

The dog barked, hackles raised, at the intruder and Meredith reached out and grabbed him.

With a glance at the animal, the man asked suspiciously, "Are you one of those travelling folk?"

"No," Meredith said, wishing he didn't block the only exit. "I'm from the dig."

"Oh, that lot!" He gave a slightly derisive snort as if being one of the archaeological team was more respectable than being a New Age Traveller, but only marginally so. He moved further into the room.

Now she could see him clearly. He was about forty years old, his skin tanned by exposure to the elements, his features undistinguished except for shrewd brown eyes. They were small and oddly bright and, when she met their gaze, they became suddenly elusive, the mind behind them unreadable, for all that they had been studying her so closely. He wore strong work trousers and a much-washed red shirt with the sleeves rolled up, and serviceable boots. But his general appearance was tidy.

"What you got there, then?"

"Nothing!" She flushed indignantly and held out her open palm so that he could see the scraps of straw.

He snorted. "Bringing rubbish in here!"

"I didn't!" Meredith denied. "I picked them off the floor! I haven't been here more than a few minutes!" She thrust the straw scraps into her jeans pocket since to throw them down would invite a further charge of making a mess.

He scowled. "Shouldn't you be down the hill with your friends, scraping about for bits of old bone and pot?"

She avoided answering directly by asking in her turn, "Are you the farmer who owns this land?"

He nodded. "One of 'em. I'm Brian Felston. I farm here with my uncle — Lionel."

"I'm Meredith Mitchell." She held out her hand.

The brown eyes flickered but he took it and shook it briefly. The skin of his palm was like smooth fine leather.

"I hope you don't mind," Meredith went on, suspecting that he probably did mind. "My investigating this folly, I mean. But I do like eccentricities and now work's held up at the dig and the travellers have left, it seemed an opportunity."

"What's held you up, then?" The voice was suspicious again.

She ought not to have said that and Meredith sought to make good the slip. "We're waiting for one of us to come back from Bamford."

He seemed to accept that and she went on quickly, trying to divert him, "The travellers have left a terrible mess at their campsite. I passed it on my way up here."

"Don't I know it?" he said grimly. "It'll take me best part of a week to clear it up! They've been in here and brought all that dirt!" His face darkened and he pointed at the scattered pebbles on the floor. "That'll be their bloody kids did that! Little devils!"

Now that credentials had been exchanged, Meredith was emboldened to ask, "Who uses this room? I didn't expect to find it furnished!"

He looked round and shrugged. "I've got a chap comes over and helps out when we're specially busy. Usually uncle and I can manage but at harvest time and so on we take on an extra pair of hands. Uncle doesn't like the idea of having anyone living at the farm so the chap lives here, just for a couple of weeks at a time, whenever he comes. But, as it happens, I've been sleeping out here for the last few nights. Since those travellers turned up, that is. I've been keeping watch on them. I didn't like that fire they'd built. I was worried it'd get out of hand. Didn't know what else they might get up to, neither!"

"They've gone now. You'll be able to relax."

"Until the next lot turn up and set up camp without so much as a by your leave! They don't seem to understand farmland is private land. They treat it like a common. And pasture or hay, well, to them that's just a field not being used! They live in the country and don't know a damn thing about it! Most of 'em are townies. Barmy, half of 'em!"

He had been growing vehement. His little bright eyes glowed. It occurred to her that the travellers had had an enemy to beware of in Brian Felston. He was still looking about the room, the button eyes searching. Then the bright gaze swivelled back to her face.

"'Tisn't what I'd call proper furnished. That old sofa," he pointed at the chaise-longue, "I brought that up here from the quarry tip a year or so back. Rest of the stuff came from the farm. We didn't use it."

"It looks Victorian and if it was done up would probably fetch a good price," said Meredith of the chaise-longue.

He seemed unimpressed. "Don't see why folks should want that when the shops are full of decent modern stuff! Might appeal to you, I suppose, if you're keen on old things. It's solid enough, mind! I only fetched it up here because it was a good 'un. I had to give the old devil down at the tip two quid for it."

"Finny? He seems to make a living from selling things from the tip! Has he any right to?"

"Of course not!" Brian snorted scornfully. "He's an old rogue. Still, he's been there years, long as I can remember, and he's a bit of the landscape you might say. I don't mind slipping him a quid or two from time to time."

But he was still casting his gaze round the little room as he spoke and she sensed an underlying restlessness. Why had he come out here to the folly, anyway? Or had he just been passing and seen the open door? She guessed he wanted her to leave but was too polite to order her out.

"I'd better get back," she said, moving towards the door.

Unexpectedly he asked, "What are all those coppers doing down there? Couldn't get the blighters to come up here when we wanted them to move on the travellers. Now they're fair swarming all over the quarry. Old Finny found the Crown Jewels chucked away down there?"

Meredith supposed that really there was no reason not to tell him the basic fact. "The police? I suppose you haven't heard yet. It's rather horrid, I'm afraid."

His eyes narrowed and his expression grew wary. "Oh, yes? What then?"

"They found a body in the quarry."

There was a silence. He looked quite shocked, frozen. At last he asked hoarsely, "What, a dead person, you mean? Someone dead?"

"Yes." She hesitated. Clearly the news

had rocked him and it wasn't the sort of thing that happened on one's doorstep every day, after all. But she really couldn't tell him any more. Alan particularly didn't want the identity of the victim to get out yet. She began to prepare some sort of evasive explanation, but it wasn't needed.

Brian must have been holding his breath. Now he let it out in a gusty sigh. "That's bad." Abruptly he wheeled round. "I'd best get back to the house. Police may turn up there next and I'd do well to warn uncle. He's getting on and can't be doing with too many shocks at his age!"

He strode out of the folly and when she went to the door she saw him making his way rapidly along the ridge towards the chimneys of Motts Farm. His head was lowered and his hands thrust in his pockets as if he were lost in thought. He didn't look back. She was sure he'd already completely forgotten her.

She must get back too. Meredith closed the door behind her and set off on her own way down the hill, the dog bounding happily before her.

Leaving the folly behind him, Brian Felston quickly covered the distance to the farm, striding along, his face grim beneath the peak of his cap. The yard was empty but the back porch door was open at the house so the old man was indoors.

Brian went into the porch, taking off his cap to hang on its usual peg and stooping to unlace his boots, both in an automatic gesture. Neither he nor his uncle ever wore dirty footwear into the house. He peered into the kitchen beyond.

The old chap was taking his afternoon tea-break, his habit. He was moving stiffly round the kitchen, a conscious precision in his actions, thinking what he was doing. Starting to show his age now, poor old devil. Must be well over seventy, thought Brian, almost with shock.

Lionel held the kettle in his hand and, as his nephew watched, poured boiling water into the old black-glazed teapot. He splashed a little on to the table. Then he took down two mugs from their hooks. Two, because without looking up he knew Brian was there. Heard him moving in the porch. Sight and hearing sound as a bell. Just the stiff joints, the slight shake of the hand, the first signs of what would be increasing infirmity.

Sadness swept over Brian. Had the old man been an animal they'd be thinking that time neared to have him put down. But human life was sacred, whether or not folk could still do a hand's turn or shift for themselves. It distinguished man from beast, that respect for life for life's sake despite the inevitable. A poor brute sent to slaughter sometimes looked at you with infinite reproach but generally accepted its fate. The old man was a fighter and would never give up.

And what of human affection and companionship? Brian didn't like to think of the farm without his uncle because then he'd be alone. He shied away from facing that it would come to that. But it must and nothing now could be done about it. All too late. Yet it might have been different. Sometimes he wondered whether he loved his uncle or hated him. A little of both, most likely.

Lionel looked his way at last. "There you are. Got a pot of tea brewing here. Don't stand gawping."

Brian came in on stockinged feet. Slowly, methodically he washed his hands at the sink, watching his uncle surreptitiously all the while. Then he dried them on a worn towel and approached the table.

Lionel had already poured the tea and seated himself. He was spooning sugar carefully into his mug. Brian watched him stir it round, seeing the purple knotted veins standing up in ridges on the old man's hand, burned walnut brown by years of work out of doors and still strong and sinewy. Strong enough. Lionel put down the spoon and reached for his book. He never lost the opportunity to read a few verses of his Bible or a paragraph or two from the old pulpit-basher's sermons.

Brian hesitated and then stretched out his hand and put it on the old man's shoulder. Lionel looked up.

"Police may come by later, Uncle Lionel. Seems there's a spot of bother at the quarry."

"Don't need 'em now, not no more now them travelling rascals have moved on!" grumbled Lionel. "Trust police to turn up when they're not wanted no more! They got that Markby with them? Clever blighter. That was a big family round here once, Markbys. I remember 'em. The old man was Justice of the Peace. Another of 'em was rector over to Westerfield. For all that he did nothing about those travelling buggers. Been dead years, the old rector and the Justice. Now his son's a policeman and the daughter's a lawyer of sorts. Funny sort of business for a woman, that. But they was always a powerful judging family. Judgement. There comes a time of judgement, Brian, you keep that in your mind!"

So there might be! thought Brian grimly. But there was no need to go running to meet it! He cleared his throat.

"They turned up a body down there. It's nothing to do with us." Brian's voice grew firmer. "Nothing at all and we don't need to say anything about — anything. They'll be asking questions, I don't doubt. If we saw or heard aught.

That's routine, uncle, and nothing to worry about." The hand Brian had on his uncle's shoulder squeezed gently, feeling how bony the old man was under the cloth of his jacket. "Don't you fret, Uncle Lionel. I'll take care of everything!"

★ ★ ★

Meredith had meant to go straight back to the dig. She might have been missed and Alan, although probably too busy, might wonder where she'd got to. But she found herself sidetracked, perhaps as a result of her conversation with Brian.

She had turned on to the wider track down the hill at the spot where the paths split. It was really an unmade road full of stones and potholes winding down to the main road. Once more she found herself passing the abandoned camp site, now on her right. She was truly sorry for Brian who had the unenviable task of clearing away the rubbish and filth. Until it was gone, the Felstons couldn't turn animals out to graze here. Offended both by sight and smell, she turned her head away and looked to the left.

In stark contrast a field of ripe wheat inclined full golden heads gently as the breeze rippled across it. This was ready for cutting. Presumably the Felstons meant to harvest it any day now. This was the reason Brian had originally furnished the folly room. The temporary hired help he'd spoken of would be joining the Felstons and they would all turn to until the crop was in. Perhaps the man even preferred staying on his own in the folly. The Felstons sounded to Meredith an uncomfortable pair to spend much time with.

Alas, there was ample evidence to be seen here as to why the presence of the travelling convoy had made the Felstons so angry. Throughout the field, wide swathes had been trodden down to make irregular paths. Some were meaningless, leading nowhere, just meandering or circular. Possibly they'd been made by dogs from the camp chasing rabbits or by the convoy's children.

But one path did lead somewhere. It ran in a fairly straight line out into the middle of the field to where a scarecrow stood with arms outstretched.

It looked from where she stood a fairly elaborate creation made with some skill and she was curious to view it closer. The damage had already been done and the crop flattened along the narrow footpath leading to it. Treading carefully so as not to make the path any wider, Meredith began to walk out to the centre of the field.

It was hotter than ever out here, a blazing expanse without shade of any kind. The scarecrow looked unnervingly lifelike and seemed to be watching her approach. Its tattered jacket fluttered and gave the impression its straw hands beckoned.

She reached it at last. It stood the height of a man and was made of bundled straw secured with twine. All except the head, which was made from an old grain sack stuffed with straw. The face had been carefully painted on. It had round eyes under surprised eyebrows and its mouth was open in a foolish grin showing both sets of teeth, upper and lower. The teeth in particular were individually painted, and suddenly, with a mixture of amusement and disgust, she realised that it was meant to represent Finny with his badly fitting dentures.

How cruel! she thought. Had Brian made it? A petty revenge for being made to pay two pounds for the chaise-longue? But perhaps he'd meant no malice and had just been amusing himself. It was unlikely Finny would ever see the scarecrow and, even if he did, he wouldn't necessarily recognise himself.

She looked down at the ground. Children had indeed beaten this particular track to visit the scarecrow, which must have fascinated them. Reprehensible though the damage to the crop was, there had been charm in their purpose. They'd held a doll's tea-party out here and it was easy to deduce that the scarecrow had been guest of honour. A set of pink plastic dolls' cups and saucers with plates lay abandoned on the flattened stalks together with empty crisp packets and a soft drink can. Meredith wondered whether they had actually been engaged in holding their tea-party when the convey had struck camp. That could explain why they'd forgotten their playthings, having been called away suddenly by their alarmed parents.

Meredith smiled, imagining them all sitting round the scarecrow out of sight amongst the tall wheat, solemnly handing round their dolls' cups of orangeade. Then she noticed the scarecrow's footwear and her smile broadened. His shoes had been put on the wrong feet. Not that he had any true feet. The shoes had simply been shoved under the, ends of his straw legs, but left where right should be and vice-versa.

Meredith's smile faded. She frowned and stooped to look closer. That was odd. The rest of the scarecrow's garments were old and faded. But his footwear consisted of an expensive-looking pair of Italian-made women's sandals.

13

THE Crossed Keys was situated in the Market Square and had previously been called The Railway Arms. Its original name had at least borne some relation to its appearance and history. The hotel had been built when the railway reached Bamford in the late 1840s to accommodate travellers by the speedy new transport. But in the present century the management had decided that old coaching inns had more appeal to tourists than ramshackle Victorian railway hotels, and so the inn had been rechristened.

The new name was unsuitable in every way. The red brick exterior and gloomy corridors with disused gas mantles still attached to the walls failed to suggest the bustle of changing horses or tales of highwaymen. Few tourists were drawn to its unpainted portals or dined in its austere restaurant.

Meredith took a room at the back

overlooking the kitchens, having been assured that this was the quiet side of the building. Clanging saucepans, shouts from the cooks and a persistent background of Radio One made this a doubtful claim. Shutting the window kept out some of this and the odour of boiled vegetables. It was not the sort of place anyone stayed in for more than a night or two and Meredith wondered how long she would be residing here. She sat on the bed which squeaked and was hard enough to delight the most orthopaedic of requirements. There was a Gideon Bible on the bedside table and a sign above the window read 'Fire Escape'.

Fire Escape? Meredith reopened the window and leaned out. Sure enough, an unstable-looking iron ladder led down almost to the ground outside. So if The Crossed Keys caught fire, all the guests would presumably come rushing through her room in their night attire to clamber out of her window. It wasn't an encouraging thought.

But neither was that of returning to Islington and Toby. Caught between these dire options, Meredith extricated her sponge bag from her travelling hold-all and set off down the corridor to find a bath or a shower unit. The Crossed Keys, having no aspirations towards any stars, did not provide rooms with such facilities as an integral fixture.

It was early evening. With the discovery of Natalie's body all work at the site had been halted. Ursula had returned to her father's house in Oxford. Dan Woollard had made a statement at Bamford police station in the presence of his solicitor and had been released. Presumably he'd also gone home. The inquest on Natalie Woollard had been set for the following Friday and would certainly be adjourned pending police inquiries. Markby was already up to his eyes in said inquiries but had promised to call by The Crossed Keys and eat a hasty dinner with Meredith, developments permitting. She was more than half-expecting a call with his excuses.

Despite her doubts, Alan turned up on time, and she wondered briefly if he was trying to prove some point. "I thought you mightn't," she said, adding, "Sorry. I knew you'd come if you could. I just thought, with a new case, you mightn't be able."

"I nearly didn't," he confessed. "And if the course of duty hadn't brought me back to Bamford, I should have rung up and cried off. But I had to go and see Mrs Salter and break the news. She took it very badly and a neighbour's looking after her. From Old Mill Street to this place is only a couple of hundred yards. So here I am."

He glanced round. "Besides which, I confess I need a drink. Breaking bad news isn't what I feel I do best. Perhaps I should have sent a policewoman. Only, I felt I should go myself."

"I'm sure you did it as well as anyone could. There's no way you could have made it less painful or horrifying."

He hunched his shoulders resignedly. "I can't stay long. This has to be a rushed meal. Is it all right to eat here?"

"Judging from the kitchen odours, I doubt it. But it will suit you best, won't it? They're offering a choice between roast chicken and fried fish followed by rice pudding or trifle."

They settled for the fish. Only two

other diners shared the restaurant with them, a dispirited pair of businessmen. The atmosphere was such that all conversation was automatically conducted in whispers across the none too white tablecloth and vase containing a fabric rose.

"There's really no need to keep you hanging about in this dismal spot. You can go back to London if you want," Markby said, prodding the fish doubtfully. "I know where to find you. Is this cod or haddock?"

"Looks like coley to me. No, I'll stay here. I'll be at Friday's inquest. But it'll be adjourned, won't it? How's it going?"

"We're trying to track her movements. I'd like to know how she got to the area and why she came. She might have come with the intention of contacting her mother. If so, she didn't. Amy's adamant. And I'd like to find her shoes."

"Shoes?" Meredith put down her fork and mentally, cursed herself for not reporting the oddity of the scarecrow's footwear. Who sticks expensive sandals under a scarecrow's straw legs? She should have known such an obvious disparity might be important to inquiries. Tentatively she asked, "They wouldn't be a pair of Italian sandals, would they?"

He looked up sharply. "What's that?"

Briefly she told him about the scarecrow. Markby threw down his knife and fork. "Damn! It's nearly dark out there already! But come on, you'll have to show me exactly where this scarecrow is! I'll call the incident room first and tell them where I'm going — but let's hope those sandals are still there!"

★ ★ ★

Blundering about in a wheat field in the dark with the aid of a torch wasn't how Meredith had envisaged spending the evening and provided an odd sort of alternative to watching TV at The Crossed Keys. She would have said anything was preferable to the latter, but now she wasn't sure. At first she had trouble in the poor light in finding the track into the wheat at all. But they found it at last, and the scarecrow and, thankfully, his strange footwear.

As Markby crouched over it shining his torch down on to the ground, a cool breeze blew over the hillside rustling the dry ears of wheat. Clouds scudded across the face of the moon. Meredith wrapped her arms around her upper body and shivered in the silvery light. In the distance car engines could be heard approaching from Bamford and then headlights swept up the track. After a while a voice, Sergeant Pearce's, could be heard shouting, "You out there, sir?"

"Yes! Bring a plastic bag! The sandals are here and will have to go to forensic!"

Pearce blundered up, flattening wheat to right and left and peered at the ground in the circle of torchlight. "Weird!" he commented.

"You should see its face!" said Meredith from the darkness.

Pearce jumped. "That you, Miss Mitchell?"

Markby flashed the torch briefly towards Meredith and then at the scarecrow's face.

"Ugly looking thing!" said Pearce.

"I think it's meant to be the old man who minds the rubbish tip down the hill on the other side of the main road, at the quarry," Meredith volunteered.

"Weird," said Pearce again. "Looks like someone's got a sense of humour."

His chief inspector growled. "Get some proper lights fixed up! We'll have to search the area."

Meredith, on the edge of the group, said, "Someone's coming down here from the farm."

More headlights were approaching and with a rattle and roar the Felstons' Land-Rover swept up and decanted both farmers.

"Get out of there! You're flattening it!" Lionel shouted, dancing up and down on the track in the headlights of his own vehicle.

Brian, flashlight in hand, made his way out to join them and asked curtly, "What's it now?"

"Possibly important evidence!" Markby moved the torch so that the beam no longer illuminated the ground and Brian couldn't see the sandals. "Sorry about the damage to the crop."

"We're cutting this field tomorrow morning!"

"Sorry, afraid not. We'll be out here tomorrow. It'll have to be put off."

"I've got a man coming out to give us a hand!" Brian protested.

"Get them fellows out of that field!" Lionel commanded from the track. "There won't be a stalk left standing to cut! First them hippies now the police as ought to know better! Is that you out there, Markby? What in tarnation d'you think you're doing? Get them men of yours out of that crop!"

"Take Miss Mitchell back to the hotel, will you?" Markby said to Pearce.

Brian started and shone his flashlight into Meredith's face. She threw up her hands to protect her eyes from the light as he exclaimed, "I've met you, haven't I? What're you doing here?"

"Long story," said Meredith. "And I can't tell you now."

She stepped round him and set off back to the track followed by Pearce. Lionel surged out of the shadow of a hedge to meet them. The moonlight silvered his grey hair and bleached his skin to a dead whiteness lending his

240

Old Testament face a haggard, unearthly aspect.

"A woman! What's a woman doing out here? 'Tis always a woman where there's trouble!"

"Crazy old coot!" Pearce said briefly. "Jump in the car, Miss Mitchell, I'll get you back to the hotel in no time."

As they drove away she turned and looked back. Lights flickered on the track and dark silhouettes moved in and out of the yellow splashes as if so many trolls had danced out of the rampart to cavort on the down by the light of the moon. One, probably Lionel, had raised its arms and swayed from side to side calling down imprecations on those who destroyed the fruit of his labour on the land. Meredith turned back her head, slumped in the passenger seat and sighed.

"Missed out on your dinner, didn't you?" Pearce sympathised. "Was it something nice?"

"No," said Meredith. "It was a bit of dried up fish in leathery batter with some rock-hard chips!"

"Oh," said Pearce. "No loss, then."

14

IT was hardly to be hoped that Meredith got much sleep for the rest of that night. In the darkness of her room at The Crossed Keys strange shapes formed. Her dressing gown on the back of the door suggested the scarecrow's untidy figure. The moonlight glinting off the mirror was oddly reminiscent of the ivory-coloured Saxon bones lying in the dark earth. The musty smell of the room recalled both Finny's cottage and the works trailer. In addition to all this, pangs of hunger gnawed at her stomach reminding her that for all her contemptuous dismissal of her dinner when talking to Sergeant Pearce, she now wished she'd had the forethought to finish it before springing her information about the sandals on Markby.

Next morning, Thursday, when Meredith sallied forth from the hostelry tired and a little irritable with just the faintest suggestion of a headache pressing at her brow, she found herself at a loose end.

She didn't like it. Her inactivity was rendered worse by it being Market Day and the little town more than usually busy. She roamed up and down the High Street and finally found herself standing before the window of an estate agency. Recession in the property market had led to several of the residences on offer being attractively priced. It was certainly the time to buy and not to sell. Meredith pursed her lips and pressed her nose against the glass and wondered if she ought to consider buying.

Buying here in Bamford? Why not. True, she'd commuted up to London from Bamford station for a while before and found it too much. But at that time she'd been living outside the town and had first to drive in from the village before catching the train. If she lived in town and could walk to the station, it would cut out that twenty-minute drive at the beginning and end of each day and the cost of parking the car all day in the station yard.

But she didn't want four bedrooms and a double garage. She didn't even want three bedrooms and a garden. She didn't really fancy a flat. Toby's flat had put her off flats. She most certainly didn't want a flimsy starter home on an estate. In short, she didn't want any of the delights in the window.

She was about to turn away when she saw it. Tucked down in a corner was a faded photo of a small mid-Victorian end of terrace labourer's cottage. Two up and two down basically, with a bathroom built on as an extension in the 1930s. The property, the accompanying blurb optimistically proclaimed, had character and offered scope for improvement. Its address put it within five minutes' walk of the railway station. It was currently empty. In a moment's madness, Meredith walked into the office and asked if she could have the brochure.

They were clearly short of customers. They offered her coffee and pressed numerous leaflets describing other properties on her. Politely declining all others, she asked if she might have the keys of the one she'd seen in the window.

"It wants a lot doing," said the

young man, impelled by some residue of honesty.

"Yes, I understand. I'd like to take a look."

"I'll come with you!" He still didn't believe she could be seriously considering the place, but he was probably keen to get out of the office and actually be doing something. "It's not far from the station, but you wouldn't be bothered with the noise of the trains. The street's a quiet one. Several of the other houses have been done up. It's moving upmarket. It's quite a bijou little place really." He was remembering that he was supposed to sell it. "It's quaint."

It wanted a lot doing all right. Bijou meant extremely small. But it was built of warm, pale gold stone with a narrow tiled forecourt in front and a tiny yard behind. Being end of terrace it also had enough space at the side for a wonky lean-to wooden garage. Meredith began to imagine it with a newly painted front door and window boxes.

The young man launched into full flow. These period properties, he confided, were much in demand. They were especially attractive to single professional people, he added with a keen glance at Meredith. So how long had this one been empty? He was vague. A sale had fallen through. Otherwise it would have gone long ago.

He opened the front door and it dislodged a yellowed stack of free newspapers and advertising mail. Meredith observed the cobwebs in the ceiling corners and thick dust on the banisters. "It doesn't look to me as if anyone else has even viewed it recently!"

He looked hurt and scooped up the junk mail. "We can't help it if so much of this stuff comes through the door. The downstairs has been entirely renovated. The bathroom's at the back in the extension but it's very spacious."

Meredith peered into the pitted enamel bath and at the cracked wash basin. A new bathroom suite was urgently needed. But the little house seemed solid enough and the two upstairs bedrooms proved larger than the exterior of the house suggested. She probed at the sash window frames without discovering soft patches and moved them up and down to see if the sashes still worked. They did, stiffly. There was no smell of rot in the cupboards. No telltale mildewed stains on the walls or peeling wallpaper. No sagging ceilings. Just neglect. She began to cheer up. For some reason she couldn't have explained she felt right here, as if she and the little house were old friends who were remeeting after a long absence.

The back yard came as a bit of a shock and dented her optimism. There was a collapsing outside toilet and a whole lot of rubbish surrounded by weeds. But Alan would have ideas about that and could advise on patio gardens and so on. The wooden garage, on the other hand, could only be described as 'condemned'. Even the agent looked depressed as they inspected it. His manner, when they returned to the house, was resigned. The client was going to back off now she'd seen the reality.

"I'd need to get a professional surveyor's report on the structure," Meredith said. "And a drains test."

He stared at her then quickly masked his surprise. "It's basically sound, very sound. Better built than some modern places, though I shouldn't say so!" Despite his enthusiasm it was clear that he personally wouldn't have lived here if he'd been paid to do it: But against all the odds it seemed he might even have a buyer for this white elephant.

"It needs new kitchen and bathroom and that garage will have to come down and be entirely rebuilt in matching stone which nowadays will be extremely expensive!" Meredith said firmly. "I take it the price is negotiable?"

He havered. "I'd have to consult the sellers."

Meredith fixed the pile of yellowed junk mail in his arms with an expressive eye.

"But I'm sure they'd be reasonable," he said hastily. "In fact, I think they might even come down a couple of thousand."

★ ★ ★

Whilst Meredith was house-hunting, Markby was continuing his own hunt for a murderer. He was doing so by a painstaking, tedious attention to detail with its attendant time-wasting which marked so much police work.

Today would see Natalie's name released as the victim. It might jog a few memories in the Bamford area but he couldn't rely on it. He stood on the track by the wheatfield and watched men sweep methodically across it. They were unlikely, too, to find anything else. But they had to be sure. As for the crop itself, that was now flattened.

Markby was uneasily aware that as the police operation was in progress it was itself under surveillance. Every time he turned his head he saw high on the ridge above them, the dark outline of a man hovering increasingly vengefully.

At last the officer in charge of the search came to him and said, "That's about it, sir. I doubt there's anything else out there. There's no other clothing, that's for sure."

"Okay," Markby said. "Stand the search down." He glanced up at the ridge again. "I'm going up to the farm."

He negotiated his car up the bumpy track, turning left along the ridge at the top, now empty of the observer, and eventually reaching Motts Farm. The entry to its yard was barred by a gate and leaning on the gate was Brian Felston.

Markby stopped the car and got out. Brian watched him approach with hostile eyes and his words of greeting confirmed that the farmer was both waiting for him and intending to delay him.

"I've been watching you from up on the ridge. I get a good view of everything all round from up there. Saw you get in your car and set off up here. We've been expecting you. I want to have a word with you before you speak to Uncle Lionel."

Markby studied him. A lifetime working on the land and exposure to wind and weather had dried and wrinkled Brian's skin to resemble that of a much older man. There was a certain feral wariness about him, a disconcerting elusiveness in his gaze. These combined with an attitude of uncompromising obstinacy which suggested he wouldn't be moved off that gate in a hurry.

"I don't want to take up too much of your time," Markby said placatingly. "I know you're busy. So am I."

Brian's mouth twisted into an unpleasing grimace. "You might be busy. We're not. And for why? I reckon you know the answer to that! Everything those hippies hadn't already destroyed, your fellows did! That was to be cut today. Now we're left sitting on our hands here. Have you any idea what that crop was worth? We hold you responsible, just you remember that! Everyone bending over backwards not to upset those blighters! As for us, we can be ruined and no one cares!"

"I'm very sorry, Mr Felston, but it was unavoidable."

"What did you find there last night, anyhow?"

"I'd rather not say just now." Markby indicated the surrounding countryside. "Yes, you do have a very good view from the ridge. You didn't happen to see anything unusual yesterday down on the main road in the vicinity of the quarry? Or even this morning?"

"No, I didn't see a damn thing and you ought to know the reason for that and all!" Brian gave a snort. "Because Uncle Lionel and I, we've had to keep our eyes fixed on those hippies! I spent all my time watching them from the moment they moved on to the hill till the moment they left, yesterday midday. We got no help from your lot!"

"It was a complicated matter," Markby said.

"It seemed simple enough to uncle and me. Anyway, they've gone now and good riddance! They left a pile of filth and rubbish behind for me to clear up. Burnt off the turf with their fires. I was worried about that fire, I can tell you. I could see that getting out of hand with the dry weather like we've had. I even had to turn out at night and sit up there keeping watch! When a man's been working hard all day, the last thing he needs is having to sit up half the night trying to make sure a bunch of nutters like that don't burn down half his crops! Only as it turned out, you coppers have trampled the entire field flat, so what's the difference!"

"Look, I understand your grievance and I sympathise!" Markby broke firmly into Brian's litany of woe. "Now what is it you wanted to say to me before I speak to Mr Lionel?"

"Oh, yes, uncle." Brian seemed recalled to his original purpose. "See here, Markby, you know the old man and how he is. Well, more or less. He rants on a bit about sin and women and so forth. He's harmless. It's a sort of kink he's got, up here." Brian tapped his brow. "But it's only up here, in his head. Reads his Bible a lot and a couple of other religious books. What I mean is, you need to ignore half of what he says. Weed it out, in a manner of speaking."

"I understand. Now may I come in?"

Brian nodded and opened the gate to let Markby through.

★ ★ ★

Lionel awaited him in the farmhouse parlour. Markby, sitting beneath the truculent gaze of the late Winston Churchill, found it a dispiritingly uncomfortable room. Furniture surfaces were dusty, the windows unwashed, the air stale. There was, however, a television set in the corner and a single armchair set right in front of it. But he supposed the Felstons must generally hardly ever use this room. He was being received in here as a mark of formality. In a way it was a compliment, an acknowledgement of his rank and standing, putting him on a par with the doctor or the vicar.

In the light of this thought, Lionel's opening words to him came as a considerable jolt.

"I knew your uncle, the Reverend Markby as was rector over to Westerfield some years back now! I mind he had a little car, Austin Seven it was, and he used to go paying parish visits in it."

"Yes, I remember that car," Markby informed him. "Though I was only a young boy at the time."

"He preached a powerful sermon."

"So I believe. He scared me!" Markby admitted.

"Didn't do you any harm, did it? Getting the fear of judgement put in you?"

"I'm not sure," Markby said cautiously. From the corner of his eye he could see Brian sitting stiffly on the edge of an old-fashioned sofa with tufts of horsehair showing through holes in the fabric.

"Chief Inspector's come about the body in the quarry!" Brian said loudly.

Markby was annoyed. He wanted to conduct the interview in his own way and let Lionel lead into the subject, something which he had been doing nicely. Obliged now to tackle it head-on, he asked, "Do you recall seeing anything unusual in the vicinity of the quarry either yesterday or the previous day, before the police arrived, Mr Lionel?"

"Unusual?" Lionel's hawkish gaze fixed him. "Apart from a horde of vagrants fornicating all over the hillside, d'you mean?"

"Apart from the hippies and, of course, the activities of the archaeological team."

"No. She'll have been a loose woman!" said Lionel briefly.

Brian stirred and looked uneasily at his uncle and then at Markby. "There's no need for that, Uncle!"

"A decent woman wouldn't have finished like that, dead in the quarry!"

"You don't know!" Brian's voice boomed suddenly loud in the drab little room. "And don't start going on

255

with your nonsense to the Chief Inspector here!"

"All right, Mr Felston! I can manage. Let your uncle say what he wants!" Markby ordered sharply.

"Nothing I've got to say will make any difference," Lionel told him, and Markby could have sworn there was a sort of malign glee in his voice. "A perverse and faithless generation! That's what it's called. The wages of sin are death. Dead she was, so she must have sinned!"

"We all die," Markby pointed out. And we all sin, he might have added but didn't.

"In the fullness of time. She was taken afore her time. It was a judgement."

"She wasn't actually what you'd call a loose woman, Mr Lionel. I am at liberty now to release her name. It was Natalie Woollard and she was a well-known novelist. She was Bamford born though not living in the town any longer."

Again Brian shifted on his sofa and looked as if he'd dearly like to speak. Markby quelled him with a look.

"I never go into Bamford," Lionel said.

"She would have been Natalie Salter before she married. Her mother, Mrs Amy Salter, still lives in Bamford."

There was a perceptible pause. Lionel nodded. "A widow woman, god-fearing and decent."

"Ah! So you know Mrs Salter?"

"I know of her. Not to speak to."

"But you didn't know of Natalie?" Markby persisted.

"He told you he didn't!" Brian snapped.

"Wrote books, eh? What sort of books?" Lionel growled. "I can guess. Lewd, most likely, like most modern writing — and that!" He pointed at the television in the corner. "All lewdness and nakedness on that!"

"He never watches it," said Brian wearily. "He doesn't know a thing about it. You're making a fool of yourself, Uncle Lionel, rambling on like it."

Dammit, what d'you think I want him to do? thought Markby furiously.

"I know nothing about the woman dead in the quarry!" Lionel said suddenly. "You'd best go and ask Wilf Finny."

"We've spoken to Mr Finny."

"Then I don't know who else you can ask." Lionel folded his arms.

Clearly the conversation was at an end. Markby accepted his dismissal, glad to be out of the claustrophobic parlour. Brian accompanied him to his car.

"I told you he goes on a bit. You don't need to take any notice."

"Did you know Natalie Salter?" Markby asked suddenly. "You'd be much of an age as she was. Do you recall hearing her name when you were a youngster?"

Brian nodded. "Aye. Went to school with her, I fancy. Old High School as it was then. Comprehensive now."

"Damn it, man!" yelled Markby, accumulated frustration boiling over. "Why didn't you say so?"

Brian stared at him phlegmatically. "I was going to, but you gave me a dirty look so I shut up. It's no help to you, anyway. That was all of twenty-five years ago. What's that got to do with now? I went to school with a whole lot of others. Want their names? But I do remember Natalie Salter on account she went to university and the old headmaster was very proud of her. Then I fancy she got married away from Bamford. Any road, she never came back. I never go near the place myself, either, excepting Market Day. And in case you've overlooked it, that's today and I haven't gone in on account of your people messing about on our land all day and my not being able to leave Uncle Lionel."

"I am so very sorry," said Markby through gritted teeth, "that your plans have been disarranged, Mr Felston."

"Having old folks to look after, that's a responsibility," Brian informed him pugnaciously.

He stood in the entry to the yard and watched as Markby drove away, a solid, stocky figure with his hands in his pockets. But it was not so much his appearance or even his surprising revelation about his schoolboy acquaintance with the dead woman which lingered in Markby's mind. It was something in Brian's tone as he spoke the last words. Defensiveness? No, protectiveness, that was it.

"I do believe," Markby said aloud to himself, "that Brian is quite fond of the crazy old fellow!"

15

WHEN Meredith left the estate agents for a second time, a little before lunchtime, she walked down the High Street with a lighter step. The sellers, contacted by phone, had been willing to negotiate. A price hadn't been decided but clearly they were desperate to be rid of the place. She'd have to get a mortgage but not one which would leave her with a horrendous financial burden. The day had not been wasted. She was looking forward to seeing Alan and telling him what she'd done. Although she knew it was extremely unlikely she'd see him today. He would certainly be much too busy that Thursday. She wondered how he was getting on. Then she contemplated phoning Ursula but decided against it. Maybe they all needed a break before the ordeal of the inquest tomorrow.

So she had time to kill. Meredith stopped and reproached herself for the metaphor which sprang so easily to mind despite the death of Natalie Woollard and the memory of Ursula's distress. Recalled now to thoughts of the interrupted archaeological excavations at the hill, she glanced at her wristwatch. It was only a quarter past twelve. Meredith turned her feet in the direction indicated by a small white arrow and the legend 'Bamford Museum'. Jackson and his co-workers would almost certainly be found there since the dig was interrupted. Besides, she was not a little curious to see the place.

She found it in a back street. It was housed in a dingy, concrete Fifties building and its display rooms deserted. She walked around the glass cases and studied the flints and pottery shards and some Tudor bits and pieces unearthed when an old building in the town had been demolished twenty years before. Some tools, a leather shoe, a dented cook's ladle. It all reminded her of Finny and his rubbish tip. Yesterday's unconsidered domestic trivia: today's museum exhibits. What did the word 'value' mean, after all?

There was a corridor running off into

the back of a building and sounds of hesitant typing came from the far end of it. Meredith followed the noise, confident it would lead her to the curator's office. All at once there was the sound of something crashing to the floor and a shrill female squeal of distress followed by the infuriated roar of a male voice.

"For God's sake, Karen, not again! Can't you look what you're doing!"

The words burst out just by Meredith's ear. She stopped. There was a door to her left, ajar, and the speaker and the commotion had come from behind it.

Karen Henson's voice was heard in reply, nervously apologetic. "I'm really sorry, Ian. I just stepped back — "

"I don't care how you did it! Pick the bloody things up!"

Meredith made up her mind and tapped at the door. It flew open. Ian stood before her and behind him was Karen, looking close to tears. An upended cardboard box lay on the floor and mounted photo transparencies which it had evidently held lay scattered everywhere. The room itself appeared to be a store. Shelves along one side were stacked with a motley collection of items.

"Oh, hullo!" Jackson said looking a little abashed.

Karen smiled timidly and crouched down to scrabble among the spilled transparencies. "I'll put them all back in order, Ian."

"Oh, never mind!" He hunched his shoulders. "They're part of our schools stuff," he explained to Meredith. "We keep a sort of lecture kit in here. It's all under various headings, Roman Britain, Mediaeval Village Life, all that sort of thing. The schools borrow it or one of us takes it out and gives a talk. None of it is valuable."

"I've just had a look round the museum," Meredith said.

"Then you know why we're so desperate to find something new!" he muttered. "Come into the office."

They left poor Karen holding transparencies to the light and trying to make some kind of order out of them. Behind another door labelled 'Curator', the source of the typing was discovered. Renee Colmar sat at a typewriter with the perplexed expression of a novice technician faced with the controls of a super jetfighter. She looked up in some relief when she saw Meredith.

"Hi! Don't get the wrong idea now, I'm no secretary! How's the murder investigation going?"

Meredith said apologetically that she didn't know.

"I thought you had an information hotline right to that handsome policeman? Gee, am I disappointed!"

"I haven't actually come to disturb you."

"What's to disturb?" growled Jackson. "The dig's suspended!" He led the way to the window where a plan of the dig was pinned out on a board. He stood looking down at it gloomily.

"You'll be able to get back to work after the inquest," Meredith consoled him.

"It's not just a question of respect for Dan's wife that's stopping us. It's money. The Ellsworth has as good as pulled the plug."

"I *am* sorry." That was a blow to his hopes. "Completely? As of now?"

"As of the end of the month. Even if we do get back to work we'll have a matter of days to find Wulfric. There's hardly the remotest possibility."

From the door a small tense voice said, "Dan's more important! The police might arrest him!"

They all turned. Karen stood there, still holding the cardboard box of transparencies in her arms. Her face crimson, she looked the picture of misery and totally disorganised. Worst of all, fat tears trickled openly down her freckled cheeks.

Renee leapt up from the typewriter and ran to put an arm round Karen's shoulders. "It's okay, really! Ian's going to apologise, aren't you?" She turned a minatory glare on Jackson.

"What for?" The curator looked puzzled.

"For boring the pants off everyone about Wulfric for a start!" Renee shouted at him. "And for upsetting Karen the way you do!"

Jackson regarded Karen without the slightest sympathy. "I didn't upset her. What's the matter with her? What's she crying about this time? It's not a woman's thing, is it? Time of the month?"

Renee rocketed across the room and pushed her pugnacious little face into his, causing Jackson understandably to start back in some alarm.

"Listen to me, you, chauvinistic creep! She isn't like that mimsy wife of yours — "

Beneath his sandy hair Jackson's face took on a clashing hue of deep puce. "No dyke is going to call my wife — "

"Hey! Don't you call me — "

It was time to break up the argument before it degenerated into a physical brawl. Meredith declared loudly, "But the police haven't arrested Dan and, as far as we know, they're not about to. So cheer up, Karen! In the meantime, who's watching over the dig?"

This was the magical question which caused them all to abandon the fray. Jackson seized on the subject which alone interested him.

"The trailer's locked up and the Felstons will keep a general eye open." He rubbed at his hair so that it stood up on end. "We'll take turns to go out there and check the place out. The hippies have gone so there's no one about out there."

Meredith thought about the police combing the wheat field but only said, "If you like, I'll go out there this afternoon. I've nothing else to do."

"Thanks." He stared down at the diagram of trenches and tapped the chart with his forefinger. "I'm looking at it, you know, Wulfric's grave. It's down here in some spot we haven't tried. I just can't find the bloody thing!"

"It could be," snapped Renee sourly, "that we're all just working our butts off looking in the wrong, place!"

"What do you know? I've spent years — "

Hostilities were breaking out again, fuelled no doubt by the frustrations of the forced abandonment of their work. Meredith decided to leave them to it.

★ ★ ★

However, true to her promise to Jackson, she collected her car from the park at The Crossed Keys and set off for Bamford Hill after lunch. Not fancying the hotel lunch, she'd found a small restaurant and ordered salad and, suppressing all thought of the calories it contained, a slice of gooey home-made chocolate cake. She didn't hurry over it and didn't hurry as she drove along the main road towards the distant rise of the hill. She aimed to get there at about three o'clock.

She didn't mind going out to check the dig — the hippies had gone and although the police might still be at the wheat field higher up the hill, the site of the dig should be quiet — yet it would be an odd feeling to be out there alone with just the excavated skeleton for company. Meredith wondered if, to carry out her task properly, she should peel back the tarpaulin over the grave and make sure the old warrior still rested secure and undisturbed in his last bed. She didn't fancy the idea much.

Absorbed in thought of this, she had arrived almost at the turning on to the hill, before she realised it, or had taken much notice of the surrounding countryside. She was just about level with the quarry, and her attention was first drawn to it by fluttering lengths of official tape across the entrance, and a notice saying that tipping was suspended for the time being pending police investigations. Then she saw two other things simultaneously.

One was a plastic carrier bag and groceries spilling out of it on the ground beneath the notice. The other was a hunched figure in a trilby hat, leaning against a tree and evidently in some distress.

Meredith braked sharply. "Mr Finny?" She jumped out of the car and ran towards him.

Finny, his face an alarming dusky red, was wheezing dreadfully. His eyes bulged and, as she came up, he opened his mouth and the porcelain teeth slipped into view, chattering together, but no words emerging through them. Pearls of sweat rolled down his forehead from beneath the hat and he was gesturing feebly with his right arm, bending it back and forth across his chest in a strange motion. Whether he was beckoning to her or trying to indicate his heart she couldn't be sure.

"Come on, Mr Finny!" she said and

grasped his arm. "Let's get you into your cottage! You remember me, don't you?"

"Ah . . . " Finny whispered. "Me shopping . . . "

"I'll come back for it."

But he began to show signs of even more distress and Meredith was obliged to gather up his small supply of necessities and return them to the bag from which they'd tumbled when he'd let it fall. Only then did Finny allow her to guide him along the track, up his own path and through the front door.

Their progress was slow and being encumbered with the shopping bag didn't help. Twice Finny sagged at the knees and Meredith needed all her strength to keep him upright. But they reached the door at last.

"The doorkey, Mr Finny?" she gasped.

"'Tain't locked . . . " wheezed Finny. "Allus open . . . "

She tried the handle and found the door was indeed unlocked. He must leave it so all the time, thought Meredith. An old country habit, but dating from safer times and unwise in this day and age.

She managed after further tussling to

get him into his parlour and on to a faded sofa. There he lay like a stranded whale and gazed up at her. His colour, however, she noted with some relief, was slowly returning to something more like normal.

"You haven't got a drop of brandy or whisky?" She looked around her.

An extraordinary sight met her eyes. Mismatched furniture in all stages of decrepitude and all styles was packed in the room, giving seating for twenty. Ornaments, chipped, broken or glued, decorated every surface. An Edwardian reproduction of Landseer's *Monarch of the Glen*, frame damaged and glass cracked, hung askew on the wall beside the Swiss cuckoo clock, not working, and a framed set of medals with ribbons. All of these things must have been gleaned over the years from the tip in the quarry below, unwanted by everyone else, but cherished by Finny.

She opened a cupboard looking for brandy but it held a stack of mouldering books and magazines. Meredith went out to the kitchen.

It was dreadfully overheated for the

time of year, due to the antique range burning even in this weather. But this detail apart, it was quite the most peculiar kitchen she'd ever seen. It wasn't dirty, but it had an overall grubbiness. The chipped enamel pans on a shelf looked as if they might have been rescued from the tip below like so much else in the cottage. There was a musty smell of earth coming from sacks and boxes of potatoes which were stacked tidily around the walls in abundance, giving the impression of a storeroom rather than a kitchen.

Meredith drew a glass of water from the tap. When she returned Finny was looking more himself and seemed to have perked up.

He sat up, took the glass, drained it and said "Ah!" again, but more strongly.

"I'll make you a cup of tea," Meredith said, "And put these things away."

Back to the furnace of a kitchen she went to stow away his few purchases. A dented kettle sat on top of the range and the water in it was hot. This was the reason for the unseasonal fire. The range was Finny's cooking stove, his hot water heater and his general supply of warmth. Meredith hooked open the little metal door, stuffed in some kindling from a supply at hand and got the flames roaring. Sweat was pouring from her own brow by now and it wasn't surprising, she reflected, that in days gone by, cooks were known to have fainted into the fire from time to time.

As the kettle began to hiss gently to itself, she found an already opened packet of tea, a teapot and a mug. There wasn't any milk.

"I don't drink milk," said Finny hoarsely when she took the mug of black tea to him, "I ain't no babe in arms. You put any sugar in that?" He peered into the mug. "I likes plenty of sugar. Gives energy, does sugar. I heard Radio Doctor tell us that, years ago."

"Yes, two spoons. Good for shock."

"I ain't had no shock. 'Tis that there new bus driver," grumbled Finny.

Meredith sat down on one of the armchairs. "What did he do?"

"What he never done! Never stopped in the right spot. Old driver, he knew me, allus put me down right outside me own house. Not this new feller. Young whippersnapper, got no manners! Took me right past and I 'ad ter walk back carrying me shopping! I told him, I gets off here! 'Isn't a regular stop!' he says! 'Tis my regular stop, I told him. But he still took me past, jest to be awkward, that's what!"

Finny sipped his tea. He now appeared more normal or what passed for normal with Finny.

"Good job you happened along. You sure you're not a district nurse?" He squinted at her appraisingly.

"Quite sure, Mr Finny. Nor am I from the council. You asked me that before."

"Ah, right, so I did. You got no uniform. Pity. They sent along one of them girl police officers to see me. She were like you, big strong lass. Good sturdy pair of legs. She had a uniform and a little hat. Suit you that would. During the war there was one of them ATS camps down the road from here. Them girls used to cycle past in their khaki and peaked caps. Sight for sore eyes. I don't know why modern girls wants to look so spindly all of 'em. You're not."

"Have the police gone from the quarry?" Meredith decided to accept what was presumably meant as a compliment at face value and firmly turned the conversation in another direction. "I saw their notice and tape."

Finny spluttered. "Ah, took 'emselves off! And left that notice behind them! What's the use telling folk not to tip? If folk don't tip, I don't find nothing! How am I supposed to make a living?"

"I don't think you need any more," said Meredith, eyeing the collection in the parlour with some misgiving. "I don't think you've got any room for it."

"I got a tidy bit," said Finny proudly. "I got books and all, you seen 'em, in that cupboard. I can't read 'em, mind! I'm not a reader. Me eyes isn't good enough. But some of 'em got pictures in them."

"And all this is from the tip down in the quarry?"

"All of it, 'cepting the medals over there on the wall."

Meredith turned her head and looked at the framed set of war medals. "Oh, where did you get those?"

"They give 'em to me," said Finny simply. "Give 'em everyone. I was on destroyers in the last war. Got blown into the water by one of them U-boats and was bobbing about fer two days before I got hauled out. It did for me legs. I was invalided out. Legs never been much good after that. They'd taught me something, though, had the Navy. I knowed about fuses and so on. That's how I got me job in the quarry. Blowing the stone out. Made a change from torpedoes."

He settled down to drink the rest of his tea whilst Meredith waited in embarrassed silence. It was easy to underestimate or just dismiss the old, to forget they had ever been young or the troubled times through which they'd lived. Easy to see Finny as an eccentric, an old man with crippled feet and a penchant for women in uniform. Less easy to imagine Finny struggling in the icy water amidst the wreckage of a sunk destroyer and the shattered bodies of his shipmates.

"Are you all right now?" she asked at last. "Would you like me to cook you something for your evening meal?"

"No," said Finny. "I cooks me own. Potaters."

"I'll peel them, if you like."

"No," said Finny again firmly. "I does me own."

To the various creaks and groans emanating from the aged sagging timbers of the cottage was joined a fresh rattle and soft scraping sound. From the corner of her eyes it seemed to Meredith that something moved, catching her attention and surprising her. She gave a start and turned her head sharply but it was only a branch of some shrub growing outside beneath the half-open window and waving gently in the breeze.

"What's up?" asked Finny.

"Nothing. I thought I saw — it was just the bush outside knocking against the window."

"You hears all sorts out here at nights," said Finny. "You finds all sorts, too!"

He fell silent, put his stubby fingers into his emptied cup and scooped out the last of the half melted sugar congealed in the bottom.

"Hear what, Mr Finny?" she asked.

Finny, sucking sugar from his fingers, only mumbled.

"Find what?" she persevered.

"I'll show you." He got up again and this time rummaged at length in a drawer. Returning to her, he held out something on the palm of his hand. "You can have it. Go on, take it. 'Tis a brooch. Needs a bit of polishing up."

Meredith picked up the battered disc of some yellow metal with a simple pin fastening. It had a curious design on it difficult to decipher for dirt and some pressure which had caused the surface of the brooch to sink and become concave. "Thank you," she said politely.

"'Tis a horse."

"What?"

"On that brooch. 'Tis a horse, you can see if you looks proper."

Meredith peered at the brooch. "Y-es. Just about."

"Needs a clean." Finny gave a malicious chuckle. "Them clever fellers, them what digs around up on the hill, they reckons they find stuff, but they never found nothing like I found."

"What did you find, Mr Finny?"

Something crackled and tapped against the glass. A curious unease rippled along Meredith's spine. She turned again to look at the window but only saw the leaves of the bushes quivering.

But Finny was having second thoughts. "I found what I found and 'tis my business and not yours!" He leaned forward. "Anyhow, I filled it in again."

"What?" Meredith almost shouted.

"What I found. 'Twas years ago. I set a snare fer rabbit. Reached me hand down rabbit burrow and old long-ears, he'd been digging about in there . . . " He fell silent. "I don't eat no meat now. 'Cepting Christmas. I goes into Bamford of a Christmas and has me Christmas dinner at the pensioners' club. Dinner is all right but company is a lot of old folk bleating on. Can't be doing with it. Keeps meself to meself out here, I do."

There was nothing more to be got by asking questions. Meredith asked a last one. "Are you going to be all right now?"

"Ah, all right tonight. But I ain't walking up to that bus stop termorrow, don't care what that police feller says."

"What policeman? What did he say?"

"That I had to go to inquest, in case I has to tell how body was found. Termorrow, it is, Friday."

"Yes, I know. You needn't catch the bus, Mr Finny. I'll drive out and fetch you and bring you home afterwards. How's that?"

"Ah, that'll be fine!" Finny brightened. "Serve that there driver right if I don't take his bus and buy no ticket! No one takes his bus and buys no tickets, he got no job and serve him right!"

"I'll come about a quarter past nine, okay? The inquest is at ten."

"Just you shout out by the door, my dear!" said Finny with a leer. "I'll be ready. Don't do to keep a lady waiting!" He put his fingers to his lips and blew her a gallant kiss.

★ ★ ★

Meredith left him chuckling happily to himself in anticipation of the outing. Outside, on the cottage doorstep, she paused and looked about her. The overgrown garden rustled and swayed in the breeze. There was a path beaten through the weeds to the privy door and another to a primitive washing line fixed up between two trees. Finny's woollen longjohns, patched and shrunk from much laundering, hung from it. She turned her head to study the bushes by the window. The one which had caused her a moment's unease was a hebe. Its thin green leaves scraped against the window-sill and when she looked down she saw a broken piece of it lying by her foot.

Meredith stooped and picked it up. It was freshly snapped off. That must have happened as she was struggling to get Finny through the door earlier. In the distance a stone rattled down into the quarry from the edge. Meredith threw up her head and the twinge of alarm returned. But there was silence. Stones must be loose all round the quarry and for ever rolling down the sides.

She walked slowly back to her car and drove up the track on the other side of the road which was signposted 'Motts Farm'. By the turning on to the archaeological site she stopped and got out.

The area was deserted. The trenches were untouched, the trailer door fast locked when she tested the handle. Meredith walked to the grave and hesitated before she stooped to unpeg the corner of the tarpaulin covering the skeleton and roll it back.

A bony foot came into view. So the old warrior was safe too. She repegged the tarpaulin and hurried away. But she felt a strong desire now for some living human company. The quiet hillside seemed to stir with something not quite human. Spirits? That's what people would have said long ago. And who was to say they weren't right?

Perhaps it was the urge to seek out the presence of others which led her, before driving off, to walk on up the track to the wheatfield which she had last seen by moonlight with the police cars gathering at its edge.

The police had finished here too and it was as deserted as the site. She felt a twinge of disappointment and her sense of isolation increased. The police tape was still in place but the search was over. The wheat was now in a terrible mess and the Felstons must be in despair. She couldn't even see her acquaintance the scarecrow. But when she walked out to where it had been, she found it lying flat, face up amongst the trampled stalks.

Its sackcloth face grimaced up at her, all teeth. She thought of the war medals on Finny's parlour wall. "You deserve better!" she said aloud to the scarecrow.

It grinned back, tattered clothes awry, straw legs straight and shoeless now. One arm still stuck out sideways but the other had been bent when the scarecrow had been unhitched from the pole which had kept it upright and put on the ground. Now its right arm was folded across its chest so that it seemed to gesture at her much as Finny had done when propped against the tree. The face and attitude combined suggested some lascivious invitation, as if it beckoned her down to join it on the spiky bed and into its straw embrace.

Around her the ears of wheat which had escaped destruction whispered secrets in a soft dry shu-shurruh. There was a sudden rustle at her feet as some creature, a mouse probably, scuttled away. She could mark its progress by a twitch of the crushed stalks and a glimpse of a shape as it burrowed its way frantically beneath them to safety.

The same urge to fly this place and seek safety assailed her. She felt it so powerfully she was sure that to remain was to invite some dreadful knowledge, that in a moment she would turn and find herself face to face with an unknown enemy. Meredith turned and hurried away down the hill to her waiting car, conscious all the way that eyes watched her, though to what they belonged she couldn't have said with any certainty.

16

TRUE to her word, Meredith set out in good time on Friday morning to collect Finny. Despite the saddening prospect of the inquest ahead, she was feeling refreshed and energetic. So many uneasy nights lately had resulted in falling into instant dreamless slumber on her unyielding couch at The Crossed Keys as soon as her head had touched the pillow.

Also it was a beautiful morning. The sun was mild as yet but promised to beat down later. At the moment the air had a pleasant early morning coolness. The grass verges were still damp and glistening with silver dew. There was a slight haze on the meadows which veiled the distant trees and snaked wraithlike around the solid bodies of the cows browsing there. All in all, a very nice day indeed.

She hoped Finny would be ready. She supposed his preparations wouldn't amount to much more than fixing the teeth and putting on his aged trilby, even giving the prospect of being collected at his door by a 'big strong woman'. Meredith grinned to herself. Old reprobate!

She pulled on to the verge by the sign for the quarry and got out. The slam of the car door disturbed a pair of pigeons which flapped noisily away but otherwise it was deathly quiet all around with a smell of rotting vegetation in the air. Meredith walked down Finny's front path, damp weeds clutching wetly at her ankles, and rapped at the door.

"Mr Finny? Are you ready to go to Bamford?"

There was no reply. She tried the door handle. As always unlocked, the door swung open with a protesting creak of hinges. Meredith took a tentative step into the dingy little hall.

"Mr Finny? Are you awake?"

Not overslept, surely? But he might have dozed off as he waited as old people often did.

She looked in the parlour which appeared untouched since she'd left him there the previous afternoon. No Finny. No Finny either in the kitchen, and an odd thing here. The kitchen range had been allowed to go out.

Meredith put her hand on it. Quite cold. She began to feel slightly uneasy. He might, of course, have decided to let it go until he returned from Bamford later but what about boiling the kettle for his breakfast tea? She looked in the dented receptacle. It was full of water but cold. A mug, the same one as she'd used to give Finny tea the previous day, was washed up on the draining board and quite dry. There was no sign of any tea having been brewed this morning.

The memory of the old man's distressed condition by the roadside yesterday came worryingly to mind. He might have suffered a heart attack, be lying anywhere. She reproached herself for not having taken him into Bamford to his doctor. He clearly hadn't been well.

Urgently now Meredith hunted for Finny. She searched the cottage. Every room was crammed with junk, items salvaged by its owner over the years from the domestic tip below. In what was Finny's bedroom his bed was neatly made. But had he risen and made it that morning, or had he not slept in it last night?

Meredith looked around her. On the wall hung a mounted eland's head much the worse for wear and labelled 'Shot by Col. S. Wilkins Barotseland, 1925'. It stared at her with a dull and disillusioned eye.

"Where is he?" she demanded of it aloud.

Out in the garden, perhaps? Gone out to the privy? To fetch in his washing? Inspect his row of spuds?

But Finny was nowhere in the jungle of a garden. The longjohns still dangled from the line, damp with overnight dew. The privy door was ajar and the amenity untenanted. Newspaper cut neatly into squares hung from a nail in the wall. He might have gone down to the quarry floor to inspect the tip.

Meredith's former good mood had quite evaporated. Getting hot, sweaty and dusty, increasingly worried and out of temper, she hurried down the stony track to the quarry floor. More police tape around the spot where Natalie's body had been found fluttered in the little wind down here. The heaps of domestic junk and garden clippings, disturbed by the police search, lay mouldering under the attention of flies. No Finny.

Meredith toiled back up to the top again. It was quite possible, of course, that given his age, Finny had simply forgotten the arrangement that she should collect him and had got on the bus despite his altercation with the driver the previous day. But somehow she didn't think that he had.

She shouted his name a few more times before returning to her car and driving slowly down the road. She passed the bus stop. No one waited at it. A little further on she reached the wayside pub, a lonely hostelry of ancient appearance built in mellow stone under a grey slate roof, its exterior brightened by hanging baskets of lobelia, geranium and fuchsia.

Meredith got out and knocked on the door, persisting until a tiny dormer window opened and a youngish woman put her head out.

"We're not open!"

"I don't want a drink. I only want to ask if you happen to have seen the old man who lives by the quarry this morning. Finny."

The woman shook her head. "No, don't hardly never see him. He came the other day, making a fuss about that body. He got Derek to phone the police. Derek's gone into Bamford to the inquest."

"I know about the inquest. I'd arranged to take Finny to it. But he's not at the cottage."

"Oh, he'll have got on the bus," said the woman dismissively. "He's a funny old bird, independent. Don't worry about him!"

She shut the window. So much for that, thought Meredith. The woman was probably right. She knew Finny better than did Meredith. The awkward old blighter had caught the bus, after all.

Seriously out of temper now, Meredith drove back to Bamford aware that by the time she reached the venue of the inquest the coroner was likely to have already adjourned it. What's more she'd promised moral support to Ursula and would appear to have welshed. She pressed down the accelerator and sped along the empty road. Alan was right. She always felt she had to help and got drawn in. Well, she didn't and it was high time she learned not to meddle.

★ ★ ★

Ursula Gretton sat miserably in the plain little room set aside for inquests. It had the look of an old-fashioned schoolroom with hard wooden chairs and a desk on a dais out in front.

Mrs Salter had arrived earlier, already established, tight-lipped and clad entirely in black in the front row when Ursula had walked in. A friend, also in black, was in attendance on Natalie's mother. Both stony-faced women were only a few feet away brooding, so it seemed to Ursula, like a pair of crows on a fence. She had gone to express her condolences but they had been received with an expression of positive hatred on Amy Salter's face. Clearly she knew something about Ursula's affair with Dan. Old ladies like Amy were as sharp as needles

291

and seldom fooled.

'I am, after all', thought Ursula, 'branded an adulteress for ever! I've just got to grin and bear it'!

Other people were drifting in but as yet no Meredith, for whom Ursula looked anxiously, longing for a friendly face. Karen and Renee came together, Karen dressed unsuitably in denim dungarees and her hair scraped back from her plain face in an unflattering ponytail. Her eyes were reddened as if she'd been crying and Renee looked harassed.

Ian Jackson mooched in, greeted them all and then seated himself scowling in a far corner. Then Brian Felston came. Ursula was a little surprised. The farmer was buttoned into a Harris tweed jacket a size too small and wore a white shirt and a tie. He looked hot and very uncomfortable. He nodded an acknowledgment towards her and went to speak to Mrs Salter.

She seemed to recognise him. Her stony manner thawed.

She took the hand he held out and said quite graciously, "Thank you, Brian. How good of you to come."

"Felt I should . . . " he muttered.

"Yes, of course, Brian, I understand. I've often wished, and especially now . . . " She broke off, glanced towards Ursula and took her hand from Felston's grip.

Felston moved away and found himself a seat. Two or three others came in and Markby had slipped in behind them. But as yet still no Meredith, and, more significantly, no Dan Woollard.

As if the thought precipitated the action, Dan appeared suddenly, filling the doorway with his bulky frame. He'd put on a suit in respect for his late wife. But he wasn't a man who cared about his clothes and although it had probably been an expensive buy, on Dan the crumpled jacket and sagging trousers looked like something from a jumble sale. She thought with some irritation that it oughtn't to have been beyond him to press a crease in the pants. He had found a rusty black tie.

Ursula glanced down at her own grey skirt and navy blazer jacket with gilt buttons. A hunt through the wardrobe this morning had produced these items as being suitable for the occasion. But the skirt hadn't been worn for a year and the jacket was one left behind by the last of her sisters to move out on marriage. 'What a shabby, awkward bunch we must look'! she thought. 'Like survivors of some disaster kitted out by Oxfam and still not sure what's happened to us'!

She watched surreptitiously as Dan went to speak to his mother-in-law, who gave him a frosty reception. Then he nodded briefly to Jackson and the girls before making his way to Ursula and to her great dismay, taking the seat next to her.

"We ought not to sit together!" she muttered.

"Why?" he retorted, but not nearly quietly enough. "Think people might suppose we're in cahoots? Plotted to kill Natalie, maybe?"

She gazed at him, shocked and angry. "Look I'm sorry about your wife, really! It's a horrible business! And it doesn't help any of us for you to talk that way!"

He said callously, "She's gone for ever. Isn't that what we wanted?"

"No!" Ursula realised she'd raised her voice, glanced around and lowered it furtively. "It's not what I wanted! This doesn't make any difference to us, Dan! We're through! We were finished ages ago and even if we hadn't been, after this, how could we ever . . . " She fell into a choked silence.

He said in a low fierce voice, staring ahead at the empty desk on the dais, "Wherever she is, Natalie must be laughing! She's won the last round, hasn't she? Stymied us for ever?"

Fortunately the coroner entered then and took up his position on the dais and Ursula hadn't to reply.

The proceedings were blessedly brief. Medical evidence was heard confirming that Natalie had been strangled manually and with some force. The larynx was fractured and there was other bruising of the throat. It was not possible to say for sure if the deceased had been surprised or put up a struggle but in the absence of signs of violence elsewhere on the body and of any foreign matter under the fingernails, it seemed likely she had offered little or no resistance. In reply to the coroner's questions, Dr Fuller confirmed that strangulation could be a quick business.

The true horror of Natalie's death had not been borne in on Ursula until that moment. Now the grisly possibilities of just how it had occurred unrolled like a piece of cinema film before her mental vision. The unsuspecting victim, the murderer creeping up, unheard. Or heard, but expected and so occasioning no curious turn of the head? For the first time a cold finger laid itself on her spine and she asked herself, who?

Beside her Dan muttered, "Is so much macabre detail necessary at this point?"

He was sweating. For a second she almost put out her hand and took his in sympathy but stopped herself in time. It would be misconstrued by anyone who saw the gesture and, worst of all, it would be misunderstood by Dan.

The medical evidence had been deemed sufficient for the moment. But a new issue had arisen. The non-appearance of any of those who had been present at the discovery of the body clearly annoyed Colonel Harbin, the coroner.

He made some sharp remarks and then announced that as proceedings had to be adjourned pending police inquiries, he would reconvene the inquest at a later date. He stomped off the dais, papers under his arm.

"So much for that!" said Dan sourly, rising to his feet.

Jackson came sidling up. "We're awfully sorry, Dan, Becky and I — about your wife."

"Yes, thanks!" was the brief reply.

"It's probably not the moment to mention it, but the dig — "

"There's no reason for it to be held up on my account!" Dan told him.

Jackson's lugubrious face under its crest of gingery hair brightened slightly, like a cocker spaniel whose owner has mentioned the word 'walk'.

"I was hoping we could carry on! I mean, you know the Ellsworth is going to cease funding at the end of the month?"

"I'm sorry about that, Ian," Ursula said. "Dan and I have both protested."

"Got to accept it, I suppose." Jackson shrugged. "It was always on the cards. But it means that we've got something like ten days left and can't afford to waste any of it. I hope you understand, Dan, that I'd like to start work again this afternoon. I don't expect you to come out yourself in the circumstances — "

"Why not?" Woollard interrupted brusquely. "I'd rather be working than doing nothing! Give me time to go home and change."

"Oh, fine then. Sula?" Jackson gave her an awkward sideways glance.

Damn! thought Ursula. The last spot I want to be is cheek by jowl with Dan in a trench! Aloud she said, "Certainly, Ian. I'll be there."

"Girls will come along too!" Jackson indicated Renee and Karen whispering in the corner. "That FO friend of yours, has she gone back to London?"

"Meredith?" Ursula shook her head. "No, I'd expected to see her here this morning. I don't know what's happened to her."

"See you both later then, at the hill." Jackson hurried off.

Mrs Salter had been led away on the arm of her friend, weeping copiously, and she and Dan were left alone now in the room. "Are you sure you want to go out to the dig?" she demanded as they moved towards the door. "Haven't you other things to do?"

"Arrange the funeral, d'you mean? They haven't released the body yet. If I don't go out to the dig I shall be obliged to call on Amy. You probably saw how she received me just now."

"All the same, it's an occasion for a family to pull together, surely?" Ursula snapped.

"Family? In Amy's view, I pulled her family apart. I married Natalie and took her away. That was to take away from Amy her most prized possession and I was never forgiven. If I go to see her at home it will be to listen to endless accusations of what a rotten husband I was."

"She knows about us, doesn't she? Don't look so surprised, Dan! I can tell. I went to say I was sorry and she all but spat in my eye!"

"She doesn't know!" Dan said obstinately. "She might suspect but she doesn't know! It's because you're good-looking and young and we work together.

It's the way Amy's mind works!"

"Stop rearranging the facts, Dan!" Ursula exploded. "I really can't stand any more of it! At least face them for once in your life! Amy knows!"

He didn't answer and she saw that familiar obstinate expression on his face. He didn't want to believe that the affair could be public knowledge.

But he was to be forced to. As they left the building and entered the carpark outside a figure surged up before them, there was a sudden loud click and the figure scurried back.

"What the — " Dan yelled as Ursula flung up her hand too late to shield her face.

"Press!" she gasped.

"Hey!" Woollard lunged after the photographer but he hadn't a hope of catching him.

"Don't make a scene!" Ursula pleaded. They had caught people's attention and faces had turned towards them. Some onlookers whispered.

Woollard stood, his hands dangling impotently by his sides, his face contorted with fury. "If I get hold of the perisher,

I'll wring his blasted neck!"

There was silence all round.

"You would have to say that, wouldn't you?" Ursula said bitterly.

"What?" He stared at her uncomprehendingly. Then understanding dawned. He whirled to face the small crowd of silent onlookers.

"Okay, everyone! In case you're wondering, I did not kill my wife! Got that? I'll repeat it. I did not kill my wife!"

From the back of the crowd a voice came, an elderly female voice cracked with emotion but ringing clear. "Depends how you look at it! If my poor girl hadn't married you, she'd be alive today! You're responsible in my eyes, Daniel Woollard, and you always will be! You and that trollop there beside you. Yes, you, miss! You needn't look down your nose at me! We all know you for what you are!"

A nightmare. It was worse than a nightmare. Head held high and features fixed, Ursula marched through the crowd. It parted to let her through. She didn't know where Dan was. But he hadn't, thank God, followed. She found her car and unlocked it, but then a brief giddiness attacked her. Ursula hesitated with the car keys still clenched in one hand, to rest the other arm on the car roof and lean her throbbing forehead on it.

It only lasted a moment. When she lifted her face the surrounding trees wobbled for a second then steadied themselves and she became aware of a face. It was a grinning face, grinning at her and, or so it seemed for a wild moment before the last of the giddiness left her, grimacing through a circle of leaves. A round brown face, spiteful and mocking.

Ursula gave a little cry of alarm. Then she recognised it and realised it belonged to Brian Felston who stood a few feet away on the further side of her car, between the trees. He was watching her, hands in the pockets of his best jacket, causing it to strain even more against the buttons.

"What do you want?" she called out angrily.

"Come to see if you're all right. No need to go squawking at me!"

Brian came a few steps forward. He

was no longer grinning, no longer had that spiteful expression. Perhaps she'd only imagined it. But she didn't think so and her instinct was to mistrust him.

"I'm fine, thank you!"

"Amy, she's upset. It's only natural. You don't want to take too much notice."

"Amy? Oh yes. Natalie's mother." Suspicion entered Ursula's mind. "You seemed very friendly with her."

"I've known Amy for a good few years. It seemed only decent to come today and show respect."

It occurred to Ursula that this was the whole purpose of his coming to speak to her. He knew she'd seen him talking to Amy in the courtroom and he wanted to explain his presence.

"Yes," she said stiffly. "I'm sure Mrs Salter appreciated it."

Brian was still dawdling there in that too-tight jacket, his neck straining against the unaccustomed confines of a tie, his shiny button-bright brown eyes watching her. He reminded her forcibly of some small wild animal, something found in ditches and hedgerows or woodland undergrowth, a stoat perhaps.

All at once she felt quite afraid of him, deep down inside herself, in an almost superstitious way. All those curious unexplained feelings they'd all experienced out at the dig as they worked in the shadow of the ancient rampart rushed back. With them mingled other fears, the sort that made you look over your shoulder when you walked alone on country paths or through a coppice, hearing a faint rustle or even worse, hearing nothing.

"Please go away!" she said loudly and very rudely.

He didn't seem to take it as impolite. He did not even seem surprised. He gave a faint smile, more of a smirk really, as if satisfied. But he did move away to her great relief.

At last Ursula got into her car and sat in the driving seat.

But she couldn't drive away, not just yet. To her dismay she realised she was trembling with suppressed emotion. Was that what he'd wanted to achieve? To frighten her, discompose her further? She dragged a handkerchief from her bag and rubbed the cold perspiration from her forehead and then rummaged for a lipstick. She was interrupted by someone tapping at the window beside her.

305

17

"**S**ORRY!" gasped Meredith as Ursula wound down the window. "I got held up. I didn't forget but the end result's the same. Obviously it's all over and I'm way too late to be any use."

"Doesn't matter," said Ursula bleakly.

Meredith eyed her friend's frozen features. "Are you all right? Was it that bad?"

"Oh, the inquest itself was adjourned. There was nothing bad about that in itself. It was — afterwards." Ursula shrugged. "I'm overwrought, I dare say. I've been thinking about Natalie so much and feeling so guilty! Amy, Natalie's mother, made a very public and embarrassing scene and I can't really blame the old lady. She accused us, Dan and me, of being responsible for her daughter's death."

"That's because she's very upset. Don't brood on it, Ursula."

"That's more or less what *he* said, Brian Felston. He came over here afterwards to ask if I was all right. I believe he could see I wasn't and he was highly pleased about it. It seems he's known Amy for years. I have to expect that they all hate me. Natalie was a Bamford girl and you know how they all are in the country. Anyone else is an outsider and they close ranks." Ursula sighed. "Even so, I admit I wasn't prepared for Amy to be quite so vicious towards me. But she obviously knows abut Dan and me. Natalie must have said something."

Possibly Mrs Salter just knew her son-in-law's habits! thought Meredith unkindly. It was unlikely that Ursula represented the first time Woollard's feet had strayed from the marital straight and narrow.

"Just to top it all, a Press cameraman was waiting outside," Ursula was saying. "So not only do I not have any reputation left in this town, pretty soon I won't have any reputation left anywhere! Most people would say I'm only getting my just deserts. I just hope Dad doesn't see the picture. It might get into the national papers as Natalie's name is so well known. Then there's the Trust. It can be sticky about respectability!" She scowled and then shook back her hair to conclude more robustly, "Well, what the Ellsworth doesn't know now, it will know by tomorrow. I might just as well stick the whole sordid story up on a hoarding in neon lights!"

"Come on," Meredith said awkwardly. "Is there somewhere we can go and have a cup of coffee?"

Ursula stirred herself and switched on the ignition. "It's okay, really. I can't take time for coffee. I've got to go out to the dig this afternoon, more's the pity. I need time alone to get myself together before I can face it. Don't worry about missing the inquest. It didn't make much difference and in a way I'm glad you weren't a witness to what happened afterwards."

"I'm still sorry. It was that silly old man's fault, Finny. I'd arranged to bring him here this morning but he must have forgotten and got on the bus. I wasted time searching for him. I went down to the bottom of the quarry and along to the pub. You say he wasn't called to give evidence, after all?"

Ursula frowned. "Finny? He wasn't there. I think the coroner was annoyed that the police hadn't been able to ensure that at least one of the people who were present when poor Natalie's body was found, turned up today."

Puzzled, Meredith asked, "You're sure?"

"Of course I am. It was only a little room and I could see everyone. There was definitely no Finny. You can't miss him."

The engine sprang into life and she backed the car slowly from its parking slot. Meredith moved clear and raised a hand in farewell.

For a few seconds she stood staring after the departed car in what she imagined was a now deserted parking lot. But the sound of a throat being cleared behind her made her realise otherwise and she turned round.

"Oh," she said, "so you're still here! What do you mean by upsetting Ursula Gretton?"

Brian moved forward but not too near to her as if he wanted to leave a clear space. So he might have approached a beast of uncertain temper. "I didn't upset her. Others did that. She had to listen to a few home truths, I reckon."

She wasn't going to discuss Ursula's business with him. Besides, she wanted to ask him something else. "Brian, did you make that scarecrow, the one in the field opposite the site of the travellers' camp?"

Brian's eyebrows twitched. "Make all our scarecrows. I make for other folk too. There's a knack to making a good scarecrow. Most people think it's easy, but it's not. The birds aren't daft. They know a dummy when they see one. You have to make it lifelike."

"Yes, it is lifelike. In fact, it reminded me of Finny at the quarry."

Brian cast her a wary look. "Oh, did it? It's just a face. I don't rightly remember how I made that one." Suddenly he seemed anxious to be gone. "I've work waiting for me at home. Goodbye."

And he was off, striding quickly across the parking lot towards his Land-Rover which she now noticed parked in a far corner in the shade of the trees. She watched him drive away and was still standing there when Markby came out of the building and found her.

★ ★ ★

Markby had had a short and not very friendly private exchange with the coroner after proceedings.

"It's all very unsatisfactory, Chief Inspector!" said Colonel Harbin irritably as he fastened his briefcase. His pale blue eyes bulged and his fleshy nostrils flared. His cheeks were mottled with broken thread veins. Old Harbin working himself up was a not unobserved phenomenon in court and had given harmless entertainment to many a junior police officer.

But Markby wasn't a junior nor was he amused. "I'll make sure everyone's there when you reconvene."

"The old fellow, Finny, should have been there if only for the form. And you're going to have to find those hippies, Markby!"

"We'll find them!" Markby had already heard all this from Superintendent McVeigh and didn't see why he should have to hear it again from the coroner.

Harbin growled. "How can you lose an entire convoy of the blighters? I should have thought they were obvious!"

"Less so than you might imagine! There are plenty of disused tracks leading out into open countryside around Bamford and it's not the only such convoy on the road! But I don't suppose they've got far. Their vehicles are slow and they probably pitch their pace to the slowest. Failing all else, there's rumour of some open-air festival to be held over the county border in a couple of weeks' time and they'll very likely turn up there. I've been in touch with all the neighbouring police forces and asked them to keep me informed. They're all on the lookout for the convoy and we do know the names of two of its leaders."

Here Markby paused and wondered whether to spring the bombshell on the coroner now or later.

Harbin was making an assortment of snuffling and snorting noises. "Well, what about this feller, Finny? You haven't lost him, have you?"

"Finny should have been here and it was made quite clear to him. I'll look into it. He's very elderly and eccentric and apt to be a law unto himself."

Colonel Harbin did not believe in anyone being outside the law of the land. "Damn it all, Markby! You should have made sure of him!"

Markby was fed up with apologising. "It's a murder inquiry and I'll do everything I have to!"

"Yes, I dare say, no offence!" Harbin placated him.

"When we do find the travellers, there may be a small procedural hiccup to overcome, however. I should mention it to you."

"Oh?" The coroner's pale eyes rolled alarmingly in their sockets.

"One of them would appear to be Miss Anna Harbin, your niece."

Any junior officer present might have observed Colonel Harbin explode like a human Vesuvius in a most satisfactory manner.

Markby left him spluttering and went

outside where he found Meredith in a brown study in the carpark.

"Hullo! What are you doing?" he greeted her. "I didn't see you in court."

"I was too late. I went to the quarry to fetch Finny but he wasn't in his cottage. I assumed he'd taken the bus but Ursula's just told me that he wasn't at the inquest either. Alan, I'm worried. When I left him yesterday he'd had a sort of 'turn'. I thought he'd got over it but he might have been taken ill again later. I think I'll go back to his place and look again."

"Hold on!" Markby put out a hand to restrain her. "It's odd, I agree, because he was told to attend and failed to show up. I'll send a patrol car out there to check on him. Don't you worry about it. I reckon — " He glanced at his watch. "I can take forty-five minutes for lunch and there's a café just across the road there. Join me?"

Meredith hesitated. "All right, provided you send off the patrol car now or I won't be able to eat in peace."

Markby signalled to his sergeant, Pearce, and gave him relevant instructions

"Come on!" He took her arm. "For forty-five minutes I don't want to talk police business! Old Harbin really would, try the patience of a saint. Tell me what you've been doing."

* * *

The little café was unfussy but comfortable and half-empty. It offered light meals. They settled for a Welsh rarebit apiece, and over it Meredith told him about the little house and her idea to buy.

"No need to tell you how I'd feel about that," he said. "I'd be delighted to see you back in Bamford for motives I admit are purely selfish! But you know how I feel. You know too that I already have a house in Bamford and there's nothing I'd like better than to share it with you."

She was shaking her head. "It wouldn't work, Alan."

It was the reply he always got. But he found himself growing angry this time because in his own way he was as obstinate as she was and as determined to win her round as she was to leave things as they were.

315

"You always say that! We could at least try and then, if it didn't work — "

"If it didn't work it would probably be because we'd got on one another's nerves or fallen out over some domestic trifle."

"Is it the police work? You said once before — "

"I know I did. I don't think that's changed, either. I admire you for the work you do. I know you're dedicated and how hard you work. I know I couldn't ask you to give it up, nor would you if I did. Quite right too. But if we were living together it would be as if, well, as if there were three of us not two of us. You, me, and a particularly tiresome mistress who insisted on having first call on you. It would be a *ménage à trois* which couldn't work long-term and it's no use saying that we could just split up and go back to being as we were before! Because we couldn't! We wouldn't be as we were before. We'd be a couple who'd parted and in that way we'd be like any other couple who'd tried to make a go of it and failed. We might not drag one another through the divorce court but it would be as if we

316

had. We'd lose one another, Alan, and I don't want that!"

After a moment he said bitterly, "Well, at least that's something and I suppose I have to be grateful."

"Don't be hurt, Alan!" Meredith reached over the table and put her hand over his. He twisted his round and seized her fingers so that she couldn't withdraw it. "You know your friendship means a lot to me," she went on unsteadily. "That's why I'm so scared I'll lose it. It's no fault of yours that I feel I couldn't make a relationship under a shared roof work. But I know I couldn't share a home with you permanently any more than with Toby, although the reasons are quite different."

Markby released the grip he had on her fingers and let her hand slip free. He was quiet for so long, staring into his coffee cup, that Meredith could only feel as wretched as he looked. Somehow that letting go of her hand seemed symbolic. He was letting her go. But to what extent? Not, she prayed, completely, at least not now, not yet. But she had to face that he might do so one day.

Suddenly he looked up and said in a brisk voice, "At least it would serve the blighter in Islington right if you moved yourself out entirely! All right, buy your own place. But are you quite sure about this particular house? It sounds as if it's in poor shape. It's a fallacy that our forebears built everything well. They were as capable of shoddy building practices as any. The problems may be structural."

Relieved that he seemed to have returned to his normal forthright self, she countered, "I think it's only superficial neglect. But naturally I'll get a proper surveyor to look it over."

"Drains!" said Markby ominously. "Always tricky in those old properties. The area's okay. I know that road. It's quiet. That's about the most anyone can say for it."

"I'll get the drains tested. I don't mind a quiet street."

"You'll almost certainly need all new electrical wiring."

"Yes, I realise! Are you going to be completely negative about this?"

He looked hurt. "Not negative, practical!"

"I won't take it on if I think it can't be all fixed." He was looking unconvinced so she went on: "I was thinking of asking Steve Wetherall to carry out the survey. You'd have confidence in any report he made, wouldn't you? He's a friend of yours."

"I'd be happier if I knew Steve had crawled around the attics. He knows those houses. But even if it's structurally sound, repairs could cost a fortune and take years to complete. I mean, really to transform the place."

"I choose to see it as a challenge!" said Meredith firmly. "For example, the back yard is admittedly in a horrible mess, a real eyesore. But I thought perhaps you could advise me on a patio garden. There's room to make a paved area and a raised flowerbed or two, somewhere to sit . . . " She saw that glazed look enter his eyes and added hastily, "Not now! Don't start thinking about it now!"

Markby returned regretfully to the present. "The back yard might be the least of your problems."

"What a Jeremiah you are! Come and see it with me!"

"I can't this afternoon. Tomorrow, maybe. We've got time for another cup of coffee." He raised an eyebrow.

"Not for me. I'd like to call back at the station with you and see if that patrol car you sent out found Finny. I feel sort of responsible for the poor old man."

"When will you stop feeling responsible for people?" Alan Markby asked her resignedly. "It always gets you into trouble."

★ ★ ★

Meredith sat in her car outside Bamford police station a few minutes later and reflected on Markby's misgivings about the house while he was inside checking on Finny.

He could be right. The house could prove an expensive mistake. There were other, newer, properties on the market. She ought, perhaps, to look further. But she was sure in her heart that no other place would speak directly to her as the little house had done.

Markby came back, frowning. "No luck!" he said, stooping down to speak through the window.

"You see? I was right to worry! I don't like it, Alan. He could have collapsed anywhere."

"My men searched the undergrowth around the top of the quarry but it's a big area. He might have wandered over the hills."

"Why on earth should he? Or could he? He's got bad feet. He was invalided out of the Navy during the war after his ship was torpedoed and he was adrift for two days. I'm going back to that cottage and looking again! He can't have vanished off the face of the earth!"

"I'll follow you down in my car," Markby said.

★ ★ ★

Finny's cottage was as she'd left it that morning.

"Door's open!" remarked Markby, trying the handle.

"He leaves it open, that's usual."

"Old country habit but not many people do it now." He walked in and gazed about him. "Good God! It's like the Old Curiosity Shop!"

"He's a hoarder. He got it all from the tip except for his own war medals, over there."

"Technically, I suppose, he's been stealing from the council all these years." Markby tentatively rocked a nearby chair.

"He wouldn't see it like that. He's looking after it."

Markby had progressed to another room and his voice drifted through the doorway. "Have you seen this stuffed animal head? Gruesome thing! Hmn, bed's tidily made, unlike the rest of the pickle. Odd."

"But the kitchen range has been allowed to go out, that's wrong!" she called back.

There was a sudden crash from outside which brought Markby precipitously back. "Did you make that row?"

At the same moment a distraught voice shouted, "Is anyone there? For God's sake, Chief Inspector, is that you?"

They stared at one another and then collided as both dived for the front door. Ian Jackson was crouched outside, rubbing his shin. The curator looked as if he'd seen a ghost. His hair was dishevelled and his eyes stared wildly from a face drained of all colour.

"What's wrong?" Markby asked in a sharp voice.

"You've got to come over to the site!" Jackson babbled, lurching towards them. "It's — it's horrible! We've just found it! Dan and I rolled back the tarpaulin."

But Markby, with Meredith at his heels, was already crossing the main road in long strides and heading towards the rise of Bamford hill.

* * *

It was, Meredith thought, very like one of those nineteenth-century paintings of country burial services. The breeze blew stiffly across the open hillside, the historic rampart which had seen so much over the centuries, and the scarred earth of the dig. The Felstons' cattle, returned to their field on the far side, stood watching with placid bovine interest. The human inhabitants of the scene were gathered silently around the excavated grave of the Saxon warrior. No one moved.

Only as the newcomers pounded up did they part and allow them through. Dan Woollard, crouched by the head of the grave, his broad hands still gripping the tarpaulin which had covered it, raised a haggard face. Markby swore softly, something Meredith had seldom heard him do. She moved out from behind him so that she could see.

The old warrior was still in his grave but no longer had it to himself. For a wild moment Meredith had the impression that some joker had brought the scarecrow down the hill and put it on top of the original occupant. There were the same stiff limbs, one arm bent across the chest, the raggedy clothes, round vacant face and the teeth. In the open mouth they'd slipped and gleamed in the late afternoon sun as if the jaw had become unhinged, just as that of the skeleton below had done.

But it wasn't the scarecrow, she knew it, and a dull angry ache filled her chest. It was Finny, neatly laid out, minus his hat but otherwise as he'd been in life.

"This is foul!" she heard herself say in a cold little voice.

A woman started to sob hysterically and she looked to see who it was. It was Karen. Renee moved capably to take care of her. Ursula was standing a little apart, arms folded, her face frozen like the heroine of a Greek tragedy, her long dark hair fluttering in the breeze.

Markby dropped on his knees and snapped, "Has anyone touched the body?"

There was silence and then they all mumbled denial, shaking their heads.

Woollard said harshly, "We've none of us been here long. We'd just assembled. We spent a few minutes discussing how best to use the remaining time at this dig. We were thinking of removing the skeleton for preservation. Ian and I turned back the tarpaulin and — and there was Finny, poor old devil!"

Jackson took up the tale, his voice shaking. "We could see your cars parked down there by the quarry. Sula said it was Meredith's car and the other one belonged to you, Chief Inspector. I ran down but I tripped and fell on the old man's garden path . . . I couldn't get to you fast enough!"

He moved forward, eyes burning feverishly in his pale face. "He's got to be mad!" Jackson's voice had risen and was now so high-pitched it was piping. "Someone is doing these things and he's got to be crazy! Natalie in a carpet, the old man under the tarpaulin. He's mad, he's got to be mad!"

"Oh, I doubt it, Mr Jackson!" said Markby, rising to his feet and dusting off the knees of his trousers. At least, not crazy in the way you mean it. I'm afraid your work here will have to be abandoned again."

"It's been doomed from the start!" Jackson shrilled.

"Someone hates us!" Ursula declared suddenly in a loud voice. They all looked at her. "Someone hates all of us!" she repeated. "Me and you, Dan, and you too, Ian, and the girls. All of us!"

It was Renee Colmar who spoke then and what she said startled and temporarily silenced them all.

"It's Wulfric!" she announced calmly.

She removed the arm she'd put comfortingly around Karen's shoulder and Karen, red-eyed, stopped snuffling and looked up as astonished as the rest.

"Yes, Wulfric!" Renee repeated. "It has to be. We disturbed one of his henchmen." She pointed to the open grave. "And he means to make sure we don't disturb him too! He meant to stop you, Ian, and he has, hasn't he?"

Woollard burst out, "Don't be so damn ridiculous!"

"It's not ridiculous!" Renee flushed angrily. "I've felt someone watched us here from the start. I'm not the only one. He's watching us now. And if we don't stop, someone else will die."

18

"**A**T least," Ursula demanded aggressively, "you surely don't think Dan did this?" She sat bolt upright on the bunk, both fists clenched and resting on her knees. Her look defied him to argue and it would have been a bold man who demurred.

Clearly in her view they were adversaries. That was, thought Markby as he faced her across the works trailer, a great pity. He had to admit, however, that possibly he had invited the present aggression by quipping heavily, "Well, here we are again!" at the outset of the interview. He offered a flag of truce.

"I don't think anything as yet, Sula! I do realise how stressful this is for you, for all of you, not just you personally. I'm sorry if I sounded facetious. That wasn't the intention."

She relaxed marginally, a handsome young woman whose features were currently drawn and distorted by some

328

inner pain. "I'm not getting at you, Chief Inspector, I'm well aware that if the situation's stressful to me then it's because I made it so. I feel so responsible for everything!"

"But you're not," said Markby sensibly. "We're seldom the important link in the chain of events we imagine ourselves to be."

"A humbling maxim!" was the dry retort, but he saw a momentary flicker of humour in her eyes.

"Let's say, a sad truth. The world goes on, with or without us, and things very often turn out as they will, again with or without our interference. Although we may prove pawns of Fate, if you like!"

"That's a very unpolicemanly attitude!" she rebuked him.

"More an argument for predestination. I thought policemen went around pointing the finger of accusation at the guilty and saying 'Anything you say may be taken down in evidence'!"

"We do say that. And I'm not a theologian, just a copper! But I've still a right to a personal viewpoint. Generally, however, I'm not fanciful and I wasn't being fanciful then. I'm just trying to underline that you shouldn't go overboard with the *mea culpa* business! As yet we don't know why Natalie Woollard died: and we certainly don't know why Finny died or where or how."

Although he could hazard a guess as to why, he thought. And so could Ursula or anyone else who cared to think about it. Natalie's body had been found in the quarry. Finny's cottage overlooked the path down to the tip. Possibly Natalie's killer knew or thought he knew that Finny had information he was likely to divulge under questioning at the inquest if he were allowed to attend. Something seen or heard? Someone seen? A suspicion? No way they would ever know now. Finny had taken the answer to the grave with him.

Literally. Markby scowled. "Incidentally, whilst I appreciate that everyone working at the site must be on edge by now, I don't think Wulfric the Saxon had a hand in any of this, with all respect to Miss Colmar! I certainly don't intend to let long-dead chieftains interfere with the work of Bamford CID!"

Ursula laughed nervously. "Renee? That was a bit over the top. But I can understand how she feels. She's right when she says we've all felt a sort of presence, someone watching us as we've worked. Sometimes the feeling's been very strong and I've genuinely felt the hairs on the nape of my neck prickle."

"Probably only the breeze. There's always a wind blowing over this hill. But you also made a surprising statement earlier. You said that someone hated you, all of you. Why d'you think that?"

"Because of the way things have been presented, all so horrible, all so deliberate and so twisted. Rolling Natalie's body in that carpet! Putting Finny in the grave! It's meant to frighten us or send us some kind of spiteful message! It's vindictive in a personal way."

"All right, take the first one. The carpet. Woollard said it was like Cleopatra. I'm no classical scholar but I seem to recall young Cleo had herself introduced into Caesar's presence in a rolled carpet. How would that tie in with the site?"

"It doesn't, unless . . . " She bit her lip. "It was making Natalie out to be

331

some kind of *femme fatale*."

"Was she? I never met Mrs Woollard when she was alive. I've only seen her dead and that's deceptive. A face with no life or expression in it tells you nothing."

Ursula looked uneasy. "I don't like talking about her, behind her back as it were. All right, I know she's dead. She was pretty and rather waif-like. Small and neat with a heart-shaped face, very pale skin and big dark eyes peering up from under a fringe. She had lots of thick dark hair, bobbed and straight. She always looked to me as if she really belonged in the 1920s, a flapper with beads, garter elastic showing beneath her short skirts! That sound bitchy enough for you?" She twitched a dark eyebrow.

"It doesn't really answer my question. I saw for myself she was petite and dark. You make her sound vivacious. Was she attractive to men?"

"You'd have to ask a man, wouldn't you? On the odd occasion she turned up at receptions held by the Trust, she buzzed in a bright sort of way. She was well known for her books, so she had a lot of experience of being the centre of attention. If people had read or even heard about the books they automatically supposed she must be a sex-kitten of the first order and were intrigued. Personally I think she just liked writing about it, not doing it. But I think she probably did turn them on, yes — until they got to know her better!"

Clearly talking about Natalie with Ursula was to walk in a minefield. Markby changed tack.

"Let's talk about Finny, then. We don't yet know where he was killed. I hope we shall find out. But why was he brought to the site? Or was he killed here? In which case, what was he doing up here? Was he in the habit of coming here to look round?"

She shook her head. "Not whilst I've been here. I don't think he leaves the quarry in case he misses anyone tipping!" She heaved a sigh. "Wrong tense. I should have said, left the quarry. He might, of course, have come up here in the evenings after we went home but we never found anything disturbed. I rather got the impression he despised us. He used sometimes to stand by the main roadside down there as we arrived or left, just by the turning to his cottage, and jeer at us. I mean laugh, but maliciously. I really didn't like him very much. But then, from his point of view, we were rank amateurs in the scavenging business, weren't we? Here we were earnestly collecting useless bits of pottery and there he was, collecting whole three-piece suites! It doesn't compare, does it?"

Markby laughed aloud and after a moment she joined in before breaking off abruptly and putting her hand to her mouth.

"We shouldn't!" she said, gazing at him with appalled blue eyes. "We shouldn't be laughing! The poor old man is lying dead out there."

"I've seen many unpleasant sights in my time," he told her. "One develops a robust reaction."

"Laugh in order not to weep, you mean?"

"More or less. It doesn't mean I don't care. I do care, very much. I particularly dislike a vulnerable old eccentric like

Finny being attacked, and I admit I can still be shocked. I was shocked when I saw him laid out in that grave."

There was a short silence, then she said slowly, "Meredith said you were a nice person and it's possible to talk to you. She's right."

"Oh, did she?" muttered Markby, feeling absurdly embarrassed. "Hum, well . . ."

There was a tap at the door and he blessed heaven for the interruption. Sergeant Pearce's face appeared at the gap as it opened.

"Okay to remove the body now, sir?"

"Yes, sure, go ahead. Tell Dr Fuller I'll see him later at the path lab."

When Pearce had gone he turned back to Ursula and saw that her face again held the earlier expression of gloom and tension. Reference to the necessary autopsy, he supposed.

"I don't mean to be self-centred or whinge," she said quietly.

"But I really think I can't take much more of this."

"That's all right. I don't need to talk to you any more now," Markby assured her.

"Sorry to put you through it. Policemen must ask questions and witnesses suffer, I'm afraid."

"I didn't mean you particularly or these interviews. I mean these two violent deaths and the macabre disposal of the bodies. Do you think Renee's right? Is anyone else going to die?"

"I most sincerely hope not!" Markby exclaimed. "However, Miss Colmar's fears were based on Jackson's determined efforts to disturb Wulfric's last resting place. That's highly unlikely now, isn't it? I understand the Trust for which both you and Woollard work is to cease funding the dig at the end of the month and we're holding up any last chance of working here before then."

"Yes, poor Ian. It means so much to him! Dan and I are both arguing with the Trust but I'm afraid the money's just run out and that's that. Besides which it's no use pretending that all the scandal, murder, affairs between Trust employees and so on, hasn't upset the Ellsworth! The dig has gained an unpleasant notoriety and naturally the Ellsworth wants none of it!"

"Who founded the Trust?"

"Oh, some enthusiastic and wealthy amateur at the turn of the century. It has a funny sort of charter with a clause stating that the Trust must aim at enhancing the standing of archaeological research in the public eye. Now that, if you were so disposed, you could interpret as a morals clause."

"I didn't realise that!" Markby frowned. "So any bad publicity would be a reason for the Ellsworth to pull the plug?"

"Yes. But I don't think, or I didn't think, the Trust would seriously seek to implement the clause in that light, even though they could do so if they wished! I never thought myself that the originators of the charter meant 'standing' in that way, as referring to the personal reputations of the workers for the Trust. I always thought, and still do, that they meant getting the public to take an intelligent interest and not think of us as treasure-seekers!"

"But Jackson knew about this clause?"

"Oh yes, Ian knows. He didn't even want Dan and me to tell the Ellsworth about the New Age travellers when they arrived, in case the Trust thought wild, lascivious, drug-demented goings-on were taking place on the hill. The sort of thing old Lionel Felston imagines the rest of the world is up to! Actually our hippies appeared to me a drearily normal bunch of layabouts. But Ian's invested so much in this dig in every way, do you see? His time, his hopes, his professional reputation, and judgement — and the future of Bamford Museum."

"Yes, I do indeed see," Markby said thoughtfully.

★ ★ ★

Meredith sat with Dan Woollard and Ian Jackson on the grassy rise above the dig and watched the ambulance jolt away across the turf, bearing within it the body of Finny. It was late afternoon by now and the sun sinking, but it was still hot enough to burn through Meredith's shirt on to her shoulders.

Beside her a depressed Jackson hunched with his head clasped in his hands and his tousled pale ginger hair blown straight up by the breeze. Woollard, head thrown back and forearms resting on his bent knees, glowered angrily down the hill towards the quarry. Neither of them had much to say. No more did Meredith who, worried as to how Ursula was standing up to another interrogation by Alan, was watching the trailer apprehensively.

Woollard, noticing her preoccupation, suddenly said, "Boyfriend of yours, that copper? So Sula says."

"Friend!" said Meredith firmly.

"That how he sees the relationship?"

That was a totally unexpected and unwelcome, if extremely pertinent, question on the part of Woollard. Meredith turned her head to look at him. He had a mocking expression on his face.

She heard herself snap, "That's my business!"

"And I've no right to ask? But you and Sula have discussed me, haven't you?"

She couldn't deny it. Flushing, she said, "Sula's very distressed. It's a very difficult time for her."

"And not for me? It's bloody difficult for me, too, in case you haven't considered that! My wife's been murdered.

People are all whispering to each other that I had something to do with it. I didn't, incidentally. But sauce for the goose is sauce for the gander, as they say. So, how pally are you with the flatfoot?"

"I know him fairly well, and I still don't see you've any right to ask me. Even if you imagine you have, I'm blowed if I'm going to answer you, so there!" she finished, she felt rather childishly.

Woollard was looking absurdly smug, flattering himself he'd upset her. He really was an irritating man. He said nastily, "You women, you're all the same. Lead a man on and then chuck him when the arrangement no longer suits you!"

"Now look here!" Meredith snarled at him. "You've absolutely no right to talk to me that way! I'm trying to make allowances for your bereavement, but if you go on like that, I'm liable to dot you one!"

"Feminine charm's not your strong point, is it?"

"You lack a certain charm yourself!"

340

she retaliated furiously.

Silence ensued. Under the general strain things were falling apart rather obviously, Meredith thought. They were taking it out on each other.

Woollard, perhaps thinking the same, said stiffly, "I spoke out of turn, sorry."

"Apology accepted and I'm sorry if I was brusque. All our nerves are pretty frayed."

"Who cares?" Jackson said in tones of sepulchral gloom.

"Eh?" Woollard looked taken aback.

"I said, who cares?" Jackson repeated with a surge of spirit. "I'm fed up with hearing people whinge about their problems! I know your wife's dead, Dan, and I'm sorry. I've said so and I meant it. But it gets my goat that no one thinks my problems matter a toss compared with theirs! Well, I happen to think they do! We're sitting here, yes, here!" Jackson patted the turf beside him to emphasise the words. "And for all we know we're sitting on Wulfric in his burial chamber! I've devoted years to tracking him down! I wrote a paper on him. I've written several articles in journals. I've staked my academic and professional reputation on finding him. I've got nearer than I've ever got before and squish!"

Jackson slapped down and annihilated a beetle crawling over the grass. "That's me, squashed flat by the Ellsworth! Just like that unfortunate creepie-crawlie. And I'll tell you, I'm just about fed up with people taking about as much notice of me as of that damn bug!"

He fell into simmering silence. Woollard said mildly, "Feel better now you've got that off your chest?"

"Yes, thanks. I do. But I meant every word."

"If you care as much as you do," said Meredith, "you'll get another chance. You'll make sure you do."

"And get it screwed up by someone, just like this time!"

Woollard grunted, got up and slouched away over the hillside.

"He's upset about his wife," said Meredith reproachfully. "I know he doesn't express it quite as people might expect. But he must be feeling very low and frightened. I understand how you feel, Ian, but do you think it was quite tactful to pour all that out just now?"

"Tactful?" Jackson swivelled round to face her. "Who gets anywhere being tactful? I've tried it and it doesn't work. I was polite to the Ellsworth, I crawled to the Ellsworth when they told me they couldn't go on funding. I should have gone straight to them and yelled at them, that's what I should have done! Told them they were passing up the chance of the discovery of a decade! But no, I wrote them a snivelling letter and made them an apologetic phone call! Well, the worm has turned!"

Pursuing this argument didn't seem a good idea. But Meredith said crossly, "Well, I've got problems too! I was last to see Finny alive, apart from his murderer! How do you think that makes me feel?"

"Lousy, I imagine. But I can't do anything about it. All I can think about is Wulfric."

"And I keep thinking about my last meeting with Finny. He even gave me a present, poor old chap. I didn't really want it. It's just a broken old brooch he got off the tip. But he thought it was

343

nice and he wanted to please me. Now I'll never be able to throw it away."

Meredith fished the brooch out of her pocket and let it lie on the palm of her hand. The evening sunshine made the yellow metal gleam dully. The battered relief of a horseman showed up more clearly than it had done in the cottage. She tilted it slightly so that the sun's rays caught it and Jackson glanced at it.

The immediate change in the atmosphere was almost palpable. A spark of some emotion sprang from Jackson to her like a electric flash. Meredith looked up. His face was deathly pale and beads of sweat had appeared on his forehead.

He put out a shaking hand and whispered hoarsely, "Show me that!"

She passed it over, feeling oddly excited and not a little alarmed.

"Where did he get it?" Jackson breathed.

"From the tip, I imagine."

"No! No, impossible! It's a Saxon dish brooch! He must have got it from up here on the hill!" Jackson turned glowing eyes on her.

"Are you sure? He said he found

344

it a long time ago. It's not rusty or corroded!"

"Of course it's not!" he burst out. "It's gold!"

He was turning it over. "Look here, this is a fairly simple common fastening for such brooches but the workmanship in general is very fine. The image of the horseman, that's done by a skilled artist. This was the property of a man of some importance! Probably a cloak fastening. It could even be . . ." He smoothed the horseman's image with sensitive, trembling fingertips. "It could even be Wulfric's! For God's sake, Meredith, where did the old man find it?"

"I don't know!" she confessed. "But he said it was ages ago. He talked about finding things. He made some sort of derogatory remark about your efforts up here, indicating he'd done better. I thought he was talking about the things he found on the rubbish tip!"

"Please!" Jackson grabbed her hand. "Think! You must! Rattle your brain, for goodness sake, and try and remember every single word the old man said!"

Meredith concentrated. "He said he

found it a long time ago. Rabbit hole, that's it! He found it in a rabbit hole!"

"What?" Jackson gazed wildly at her.

"He set a snare for a rabbit. He put his hand into the rabbit's burrow and in the loose earth the rabbit had kicked out of the hole, there was that . . . " She pointed at the brooch.

"Where?" asked Jackson faintly. "Where was this rabbit hole?"

"I honestly have no idea. He didn't say. Whether he found anything else I don't know, but if he did, it will be down there in that cottage amongst all the other stuff. He wasn't one for throwing anything away. He may have done a bit more digging, now that I think about it!" Meredith's voice gained enthusiasm. "Because he said that he had filled it in again."

Jackson's mouth opened and shut wordlessly for some moments. He looked dangerously close to hysteria. At last he managed to whisper, "Are you telling me that the old madman down there found Wulfric's grave years ago? And that having opened it, he then filled it in?"

The curator's voice rose shrilly. "Are you telling me he stumbled on its location and having done so," Jackson's shriek echoed over the hillside, "he then deliberately made sure it was lost again?"

19

"**T**HANKS to your having shown Jackson that brooch," Markby said on Monday morning, sipping gloomily at a cup of The Crossed Keys' coffee, "he's now spending his time either besieging my office with a demand I give him immediate permission to search Finny's cottage from top to bottom, or he's down there at the cottage trying to persuade the officers on duty to let him in. He's convinced that we'll destroy or throw away some valuable ancient artefact. I've had to give clear and unequivocal instructions that he isn't to be allowed over the threshold. The man's a pest!"

Meredith wondered if a spur of the moment decision to take a further week's leave and stay on had been wise. She couldn't have concentrated on work with so many unanswered questions still plaguing them all. But The Crossed Keys appeared twice as doleful today. In mid-morning it wasn't exactly a-buzz with activity, though distant sounds of vacuum cleaners indicated that the maids were attacking the worn carpets. There was an argument going on behind reception about deliveries to the kitchens. A frustrated businessman complained into the public telephone about a broken appointment, and a dog had appeared. Fat, elderly and wheezy, it waddled around the place sniffing at people's ankles and ignoring their overtures of friendship. It passed by Meredith now. True to form, it brushed against her leg clumsily, oblivious of the hand she stretched down to pat its plump back. Her move caused interesting shapes to appear against her turquoise jerseyknit shirt. Markby, in no way oblivious, heaved a mental sigh and let his mind wander.

"It's deaf," she said apologetically.

"What is?" He blinked and dismissed the images. "Oh, the pooch. I know that. It's been here years. At one time it had a habit of sitting in the middle of the Market Square constituting a hazard to traffic. The owners were warned. As for deafness, I'm developing that with regard to Jackson."

"Poor Ian, you can't blame him! Finding Wulfric has been his dream. Now it seems Finny beat him to it. Jackson's pestering me too, you know. He keeps ringing up and asking if I'm sure Finny didn't say where he found the brooch, and have I remembered anything else. Of course he's keen to get into the cottage. It might well contain a clue to where Finny found the goods! Will you let him in when you've finished?"

"I'm not sure I can! As yet no one has come forward to claim Finny's estate, but that's not to say he doesn't have heirs somewhere. We've got in touch with the Navy as he was a naval pensioner. They may have details of his family. And there's a notice to go out in the legal column of the *Bamford Gazette* asking anyone connected to get in touch with a local solicitor."

"And they may hear something to their advantage?" Meredith quoted, relinquishing her cup half drunk. She leaned back in the balding velveteen armchair and stretched out her legs.

Appreciatively, Markby eyed the legs — nicely suntanned and nicely shaped. More distracting images returned. He forced his mind back to work. "Not so much gain advantage as get a horrible shock! If anyone thinks he's come into a fortune, all he'll find is a tumbledown cottage full of rubbish and even that's got a demolition order hovering over it. The council's been trying to enforce it for years."

"But there could be valuables in there," Meredith said thoughtfully. "Amongst so much junk, there almost has to be something worth more than it looks. Take the brooch. It looked like nothing, yet it was gold. Suppose he took other things from the rabbit burrow before he filled it in?" She reached down and scratched her ankle. "Hey, do you think that dog has fleas?"

"If anything more is found, heaven forbid, ownership will almost certainly be disputed. It will mean establishing exactly where the burrow was, on whose land, whether the objects can be classed as treasure trove and a dozen other complications I don't want to know about, thanks! What I meant was, if Jackson wants to search Finny's effects, he'll have to do so by arrangement with Finny's heirs and as yet, none has come forward."

He stopped and peered at her calf. "No, those aren't fleabites. Nettlerash. You're sidetracking me very nicely, you know."

"By persuading you to gawp at my legs?"

"Who needs persuading? But I've come here this morning not to dally pleasantly with you or talk about Jackson, but to do as he's been doing and ask you if you're sure you can't remember anything from your last meeting with Finny which might give a clue to his killer! You didn't see anyone hanging round the cottage as you arrived or left?"

She sighed and shook her head so that her dark brown hair flopped forward in a glossy mop; Markby fidgeted in his chair. "No. He was in the habit of leaving the door unlocked. Anyone could have got in. Perhaps someone did think he had something of value there."

"Murder in the course of a robbery?" He

looked dubious. "Nothing was apparently taken. Nothing disturbed, no obvious search and no sign of a struggle. Either the old fellow was surprised or he knew his killer."

Meredith asked hesitantly, "Are you releasing the cause of death before the inquest?"

"Strictly between us, it looks like suffocation. There's a pillow undergoing further forensic tests right now."

"You mean the poor old man was in bed?" she asked horrified. "But the bed was made. I saw it."

"But not who made it. To me it looked suspiciously well made, too tidy. I sent all the bed linen to the forensic lab and not just the pillow. Also the bedside rug. No need to spread that about although forensic tests are routine anyway."

But Meredith was seeing in her mind's eye the image of the stuffed eland head above Finny's bed. Had that thing's glass eyes been the only witness of such a horrible deed?

"It's foul. It really is. You know, there is just one thing. When I was talking to him that last time I had the funny feeling we were being spied or eavesdropped on. It was probably my imagination. That feeling of being watched is very strong out there everywhere, just as Renee Colmar said."

"But you felt it in the cottage? Isn't that a little odd? Did you hear anything?"

"Only a twig tapping at the window pane. I was already pretty agitated at finding Finny collapsed. I was jumpy. Ignore it."

"Oh well . . . " Markby made half-hearted preparations to leave. "So what will you do today? Visit that house you're thinking of buying?"

"Going to see Wetherall about a survey. Yes, probably go there if I can get the key off the agent."

"Sure you can! The man's probably delighted with you."

"I wish you'd come and see it yourself."

"I will." He leaned forward, his long, narrow face managing to look both earnest and frustrated. "We never seem to get any time, you and I, no time to do the things that matter to us! Work always seems to take charge and get in the way.

I suppose I have to accept we won't be sharing a roof but we never seem to get round to sharing any damn thing! Well, not as often as I'd like!"

She grinned at him. "We're workaholics, you and I. But I wish events didn't always get in the way, too. When this case is finished and if I do move back to Bamford, we'll have plenty of time."

"I'd like that." He put out a hand to tuck the fringe of rebel brown hair behind her ear. "Excuse me, but I've been wanting to do that for the past five minutes."

"Hair is a bit of a mess. I was going to have a trim during my week off before Toby turned up and Ursula called with her tale of woe."

"I wasn't indicating you looked a mess!" he said indignantly. "As if I would! And you don't. In fact, that's not the effect that rumpled look has on me at all. To say nothing of the legs and all the rest of you. Something quite different!"

"Oh?" She propped her chin in her hands. "Got time to come over here and have dinner tonight?"

"I can do better than that. Take you out somewhere where they don't serve steel chips. Or else, of course, there's my place."

"Okay, your place. No talk of work, no talk of Toby, no argument about buying my own place here, just us."

A male outline filled the lounge door and approached purposefully across the carpet.

"Pearce," said Markby resignedly. "You never fail."

"Thought I'd find you here, sir. Good morning, Miss Mitchell! We've had a call about those hippies. Seems they've been located, and the local force there has them under obbo."

"Where?" Markby asked sharply, getting to his feet.

So much for romantic dinners and anything which might follow, thought Meredith. He's going haring off across a couple of counties after his missing witnesses! May you rot, Sergeant Pearce!

"Some miles over the Welsh border. They were probably looking for somewhere really remote, but they made the mistake of trespassing on private land again. The landowner called the local police. They went down to the camp and took a few names and turned up — "

"Anna Harbin and Pete Wardle?"

"That's them!" said Pearce. "They took 'em in for questioning. The Harbin girl is raising merry hell by all accounts!"

* * *

There was a distinct odour of woodsmoke permeating the air of the interview room at the small Welsh police station by the time Markby arrived in early afternoon.

"Sorry it's a bit whiffy in here, like!" said the local sergeant to him. "It came in with them!" He pointed to the defiant figure of Anna Harbin. "And the other one smells worse, terrible it is."

"We don't smell any worse than you do!" retorted Anna vehemently. She sat on one chair with her feet propped on the stretchers of another, arms folded across her chest, eyes glaring from beneath an untidy fringe.

The local man gazed with a mixture of awe and disgust at her stout, mud-smeared footwear. "Get all sorts in here

357

but not many like her, mind you! Won't answer questions but bend your ear terrible otherwise! Never stop!"

"You needn't think I'm going to answer questions fired at me by some fascist police thug!"

"You mean me, do you?" Markby asked her, seating himself.

She flushed, and tossed tangled long hair. "You're worse than these local pigs! They're just thick! You're, oh, so quiet and polite! And then you strike, just like a snake! I trust you even less than this lot! What have they done with Pete? They won't let me see him! You do realise that keeping us here is an infringement of our civil liberties? Not that you'd care! You'd like a police state with everyone carrying identity cards and residence permits!"

"I don't feel like a cobra," he said. "I feel tired after a long drive in the heat, annoyed because I fancy my plans for the evening have just gone down the plug-hole, and more than fed up with your childish attitude! It's your own fault you're here. If you'd stayed and made a statement or been available around Bamford, neither of us would be here now! I've been obliged to make a long journey at considerable inconvenience, and I'm not going to be put off with pseudo-political twaddle, and what's looks to me remarkably like a nursery tantrum! I had thought you fairly intelligent."

She glowered. "Poor Pete's being given the third degree somewhere else in this dump, I suppose? He's a very sensitive person. This will do him terrible damage. We ought to sue you!"

"I take it back. You're not as intelligent as I thought, just rather boring. I suppose you imagine you're making some kind of social statement by not conforming in any way or being even marginally polite. But no one who has to work so hard at being different is a natural eccentric. You're a deeply conventional young woman trying to prove a point and not doing it very well!" Markby concluded crisply. "Cut it out, Anna. You're wasting your own time as well as mine!"

The Welsh sergeant chuckled.

She clenched her fists, took her boots from their rest and swivelled to face him. The volley of abuse which followed was unoriginal but not unexpected. He let it flow over him. When she saw she was making little impression, she yelled, "We can't help you! We don't know anything! And I'm not saying another bloody word until I see Pete for myself and know he's okay!"

Markby hesitated, then turned to the sergeant. "Is it possible to have Wardle in here? I think it might be useful to talk to them together. They calm one another down."

"Anything you like," said the sergeant amiably. "Just so long as it doesn't go on too long. Got choir practice tonight, see?"

Markby longed for Pearce but Pearce was back in Bamford. The sergeant ambled to the door and spoke to a constable on duty. After a few minutes Wardle was shown in, looking badly frightened, and sat down, twitching.

The girl whispered soothingly, "It's all right, Pete!" and took his hand.

"It's not all right, Anna!" replied Markby firmly, before Wardle could answer. "It's very much all wrong! When the body was found in the quarry by you and your friends, you should have stayed there until the police arrived."

"We made sure the old man would phone the police! What else could we do? We didn't put her there, the dead woman!"

Wardle, gripping Anna's hand tightly, ran a tongue over his dry lips and made his first contribution. "She was rolled in a carpet!" His voice was husky and the words difficult to make out.

"Yes. The old man did contact the police but he had to walk a quarter of a mile to the nearest pub to do it, and you didn't know that he would. Where are the other two? Lily and Joe, isn't it?"

"We don't know! They left us!" Anna said sullenly. "We wouldn't tell you if we did know, but we don't, so we can't!"

He thought she was probably telling the truth. Lily's and Joe's streetwise instincts admitted no loyalties. They would distance themselves as fast as possible from any compromising situation or companions.

"They, we, didn't have anything to do with it!" Wardle croaked.

"Ask the old man!" Anna snapped.

"He saw what we saw! He can probably tell you more than we ever could. He's always hanging round that tip. He lives there!"

"The old man is dead, Anna. I'm afraid we can't ask him anything."

He meant to shock and he had. They gazed at him popeyed. Wardle looked as though he would throw up. He moaned and put his hands to his temples, pressing against his head as if it would explode.

The girl, as always, rallied first. "How did he die? Heart or something?" Her face beneath the tangle of unkempt hair was as sharp as a ferret's.

"No, foul play."

"We had nothing to do with it! We weren't even there in the vicinity! We were already miles away. He can tell you when we got here! He had his flatfoots all over our camp inside half an hour of our arrival!"

He — the local sergeant, who had been stolidly examining his fingernails throughout — stirred and nodded corroboration. "Got a call, see, from Major Anderson, the landowner. Very upset. I sent a couple of my boys down there straight away. Very nice gentleman, the major. Always very generous to local charities."

"Listen, Anna," Markby leant forward. "And you, Wardle. You both understand how important it is that you cooperate. No one is accusing you of anything other than trespass and right now I couldn't care less about the trespass. I'm dealing with two murders. You know what's involved, don't you? Your uncle is a coroner."

The local sergeant stopped examining his fingernails and looked up, first at Markby with surprise and then at Anna with downright incredulity.

"Yes, I understand," she mumbled. "We have to do as he says, Pete."

Wardle looked relieved at receiving her permission. "Of course we want to help!" he assured them.

"All right. Now I want you to take me out to your camp and speak on my behalf to your fellow travellers. Explain the situation to them. I want to talk to the children. I'll need the parents' permission. I'm relying on you."

"The kids?" Wardle spoke unprompted.

363

"What have they done?"

"They're not in trouble but I fancy they know something I'd very much like to know. Okay?"

* * *

The New Age convoy had chosen to pitch its camp in rough pastureland enclosed by pearl-grey drystone walls and situated in a wide flat basin overlooked on three sides by the mountains. It was being watched by two constables in a police car, parked strategically at the entrance to the field so that the travellers couldn't leave.

All the figures, vehicles, people and animals, appeared as tiny models in a huge diorama. The stark contrast between this Welsh landscape and the rolling Cotswold hills he had left, never failed to make Markby catch his breath. The lower mountain slopes were clothed in bottle-green forest. Above the treeline the inhospitable crests were olive and tawny-brown in the late afternoon sunlight, patched here and there by outcrops of bare grey rock. The peaks were decked with mist, even though it was sunny here below. The weather was notoriously changeable in these parts as many unwary walkers and climbers had found to their cost. That thin veil drifting across the high ridges up there could descend in the matter of a quarter of an hour, creeping relentlessly and with deceptive speed down to the valley floor, throwing its thick, drizzling, damp mantle round you with a clamminess which seeped into your bones. Then the very mountains themselves would seem to move closer, bending their slate grey heads over the roads which clung to their flanks. But now, thought Markby, they were just beautiful in their wild defiance.

He walked towards the grouped trailers and buses. Sheep which had been grazing on the sparse grass scampered out of his way. If there were dogs in the convoy they had been tied up. The travellers were being careful.

They had gathered in a watchful crowd and in this untamed setting they looked just right in their weird clothing and with their long hair and beards. It took Anna a good ten minutes to persuade them to cooperate and allow Markby to talk to the children. But she was a forceful orator and a strong personality. Markby was glad that she was, in a manner of speaking, on his side.

Accordingly, some twenty minutes after his arrival, he found himself sitting on the turf surrounded by a circle of young children who watched him intently as if he were a magician about to entertain them with some baffling trick.

He asked them if they remembered the last place they had stayed, where there had been people digging in a field for old things. Clearly they remembered it very well and for an obvious reason.

"There was a skellyton down there!" one infant assured him, round-eyed. "I was scared of it. I thought it would get up and walk about."

"I didn't like that place, said another. "It was creepy."

"But you didn't see the skeleton, did you?"

"No," said the first speaker. "But we saw the witch."

That odd prickle ran down Markby's spine which meant he was getting close now. "I've never seen a witch. How do you know she was a witch?"

They wriggled about and looked at one another. "She shouted at us when we went to look at the castle."

"Castle?" Markby paused and then quickly made a sketch in his notepad. He held the sketch out. "Did it look like that, the castle?"

"Yes!" they all solemnly agreed.

He had shown them a drawing of Motts Folly. "And you think she lived in there, the witch? What did she look like?"

Some consultation here. The resulting consensus was that the witch had been small and bad-tempered with dark or black hair cut short in a bobbed style. She had uttered bloodcurdling threats and they were sure she could have carried them out.

"We used to dare one another, to go up to the castle and try and see her before she saw us!" one of the older girls volunteered.

Another girl burst out, "We threw some stones in the door to make her come running out but she couldn't catch us!" The others hissed her to silence.

"But she wasn't there when you left, was she?" Markby prompted.

"No." They stared at him. "She'd gone."

"How d'you know?"

"We went up there," said the girl who'd spoken of the dare. "We crept up and looked in the windows but she'd gone. She really had, we went in and made sure. The door wasn't locked. She'd left her shoes behind."

"What did you do with the shoes?" That had been badly phrased. They looked obstinate and chorused, "Nothing!"

"I bet," he said. "You did something funny with them."

They giggled. Sly glances were exchanged. Much whispering. Eventually one asked, "If we tell you, you won't tell that farmer?"

"If you tell me, it's for me."

"We put them on Harry!" said the girl triumphantly.

"Harry?" Markby was temporarily taken aback. "Which one of you is Harry?"

He'd made a gaffe. Roars of infant laughter. "Harry's not a who!" said the girl scornfully. "He's a scarecrow!"

"He's in a field near there," a boy added. "We called him Harry because he looked so real, like a person."

"He looked like the old man who lived in the cottage down on the road," the girl said.

Markby reflected, not for the first time, that children seldom missed a trick. He wondered at what stage in our development we lost that natural faculty to observe without effort and automatically store the most trivial detail away in memory.

"When you left, where were the shoes?"

"Still on Harry . . . " the girl said vaguely. "We were playing tea-parties but we had to go quickly. We left them behind."

"This is very important," Markby said carefully. "When did you find the shoes?"

"That morning," said the girl. "The same morning we left."

"Was the witch in her castle the day before?"

They responded with frowns and vague nods. They thought so. No one had dared to go up there and check. They'd gone up early in the morning of their departure and found the witch had gone, leaving her footwear. They'd carried it off in triumph to prove to their friends that they'd really been in the castle and that the witch had really gone.

"I expect," the first infant said sagely, "she flew away and didn't need her shoes."

She didn't need them when she left, that's for sure! Markby thought grimly.

★ ★ ★

A little later he sat with Anna in the converted bus which she and Wardle called home. It was more comfortable than he'd imagined. They'd been ingenious to arrange it conveniently and it compared very well with more conventional caravans.

Perhaps it appeared so cosy because outside, as he'd feared, the mist had crept down the mountainside while he talked to the youngsters. It had brought a fine insistent rain like spray which hid the sun and turned the air chill. Anna had brewed up tea and he was glad of it, watching her as she performed the task in silence but with great competence. Finally she handed him his tea in a large enamelled mug hand-painted with flowers. He wrapped his hands round it, grateful for the heat though it almost burned his fingers.

She sat down across the interior of the bus from him, arranged her long skirts and looked up at him in her forthright manner.

"If we come back to give any evidence at an inquest, will I have to give mine to Uncle George?"

He shook his head. "Unlikely in view of your relationship I think his deputy will probably conduct affairs."

"Good. I don't think I could do it if I had to face Uncle George."

"Anna," he said curiously. "Why are you running away from your family? You must be of age. You're not, forgive me, a shy violet. Do they object to Wardle? Does it matter if they do? To be independent you only have to stand up for yourself and I'm sure you're more than capable of that! Why have you and Wardle chosen this life?"

"Because it's what we want. We can't explain it to you."

"No, I dare say not. But don't you ever think about your families? Never miss them? They must be worried."

"Not worried, just shocked," she said dismissively.

He took a cautious sip of his tea. "I don't know that I can agree with that. Surely they love you? If you love someone, you naturally worry about them."

She gave him a strange, sidelong look. Then she shook her head.

"Love, real love, doesn't ask a price, does it? But they always wanted a price for their love. I always knew that. When I was a little kid it was being prettier or more clever or best at dancing class."

"No!" he protested. "Naturally any parent, well I'm not a parent so I can't speak from experience, but I imagine any parent is proud of a child's achievements."

"Why? For the child's sake, or for the parent's? Look," she leaned forward earnestly, and bitterness entered her tone. "I never had any illusions. They loved

372

me provided I measured up to what they wanted! One year, when I was about six, I wasn't chosen to be Mary in the Nativity play. I'll never forget. My mother said, 'They didn't choose you because you were so naughty at school! If you'd been good they'd have chosen you and I would have been able to make your costume! I'm so disappointed'!"

"She didn't mean — "

"I know what she meant! She didn't ask if I minded! I did, as it happened. I cried buckets because I'd set my heart on being Mary! But all she said was that she was upset and it was my fault. Not my fault I wasn't chosen, my fault she was upset, was what she meant! As I got older, it just changed a bit but it was always the same! I had to be bright at lessons and good at sports and head girl! I also, mind you, had to be pretty and attract all the right sort of boys! I had to be bloody wonderwoman, that's what I had to be! And if I ever argued about any of it I was told they were spending so much money on my education! They'd made so many sacrifices. They'd always tried so hard so that I could have

373

everything. I was so ungrateful! I was saying things to hurt them on purpose! Hurt them? They hurt me!"

She shouted the last words. "They never asked me if I wanted to be what they wanted me to be! They said they loved me but I always had to earn their approval, their love! I wanted to love them but it was as if they'd attached leeches to me and the leeches had sucked out all the love I had for them and it was gone! I didn't care any more."

There was an uneasy pause. "So that's why I left!" she said briefly. "I couldn't live in their world. Now I live in mine. I'm happy. I don't need anyone's approval any more. You were wrong in what you said about me, back there at the police station. But I don't give a damn what you think. In this life with the travellers it doesn't matter."

"And Wardle, where does he fit into this?"

"Pete?" Her expression and tone softened. "He's the only person who's ever said 'I love you' and meant it with no strings attached. He just loves me, that's all. He doesn't want something from me."

Oh yes, he does! Markby thought, but didn't say it. He wants constant reassurance and propping up! He wants you to be his strength! I just hope your strength holds out, Anna!

She said, "If you see Uncle George, tell him I'm going to cooperate, won't you?"

Markby said gently, "Yes, I'll tell him."

She understood. She gave a sad little grin. "Still seeking approval, aren't I? It's bred in me now. Can't shake it off. But none of those kids, the ones you were talking to out there earlier, will grow up with that sort of burden. They'll be their own persons. Free."

"No one's free, Anna," he said. "You can always choose to be your own person, but each of us carries his own burden. That's part of the deal. There are just different burdens, that's all."

There was a creak and the bus floor quivered. Wardle appeared. "Is it all right now?"

He was hovering uncertainly and

Markby found himself irritated by him. "For the time being!"

"You can't blame us for taking off, you know! We were scared. You'd be!"

"All right, Wardle, we've gone into that."

But Wardle was unwilling to let it go. Now he'd got over his initial fright and matters seemed to be smoothed out, he was attempting to justify his own poor showing and obvious dependence on his girlfriend by a display of bluster.

"People pick on us. We don't mean any harm! Those two farmers at the last place, one of them came waving a shotgun at us. I mean, all we wanted to do was camp on the open hillside."

"And light fires, leave rubbish and filth and trample his crops!" Markby said, not meaning to be drawn into it again.

"True New Age believers like us don't do that! We respect Mother Earth. We live in harmony with the natural world. It's the others who tag along with us for the raves and parties. Some just drive out in expensive cars for the one night at our festivals, cause a riot, get us in trouble with your flatfoots and then take off again! We get the blame. They don't share our philosophy. Even a lot who join us meaning to stay don't stick it for long. They drift back to the towns."

"Like Joe and his girlfriend, d'you mean?"

Wardle shrugged. "Like them, if you like. But they weren't so bad, they pitched in and shared chores." Aggression returned to his pale face. "Anyway, what about that farmer? He harassed us too! Or is it all right for him to do it? He kept spying on us! You could feel him watching all the time."

"The old man, Lionel Felston?"

"Not the old one, the young one. And what kind of a weird set-up is that, anyway? That younger one, he was a mean bastard. The old man was just crazy, but the young one was a real sod. The night before we left he went driving up and down in his Land-Rover in the middle of the night, just to disturb us and wake our kids."

"Oh?" Markby said slowly. "How do you know it was Brian Felston?"

"Looked out and saw from the shape it was a Land-Rover. Besides it came from up there on the ridge. Who else would do it? Who goes driving about at two, three in the morning? There's no reason for it but spite, and he was a spiteful blighter, I told you."

"Oh, he may have had a reason," said Markby, getting to his feet. "There's always a reason."

Like moving a dead body, for instance.

20

WHILE Markby went hotfoot after his hippy convoy, Meredith called on Steve Wetherall the architect to arrange a thorough survey of the house. Steve was interested to hear her plans and willing to do the work, but had a full schedule and couldn't go before the end of the week. House-purchase held up for the time being and her presence no longer required for immediate police inquiries, Meredith was left at The Crossed Keys twiddling her thumbs.

She ought not to have opted to spend the extra week's leave in Bamford. The time had clearly come to return to London and the flat; plus Toby and all the other problems she'd thrust into the background when she'd undertaken, perhaps rashly, to dash to Ursula's aid. It might be better to act more prudently this time and warn Toby of her impending return. It was just possible that in her

379

absence some girlfriend or other had moved in. She couldn't contact him before that evening so return to Islington would have to wait until tomorrow. That left her with the rest of Monday to spend in Bamford on her own.

Discovery of Finny's body had interrupted work at the archaeological site and Meredith didn't know whether anyone from the Trust or from the museum would be out there. She tried ringing Ursula in Oxford but no one answered the phone. She could call round at the museum, but really didn't want to. If Jackson were there he would begin to quiz her about the brooch again and there was nothing more she could tell him. Karen would be wandering around looking miserable and Dan, if he was anywhere in evidence, was company to be avoided.

But in the end, sheer boredom led her to get into her car in late afternoon and drive out to Bamford Hill.

She wasn't surprised to find the site occupied only by two young men who were familiar to her as workers on the dig. They were sweaty and grimy and sitting on the turf drinking lager from cans, mud-caked spades abandoned on the ground beside them. They had been busy filling in the trenches, they informed her, and evidence of their industry was behind them. Clearing and tidying a site was a tedious and time-consuming business. Since the team wouldn't be excavating any further, Jackson had sent them up to begin the necessary restoration work. They couldn't touch the grave with the skeleton, of course. The bones themselves had yet to be removed and Jackson would supervise that together with Dr Gretton. As of now, fluttering police tape still surrounded the grave. They supposed the bones would be removed when the police said it was okay to do so. They were restricting themselves to making good the exploratory trenches cut near the trailer. It was a pity, they said, that they hadn't found Wulfric. But finding the other skeleton had been good going.

"Sometimes, you don't find anything," one said.

Meredith said she supposed she could handle a spade as well as anyone else and offered help. But it turned out more tiring and indeed more skilful a task than she'd anticipated. After an hour during which she gained backache and blisters, her young friends kindly said that they could manage without her. With some relief, she packed up, left them to it and walked back to her car.

Now that the hill was empty and quiet but for the sounds of earth still being shovelled into the trenches behind her, it was possible to imagine what it was usually like up here. Certainly the countryside had seen more than enough activity for the time being and the filling in of the trenches now seemed highly symbolic, as though life were returning to normal. The Felstons in particular must be mightily relieved to see all their visitors, invited and uninvited, depart. Wulfric, if Renee's theory was correct, would be more than satisfied and his spirit was probably dancing in glee on the rampart, making suitably Saxon gestures of derision.

Thoughts of the Felstons caused her to raise her eyes to the skyline and the eccentric silhouette of Motts Folly. At least Brian wouldn't have to sleep out there any longer to keep watch on the hippies, and thanks to the activities of the police in the wheatfield, the man who helped with the harvesting wouldn't be sleeping there either. In her mind's eye Meredith saw the stone-flagged room with its motley collection of furniture. It must be windproof and dry up there and probably staying in the folly wasn't dissimilar to staying in a weekend cottage. It was clean.

Meredith frowned. The folly floor, as she recalled it now, had been in surprisingly good condition, despite the dust and scattered pebbles on the pale stone. Surely if Brian and the hired man had walked across it in their boots, its appearance ought to have been more worn? It was almost as if it had had a covering. Like a carpet.

She had been about to open the car door. Now she put the keys back in her pocket. Why not? Brian had furnished the folly with old bits and pieces from the farm. Might those not have included an old carpet put down to reduce noise and take the chill off the stone flags?

And Natalie herself? A curious shiver ran up Meredith's spine. Where had Natalie been for the unaccounted days between walking out of her home and the appearance of her body on the tip? Was it possible that she'd been hiding in the folly?

It was, but only with the connivance of Brian Felston. But was that impossible? Natalie was Bamford-born, a local girl. Had not Ursula said that Brian had come to the inquest and greeted Amy Salter, being received by her as an old acquaintance?

She said aloud, "There's more here than meets the eye!" and without more ado, set off briskly to walk up the hill to the folly.

She wasn't sure what she was going to do when she got there. The door was still unlocked. When she examined it she saw that it couldn't be locked from outside. On the inside, however, was a simple bar and bracket arrangement which meant that anyone sleeping there could render himself — or herself — secure from intrusion. Meredith went in and looked about her. The open door let in the breeze which blew gustily across the hilltop. To search the little room didn't take long. There was nothing here which hadn't been here last time she'd visited it.

Meredith put her hands in her pockets and sighed. She would have to tell Alan about her idea. If a forensic team went over the folly, they would have far more chance of finding traces of Natalie than she ever could. A few hairs perhaps? Smears of make-up?

Behind her the door swung silently to and only made a click as the latch connected followed by a rattle as the bar dropped into place, locking it. She spun round and gave a short shriek of alarm.

Lionel Felston stood inside the now barred door. She had no idea how he had managed to approach so silently, but then so had Brian on her previous visit and, indeed, the turf outside absorbed any footstep. Lionel was a tall man, taller than his nephew. His shaggy grey locks hung round a narrow bony face in which deepset eyes glittered at her. If Wulfric himself had appeared, he would hardly have been more unnerving.

"I knew there was a woman," he said. "I can read that boy like a book."

"Just a minute!" Meredith began nervously. "I think you may have misunderstood — "

He shook his head, cutting short her explanation. "The boy thinks I don't notice, but I knew something was amiss. Creeping about at night! He said he was going out on account of those hippies. But I got to thinking. He's not been himself these past days. Got you tucked away up here, has he?"

"No, he hasn't!" Meredith burst out vigorously. "I've been working down at the site. I was helping fill in the trenches. Look — " She held out her blistered hands. "And I just — just came up here to take a look before I went back to Bamford."

"Women are nothing but trouble!" He ignored her explanation. "The cause of all misdoing and men going wrong. It's been so since the Fall. Eve gave Adam the apple and he, poor daftie, took it and ate it. 'Tis the same with Brian. He's not got the brain to take care of himself where women are concerned! Women are the cause of man's fall."

"Rubbish!" Meredith said. "A lot of nonsense! That's a mediaeval attitude. Men are quite capable of going wrong all by themselves! Only they like to have someone to blame for it!"

She'd meant only to refute his argument but she saw at once that she'd somehow struck nearer to home than she'd intended. Lionel's face darkened with an angry flush and the glitter in his eyes intensified.

"They lead a man astray! 'Tis the smell of their skin and the way they move their bodies! A man can't control his instincts! And when a man's a religious man, it's not only his body is defiled but his soul endangered!"

This was not a good situation to be in. The folly's walls were thick, its windows small, its one solid door barred, and the way to it blocked by Lionel. He was elderly but sinewy and a lifetime's hard physical work had toughened him. Besides, Meredith thought gloomily, he was clearly as mad as a hatter, or at least, as far as women were concerned and she, unfortunately for her at this minute, was a woman. If she could just get them both outside. The two young men working down at the site might just hear her cries, or she might be able to run down the hill towards them and they might see her.

"Mr Felston," she said. "Perhaps we should go back to the farm."

It was unlikely he even heard her. He seemed to be transported to some world of his own. He had begun to sway. "They have white skins and smell of perfumes!" To the swaying was added a monotonous humming, as if Lionel tried to recall some hymn tune but couldn't get it right.

Meredith wondered whether it would be possible to edge round him. He might have been in a trance for all the awareness in his eyes. But just then there was the cough of a car engine outside, a short distance away. Someone had stopped at the point where the main track forked. Would they come this way? She held her breath.

Then the door handle rattled and before Lionel could prevent her, she shouted out, "In here! We're in here!" and dashed past Lionel to lift the bar before he could interfere. She dragged the door open, looking out eagerly.

She didn't know whom to expect. But when the door swung open she saw, not surprisingly, Brian. He walked past her into the folly and looked from one to the other of them.

"Uncle Lionel?" His voice cut loudly into the dirge-like song coming from his uncle's throat.

Lionel blinked and some kind of awareness returned to his face. He turned his prophet's head and regarded his nephew. "'Tis you, then, boy."

Brian looked exasperated and, Meredith thought, worried. "What nonsense are you up to?" He glanced briefly at her. "You all right, what's your name, Meredith?"

"Yes, thanks. I think your uncle is, um, a bit muddled."

"You go home, Uncle Lionel!" Brian said firmly.

"I'll not leave you," Lionel declared. "Not with this woman! She'll lead you astray!"

"Go home!" Brian bellowed.

Lionel blinked again and, somewhat

to Meredith's surprise, obediently walked out of the folly.

Brian, breathing heavily, turned to her. "What the hell are you doing here?"

"I only — " What could she say? "I'll be leaving soon and I was just taking a last look."

"At what? There's nothing to interest you! What was the old man saying?" Brian regarded her fiercely.

"He — it was sort of religious. He's got a thing about women."

Lionel was raving nuts, she thought. And why should Brian ask if she was all right? Shouldn't she be, with Lionel?

Suddenly a terrible possibility struck her and before she could stop herself, she blurted, "Brian, he didn't kill Natalie, did he?"

"Hold your tongue!" Brian shouted. "You're not to say that!"

There was silence as his voice echoed round the little stone room.

"Did you kill her?" Meredith asked quietly.

"No!" He spoke as vehemently but more quietly.

"You put her body in the quarry

though, didn't you?" When he didn't answer, she pointed at the floor. "Wasn't there a carpet here? It's very clean apart from a little dust and those stones. When I was last here and you came in, you seemed to be looking around, as if you'd lost something. Were you looking for Natalie's sandals?"

Brian stared at her. "Sit down!" he said abruptly.

It was an order not to be refused. Meredith sat down on the chaise-longue. Brian pulled out a wooden chair and took a seat between her and the door.

"You a friend of Markby's?"

"Yes. If you've got a problem, Brian, you can talk to Alan, to Chief Inspector Markby. He'll listen."

"You listen!" Brian swallowed and pressed his work-hardened palms together. "See, 'twas like this. When I was eleven or so I started to go to school in Bamford, old High School. Before that I went to local primary school. It was in Westerfield then, but that's closed down long since. Anyhow, I used to get the school bus. It stopped down there on the road for me. I'd walk down from the farm every morning."

He paused. Meredith said, "And at the High School you got to know Natalie Salter."

He nodded. "She was the prettiest little thing. I'd never seen anyone like her, nor have I since! I'd hang about the gate to carry her books. She was brainy, mind! Really clever. When we got a bit older, it was clear how things would go. I'd come back here and farm and she'd go on to the university and make something of herself. I'd have liked it if I could have married her, but she'd never have been happy at the farm. She knew how I felt, but she didn't feel that way and that's all right. She was worth something better!"

Brian was getting agitated and Meredith wondered if something of his uncle's craziness hadn't rubbed off on the nephew.

"Only she didn't get anything better! She got that Dan Woollard and he deceived her and made her miserable! She changed, did Natalie. Folk who didn't know her before, when she was a youngster, they can't imagine how much. He was responsible for that. To me it was always as if she'd had a sort of light shining in her. But he put that out! He sort of killed her, that's what he did. She was walking about looking like Natalie, but it wasn't the old Natalie, it was a different one! Well, a few days ago she phoned me from Oxford. She'd had a row with him over his latest fancy piece. She'd run out of the house and just had a few coins in her pocket, enough to phone me. She asked me to come and fetch her. She didn't want to go home right away and she didn't want to go to her mother. She thought Woollard might check round her other friends.

"So I drove there and got her. I brought her out to Bamford, thinking that she'd change her mind and want to go to her mother's, after all. But she reckoned no. She wanted to get right away for a bit where no one knew. She was thinking of getting a divorce and she wanted to think it through. I'd already thought of the old folly here as she spoke and I said, she could stay here, it was warm and dry and I'd make sure she had food. Only it was near to where her husband and his fancy piece were working down on the hill so maybe she wouldn't like it. She began to laugh. She said it would be funny if she was hiding up here and watching them and they didn't know. It would be a sort of revenge, getting her own back. She said, 'Come on, Brian! Let's do it! It'd be a marvellous joke'!"

Brian shrugged. "And I wanted to help her, I wanted her to get her own back on him and on his fancy piece, so I brought her here and hid her. And it was — it was a wonderful few days."

His voice filled with a kind of wistful wonder and Meredith felt a rush of pity.

"I had her to myself, see? I'd walk out here after nightfall and sit with her talking, because she didn't like to be alone up here in the dark, especially after the hippies came. Uncle Lionel, he never came to the folly, so I reckoned he wouldn't know."

Not just sitting up here talking, thought Meredith regarding the chaise-longue on which she sat. It went a bit further than that. Poor Brian. She asked quietly, "What happened next, Brian?"

He opened his mouth to continue his story but they were interrupted. There was the sound of another car, climbing the track. Then men's voices. She heard someone call out, "Brian? Are you in there?" and to her surprise recognised Markby's voice.

Brian jumped to his feet and dashed to the door. Meredith followed him.

Markby was outside with Pearce and another constable. A police car could be seen at the end of the footpath to the folly where it joined the track down the hill. The sun was going down over the hill now and the roof of the police car sparkled with a pink glow. Alan looked as if he'd been hurrying. He stared at Meredith in surprise.

"What are you doing here?"

"Brian and I were talking. Alan, I think — "

"It's all right. Leave it to me. Brian, I think you ought to come to Bamford with us. You and I should have a talk, at the station."

Brian said slowly, "All right, then. Your car is it, down there?"

They set off along the path. Its

narrowness meant going Indian-file. The constable led the way, with Brian behind, Markby and Pearce behind him and Meredith bringing up the rear. As they reached the police car she could see Brian's Land-Rover parked beyond it.

Brian stopped. "I'd best go, up to the farm and let Uncle Lionel know what I'm doing."

Markby said, "You can phone him from the station."

Brian didn't argue, only nodded again. He walked forward and then, without warning, he broke into a sprint.

He moved fast and he took them all by surprise. The constable shouted and plunged forward but tripped and fell. Meredith yelled, "No, Brian! Don't!" But Brian raced across the turf and jumped into his Land-Rover. It roared into life and he began to drive off down the track to the main road at breakneck speed, the Land-Rover rattling and bouncing dangerously over the ruts. Markby, Pearce and the constable piled into the police car and set off in pursuit. Meredith, apparently forgotten by them all, found herself on the hill alone.

It had happened within the space of a couple of minutes. She was half dazed by the speed of it, but pulled herself together and began to run down the track back to where she'd left her car. She'd be too late to join in the chase, but not to see the end of it, or so she hoped.

★ ★ ★

"Where's he going?" Pearce gasped, gripping at the dashboard to steady himself.

"Towards Bamford, looks like it!" said the constable at the wheel.

They had reached the main road. The Land-Rover turned on to it with a roar and they followed.

Markby, leaning over the seat from the back, snapped, "Don't lose him, for crying out loud!"

He'd phoned ahead from the Welsh station to let Pearce know his intention, but he'd wanted to be here himself, and told them to await his return. Perhaps, thought Markby grimly, he'd been wrong. He should have told them to go and pick up Brian straight away.

"Watch out!" Pearce shouted. "He's turning! He's not going to Bamford!"

They were level with the entrance to the quarry. Ahead of them, Brian wrenched at the wheel. The Land-Rover plunged down the track to Finny's cottage and stopped. They saw the driver scramble out as they pulled up with a screech of tyres. Brian, with a backward glance, set off between the trees.

"Watch out, sir!" the constable gasped as he, Markby and Pearce raced in pursuit. "The quarry edge is just about here — "

Even as he spoke there was a yell from ahead of them and the sound of falling stones. Then another noise, slithering horribly, on and on . . . and then silence.

"My God, he's gone over!" Markby exclaimed.

They had reached the edge. The wire fence round it had been snapped and the turf at the very edge broken off clean. Brian was rolling down the side of the quarry looking like a piece of discarded rubbish and not a human being at all. A small avalanche of pebbles and dust descended with him and they watched, frozen with horror, as the falling figure turned over and over, until it reached the bottom. It came to rest motionless, close to the spot where Natalie's body had lain.

There was the sound of another car behind them. Then Meredith came pushing her way through the undergrowth and calling. When she reached them she was panting.

"Oh no . . . " She gazed horrified into the quarry depths. "Oh, Alan, he was explaining why he hid Natalie! He was just going to tell me why he moved the body! Why couldn't you have come ten minutes later?"

Pearce was already halfway down the gravel track to the bottom of the quarry and they scrambled after him.

Brian lay on his face, one arm under him and one reaching out above his head. Meredith whispered, "Is he dead?"

But the prostrate figure moved as she spoke. Brian moaned and flexed the fingers at the end of his outstretched arm. The tips scrabbled in the quarry dust. He muttered, "Nat-al-ie . . . "

21

"YOU can certainly talk to him," the doctor said. "Provided you keep it reasonably brief. He's sustained a severe blow to the skull. We'll need to keep him in for another twenty-four hours, just to make sure. Besides, he's cracked a couple of ribs and sprained a wrist and there are multiple abrasions. Actually, I fancy you'll find he's anxious to talk to you."

"Oh?" Markby raised his eyebrows.

The doctor looked enigmatic. "I think there's something he wants to get off his chest. By the way, do you have to leave that constable on duty in the corridor? It's alarming other patients and I honestly don't think Mr Felston is likely to go anywhere in his condition."

"Well, I want to be sure. He's already tried to give me the slip once!" Markby said firmly.

The doctor looked askance at him. "And is that when he fell down the side

400

of the quarry?" The word 'fell' carried a multitude of undertones.

"We've not yet established exactly how he came to fall. That's one of the things I want to talk to him about."

The doctor sniffed. Clearly this episode was understood at least by him to be an example of that notorious police brutality recorded by investigative journalists. But he shrugged. He had enough problems.

Markby, followed by Pearce, walked briskly down the corridor. The constable rose from his chair at their approach.

"He's quiet as a lamb in there, sir. Subdued but sort of fidgety at the same time. He doesn't say much, only to ask when you're coming. Seems to be sitting there in bed thinking a lot. Might be something to do with the bang on the head. He asked me — " The constable paused and looked a little confused. "He asked me if you were ever married,"

"Did he? And what did you reply?"

"Said I thought you had been once, sir. Didn't know what to say really. Hope I got it right."

"Yes, you got it right!" the chief inspector told him.

Brian was propped on pillows with a large plaster on his brow and more tape visible round his ribs through his open pyjama jacket. One side of his face was swelling and turning purple.

"I've been waiting for you!" he greeted Markby.

"So I hear." Markby took the chair by the bedside and Pearce stationed himself unobtrusively by the wall. "How are you feeling, Brian?"

"As if a horse had kicked me in the guts and I've got a bloody sore head as well."

"Where did you think you were going when you ran towards the quarry?"

Brian fixed him with a stony gaze. "I don't know. Out into the woods behind. Didn't realise I was so near the edge till I slipped. Anyhow, it doesn't matter."

"Miss Mitchell repeated to me what you told her about agreeing to hide Natalie Woollard in the folly."

"I can't ever call her by that name." Brian shifted painfully on his pillows.

"Natalie Salter she was always to me, always will be."

"Want to tell me some more, Brian?"

Brian moved his head slightly so that he could see Markby better. "If you've spoken to your girlfriend, then you already know all there is to know about Natalie and me."

"Never mind Natalie," Markby said. "Tell me about the farm, your father and your uncle. Tell me about your mother."

The farmer twitched and then muttered in pain. "Bloody sharp, aren't you? And don't mind poking your nose in other people's business! That's how you got to be a chief inspector, I suppose."

Pearce forgot himself so far as to chuckle and cast Markby an apologetic glance.

"All right, then!" Brian went on suddenly in a firm voice. "It's like this. My father and Uncle Lionel, they were brothers and always very close. They took on the farm together. The war hadn't been long over, it'd be 1948. They decided they needed a woman to look after the house and do the cooking

403

and such, lend a hand with the small livestock like the chickens. They couldn't both afford to get married. Farm wouldn't have supported two wives. So they drew straws and my father, he won. He knew a girl in Westerfield. She'd been a landgirl during the last year of the war on a farm where he'd worked. She'd enjoyed herself and she had good memories of farmwork. Besides, late 1940s were times of shortages, still got rationing on a lot of things. Life on the farm must have sounded good to her. So she said yes when he went down and asked her."

Pearce was looking incredulous, but Markby merely nodded. He was long past finding anything people did strange. And as for making important decisions, people did that in the most hit or miss ways.

Brian looked away from him across the room as if unwilling to meet his eyes. "Only trouble was, Lionel seemed to resent her being there. That's how I saw it when I was a nipper. He'd sit staring at her with a real fierce look. She'd get upset and go out of the room, couldn't stand it."

He cast the two police officers a

sardonic look. "Looking back on it now, I can see it wasn't resentment, it was something else! And it couldn't be helped, I suppose, because Lionel, he was a young man then too. Mother was pretty enough in those days. He got restless, as it were, like a bull when you put him in a field too near the cows. But he'd struck a bargain with my father. Only one of 'em would marry."

From the corner of his eye Markby saw Pearce stir uneasily. Brian too had begun to look shifty. He moved on his pillows and put a hand to his bruised face.

"Do you want me to call the nurse?" Markby asked.

"No, it's all right." Brian paused. "But it wasn't all right back then, was it? It was all wrong. All that unhappiness and that wanting, the wrong sort of wanting. She saw it in his face and I felt it in the air, when I was a kid. But I couldn't make sense of it. But it was clear to me she was downright miserable and got more and more so as the years went by. So I wasn't surprised when she walked out."

Brian's tone grew reminiscent. "You could sense her misery, it seeped out of her. I hardly ever saw her smile. And her looks went too. She got thin and white as a sheet. And who's to wonder at it?" Anger entered his voice. "A drudge, that's all she was. Up at crack of dawn and work all day. If she did sit down it was always with some sewing or knitting! Then one day when I was about fourteen, I was driving the cows in for milking. And she came out of the house and called me over. She looked old, though I doubt she was as old as I am now. But I could see there was something different about her, as if she'd made up her mind to something. She said, 'Brian, I can't take no more and you can manage without me now. So I'll be going'. And I saw then she had an old suitcase with her. I wasn't surprised but I said I was sorry. She said, "'Tisn't your fault. But if I don't go now on my own two feet, I'll go out of here in a wooden box'. So I offered to carry the case down to the bus-stop for her. But she wouldn't have it, said she could manage. So she left. I don't know where she went, and as far as I know, neither did my father. She never wrote as I know of. I hope she was happy wherever she went. I don't blame her. I wish I could have helped her, but I was only a kid and she had to help herself. She only stayed as long as she did on account of me."

There was silence. Brian was staring unseeingly into middle distance, lost in his memories.

"How about your father during all that time? Didn't he notice that Lionel was making a nuisance of himself where your mother was concerned?" When Brian didn't answer, Markby stretched out a hand to touch his sleeve. "Brian?"

Brian slowly turned his head. "Oh, Dad. He wasn't one for saying much. Besides, he and uncle were close, as I told you." A twisted smile crossed the farmer's weather-tanned face but there was no mirth in it. "One of our cows once, she calved early, twins. Joined together they were, like human Siamese twins. They were both dead and we nearly lost the cow. But when I looked down at that abort on the straw, I remember thinking that that's how Dad and Lionel were. They were sort of joined, not in their bodies, but in the spirit, if you take my meaning."

"I think I do." It was Markby's turn to sit silent for a while, before he asked, "And how did Lionel react to your mother's leaving?"

"Turned him funny!" said Brian firmly. "He was always a bit odd in his ways but after that he got worse."

"Anyhow, it was another reason for me to help Natalie, when she came to me. Woollard treated her badly, always running after other women. She was entitled to get her own back and make him sweat a bit. I was never able to help my mother but I could help Natalie and I did. I hid her in the folly, like I told Miss Mitchell. Lionel never went near that folly. He sort of avoided the place so I thought it'd be all right. But I was wrong, I reckon."

"Brian, are you trying to tell me your uncle killed Natalie?"

Brian's whole body twitched. "I didn't say anything about that!"

"But do you think it? Would it make sense? Was he punishing her because he couldn't punish your mother for her desertion?"

Brian fixed his hostile gaze on Markby. "I don't know exactly what happened, and that's the truth! While Natalie was in the folly, I'd go there at night to be with her. On the Tuesday night when I got there, she was dead, lying on the floor. I saw it as soon as I walked in but I couldn't believe it, first off. Not my Natalie, so pretty and full of life. She'd been her old self again, with me there in the folly, away from him. I knelt down beside her and I lifted her up. She was already cold and her face was turning blue but I thought maybe I could do something, like you hear about. Kiss of life. But I knew as soon as I put my mouth on hers that I was kissing a corpse."

Pearce shifted awkwardly again. Markby asked in an expressionless voice, "What time was that?"

"About ten, ten-thirty. Uncle Lionel had gone to bed. I didn't know what to do. Panicked, I suppose. I knew I had to get rid of the body. But where? It was dark but those hippies had their fire going and were dancing round it. I couldn't go digging a grave. I thought, if

I'd wanted to hide a sheep, I'd have put it in a flock of others. So later, when all was quiet, I tied Natalie's body in the old carpet off the folly floor, put it in the back of my Land-Rover and drove down to the quarry turn. I thought if I hid it on the tip it would just be another bit of household rubbish and later I'd be able to get it back and bury her up in the woods. I was afraid old Wilf Finny might hear, though, so I left the Land-Rover up on the road and put the carpet with Natalie over my shoulder. Fireman's lift, they call it. I got down to the bottom of the quarry somehow. It was difficult, I can tell you! She was only a little slip of a thing, yet dead she was heavy! But I've lifted a few animals in my time and there's a knack to it. I left the carpet there and I came home."

"And all this," Markby persisted quietly, "because you think your Uncle Lionel found Natalie at the folly earlier in the day and killed her in an attack of righteous wrath?"

"Look!" Brian leaned forward on his pillows unwarily, swore and fell back putting a hand to his bandaged ribs.

"Look — " he repeated panting. "He's cracked! When it comes to women, that is! That's why I told you about Mother, how he came to be like it! If he did it, he didn't rightly understand what he was doing!" Brian jabbed a finger at Markby. "But it went wrong, my plan! Those hippies went poking about in the quarry the next day and found her! Then your lot were there, all over the place! To make it worse, I'd lost her sandals. I remembered when I got home she'd not had any shoes on when I rolled her in the carpet. They must've fallen off. Fancy little foreign jobs, they were. I went back to the folly to look for them but they weren't there. Your girl was though, rummaging about in there. She it was told me a body had been found. I ran off back to the farm and told Uncle Lionel to let me handle it."

"And did he say anything, Lionel? Did he admit it?"

Brian shook his head. "No, not a word."

At that moment there was a crash from outside the room as if the constable's chair had fallen. The next moment the constable himself could be heard in authoritative protest.

"I'm afraid not, sir! You can't go in there!"

"You stand out of my way!" Lionel's voice shouted.

"He's here!" Brian began to struggle on his pillows as if he would get out of bed.

Markby moved to restrain him as Pearce moved towards the door. But it flew open and, grey hair streaming about his haggard face, Lionel erupted into the room dragging the constable with him.

"Brian! You say nothing, boy!" he bellowed. "You hear me? And you, Markby, you stay away from him! He's injured and not fit to answer your questions!"

"All right!" said Markby sharply to the constable. "Let him be. Now then, Mr Lionel! This is no way to behave, creating havoc in a hospital!"

A diminutive nurse had appeared and hopped into the room ruffling her starched apron like an angry sparrow its feathers. "You'll have to keep the noise down! You're disturbing other patients!"

"Yes, yes!" Markby urged her out again, and closed the door on her.

"The boy's not responsible!" Lionel shouted. "She turned his head! He was led astray by a loose woman! He's not the first. Women turn a man's head, they make him forget what's right and wrong! You can't go blaming him for killing her!"

There was stunned silence. Then Brian, oblivious to his painful ribs, bounced out of bed and roared, "Kill her? Me? I didn't kill Natalie, you crazy old fool! You did!"

"I, boy?" Lionel looked bewildered. "I never knew she was there! Though I suspected you were up to something, mind! But I didn't finally go to look until earlier on today and it wasn't Amy Salter's daughter, 'twas that other woman I found! But now everyone's saying you had Amy's girl hid there and you killed her and put her down in the quarry and police have arrested you!"

"Just a minute!" Markby yelled and silence fell. "No one, Mr Lionel, has been charged! So let's get this cleared up. Brian! — Shut up, Mr Lionel, if you don't mind just for a minute! — Brian, you told me you thought your uncle had killed Natalie. Just answer yes or no."

"Yes!" Brian growled.

"And you, Mr Lionel," Markby turned to the older man. "You came here thinking your nephew had killed her?"

Lionel had begun to look confused. "Yes. Didn't he?"

Markby heaved a sigh. "It's beginning to look as though neither of you did!"

"Oh," Brian said in a flat voice. "Then I needn't have killed old Wilf Finny!"

22

IT was nearly midnight. Meredith sat with Alan Markby in the latter's kitchen, a bottle of wine and the remains of a pizza between them.

The whole kitchen, Markby reflected as he observed it with a critical eye, and probably the whole house shouted out that here lived a man on his own. One who, so long as he had a roof over his head which didn't leak, basically didn't care about his living space and kept his creative talents for his garden. There was a row of neat new geranium cuttings standing over there on the Welsh dresser between a rack of crumpled envelopes and a toaster. Spiders lived happily in the corners of the ceiling because the woman who came in and cleaned twice a week for him never bothered to 'do' above eye-level. The curtains were faded. How could this mess attract a woman to come and live in it? No wonder Meredith wanted her own place. Regardless of his role, if any, in the scheme of things.

One thing he was pleased about, and that was that he'd never shared this house with Rachel but had bought it after his divorce. To have the ghost of Rachel hovering in the corner giving proceedings a supercilious eye would have been the last straw. Old loves, lost loves, ex-loves, dead loves. Natalie would always be at Brian's shoulder, just as she'd been all his life.

"A true and doomed love!" he said suddenly.

He saw Meredith's hazel eyes blink and widen and felt himself redden. "Brian and Natalie. I didn't mean you and me." Before she could reply to this he went on hastily. "I've got Brian on my mind at the moment."

"A thoroughly unpleasant man!" Meredith said vehemently. Then she added with some reluctance, "Although I suppose he's a sad figure in his way, despite what he did to Finny. But he went out of his way to frighten Ursula after the inquest. He must hate everyone, be burned up with bitterness, nourishing just that one little flame of love for Natalie when she was alive."

"He doesn't hate Lionel. Perhaps he should . . . " Markby's voice tailed off as he scowled down at his glass of wine.

"A pity Brian didn't find himself another girl. It didn't help Natalie to have him so ready to fall in with any crazy scheme she dreamed up!"

Markby picked up the wine bottle. "He didn't want another girl. We want what we can't have, don't we? Another glass?" He raised his eyebrows questioningly.

He was right, of course, thought Meredith with a sigh. But she felt herself flush because he was talking about them and not Brian and Natalie.

Perhaps Markby saw her discomfiture because he went on briskly. "Brian had a hell of a shock when Natalie's body was found so soon. He'd reckoned on retrieving it and burying it somewhere with a sort of decency. He must have been half out of his mind with grief and panic."

Meredith propped her chin on her hand. "I can't help wondering whether, during all the years Brian was working from dawn to dusk around that farm, he didn't escape in his mind to a make-believe world in which he and Natalie were together. They were together for a very little while in the folly. But it couldn't last, like Romeo and Juliet's shared time. Despite everything, I can't help hoping the memory is of some comfort to him."

"Save your sympathy!" Markby advised her. "Natalie's death may have destroyed Brian's dreams. But he had no pity for Finny, and don't forget that!"

"I haven't forgotten it. How could he kill that harmless old man? He'd known him all his life!" Meredith burst out.

"Brian was scared. He nursed a nagging fear Finny knew he'd put the carpet on the tip. He was up on the rampart when Finny was taken ill and saw you stop your car and help the old chap to his cottage. Brian followed you down and hid outside and listened. He couldn't make it all out, but clearly Finny had taken a fancy to you and was chattering away. Some of the things he said made Brian very uneasy. Then he heard you arrange to take Finny to the inquest the next morning. He felt he couldn't risk it. He went back later that night and silenced the poor old fellow."

She shivered. "I felt I was being watched. Why did he put Finny in the Saxon grave? Did he think he wouldn't be found?"

Markby hunched his shoulders. "He may have wanted to delay the body being found. I fancy he did it out of pure spite. He wanted to frighten Dan Woollard and put pressure on him. Brian does hate Woollard."

"Spite, yes." Meredith thought of the scarecrow's painted face.

"But we still don't know who killed Natalie!" Markby went on. "That's if both Lionel and Brian are telling the truth, and I believe they are."

Outside the church clock could be heard in the distance, striking midnight. Bamford was dark, shuttered and deserted. The last pub clients had wended their way home and the kebab van had shut up shop and driven off now that late-night trade had noisily dispersed.

"Oy!" he said firmly. "We're not going to sit talking about it for the rest of the night, are we? This isn't how I'd imagined the evening. Though when I saw Pearce walking my way in The Crossed Keys this morning, I knew work was going to get in the way again."

"You started this conversation. You said you had Brian on your mind!"

"I've got you on my mind, too."

Their eyes met across the gnawed pizza crusts. Meredith leaned across the table and took his hand. "I don't want to talk about the Felstons any more tonight, either! I'm going back to London tomorrow, remember?"

"And what," asked Markby, "are you going to do about Toby when you get back to London?"

"Hey! If we're not to talk about the Felstons, we're not to talk about Toby, either!"

Markby trapped her other hand. "You can't expect me not to brood darkly over it. How old is this happy-go-lucky young stud?"

"Oh, he's about thirty. Don't look so glum. I don't fancy him. He drives me bonkers. He plays rock music full volume and he turns the place into a pigsty."

"Good looking, is he?"

"I suppose so. But he already has loads of girlfriends. I promise, I'll tell him he's really got to go and find somewhere else. Perhaps he can move in with one of his girls — if any of them will have him."

"And what about you? Do you want me to take you back to The Crossed Keys tonight?"

"Do you want me to go?" She met his gaze and twitched an eyebrow interrogatively.

He whispered, "Don't be daft. Of course I don't!"

"Well, then, I'll stay here." She reached out and picked up the wine bottle. "And you really didn't need to ply me with this stuff, you know!"

23

"TOBY!" yelled Meredith and hammered on the bathroom door more as a release for her feelings than to gain attention. If he hadn't heard the yell, he must be stone deaf. "Come out of there! I'm going to be late for work! You're going to be late!"

A muffled reply suggested Toby's head was enveloped in a towel.

Muttering curses, Meredith subsided on to a chair by the telephone in the narrow hallway. She eyed the instrument, redirecting her frustration from the door to the bland little plastic block with its neat array of numbered buttons. What a useless invention. It had rung for her only twice since her return from Bamford, a week now, and neither call had been from Alan. He was probably busy on the unsolved Woollard murder and with the charges to be brought against Brian Felston over Finny's death. But he could have rung, all the same.

How long did it take, five minutes? That was men for you, even the best of them. A mutually satisfactory night and affectionate following morning farewells and then zilch. Not a single miserable phone call.

Steve Wetherall the architect, however, had phoned to say he'd be sending along his report on the house. Summarising it for her, he declared it to be structurally sound, but replacing the bathroom and kitchen fittings was going to be expensive. Also there was the matter of boarded up fireplaces in both bedrooms. In neither case had air-vents been left in the boarding and this, it seemed, caused dreadful developments in the accumulated ancient soot in the sealed chimneys. But she was beginning to wonder if she did want to go and live in Bamford, after all.

Meredith sighed and glanced up at the calendar pinned to the wall above the phone. 'A happy Christmas from your milkman'! read a legend above a picture of a robin standing in snow beside a bottle of presumably frozen milk. 'Don't forget that extra pinta! Come sun or snow, you'll be glad of it'!

Annoyed by the unwitting hint of *double-entendre*, she reached up and ripped off the small paper sheet with the current month's dates. It was, after all, the last day of the month. The day, in fact, that the Ellsworth ceased financial support of the Bamford Hill project. Wulfric could slumber on undisturbed, safe and triumphant. Although Ursula — the other of the two phone calls Meredith had received — had told her that in view of the evidence provided by the brooch, Ian Jackson was planning a last-ditch appeal to the trustees of the Ellsworth, and had got them to agree to a meeting. It would be a storming of the ramparts akin to Wulfric's, and it seemed equally likely to end with Jackson retiring mortally wounded. There wasn't the proverbial snowball's hope, said Ursula, of getting the Trust to change its mind.

There was a click of a bathroom bolt sliding back and Toby, in an inadequately fastened towelling robe, appeared surrounded by clouds of steam, like something in a science fiction film.

His hair stood on end and he smelled equally of Meredith's shampoo and mint-flavoured toothpaste.

"About time!" Meredith informed him. "And make yourself decent. I haven't had my breakfast yet and it's enough to put anyone off!"

"Stop flapping. There's no rush. I'll make the breakfast!" he offered unabashed and ambled towards the kitchen.

When she'd showered, dressed and joined him shortly thereafter, he was still in the towelling robe and seated at the table reading the previous evening's *Standard* while munching toast and marmalade. He was a messy eater. Crumbs covered the table and marmalade stuck to the front of the bathrobe. He'd stirred his coffee and returned the wet spoon to the sugar bowl.

"You said you were going to move out!" Meredith said to the *Standard* as she cleared a space for her coffee cup and searched through the toast for a piece which wasn't charred.

Mumble. "I know I was." The paper rustled and he put it down. "But I've been thinking, what for? I mean if you're

425

dead set on buying that house out in the sticks, you'll be moving out anyway. Then I'll move back in again. Waste of effort. Makes more sense for me to stay here, surely?"

"I shan't be moving out for quite a while, Toby. Oh God, you are disgusting! There are bits of butter in the marmalade again!"

Leaning his elbows on the table and ignoring her complaint, he said wistfully, "You're hellbent on joining that police Lothario, are you? What is it about him turns you on? His police boots or that special social polish provided by Hendon Police College?"

"I'm not joining Alan, not as such." Join a man who can't be bothered to phone? Ha!

"Like heck! What else could take anyone out to that benighted neck of the woods, littered with mad farmers and wives' bodies dumped on rubbish tips? Why can't you stay here? I've always thought we got along very well. What's he really got, this copper? What's wrong with me? I've always fancied you, you know."

"Oh, for crying out loud!" Meredith put her head in her hands. "Doesn't anything I say get through? Anyway, I'm too old for you. You're just suffering from an older woman complex."

"I've seen your passport. I'm only six years younger than you."

"When I want a toyboy, chum, rest assured you won't be it!" she told him unkindly.

"I might amaze you. There are sides to my character of which you know absolutely nothing. Depths unplumbed. You don't even try and find out what I've got!"

"I can see what you've got from where I'm sitting. Eat your toast and go and put some clothes on — especially the clothes!"

★ ★ ★

Ursula was also facing a day of problems. She coasted on her bicycle into the asphalted area before the building which housed the offices of the Ellsworth Trust and dismounted. She wasn't looking forward to the meeting. Officially it was to hear Jackson's appeal. But she had a shrewd suspicion that unofficially other matters would be raised at some point.

Certainly as far as the dig itself was concerned, the meeting was a waste of time. *Pace* the luckless curator, neither Ursula nor Dan thought it likely the Trust would change its mind. They had both been summoned to give their views today. It would be the first time she and Dan had met in the presence of the trustees since Natalie's death and the first time they met at all since Finny's murder had stopped work on the hill.

Dan, she knew, had been offered compassionate leave but had refused it. Ursula thought that unwise of him. He was undoubtedly under strain. Yet, at the same time, his refusal made him look callous. Goodness only knew what the trustees made of it. She had an idea she'd soon find out.

"Sula!"

Ursula, who had been stooped over her bike fastening the security lock, jumped at the sound of Dan's voice. She straightened up and turned round,

428

carefully assuming a nonchalant expression. He was striding across the open area towards her and wearing that crumpled suit again. She didn't know whether the attempt at formal dress was intended to impress the trustees, or whether in some way it was meant to indicate Dan's widower status. He'd abandoned the rusty black tie, she noticed, in favour of a more jazzy one in mottled turquoise and navy. Half-mourning, then.

"Where's your car?" she asked as he came up.

"I jumped on the bus. How are you?" His eyes searched her face.

"Prepared."

"They might not — "

"They will!"

He shuffled his feet and looked away from her. "Sula, look, I'm sorry!"

She sighed. "For what, Dan? I got myself into all this. You're not to blame."

"No one's to blame!" he burst out passionately. "We fell in love!" When this elicited no reply from her, he added more quietly, "Don't ask me to give you up, Sula, because I can't. I can't just stop loving you. It won't turn off

429

like a tap. I'm not going to make a fuss in there, no matter what anyone says. But I'm certainly not going to let you suffer because of anything that's happened."

"They're unlikely to refer to it in front of Jackson or any outsider." She met his gaze. "I think after this, Dan, you should take some leave. They did offer it and you do need it."

"So that I can sit at home and brood? I still think that crazy old man killed Natalie. Why the hell don't they arrest him?"

"Lionel? The police seem sure he didn't. I'd be more inclined to think Brian did it, crime of passion. He's been charged with old Finny's death. But Markby seems unwilling to believe he killed Natalie, so neither of the Felstons looks like being charged. Maybe it means the police know something we don't."

"What it means is that the finger of suspicion still points at me!" Dan said soberly. "Markby'd dearly love to nail me with it! I can see it in his eye. I didn't do it, you know, Sula."

"Yes, I know that now. I wasn't sure

at first. It's my fault they suspect you at all, Dan."

He was shaking his head. "No, it's not. The way things were between Natalie and me, well, something drastic had to come out of it in the end! But to think of her sitting up there in the folly watching us, watching me sweat. She was an imaginative bitch, you've got to hand it to her!"

"Brian put her up to it. I've always thought he has a spiteful look to him!" Ursula defended the dead woman.

Woollard shook his shaggy head. "No, she just used him. Poor blighter, I feel almost sorry for him. Well — " He squared his shoulders. "I suppose we'd better go in and face the music!"

Impulsively she reached out and took his hand. "It's going to come out all right, Dan! It will, in the end."

He squeezed her fingers. "Sure. I hope it does for you, at any rate, if not for me." He lifted her hand to his lips and before she could prevent him, briefly kissed it.

At the same moment a car swept into the forecourt. Dan quickly released

Ursula's hand, but not, she feared, before the occupants of the car had seen the kiss. It screeched to a halt and decanted Jackson, Karen and Renee.

"The girls have come to give me moral support!" Jackson sounded excited and his voice and agitated manner boded ill for the meeting ahead. "What d'you think our chances are?" he demanded eagerly of them. "Renee's going to tell them she's writing a thesis on Wulfric for her American university. That should impress 'em!"

Renee, in the background, nodded vigorously.

"Don't bank on it, Ian!" Dan said brusquely. "We'll do our best. But you know it's an outside chance, don't you? The Trust doesn't usually change its mind."

"Oh, but now there's the brooch!" cried Jackson with an absurdly childish air of triumph. "That's an entirely new development and changes everything! When the Trust said it was pulling out, that was before the brooch turned up! They can't ignore it."

They had walked into the entrance hall

as they spoke and halted at the foot of the staircase. Jackson spoke again with his voice lowered furtively. "I've brought it along, Sula. Your friend Meredith has let me have it for the museum, anyway, which is very decent of her. It's tangible proof! The old chap must have found Wulfric's grave. He couldn't have got it anywhere else! Oh, it's out there all right, just as I've always known!"

He had pulled a small box from his pocket as he spoke and they could see it was printed with the name of a local jeweller. Ursula wondered what it had originally held. Jackson opened it. The little gold brooch lay inside packed with tissue.

"We can't prove the old man found it at the site, Ian," Ursula felt impelled to point out.

"He must have done!" Jackson's eyes gleamed feverishly. "Where else? Oh God, what I'd give to know the location of that confounded rabbit burrow!" He put the lid back on the box, his hand trembling visibly, and returned it to his pocket.

Dan and Ursula exchanged glances. Ian was clinging to the discovery of the brooch as his lifeline. When the lifeline snapped there was no telling what he'd do and neither of them fancied witnessing the scene.

Dan grasped the nettle by saying loudly, "Let's go up. Better not be late!"

"No, no!" Jackson agreed. He glanced round. "Where's Karen got to? We'll have to go up without her."

Karen's ungainly form appeared in the main doorway. "It's okay, I'm here." She spoke to Jackson but her broad red face was turned to Dan. She was perspiring and something in her eyes as she gazed at Woollard made Ursula crawl with embarrassment. It wasn't the outright hero-worship, it was the accompanying apology for it. Surely Dan had noticed? He didn't seem to.

He smiled and said, "All right then, Karen? Ready to say your piece?"

"Oh, yes!" Her face lit up. "Oh yes, Dan! Anything you want!"

★ ★ ★

In the event, it all turned out much as Ursula had feared.

"I'm sorry, Mr Jackson!" said the Director firmly. "Of course we understand. Dr Gretton and Mr Woollard have both made representations to the Trust on your behalf and we've taken all your arguments into consideration — "

Jackson, his features twitching and gingery hair on end, burst out, "No, you haven't! "The brooch — " He thrust it forward on the table around which they all sat, pushing it under the Director's nose.

"Yes, yes, very interesting, Mr Jackson. But we just don't know its provenance. The old man who found it was in the habit of foraging on the rubbish tip. He might have found it there, thrown away as useless by someone who had acquired it elsewhere and was unaware of its significance."

"Surely that's unlikely, too much of a coincidence!" Jackson seemed dazed. "He said himself he found it in a rabbit burrow!"

"So he told the lady to whom he gave it. But the lady isn't here and neither is the old man. Indeed he can't be here and we can't ask him because he's dead!"

The Director glanced awkwardly at Dan. "This is all hearsay, Mr Jackson. Third-hand information. It cannot be relied upon. I'm afraid there's nothing more to be said."

Jackson stood up, pushing back his chair with a teeth grinding scrape. He snatched up box and brooch, thrusting them into his pocket. His face and hands twitched alarmingly, his eyes watered and he looked quite ill.

"It's bloody stupid! Bloody short-sighted! After all our work, our finding the other skeleton! It's there, it's got to be there! The old man found it and I can find it. But I've got to have more time!"

"By which you mean more money, Mr Jackson. I'm sorry but the Trust simply can't support this dig any further."

Jackson stood frozen, then let out a strangled cry and stumbled from the room. The girls ran after him and all three could be heard making a noisy descent of the staircase, inarticulate shrieks from Jackson and crooning sounds of consolation from the girls punctuating the clatter of their feet.

The Director wiped his forehead. Dan and Ursula exchanged glances and got to their feet. Not quickly enough. The Director said briskly, "One moment, please! Dr Gretton, Mr Woollard!"

They sat down again.

The Director took off his spectacles and began to rub the lenses with his handkerchief. "A distressing scene, very distressing. But not the only, ah, unfortunate business to be tackled. This is very awkward for me, most difficult. I have to speak to you both on behalf of the Trustees. I've no wish to increase your burden of grief, Mr Woollard, or add to your present distress in any way. But you should know that the board is unhappy. There has been — " He struggled for a word he felt appropriate. "There has been public comment about your friendship with Dr Gretton. You cannot, of course, be held in any way responsible for the circumstances surrounding the sad death of your wife, but — "

Dan said loudly and harshly, "Save it! I resign!"

The Director looked relieved but Ursula said sharply, "You can't!"

"Yes, I can and I just have." Dan fixed the Director with a glare which made the man wriggle uncomfortably. "Only if I go, Dr Gretton stays, all right? It's not her fault and it's a condition of my resigning now, on the spot."

"Hang on!" shouted Ursula. "You can't do this, Dan! You can't go just now!"

She turned on the Director who quailed before her. "He can't resign now and you can't ask him to, not while police investigations into Natalie's death are incomplete! It looks as if you're pointing the finger at Dan, showing your lack of confidence! It makes it look as if you and the board know something the police don't and Dan has something to hide. Shut up, Dan!" He was trying ineffectually to interrupt her but she turned on the Director again. "You just go back to the board and tell them that when all this is settled, Dan and I will both go. But we can't go now!"

"No, Sula, not you!" Dan cried out.

"Yes, me too if you go! Both of us or neither! Got that?"

The Director nodded so fast it seemed

his head would fall off. He scrabbled for his spectacles and fixed them crookedly over his ears. "I'll report all that you say to the Board of Trustees, Dr Gretton. I certainly take your point. I'm sure the board doesn't wish to damage — er — prejudice police inquiries. We'll put it all on hold, shall we?" He peered at them. "Till the police are, er, satisfied."

Dan and Ursula descended the stairs in simmering silence.

"Till the police are sure I didn't do it! That's what the old fart was going to say!" Dan glowered at her. "You shouldn't have said all that, Sula."

She didn't answer but marched outside and began to unlock the bike's safety chain. Looking up from the task, she said briefly, "Yes, I had to!"

"I appreciate it, anyway." His mouth twisted in a rueful grimace.

Ursula lugged the bicycle round to face the exit. "It's not being nice to you, Dan. It's a matter of principle! The board has no right to pronounce on our private lives! That's misusing the clause in the charter and they know it! If I quit the Trust, I quit on my terms!

I'm not going to be hounded out like some Victorian fallen woman! They'll be wanting to flog us through town at the cart-tail next!"

Dan's battered features broke into an unexpected grin. "Okay, we fight 'em!"

"You bet we do! See you!"

She pushed at the pedals and rode out of the entrance. Turning into the main road she knew she still boiled with anger. She tossed back her long hair and pedalled furiously, trying to work off the energy built up in her like a real head of steam. A mist of wrath clouded her vision. It was lunchtime and the traffic dense. Suddenly a car swerved ahead of her. Ursula braked. But the wheels kept spinning. Something was wrong. She braked again, then tried to back-pedal, twisting the handlebars to avoid collision but in vain.

There was an impact which wrenched the handlebars from her grip. The bike reared like a bucking bronco. Helpless, she was thrown into the air and to one side. Car brakes squealed. A woman shrieked. Then the shock of striking the ground knocked all the breath from her body and brought darkness rushing in from all sides.

* * *

When she opened her eyes, she was lying on the pavement. Someone had thrown a car rug over her. She squinted up and made out Dan's face emerging through haze.

"Sula!" he was shouting. "Oh God, Sula!"

"What?" she mumbled. "My bike . . . " She tried to turn her head. It hurt and she gave a moan.

"Don't move! The ambulance is on its way." He put his hands on her shoulders, gently restraining her.

"Where's my bike?" Suddenly it seemed to matter so much.

Dan glanced at a heap of tangled metal nearby. "Written off, I'm afraid. But you fell towards the pavement, thank goodness, and not into the path of the traffic!"

Or I'd be written off, too! she thought to herself. Oh damn, what have I done? Have I broken anything? She tried to move her feet and was relieved when that hurt too. Better pain than the dreaded numbness.

A policeman's face, absurdly young and fresh, appeared in her line of sight, replacing Dan's. "Take it easy, Miss! Ambulance will be here in a jiff!"

"It was an old bike!" she whispered. "I ought to have given up riding it ages ago. I knew it wasn't safe."

The two-tone cry of the ambulance announced its approach. People cleared the way. She felt herself being lifted. Faintly, as she was loaded on a stretcher through the ambulance doors, she heard the policeman's voice as he spoke into his radio.

"Yes, sarge. I just had a quick look at it. Brake cables cut deliberate, no doubt about it. Girl was lucky! Lunchtime traffic and all. She ought to have been killed!"

★ ★ ★

Toby got home before her that evening. Meredith, who had stopped off at a late-night supermarket, fell through the door with two bulging plastic sacks of groceries and found him waiting for her in the hall. He took the sacks from her with unwonted alacrity.

"One inane remark," she warned him, puffing, "and murder will be done right here, in this very flat, I promise you!"

He gave a sort of shifty smile. "Your copper pal phoned."

At last! Her heart rose and then rancour took over. About time too. "When?"

"About ten minutes ago. He said, would you call him back?"

It began to dawn on Meredith that Toby seemed unusually sombre and very slightly official in his manner. He was eyeing her as he might a Distressed British Subject.

She asked tightly, "Okay, what's happened?"

"Your archaeological friend, Ursula, she's had an accident on her bike. Well, not so much an accident, really . . . "

"What do you mean? Was it an accident or not?"

"The police seem to think it was attempted murder."

443

24

"I SUPPOSE," Ursula said with a wry smile, "that you could say I've had a narrow escape."

She was propped in a deck-chair in the back garden of her family home with her feet on a cushion which in turn rested on a large upturned flowerpot.

"So how are you feeling now?" Meredith asked her.

"Everything hurts. But it's all bruises, so they tell me. They were a bit worried about the crack on the head but, apart from my skull being very sore, that's all right now. I just have to rest up, which is a nuisance because I've a hundred and one things to do. The bike's a total wreck and perhaps it's just as well. I'm giving up bike-riding. I'm going to buy a car. I'm sorry about the ozone layer getting thinner and all our lungs shrivelled up with pollution and all the rest of it. But I've done my bit to save the environment, riding that wretched bike for years, and look where it got me!"

"With a little help from someone who is not among your friends!" Meredith pointed out.

Ursula sighed. They were sitting in the dappled shade of an old apple tree. A child's swing which had been fixed with twin ropes to one of its venerable but sturdy branches had been looped up out of the way. The wooden seat dangled above Meredith's head and she kept one eye on it. Bees buzzed happily around a nearby flowerbed and a little white cat had found a smooth warm stone in the rockery and draped herself over it to sunbathe and snooze. She did not even stir for a blackbird which, as if realising the cat was too lazy to bother, hopped about the lawn within a few feet of his enemy's whiskers.

"The police here are now saying it could be a random thing. There's been a lot of hooliganism in that area recently. Break-ins and young kids stealing cars to hot-rod round the streets. The forecourt where I left the bike was open to the road and unsupervised. Anyone could have walked in. Both cables were cut almost but not quite through. They hung together by a thread so that I probably wouldn't have noticed even if I'd been more observant. But I wasn't looking because I was talking to Dan and in such a stew over what had just happened. As soon as I rode off and started using the brakes, the cables parted almost at once. Result, one spill."

It didn't sound like a random if malicious act of vandalism to Meredith, but she forbore to say, so for the moment. "Feel like telling me about the meeting?"

"Sure. Why not? Nothing that was said there was unexpected. I could have told you before I went what would happen."

"Perhaps," Meredith persisted gently. "But if you started right at the beginning, with your arrival on your bicycle, and told me everything that took place before the meeting as well as after it."

Ursula cast her a shrewd look. "You think someone's tried to bump me off, don't you? Me specifically — and it was someone at the meeting. It's not a nice thought. I've been working with all those people for several weeks."

446

"What about Alan Markby, what does he think?"

"He's not actually investigating my accident. The city police are doing that. But they're keeping him informed and, for all I know, they may be doing more than that. But if so, they don't let on. Markby did come here and talk to me. He's got a very professional and soothing bedside manner. Quite the old-fashioned family doctor. I can see him as that, if he weren't a policeman. But he plays his cards very close to his chest; although I suspect he thinks as you do. He is rather dishy, you know. I think in other circumstances I could quite fancy him myself, if you don't want him! Don't answer that! I can see a gleam in your eye and, according to you, I've already got one mortal enemy, so I don't need another! I'll tell you about the morning I had my accident."

Meredith listened. As Ursula came to the end of her tale, voices were heard from the house, one of them familiar. Meredith glanced that way and observed, "That sounds like Dan."

Ursula shifted awkwardly in her deck-chair. "It probably is. He's come to visit me every day since the accident. It's a funny thing with me and Dan. I thought we were finished, or at least we were as far as I was concerned. But now, with all the fuss and the Trust being so bloody-minded, well, people link us and it's as though Dan and I are stuck with one another come hell or high water. Life plays odd tricks."

Woollard was striding towards them across the lawn. The blackbird flew up and away clucking indignantly. The cat opened one eye and lazily beat her tail against the rockery stones.

"Hullo, Meredith!" he greeted her, thrusting out one large powerful hand. "Nice of you to come all the way from London! Tell her she's got to rest, will you? She keeps trying to get out of that deck-chair and rush around. She won't listen to me."

Meredith, finding his proprietorial manner irritating, stood up. "I've promised to meet Alan in Bamford later so I'd better be going. I'll call and see you again, Ursula, before I go back to Town."

As she left she looked over her shoulder and saw Woollard had taken the seat by Ursula and was bending solicitously over her. She still didn't like him but his devotion to Ursula wasn't to be questioned. One couldn't run other people's lives. It was up to Ursula to decide what she wanted. Besides, just now Meredith had other things on her mind.

* * *

Bamford was quiet when she arrived there an hour later, drowsy in mid-afternoon sunshine. The museum, however, had just had visitors, a noisy collection of ten-year-olds. They were being shepherded away as Meredith arrived. Ian Jackson was standing in the doorway looking harassed. His expression cleared when he saw Meredith approaching.

"Little monsters! But at least they're interested. Nice to see you again. We've got your brooch on temporary display until I can get a proper cabinet for it. You'd have thought those blighters at the Trust would have been persuaded by it, wouldn't you? But they weren't! They just quibbled about where Finny could have found it. As if he could have got it anywhere else but up on the hill site!" he snorted.

"So I heard from Ursula. Sorry you had no luck. Is Karen here, by any chance?"

He looked vague. "Oh, somewhere about. In the storeroom most likely, putting away some of the replica stuff we got out to act as visual aids during my lecture to the kids."

★ ★ ★

"Karen?" Meredith put her head round the storeroom door.

Karen Henson was standing insecurely on a box trying to push another box on to a high shelf. She glanced down, red-faced with exertion, and puffed, "Oh, Meredith! Just a sec!"

She gave the box in her arms a powerful heave on to the shelf and clambered down, dusting her palms. "We've had a party of children in."

"Yes, I saw them leaving. They looked

as if they'd enjoyed their visit."

"I think they did. Ian talked to them. He's very good with children. We show them exhibits and illustrate the talks. There are also these things, of course." Karen stretched out her hand to a nearby box and took out a small but efficient-looking axe. "This is one of our Bronze Age visual aids. It's not a real Bronze Age axe, but it looks and feels like one, and is about the same weight. The children can handle it and it fires their imaginations." She replaced the axe on the shelf.

Meredith closed the storeroom door. "I'd like a word, Karen, if you've time. This seems as private a place as any."

Karen looked mildly surprised. "All right. What about?"

Meredith avoided a direct answer. "I've just come from Oxford. I've been to see Ursula. She's getting along all right."

The girl's face took on an even darker flush and her mouth turned down sullenly. "Is she? Good."

"You don't sound terribly pleased."

"Of course I'm pleased," was the wooden reply.

"Dan arrived to see her as I left. I

think he's been every day."

It was a low blow. She felt mean but it had the desired effect.

"Look!" Karen burst out. "I'm glad she wasn't badly hurt! But she's not my friend, she's yours. As far as I'm concerned she's been rotten to Dan! He loves her and she doesn't care about him, not one bit!" Her voice shook and her pale eyes filled with unshed tears.

"Oh, Karen!" said Meredith with real pity. "Why on earth did you do it? Cut the brake cables, I mean."

Karen slumped to sit on the box on which she'd been standing. "I didn't plan it. But when Ian drove Renee and me into the carpark by the Trust, we saw Dan kissing Ursula's hand. I hated her so much at that moment I just wanted to hurt her the way she keeps hurting him! After all he'd gone through, she was just going to make him suffer more. And right then, feeling like that, I saw I had the opportunity.

"They'd all gone inside and were huddled in the hall looking at that brooch you gave Ian. I was alone with Ursula's rickety bike. I thought no one would be surprised or suspicious if she had an accident on that old wreck. In my bag I still had a little pair of pliers I'd used to dismantle some temporary shelving I'd rigged up in the works trailer. Renee jokes that I ought to have gone in for carpentry. I cut the cables nearly through and left it." Karen frowned. "When I heard she'd really had an accident, I wasn't sorry!" she burst out. "But I was scared and horrified to think I could have done it. I think I must be a really dreadful person. I don't know why. I can't help it."

Meredith pulled out another box and sat on it gingerly. "Karen, it's not the only dreadful thing you did, is it?"

Karen looked up with frightened eyes. "What d'you mean?"

Meredith put her hand in her pocket. "The day Natalie's body was found in the quarry, I went up to the folly while the police were questioning the others. I had a good look round inside it before Brian Felston came along and very nicely chucked me out! But I'd already found these."

She stretched out her hand and opened her palm to reveal the scraps of coloured straw she'd retrieved from the folly floor. "I didn't know what these were at first. But now I've realised they come from that old hat of yours."

Karen's gaze drifted upwards and Meredith saw the hat in question hanging on a nail. She stood up and held one of the pink straw scraps by a raffia daisy decorating the brim. "That's it, see? A bit of loose raffia. You hadn't lost it in the folly that morning because we were all working at the dig and you didn't leave. So you must have lost it from your hat on a visit on a previous day. But if you went up there on a previous day, then you must have found Natalie because she was hiding there." She sat down again and waited.

Obstinacy crossed Karen's face. "No, I didn't."

"So how did these raffia scraps get there? Did you struggle with Natalie and, during it, did the hat fall off?"

Karen got to her feet, rubbing her hands together with a jerky motion. "I told you, I don't know how they got there! I — "

She moved so quickly she took Meredith

completely by surprise. One hand was flung out and snatched up the replica axe and at the same time, Karen leapt towards her, the axe held high, her face distorted with rage and panic.

Meredith was as tall and as strong as her assailant but she was still seated and caught off-balance and by surprise. She fell to the floor and they wrestled together, Karen kicking and even biting in a complete frenzy. Meredith's prime concern was to protect her face and head from blows of the axe, quite capable of inflicting a nasty wound. But Karen seemed to have as many arms as an Indian deity. As the axe skimmed past Meredith's ear, the strong fingers of Karen's free hand crept relentlessly towards Meredith's throat.

Around them, objects of all kinds tumbled to the floor with a clatter and Meredith realised she was getting the worst of it and that just possibly she couldn't get free. Mad people were said to have the strength of ten, and Karen certainly qualified as mad just at that moment. It was no time for considered reflections but one unpleasant thought did crowd into her mind as she tried to shove Karen away. Alan had told her that a murderer tended to repeat a successful method. Karen knew how easy it was to throttle. Was she to die as Natalie had?

Suddenly the storeroom door flew open and Renee Colmar appeared in the entrance, yelling, "What the hell is this?" She dived forward and, summing up the situation, immobilised Karen by the simple expedient of grabbing her hair and jerking back her head.

Karen froze and Meredith took the opportunity to scramble to her feet. Karen, released by Renee, uttered a moan and curled into a disconsolate ball, dropping the axe.

Renee swiftly scooped it up. "Okay, what's going on here?"

"Karen has something to tell us!" Meredith panted.

Karen's voice emerged from the huddled form on the floor. "I'm so clumsy and so stupid. I break everything. Nothing goes right . . ."

"Okay, okay." Renee again moved to take charge, raising Karen and seating her on the box again.

Karen looked up, her cheeks tear-stained and her eyes fixed beseechingly on Meredith. "You see, I love Dan. I really do. I love him so much it hurts. He'll never love me, I know. Why should he? I'm not pretty or witty or anything. But I hated seeing him so unhappy. They both made him miserable, his wife and Sula Gretton. But at least his wife was his wife, if you understand me. I could have accepted it, I think, if he hadn't fallen for Sula. Then they were just two women and I hated them both. When his wife disappeared, I saw how everyone looked at poor Dan, accusing him with their eyes. And Sula, she did worse! She accused him outright, she talked to you, Meredith!"

"Yes, she did," Meredith admitted.

"You see? They treated Dan so badly, both those women! And he's so defenceless. Dan *can't* defend himself. You're right. I did come across Natalie in the folly. I went up there towards the end of the afternoon just to take a look at it. I'd been meaning to do that since we began work at the dig, but I hadn't got around to it. That day I felt so unhappy and I just wanted to walk away from the dig, anywhere. Somehow I fetched up at the folly. I opened the door. And there was Natalie sitting there, reading a book. Natalie!"

Karen's eyes and voice still showed the incredulity she'd experienced at the discovery. "Just sitting there! She was surprised to see me, too, you can bet! I asked her what on earth she was doing there. I said everyone thought she was missing and Dan was getting blamed. She just laughed. She said it was a joke she and Brian Felston were playing on Dan! A joke!" Karen almost choked in anger and her pale eyes blazed so that they seemed to glitter in a way which was disconcerting and even not quite human.

"I was so furious! I yelled at her. I told her she had to go down to the dig immediately and show herself, confess what she'd done. But she just told me to mind my own business and she said other things too, horrid things, about me and how I felt about Dan. How stupid I was because he'd never look at me in that way." At this Karen's voice finally faltered.

"She's crazy about him," Renee, at Meredith's elbow, said quietly. "I knew it all along. Much he cares. Poor kid."

"I grabbed her," Karen whispered. "I wanted to drag her out of the folly and back down the hill with me to the dig. But she struck out at me and my hat fell on the floor. I was so angry with her already that a silly little thing like her knocking off my hat made me boil over. I put my hands round her neck. She just sort of collapsed. I thought at first it was a trick. Then I thought she'd fainted. I was scared. I ran out of the folly and went back to the dig and didn't mention it to anyone. Then the next day they found her body in the quarry. They said she'd been strangled. I didn't know how her body got to the quarry, but I knew I must have strangled her. I'd killed her." Karen's voice took on a note of wonder. "I didn't realise it was so easy to do that, to kill someone."

There was silence. "So what now?" Renee asked directly of Meredith.

There were a lot of things Meredith could have said in reply. That there were two kinds of justice, the sort the courts

459

dealt in and the sort life gave out. Karen might get justice before the law, but in the court of life she'd always get the same raw deal she'd got up to now. Karen was a loser. People like Dan, on the other hand, always managed to avoid responsibility for what they did. Ursula wasn't guiltless, certainly, nor was the dead woman, nor Brian nor anyone else involved in this sorry mess.

What she did say was, "I think she should go and get herself a solicitor and then go with him to see Alan Markby and make a statement. If she doesn't, someone else, someone innocent, could be charged with Natalie's death."

Not that words like innocent or guilty were as easy to define as all that.

Renee heaved a deep sigh. "I'll go with her." She stooped and touched Karen's shoulder. "Come on, let's go and find you the best lawyer this one-horse town can provide!"

Karen had begun to sob in an unattractive way. It made her ungainly, unkempt appearance even worse. Her nose reddened and shone and her eyelids had begun to puff up.

Renee said in some exasperation, "The guy isn't worth it, Karen! He's a louse!"

"When did that ever make any difference?" Meredith heard herself ask with some asperity.

Renee turned on her, hostile. "How would you know? You've got that handsome police inspector sweet on you! Try falling in love with a heel some day!"

25

"YOU should have given me those scraps of raffia straight away!" Alan Markby said, not for the first time.

He'd been muttering on about it all morning and Meredith, who had finally managed to drag him to view her prospective house-buy, was more than a little fed-up with it. One can only eat so much humble pie.

"I'm sorry!" she said, allowing her irritation to creep into her voice. "But I didn't realise at first what they were."

"If you'd brought 'em to me, I might have realised what they were!"

"And you might not! All right, I know they were not the colour of normal straw. But I didn't identify them or realise they meant anything special. There was other small debris on the folly floor, dirt and stones. It wasn't until Ursula described to me the events of the morning of her accident that I realised Karen must have cut the cables. That made me think she might have killed Natalie too, perhaps not intentionally but just out of clumsiness. She is ham-fisted. So when I thought about Karen, I thought about the hat because when she was working at the dig, that's what she wore. Then I remembered the straw scraps still in my pocket."

"So when you'd worked all this out, then you should have come to me!"

This kind of argument was likely to go on for ever, round and round in a circle. She said wearily, "Yes, I know and next time, I promise, I'll come to you straight away and badger you with every little bit of meaningless information I come across."

"I trust," said Markby loftily, "that there won't be a next time!"

"You know, it's at times like this that I'm very glad I'm not moving in with you. You can be as bad as Toby in your own way!"

That annoyed him. He scowled and glared round the empty living room in which they stood, probably, she thought, looking for some glaring deficiency in the house so that he could get his own back.

But he didn't say anything and she was obliged to satisfy her own curiosity by asking, "Has Karen made a statement?"

"Yes, she has."

Nuts to you! thought Meredith. "All right, what is it? Don't you like this house? If so, perhaps you'd like to descend from that high horse and tell me what it is you object to?"

Grudgingly he said, "The house is all right. It needs a lot doing to it. But it's probably a good buy at the price you've negotiated. Steve Wetherall seems to think so."

She waved her arms in exasperation. "So what's wrong? What are you brooding over? Is it just because I held out on you over Karen? Is it still because I'm buying my own place and not moving in with you? I thought we'd sorted that out. It won't change anything between us. We'll still see more of each other. We both want that, don't we?"

Markby wheeled round and gave her flushed face, half-obscured with a lock of dark brown hair, an appraising stare.

464

"Yes, we do. I do, at any rate." He relaxed, put out his hand and tugged gently at the unruly lock of hair. "It is nothing to do with the house, nor the fact that you withheld evidence, Miss Mitchell! It's something else."

She pulled a face at him. "So what is it? Tell me for goodness sake. Don't seethe moodily all by yourself, interesting though it makes you look, I must confess."

A smile tugged at the corner of his mouth. "You look pretty interesting yourself. Got any furniture in this place?"

"No bed, if that's what you mean and this floor looks a bit too full of dust and splinters to me. Control your instincts, Chief Inspector. Think sobering thoughts."

"Anyway," said Markby briskly, moving slightly away from her. "I can't actually confide in you just at the moment. There is something worrying me, and it results from a talk I had with Fuller, the pathologist who conducted the post-mortem on Natalie Woollard. A bit like those raffia scraps, you know, it's got me thinking." He glanced at his watch.

"D'you mind if I leave you here? There's someone I really ought to go and see."

"Go on, then!" she said crossly. "Ursula said you played your cards close to your chest! Come back and tell me when you decide it's not a secret any more!"

She watched him drive away through the window of what would be her own home fairly soon now. It really wouldn't make so much difference not living under the same roof, she thought. The frustrations of his work would still be there. He'd still be breaking dates and dashing off at the drop of a hat without a word of explanation. Brooding over things he couldn't discuss with her and she couldn't or shouldn't ask about. Forgetting to phone. She'd still be a policeman's wife in everything but name.

"I wonder," she muttered aloud resentfully, "where he's gone?"

★ ★ ★

Dan Woollard was about to leave his house when Markby arrived. He looked

466

surprised to see his visitor.

"Hullo, Chief Inspector! Off your patch, aren't you?"

"Your wife's murder is my case," Markby reminded him. "So the local force here is giving me every assistance. Can I come in and talk to you for ten minutes? Or are you rushing off to an urgent appointment?"

Woollard hesitated fractionally. "I was on my way to see Sula, but ten minutes won't make much difference. Come in."

Markby followed him down the cheerless hallway to the untidy study, thinking as he did so much the same as Ursula had done. Markby was aware of the shortcomings of his own bachelor establishment but it wasn't as uncared for in appearance and feel as this house. It told a lot about the Woollards' marriage.

"Drink?" Woollard inquired. "I've got whisky."

"No, thank you."

"Ah, on duty, I suppose!" Woollard attempted a hearty laugh but then thought better of it. "Look, I realise my visiting Sula Gretton every day when my wife is, as they say, hardly cold, doesn't look good. But I'm past caring about that. There's nothing secret now about the way I feel about Sula, and she had a narrow squeak in that accident. If I could get my hands on — " His large hands curled. Then he recollected himself, sat down on the edge of an armchair and dangled his hands over his knees. "Okay, what can I do for you?"

"I'd like to clear up one or two points in Karen Henson's confession."

Woollard raised bushy eyebrows. "Thought that was already cleared up? It shook me, mind you. Who'd have thought it of Karen?"

"She's very keen on you and upset because she felt your wife had made you suffer unjustifiably. And she was jealous of Dr Gretton, so she cut the brake cables on impulse."

Woollard scowled. "Yes, the little bitch! Sula could have been killed!" His expression which had changed from regret to anger now seemed to show a dawning satisfaction which was not lost on Markby. "She was responsible for everything, all of it! The girl's a maniac!"

"Well," said Markby, watching him closely. "She cut the cables, certainly, and is responsible for Dr Gretton's accident and she also says she strangled your wife. But there is a small inconsistency which worries me because I can't get around it."

"Karen's story is feasible up to a point. There's no doubt that she believes she's the killer, and there's some evidence to back up her account. A case could be made strong enough to go to court on. But I've had a word with the pathologist. Forensic evidence doesn't entirely bear her story out, at least not as she tells it. She may, of course, not be telling it quite as it was. The struggle with your wife may have been more violent. She could be playing it down instinctively to protect herself, making Mrs Woollard's death look an accident which would carry a lesser charge."

Woollard's burly frame had stiffened. "So what's your problem?" he asked brusquely. "It sounds pretty straightforward to me! She says she did it. She's described how."

Markby gave him a smile which was

positively benign. "Oh yes, she has described exactly how, and in doing so, she's raised the problem. She says she grabbed Mrs Woollard by the neck and Natalie collapsed almost at once. That's quite feasible and, indeed, she could have been dead. Pressure on the carotid artery. But when the post-mortem was carried out, your wife's larynx was found to be fractured. Now that's another matter. That indicates a far more brutal and deliberate attack."

"So she was more violent than she admits!" Woollard almost shouted. "Chief Inspector, I find all this very distressing! We're talking about my wife!"

"Yes, I realise that. I wouldn't do so if it weren't necessary. Murder investigations are painful to all concerned. Believe me, as investigating officers, we are well aware of the burden we place on those already grieving."

Woollard looked very much as if he'd like to refute this assurance. He grunted.

"So," Markby said in the same mild but remorseless way, "I suspect what may have happened is this: Karen discovered Mrs Woollard as she described. There was a quarrel. Karen grasped your wife by the throat. Mrs Woollard fell to the floor. Karen ran away, believing Natalie had fainted. Only later, when the body was discovered, did Karen think she'd killed her.

"Now, perhaps Karen was right in the first place and Mrs Woollard had blacked out temporarily. After a few minutes, she started to come round. At this point a third party appeared on the scene. Someone, perhaps, who had seen Karen return to the dig in some distress and become curious. That person climbed up to the folly and found Natalie semi-conscious. That person was well aware of the feelings Karen so plainly showed for you and so to work out what must have happened wasn't difficult. But that person was also very angry and bearing a grudge of his own. That person saw Natalie as an obstacle and himself presented suddenly with an opportunity to clear the obstacle out of his life for ever. He decided, in fact, to finish the job, knowing Karen would be blamed if it came to naming a murderer. Indeed, she was likely to confess eventually because she isn't a criminal, but a frightened young woman not good at hiding her emotions. So that person put his hands round the semi-conscious woman's throat . . . and made sure she died."

Woollard stirred. "This is pure speculation."

"Not entirely. Forensic evidence does show a far more deliberate act than that carried out by Miss Henson."

There was a silence, then Woollard growled, "Then if what you say is so, Markby. And mind you! I still think this is just you quibbling about the evidence! Well, then, if it's so, then one of those crazy farmers did it! Lionel, most likely. But it could have been Brian. Yes, most likely it was Brian. He's been obsessed with Natalie all his life, or so I've now learned!"

"I don't think it was either of the Felstons, Mr Woollard. Brian wanted Natalie alive. He had no reason to kill her. Lionel is a religious fanatic but, if he'd found Natalie, I think it far more likely he'd have driven her away with a torrent of condemnation and a promise of hellfire! It had to be someone with a very strong motive to want her dead. You, for example.

"As it is, Karen is likely to be charged. She is genuinely in love with you, you know. Quite devoted to you. A very innocent, harmless sort of girl, really, despite the incident of the brake cables. Not well able to cope with strong emotions. Excessively loyal to the object of her devotion. I think that even if she were told what I believe to be the truth, she would still lie to protect you. The thing is, are you going to let her?"

Woollard's face was crimson. He yelled, "Look here, you've no right to say any of this! I deny it! Of course Karen killed Natalie! Look what she tried to do to Sula!"

"Yes, she tried and failed to harm Dr Gretton. Miss Henson, I fear, is one of those people who fail at pretty well everything they attempt. She saw you kiss Dr Gretton's hand and after all that had happened, believing she'd already killed your wife, it was too much for her. Her action aimed at harming Dr Gretton is nonetheless criminal because it was unsuccessful. Should she, however, take the blame on that account for a successful murder she didn't commit? She's a young woman and even if she's able to plead that she didn't know what she was doing at the time, her life will still be ruined. Others will believe her a killer. She'll believe herself a killer. But you know, Mr Woollard, truth does have a funny way of coming out in the end. Ursula Gretton is a very intelligent person. She'll work it out, sooner or later."

This time the silence lasted much longer. Then Woollard said bitterly, "It's not bloody fair!"

"No, Mr Woollard. Life generally isn't, I'm afraid."

"You don't know what Natalie put me through!" He swallowed and made a visible effort to control himself. "All right! What I told you was basically true. Natalie did storm out of the house that day. I didn't know where she'd gone. I didn't then know Brian Felston had been her childhood sweetheart. I certainly didn't know she was hiding in the folly!

"Karen had said a couple of times

474

she'd like to explore the folly. I saw her go off up the hill towards the hippy camp that Tuesday, late in the afternoon. I knew, of course, she was stuck on me. She was always mooning around gazing at me like a sick spaniel. I was amused at first, then embarrassed, and to tell the truth, in the end I got pretty fed up with it. But there wasn't anything I could do and it was, after all, the least of my worries! I thought she'd grow out of it. But when she came back to the dig later on, she looked quite dreadful, white as a ghost. She hid away in a corner and didn't speak to anyone. I thought at first the hippies might have given her a fright. But it seemed it must be more than that. I was feeling pretty down in the dumps myself. I chucked in work for a bit and walked off. I decided to go and look at the folly for myself, just in case there was something there which had frightened Karen.

"What I found was Natalie lying on the floor! I couldn't believe my eyes! She'd been up there all along, spying on me, watching me sweat! I was in a real fog of rage. I couldn't think straight.

I knelt over her and she began to stir and moan. Her eyelids fluttered and I thought that at any moment she'd open her eyes and see me. And she'd laugh. I was sure she'd do that, laugh to see how angry I was and how well she'd fooled me! I thought, Oh, no, you don't! And I — I put my hands round her neck and — finished the job. She didn't know anything about it. She hadn't come right round. She didn't suffer."

He rubbed his hands over his bearded face. "I left her there on the floor. When your sergeant came to the dig the next day to say a body had been found on the quarry tip, I was dumbfounded. I really thought at first it couldn't be Natalie's. How could it have got there? I hadn't moved it. Karen couldn't have moved it alone. But it was Natalie." He met Markby's eyes. "Did you think all along I'd done it, Chief Inspector? I'd really like to know."

Markby took his time before answering. "When I saw the dead woman was Mrs Woollard, then of course, it had to be a distinct possibility, even probability. Murder is basically nearly always a straightforward business. People are killed by those who are in the same close social circle, not by strangers, despite the occasional killing by a sex attacker or mugger which hits the headlines. And why do people kill? Well, for love or lust, greed or revenge. The details may vary but the underlying pattern doesn't. You loved Ursula Gretton. You hated your wife who was in the way. You wanted to pay her back for making you suffer, as you saw it. Pretty well a classic case, really.

"Then there's another thing. People sometime talk of 'an accident waiting to happen'. I've often seen situations which were murders waiting to happen, felt it in my bones and been helpless to prevent it. I didn't know you or your family situation well when I came in on this. But Ursula Gretton did, and when your wife disappeared — even though at that time she was still alive — Ursula's immediate fear was that you might have harmed her, even killed her. She'd already recognised a situation which was a murder waiting to happen, you see. Now, I admit I didn't take her story seriously at first. That was my mistake. I was annoyed because I felt Ursula was dragging a friend of mine into a rather nasty domestic squabble. I should have taken her seriously."

Woollard gave a bark of laughter. "So Sula did for me, after all! And I did it all for Sula, you know. It was all on her account!"

"Did you? I don't think so. I think you did it for yourself. We often try to deceive ourselves first, before we try deceiving others. Trying to salve our consciences, I suppose. Knowing we're doing wrong and trying to shift the blame elsewhere. But metaphysics isn't my department. Murder is. Shall we go?"

26

MEREDITH stretched out on the dry grass of Bamford Hill and watched a sparrowhawk, high up in the sky and hovering over something on the ground some way to their left. Alan had been quiet for so long she thought he might have fallen asleep. She turned her head. His eyes were shut, his breathing even, his appearance peaceful. Then a fly settled on his face. He muttered and put up a hand to brush it away.

"I was thinking," she said. "You know, Dan Woollard's excuses were like Adam's. When he blamed Eve for giving him the apple."

A drowsy mumble was all the reply to this.

"I mean," she persevered, "he blames the women in his life for his own weakness. After all, Adam could have refused to take it but he didn't."

At last a response. He opened his

eyes, screwing up his face in the bright light. "How much of that wine did you drink?"

"I was only making an observation."

He sat up with a sigh, and leaned his forearms on his knees. "I don't fancy being drawn into some fearful feminist argument. Apart from anything else, it's work-connected and I don't want to talk work. All the papers on that case have been sent away and until they get back I'd like to forget the whole tangle!"

"All right, all right, you don't have to be so touchy!" She sat up and picked the dry grass from the back of his shirt. He obliged by doing the same for her. "Like a couple of chimps!" she said.

Alan picked up an empty plastic box and put it back in the picnic hamper. Then he held the wine bottle up. "One of us has drunk it. We'd better go for a walk and sweat it off."

"Such a nice way of putting it!" She put her hand to her eyes and peered into the sunlight. "We're not the only ones walking up here today. There's a couple with a dog over there, where the dig was

Hey, that's Ursula and that looks like Ian Jackson with her! Surely that's Karen's dog?" She waved her arm energetically and shouted, "Hi!"

The two figures waved back. Meredith and Alan Markby climbed to their feet and began to walk towards the others and the dog, seeing company approach, bounded forward to meet them.

"We've come out to check that all's tidy," Jackson said as they came up. He indicated the ground around them. A rectangle of yellowed grass alone showed where the works trailer had stood. The excavated area had been returfed with the grass sods lifted from it forming a patchwork of scars which hadn't yet healed but would do soon. "That's it. Another year's fieldwork over and done. It wasn't too unfruitful in the end, though it didn't turn up what I'd hoped."

"How are you getting along?" Markby asked, turning to Ursula.

She pushed her hands in her pockets and tossed back her long dark hair in a gesture of sturdy independence which Meredith suspected cost some effort. Ursula must be feeling as if her world had collapsed but she was putting on a good face.

"How am I bearing up now I know that Dan did kill poor Natalie? I'm over the initial shock. At least the guilty feeling I had about accusing Dan has gone. I was right when I thought he might harm Natalie. I should have made a lot more fuss, really raised a stink! That's the only thing I'm sorry about, knowing he was lying but not insisting he tell me the truth. I might have saved her, because, at that time, she was still alive. I could have changed the whole course of things and — well, I'll always feel guilty about that."

"Never say 'if only'," Markby advised her. "In my experience it's a waste of time. And I suspect you're underestimating the strength of his desire to be rid of his wife. You weren't the cause of his action, you were just the motivation at that moment. If it hadn't been you, it would have been another at a later date. Any more talk of trying to force you to resign from the Ellsworth?"

"On the contrary. They're being very nice to me for some reason." She pulled a wry face. "I suspect they took legal advice when I said I'd fight any suggestion that I resign purely because of an incident in my private life. The one thing they fear more than anything is any more notoriety. An unfair dismissal case is the last thing they want. They're being so nice, in fact, that if I suggested reopening the dig next summer, they might listen."

Ursula kicked at a lump of turf gouged out of the ground by the passage of one of the many vehicles to have driven over the hill.

"I'll put in a plea on Ian's behalf. But I don't think I shall be returning to work here. It would be too traumatic. Besides I've half made other plans."

She saw the other two eyeing her, Markby with curiosity and Meredith with some trepidation, and gave a little laugh.

"Don't panic! No more disastrous love affairs for me! After Dan, I shall be extremely wary! I came within an inch of going back to him, too, after the row at the Ellsworth! I thought I was being loyal but all I was being was gullible. Well, I've learned something from all this! It's taught me that I should have pushed out my own boat long ago, stopped living at home emotionally stuck in adolescence! I used to tell myself my, father needed me. Of course he didn't. What's more, if I'd got out from under his feet he might have looked round for someone new to share his life, even remarried. I was claiming to take responsibility for his life when I'd never taken responsibility for my own! It's high time I did."

"It sounds as though you already have . . . " Markby said mildly.

"Yes. I've applied for a job in the States. I've been talking to Renee. They're hoping Karen will get a suspended sentence and that it won't prevent her returning to her studies there. Renee will stay over here until it's sorted out and when they go back, I'll be going too. Even if I don't get the job. I'll go anyway and take an extended vacation. I haven't yet resigned from the Ellsworth and they say I can take a sabbatical. I'm looking forward to it."

"You're doing the right thing!" said Meredith firmly. "Getting away and

484

meeting new people!"

"I'd rather you stayed here," Jackson put in. "Having a friend at the Ellsworth is a big advantage to me."

The dog had been circling them during this conversation trying to attract attention. Meredith scratched his head and he wagged his tail furiously, uttering little barks of excitement. "What's he doing up here with you?"

Jackson looked slightly embarrassed. "I've taken him on. Where I live is pretty isolated and now we've got a baby, my wife Becky's stuck out there on her own. She'd like a dog. Karen's got enough on her mind without worrying about the animal. Her case comes up next month — for the attempt to endanger Sula's life, that is. What's happening about her attack on Natalie, Chief Inspector?"

"She'll be required to give evidence at Woollard's trial. But the only charge she can face is of sabotaging Dr Gretton's bicycle. Brian Felston interfered with evidence and moved a body with intent to prevent Christian burial. I dare say he'll get a suspended sentence. All tidied up really, for the time being, until Woollard's case gets to court. That won't be for some time."

They had walked on together as they spoke, straggling out in a line across the grassy hillside. The dog ran ahead sniffing at interesting tufts and pushing his nose into holes in the turf.

"You know, do you," Jackson announced at large, "that some old dear has turned up claiming to be Finny's sister and heiress? I'm buttering her up, trying to get into that cottage. She's got to clear it out as the council are going to pull it down, so I've suggested I go through all the stuff with her."

"What does she look like?" inquired Meredith curiously.

"Believe it or not, just like Finny. If you can imagine Finny with better fitting teeth. She's the same build, about the same age and has got the same rolling walk. She wears grubby old cardigans and carries a huge old leather handbag which she keeps rummaging in furtively. Lord knows what she's got in there. A never-ending supply of throat pastilles, I think. She sucks them non-stop and I always know when she's arrived at the museum by the smell of menthol which precedes her! Never mind, all in a good cause. How's the house-buying going, Meredith?"

Meredith groaned. "Don't ask. I never knew it was so complicated! But I should be able to move in by Christmas. I'll have to get some basic furniture, just to tide me over until I can look for proper stuff. I need to get the bathroom and kitchen fixed up first. I couldn't face using the present facilities."

"You need to talk to Mrs Wallace, that's Finny's sister. She'll sell you Finny's furniture for a tenner. She says she doesn't want any of it. All she wants are his war medals and that reproduction of the *Monarch of the Glen*."

"Many thanks. I don't fancy sitting on Finny's chairs. Too many unpleasant associations. What's that dog doing?"

They had reached the ancient rampart on their stroll and the dog had run ahead and was digging in the long grass which grew in a clump at its base. Jackson whistled but the dog took no notice.

"He's not very well trained," Jackson apologised. "But Becky's going to take him to obedience classes. Oy!"

The dog recognised the last cry and backed out of the grass to stand, tongue lolling and panting, his head turned towards them. He yelped shrilly.

"Looks like he's found something!" Markby observed.

They began to walk toward the dog which, as soon as he saw that he'd attracted the humans, dived back into the grass and disappeared.

"Where's he gone?" Jackson exclaimed. He shouted out again.

The replying bark sounded muffled.

"He's in there," Ursula said, pointing at the grass thicket. "But I can't see where. He's disappeared!"

"Hang on!" Markby parted the grass and pushed his way through it. "I can see his tail — the daft brute!" He looked up. "He's got himself wedged in the bank, in an old rabbit or foxhole!"

The other three rushed forward with cries of dismay.

"How are we going to get him out? Can you reach him?" Meredith demanded, on hands and knees and trying to see into the hole down which the dog had crawled.

"We may have to dig him out. I've got a spade in the car, I'll go and get it!" Jackson set off back down the hill at a run.

"Hurry, he'll suffocate!" Ursula yelled, scraping at the entrance with her hands. "Silly thing, he's much too big and fat to get down there! You'd think he'd realise it!"

A doleful yelp from beneath the earth suggested that if the dog hadn't realised it before, he was realising it now. They could hear his paws scrabbling and his back end heaved but to no avail. He was firmly wedged. His plumed tail, all they could see of him, drooped miserably and a sad whine sounded desperately in their ears.

Jackson came running back up the hill, red in the face and carrying a small pointed spade. "No, let me!" he gasped as Markby offered to begin the task. "I'm used to digging holes! One thing about my line of work, you learn to turn your hand to any variety of odd jobs!"

He attacked the edge of the burrow efficiently and after a quarter of an hour's work, the entrance was widened sufficiently to allow the dog to scramble out backwards by his own efforts. He looked very sorry for himself, covered in earth and crestfallen.

"You'll have to give him a bath!" Ursula said laughing and trying to dust him down.

But Jackson was still on hands and knees and peering into the widened entrance. He reached in with the spade and scraped out a little more earth. "Anyone got a match? Hang on, I have."

He struck the light and stretched his arm into the tunnel with the flickering little flame, following it with the rest of his body as far as he could. "There's something in here." His voice sounded faintly. "It widens out further along into a sort of cave."

"Take care!" Markby warned. "The earth's been made unstable by the digging and could collapse round you!"

The curator had wriggled forward on his stomach and his head and shoulders had disappeared, so that he was now in the hole from waist upwards.

"Ian!" yelled Ursula. "Don't be silly!"

Jackson's body began to jerk and he

slithered out, dirt-covered, breathless but gripping something which he held high, unable to speak for the moment.

"Animal bone," said Meredith. "It must be a foxhole. It's a fox's den at the far end and that's the remains of Renard's last dinner!"

"No . . . " Ursula reached out and took the bone from her colleague's hand. "No, that's not an animal bone!"

"Let me see!" Markby said sharply.

The bone lay on Ursula's outstretched palm, yellowed and dry. "As a forensic palaeontologist," she said slowly, "I'd say it was a human collarbone."

Jackson dropped on to his knees again but Markby grasped his arm and hauled him upright again. "Sorry! No more rummaging about in there! If it's human, I'll have to get my people out and open up the bank here!"

"But Markby!" Jackson whispered excitedly. "Don't you realise what that could be? Finny found the brooch in a rabbit burrow! It's so obvious! Why on earth didn't I think of it? Wulfric was mortally wounded while leading the assault on the rampart here. So where else should they bury him but where he fell? They dug into the rampart, made a burial chamber and sealed him in it!" Jackson began to jump about excitedly. "My God, he's in there! Wulfric! I've found him! Sula, you've got to get on to the Ellsworth! Oh heck, I'll have to get permission from the Felstons to start work again!"

"Calm down," said Markby, "whether it's Wulfric or not, you don't need the Ellsworth. This dig's going to be at public expense and the Felstons don't have any say in it!"

They set off down the hill, Markby striding out and Jackson running alongside, pleading, "But your coppers don't know how to conduct a proper dig! They'll just hack the blasted rampart to bits! It's got to be marked out and a trial shaft dug, then it comes off in layers! Every spade, of earth has got to be searched for remains or evidence . . . "

"And just what do you think a police excavation does?" came Markby's irritated reply. "Of course we'll go slowly and sift the soil for evidence! It might be a more recent burial, you know!"

"The trouble with you coppers is, you see murder everywhere! I tell you, that's Wulfric . . . "

"Let them argue it out," Meredith said to Ursula.

"I hope it is Wulfric," her friend replied. "I think Ian deserves the break." She gave a wicked grin. "Think you'll like living in Bamford, Meredith?"

Meredith grimaced. "I have to admit to the odd doubt!"

They had reached the roadside where both cars were parked. Jackson was putting the spade back in the boot of his while still yelling his protests to Markby. The chief inspector, ignoring the curator, was sitting in his car speaking into his radio.

When he'd finished, Meredith opened the door and slid into the front passenger seat beside him. "Alan, you're not really going to set up a police operation?"

"Of course I am!"

"But it has to be Wulfric, surely? Or at the very least, another one of his warriors! Who else could it be?"

Markby turned towards her, resting his elbows one on the steering wheel and the

493

other on the back of his seat, fingers laced. His grey eyes fixed her face and his fair hair flopped forward untidily as it always did when he was busy.

"How about an unhappy wife who walked out of the house one day and was never seen again?"

"Now listen!" Meredith said crossly. "That's being flippant and underhand! You mean, I made a fuss about Natalie so you can make a fuss about one old bone in a rabbit burrow!"

A faint dry smile touched his mouth but wasn't reflected in the grey eyes. He leaned forward slightly. "I wasn't referring to Natalie, as it happens. You're way out." His voice sank so that there was no possibility of either Jackson or Ursula overhearing. "I was referring to the late Mrs Felston!"

She stared at him, taken aback at first and then with horrified incredulity. "You don't really think that? But Alan, Brian told you — "

"Brian's mistake was that he didn't escort his mother to the bus stop!" Markby said grimly as the radio crackled into life again.

27

TRANSCRIPTS of conversations between Lionel Felston, 76, farmer, and doctors of Bamford Psychiatric Hospital. An account of events leading to the death of Mrs Eileen Felston, 36, on 3 June 1963.

★ ★ ★

"We were always close, my brother Frank and I. He was eleven months older than me but smaller and not so solid. When we were little 'uns people took us for twins, or so Mother always used to say. She got into the way of treating us like that, as if we were twins, and so did other folk. We could wear each other's clothes right through childhood, even at school, being always of much the same size. At Christmas when we were children people gave us one present between us. I can't remember what happened on birthdays. No one ever made much of birthdays in those days, leastways, not in our house.

"Mother was a widow. I never knew my father and Frank was too young to have any memory of him. He was lost on the Somme in September 1916. He went off to war with a Pals' Brigade from our town. They all got blown to kingdom come together. Hardly a house in our street wasn't in mourning, so Mother said afterwards.

"I wasn't born when the news came. She'd started me when he'd last been home on a spot of leave and she was six months gone with carrying me when news of his death came through. I put in my appearance on January 6th, 1917, and Frank, he was still sitting in his pram at the time.

"It made things very hard for her, two babies. She wanted to keep us with her and not take us to the orphanage like a lot of women in her situation found they had to do. She had to go out to work because there weren't the good pensions then like now. She got no help from the government. So when I see those New Age travellers, as they call themselves, flitting around the country and trespassing wherever they think they will, and drawing money off the social while they do it, I haven't patience! Do you think anyone of my generation is going to be persuaded that can be right? Of course it's not!

"Well, as I was telling you, Frank and I were left with neighbours while she went out to work. The neighbours were busy women too, and had no time for us except to keep an eye open to make sure we didn't fall in the fire or stray. So Frank and I, we got to depend on each other, not having anyone else, as it were. Later on when we went to school, it was the same. We stuck together.

"When we were coming up to eleven and twelve years old, Mother left the town. She packed up and came back to the country where she was born, over towards Westerfield. She came home to look after old Grandad and took us along. The old chap died and he left the cottage to her. She stayed on there and Frank and I, we left school at fourteen and went to work on the land. There was nothing else. We liked it, though, and we reckoned we'd get a farm of our own one day. We did, in 1948. Mother had died by then, so we sold up the cottage and its bit of land to the Council for the new council housing being built then. Compulsory purchase it was, but we reckoned it a fair price since we were wanting to sell anyway.

"Land was cheap then compared to now. Frank and I bought Motts Farm and it didn't cost us more than we had, but on the other hand, we hadn't that much! So by the time we'd got settled at the farm, there wasn't any spare cash around. We didn't miss it because we'd never had spare money in our pockets to spend. What you've never had, you don't miss!

"We worked hard but we were used to that. But there wasn't time for running round the house or seeing to cooking and mending, even if either of us had been a dab hand at it. Finally we talked it over and decided what we wanted up there was a woman, someone young and strong. She could take over the poultry too and lend a hand in the dairy. In those days we couldn't have a woman living up there with two men unless she was married to one of us. It wasn't respectable and quite rightly so! There's no decency nowadays. Now 'tis all wantonness and depravity. But then folk kept decent homes.

"So, any road, we drew straws and Frank won. He went and asked Eileen to marry him. She was just on twenty-two years old at the time. She worked on a farm in the last year of the war as a land-girl and so we reckoned she'd do.

"She was a fine-looking woman, Eileen. But she knew how to stir the lust in a man's loins! She had a way of moving, swinging her hips, and when she leaned forward you'd see her bosom pushing against her frock. She knew it, too. And like I said just now, it's true that what you've never had, you don't miss. But once you've had a glimpse of it, it's different. Then you thirst for more!

"All that first summer they were wed she worked in the house or out and about in the yard, and I'd watch her. I'm a God-fearing man. We were raised well by Mother! Mother was a religious woman and went regularly to the Primitive Methodist chapel. Old Grandad, he'd been a lay preacher! So if I lusted after Eileen, it wasn't for deliberate breaking of any commandment. It was because it's a man's nature and she led me on! Curling her hair and putting on lipstick, even though Frank told her not to. She was always wanting Frank to take her to Bamford on a Saturday night to go dancing. And her a married woman! But Frank, he wouldn't take her and so in the end she saw it was no use and she stopped asking.

"I watched her every day, and every day the urges in me grew stronger. I could smell her hair, a smell of soap and flowers, when she leaned over to pour out the tea. She'd hang up her smalls of a Monday morning on the washing line in the yard, drawers and petticoats and such. Stockings, too. When she stretched up to peg the wash out, her skirt would go up and I could see her stocking tops and her thighs, white like ivory. Then the blood pounded in my head and the pictures came in my mind! It was devil's work! But she didn't care, though she knew it had the effect on me. She was a fast hussy!

"Now I told you that Frank and I, all our lives we'd shared. Clothes and toys when we were young and later the work on the farm and the money we made. One day Frank said to me: 'I've seen you looking at Eileen. We've always shared, you and I, so it's only fair you should have a share in her, since the farm can't support another woman for you to marry. Turn and turn alike, like everything else. It's right and proper and I'll tell her so.'

"So he did tell her. But first of all she refused, kicked up a fuss even though it was her lawful husband had told her what to do! Frank, he was a quiet sort of chap. He let her get away with it at first, though he felt bad since he'd told me it would be all right. 'Give her time,' he said. 'She'll come round.'

"Only she didn't. She was obstinate and she'd never agree, not of her own accord. I saw Frank was too easy with her and wouldn't insist so it was for me to take matters into my own hands, let her see she had to do as she was told by her menfolk.

"It was an evening in early autumn.

I mind it well. I walked out along the ridge and I saw Eileen blackberrying in the bushes by the old folly. She saw me and she called out, 'Lionel! You come and hook this stem down for me so I can get at the fruit!'

"And I thought, there's more than one fruit to be picked out here! So I caught hold of her and pushed her along ahead of me into the old folly. She struggled like a mad thing and even bit me! Used language too like I'd never heard from a woman. A decent woman like Mother would have spun in her grave to hear it! So I gave her a slap or two and she went quiet. I pushed her down on the floor and took her there. She didn't say anything afterwards. Snivelled a bit. Then got up and pulled down her skirt and went out.

"I reckon she went complaining to Frank but he told her to stop her noise, 'twasn't anything to make a fuss over! After that she didn't make any more trouble and we shared her, like Frank had said we should. She'd seen who was boss. You have to let a woman see that.

"Less than a year after that, the boy Brian was born. Frank and I, we both looked on him as a son. He was always a good boy.

"Now, what I'll tell you just goes to show you can't trust a woman! Eileen hadn't been any trouble for years but one day, when the boy was about fourteen, I was coming up Bamford Hill and I saw Eileen walking down the track to the main road carrying a suitcase, hat and coat on. I asked her what she thought she was doing. She said she was leaving the farm. Just like that! With work in hand and two men and a boy to care for! She was a hussy, like I told you!

"I told her to go back home. She wouldn't do it, said she meant to go and I couldn't stop her! But I could. I had to. She would have ruined our good name! So I did. I put my hands round her neck and give it a squeeze and a bit of a twist. She just sagged down. I dragged her body under the bushes and went and told Frank.

"We had to keep it secret from the boy. Luckily she'd told him herself she was leaving. Told her own child, mind! Our mother would never have left Frank and me when we were young 'uns. Anyhow, we talked it over, Frank and I, like we talked over everything. 'See here,' I said to him. 'The one place on the farm no one's ever going to plough or dig over is the old rampart, on account it's historical and it's not allowed to tamper with it'.

"So that night when we'd made sure the boy was asleep, we went down and dug into the side of it. It wasn't difficult because there were any number of rabbit warrens and once we'd opened it up, it was just a question of knocking out the old tunnels into a sort of long slot we could slide her in. Funny thing, though. While we were digging it out for Eileen, we found a lot of other old bones, and some bits of jewellery, or that's what it looked like! A knife, all corroded away, and bowls and cups, dented and damaged. Any number of strange things, all useless. We sealed Eileen's body and the other old bones into the rampart. We took the other things back to the farm and had a good look at them but they had no value. So the next morning I took them back to the rampart and pushed them down another rabbit burrow some distance away from where Eileen was.

"Frank and I, we never spoke of it. As for the boy, he never mentioned his mother. He thought she'd left on the bus. I had a fancy he looked to see if the post van would bring a letter from her to the farm for a few weeks, but when it never did, he lost interest. Frank died in 1978. The lad Brian and I stayed on at the farm and we managed all right.

"When those archaeologists came wanting to dig it didn't worry me because I knew they weren't meaning to dig near where Eileen's body would have been. Anyway, after nigh on thirty years I didn't reckon there'd be much left of her. It gave me a bit of a turn when they uncovered that Saxon feller's skeleton. You know, to think it could survive all of a piece like that for so long! But still, they'd never have found Eileen, only by chance and that was pure bad luck.

"A pity that policeman Markby was with them when they found the first bone. And that clever hussy, the woman archaeologist. Of course they saw straight off it wasn't an animal bone and went digging the whole lot out. They found Eileen then, and the other old bones all mixed up with hers. Some Saxon king or other.

"That Chief Inspector Markby, he's a tricky one. He guessed straight off it would be Eileen in the rampart. His uncle was rector over at Westerfield about the time Eileen died. I remember him well, the old Reverend Markby. He preached a powerful sermon!"

★ ★ ★

Note from Chief Inspector Markby to Superintendent McVeigh:

All the experts who have examined Lionel Felston are agreed as to his state of mind and nothing in my own experience of him suggests any reason to disagree with their findings. It seems likely that he has suffered from a severely disturbed personality all his life. A deprived childhood, an extremely strong-minded mother and a closeness between brothers which bred an unhealthy attitude towards the world outside their own family, was made much worse by a form of religious mania springing from years of suppressed guilt feelings.

I'm sure the DPP is right on this one. Lionel is unfit to plead. I'm glad to close the file on a truly tragic affair.

"For me the worst of it," said Meredith, "is thinking how everyone who was ever dear to Brian has been taken from him. I'm not surprised he's so sour and spiteful. First his mother, then Natalie and now even horrid old Lionel is locked up in a psychiatric ward!"

"Where, no doubt, he's frightening the other patients out of their remaining reason with tales of imminent Doom!"

"Don't joke about it, Alan! It's not as though poor Brian is like any of us, rootless professionals. If we have a bad emotional experience we can pick up the pieces and walk away to begin again somewhere else. He's tied to his livelihood in one place. Every day he'll walk out of that gloomy farmhouse and see the folly on the horizon, reminding him of Natalie and everything else. How did he take learning the truth about his mother's death?"

"Calmly. There may have been a moment during his adult life when, thinking it over, he began to suspect. If so, he buried the suspicion deep inside him because if he'd acknowledged the truth, it would, as you say, have taken old Lionel away from him and the old chap was all he had left. For him to disturb the past was far too dangerous! There might have been a lot of old horrors lying quiet, just waiting to be stirred up. Brian decided it was best to let old bones lie! But of course, when he found Natalie dead, his suppressed suspicions flooded to the surface and his first thought was that Lionel had done it.

"I do understand Brian and I can even dredge up a little sympathy for him, Meredith, because like him, I'm afraid of losing what little I have. Oh, I know I've got my sister and her kids. And I did pick myself up after my marriage failed and walk away to a new life. But what does worry me, frightens me really if I were truthful, is that you'll walk away one day. I think about that a lot."

"Oh. Well, I won't. I know I'm not moving in with you in Bamford, but that's because I need my space, not because I'm uncommitted. Please don't ask me to say 'I love you!' Because I get the most awful jitters about that word! But I'd hate it if you walked away and it worries me, too."

"Oh well, a shared neurosis is as good a basis as any for a relationship, I suppose! Can you reach the light switch?"

"Only if I fall out. I tell you one thing: one of us is going to have to buy a wider bed!"

THE END

Other titles in the Ulverscroft Large Print Series:

TO FIGHT THE WILD
Rod Ansell and Rachel Percy

Lost in uncharted Australian bush, Rod Ansell survived by hunting and trapping wild animals, improvising shelter and using all the bushman's skills he knew.

COROMANDEL
Pat Barr

India in the 1830s is a hot, uncomfortable place, where the East India Company still rules. Amelia and her new husband find themselves caught up in the animosities which seethe between the old order and the new.

THE SMALL PARTY
Lillian Beckwith

A frightening journey to safety begins for Ruth and her small party as their island is caught up in the dangers of armed insurrection.

THE WILDERNESS WALK
Sheila Bishop

Stifling unpleasant memories of a misbegotten romance in Cleave with Lord Francis Aubrey, Lavinia goes on holiday there with her sister. The two women are thrust into a romantic intrigue involving none other than Lord Francis.

THE RELUCTANT GUEST
Rosalind Brett

Ann Calvert went to spend a month on a South African farm with Theo Borland and his sister. They both proved to be different from her first idea of them, and there was Storr Peterson — the most disturbing man she had ever met.

ONE ENCHANTED SUMMER
Anne Tedlock Brooks

A tale of mystery and romance and a girl who found both during one enchanted summer.

CLOUD OVER MALVERTON
Nancy Buckingham

Dulcie soon realises that something is seriously wrong at Malverton, and when violence strikes she is horrified to find herself under suspicion of murder.

AFTER THOUGHTS
Max Bygraves

The Cockney entertainer tells stories of his East End childhood, of his RAF days, and his post-war showbusiness successes and friendships with fellow comedians.

MOONLIGHT
AND MARCH ROSES
D. Y. Cameron

Lynn's search to trace a missing girl takes her to Spain, where she meets Clive Hendon. While untangling the situation, she untangles her emotions and decides on her own future.

DEATH ON A
HOT SUMMER NIGHT
Anne Infante

Micky Douglas is either accident-prone or someone is trying to kill him. He finds himself caught in a desperate race to save his ex-wife and others from a ruthless gang.

HOLD DOWN A SHADOW
Geoffrey Jenkins

Maluti Rider, with the help of four of the world's most wanted men, is determined to destroy the Katse Dam and release a killer flood.

THAT NICE MISS SMITH
Nigel Morland

A reconstruction and reassessment of the trial in 1857 of Madeleine Smith, who was acquitted by a verdict of Not Proven of poisoning her lover, Emile L'Angelier.

CHATEAU OF FLOWERS
Margaret Rome

Alain, Comte de Treville needed a wife to look after him, and Fleur went into marriage on a business basis only, hoping that eventually he would come to trust and care for her.

CRISS-CROSS
Alan Scholefield

As her ex-husband had succeeded in kidnapping their young daughter once, Jane was determined to take her safely back to England. But all too soon Jane is caught up in a new web of intrigue.

DEAD BY MORNING
Dorothy Simpson

Leo Martindale's body was discovered outside the gates of his ancestral home. Is it, as Inspector Thanet begins to suspect, murder?

NURSE ALICE IN LOVE
Theresa Charles

Accepting the post of nurse to little Fernie Sherrod, Alice Everton could not guess at the romance, suspense and danger which lay ahead at the Sherrod's isolated estate.

POIROT INVESTIGATES
Agatha Christie

Two things bind these eleven stories together — the brilliance and uncanny skill of the diminutive Belgian detective, and the stupidity of his Watson-like partner, Captain Hastings.

LET LOOSE THE TIGERS
Josephine Cox

Queenie promised to find the long-lost son of the frail, elderly murderess, Hannah Jason. But her enquiries threatened to unlock the cage where crucial secrets had long been held captive.

THE LISTERDALE MYSTERY
Agatha Christie

Twelve short stories ranging from the light-hearted to the macabre, diverse mysteries ingeniously and plausibly contrived and convincingly unravelled.

TO BE LOVED
Lynne Collins

Andrew married the woman he had always loved despite the knowledge that Sarah married him for reasons of her own. So much heartache could have been avoided if only he had known how vital it was to be loved.

ACCUSED NURSE
Jane Converse

Paula found herself accused of a crime which could cost her her job, her nurse's reputation, and even the man she loved, unless the truth came to light.

THE TWILIGHT MAN
Frank Gruber

Jim Rand lives alone in the California desert awaiting death. Into his hermit existence comes a teenage girl who blows both his past and his brief future wide open.

DOG IN THE DARK
Gerald Hammond

Jim Cunningham breeds and trains gun dogs, and his antagonism towards the devotees of show spaniels earns him many enemies. So when one of them is found murdered, the police are on his doorstep within hours.

THE RED KNIGHT
Geoffrey Moxon

When he finds himself a pawn on the chessboard of international espionage with his family in constant danger, Guy Trent becomes embroiled in moves and countermoves which may mean life or death for Western scientists.

TIGER TIGER
Frank Ryan

A young man involved in drugs is found murdered. This is the first event which will draw Detective Inspector Sandy Woodings into a whirlpool of murder and deceit.

CAROLINE MINUSCULE
Andrew Taylor

Caroline Minuscule, a medieval script, is the first clue to the whereabouts of a cache of diamonds. The search becomes a deadly kind of fairy story in which several murders have an other-worldly quality.

LONG CHAIN OF DEATH
Sarah Wolf

During the Second World War four American teenagers from the same town join the Army together. Forty-two years later, the son of one of the soldiers realises that someone is systematically wiping out the families of the four men.

A GREAT DELIVERANCE
Elizabeth George

Into the web of old houses and secrets of Keldale Valley comes Scotland Yard Inspector Thomas Lynley and his assistant to solve a particularly savage murder.

'E' IS FOR EVIDENCE
Sue Grafton

Kinsey Millhone was bogged down on a warehouse fire claim. It came as something of a shock when she was accused of being on the take. She'd been set up. Now she had a new client — herself.

A FAMILY OUTING IN AFRICA
Charles Hampton and Janie Hampton

A tale of a young family's journey through Central Africa by bus, train, river boat, lorry, wooden bicycle and foot.

THE PLEASURES OF AGE
Robert Morley

The author, British stage and screen star, now eighty, is enjoying the pleasures of age. He has drawn on his experiences to write this witty, entertaining and informative book.

THE VINEGAR SEED
Maureen Peters

The first book in a trilogy which follows the exploits of two sisters who leave Ireland in 1861 to seek their fortune in England.

A VERY PAROCHIAL MURDER
John Wainwright

A mugging in the genteel seaside town turned to murder when the victim died. Then the body of a young tearaway is washed ashore and Detective Inspector Lyle is determined that a second killing will not go unpunished.